DEAR BANKS

CW01522427

This novel is written in recognition (....ps and vulnerabilities facing young care leavers.

I wish them good luck and good fortune as they venture out on their future journeys. Any profits raised will be donated to The National Youth Advisory Service (NYAS), an organisation that works tirelessly to provide ongoing support for young people as they transition out of the UK care system.

Thanks are extended to …

All of you who have patiently listened to my doubts and ramblings along the way. As always, to my close family, who are always there to cheer me on, but especially my enduring husband, Tom.

Thanks to my fellow writing companions from Curtis Brown and Liverpool Red Brick Writers, who are always ready with much-appreciated support and encouragement. Also, Gary, Annette, Chris, Channy, Anna, Phil, Marlon, and Val for providing invaluable critique and feedback. Special thanks to Patsi for her editing diligence and Georgina Parfitt for the incredible book cover.

Finally, a tribute to the master, Banksy, who never fails to inspire with his unswerving satirical creativity.

Countdown: Day 12

There was no sign of Grace at the Harbourside pickup point, where intersecting narrow streets were already choked with anticipation for Bristol's New Year fireworks display. A 'Get Brexit Done' banner was pushed into Anne's face by a sweating man with bulging eyes, one of an army of protesting Brexiteers clashing with festive party goers in their saintly luminous halos. Emerging from the crowd, she finally saw the straggling line of vaping girls under their strawberry cloud, waiting to board a battered minibus, exactly as Grace had described.

The feeling that someone was watching her made her turn. A pair of eyes shone out of a large spray-painted silhouette. Haunted eyes that implored, 'You don't belong with them. Turn back.' She'd forgotten about this piece of Banksy's artwork, hidden from view like much that went on in these backstreets. 'A skit on a famous Dutch painting,' Billy had once told her, admiringly. The eyes of the girl looking out from under a scarf bound around her head seemed to search for something beyond the crowds. Had those knowing eyes ever seen Fleur standing in this same queue?

Uneasy, she pulled her purple leather jacket around her; the comforting perfume ingrained in the soft hide grounded her, along with Fleur's sensible ankle boots, good if the weather turned bad, and good if she needed to run. She had no idea what she was letting herself in for, but if she were to find Fleur, she had to board that minibus.

'Hiya Rudi,' a young girl in a backless minidress high-fived a gaunt man, smoking with the driver, who pinched her bum as she boarded, making her squeal. She recognised the girl as one of Grace's crowd who worked the Blind Fox. Pills were being passed around, which she declined to an affronted 'suit your fuckin' self, then.' Where was Grace? Her heart sank as an arm was placed in front of her. 'Not seen you before?' Rudi's sinewy barrier stayed firm.

'No, I was going to make my own way there, but then my lift went tits-up. Grace said to tell Rudi that she'd sent me.' Her fingers were crossed behind her back.

'You know Grace?'

'Yeah, we work together down at the docks.' Rudi, with his feral, pale blue eyes, sized her up and down before nodding her on board. Opting for a seat at the back, she breathed to steady herself, gnawing at nonexistent nails, and looked out at the silhouette on the wall, the warning eyes following her with a new sense of urgency: 'Get off the minibus.' She knew this lift came with conditions. But time was running out. With only three days left to find Fleur, it was too late to turn back now.

1

#Banksy: 'Rose In A Mouse Trap'

Three weeks earlier.

Speeding up, she pounded across the park toward their flats, the beat of her backpack whiplike, lengthening her strides. Anne told herself to be rational. *There was nothing to worry about.* But the voices niggling away all day told her otherwise. Getting nearer, her prayers came in rhythm with her strides. *Dear Banksy, let me be wrong ... wrong ... wrong.*

If asked, Anne wouldn't know when she'd started praying to Banksy in place of the cruel God of her Sunday School days with his halo and flowing robes, and his lies. It probably happened somewhere between the troubles in her last foster home and the terror that engulfed her when told she was about to be cast from the care system on her eighteenth birthday. Banksy's words had provided comfort. *There is Always Hope,* a phrase he crafted and which she clung to.

Stopping only to shoo away a sharp-eyed magpie feasting on something dead, she cursed the keys still strange to her trembling fingers and burst into their room. A forensic scan settled on a scattering of Fleur's clothes, recklessly discarded along with any hopes for their fresh start.

What do you wear on the day you plan to die? Such a dilemma would have thrown Fleur, wrecked her pretty head.

Slamming the door, she dashed to the place she'd hoped never to have to return, resorting once more to her pounding supplications: *Dear Banksy, please let me be wrong ... wrong ... wrong.*

She strained to see the top of the brutal multi-storey car park, where a shape hung precariously between floors, floating in the mist like a holy relic. She blinked at Fleur's earlier 'Help Me' message, the words blurred on the illuminated screen, before making the dreaded call for help.

'Fuck off,' she screamed at a car exiting the car park, honking accusingly at her, spewing out diesel fumes that clung to her skin like the fungus that used to kill off Billy's fish. Clawing through thick air, she pounded the ramp higher and higher until her muscles burned. Out on the roof, she gulped up the murky evening air.

'Hang on, Fleur, help's coming ...' Her breath caught as she looked over the terrifying precipice to where Fleur clung to a thin metal rail. Dropping to her knees, she needed to lie down, suddenly lightheaded. A distorted reflection mocked her, bouncing off discarded laughing gas containers - youth's silver bullets.

It can't end here Fleur...

Anne had always loved Fleur. Ever since they'd hung upside down from monkey bars together, their hair brushing concrete as fractured as their lifelines. They'd preferred life upside down back then, the blood rushing to their head as the inverted blocks of council flats transformed into drifting fairy castles. The carefree days before the scrubbed-faced, Birkenstocked social worker snatched her away. The shimmering days before the fire, when Billy was still around to make things right.

'Fleur, make your way back to the ladder, I can reach you from the top …' but the wind flung her words back in her face.

Looking beyond, she spotted the top of her mum's old flats clinging scab-like ugly on the landscape and felt blinding hot anger. A searing fury that they'd survived, holding onto all the bad things. All those secrets. Narrowly escaping demolition, they were saved only by the arrival of the asylum seekers, and after that, the overnight appearance of a mural everyone seemed to be arguing over.

'It's him,' Billy had said, knowingly, claiming to have met his idol Banksy at school. But then he used to say a lot of mad things. 'We're all a product of our environment. It shapes who we are,' he once told her. Looking out, she fucking hoped not. The freezing wind was making it hard to stay concentrated. 'Fleur - please come back up here to me.'

'No, I want to fly, come on, Anne, fly with me,' tinny words floating like translucent bubbles just beyond her reach.

'Just climb back up the ladder,' she pleaded, but her zigzag wrists flopped limply as Fleur edged further away on the sorry narrow ledge, her worn trainers breaking free cement shards, as jagged as their shed baby teeth.

Please don't do this Fleur, you're all I've got.

She turned in response to a shuffle behind her. 'At last.' But at least there were no blue lights this time.

'I'm PC Wright … never been to one of these before,' a constricted disembodied voice floated above a badge flashed hesitantly in her direction.

Oh God, he looks about twelve and shit scared. I'm on my own here.

His radio buzzed.

'Turn that thing off. And stay back there 'til I need you.' It wasn't just Fleur's life at stake here. He approached warily and kneeled beside her, his gripped knuckles turned white as they peered over the edge, down to where the wind was whipping Fleur's hair, giving her a crazed appearance like she'd been electrocuted. Anne smelled his cinnamon-scented aftershave tinged with terror, and felt short-changed.

They froze as Fleur turned and looked up at them, wild eyes in a white pancake of a face.

Shit, what's she taken this time? She's completely out of it.

A plastic bag waltzed between them, hypnotizing, like the tiny parachutes they used to tie to their Barbie dolls before throwing them from the tenth-floor landing, running to find them, legs splayed and eyes startled.

'Where do you want to fly to, Fleur?' she shouted against the unruly wind.

'I want to go to Spain with the others.'

'No, fuck them, let's go to Ibiza, let's go clubbing.' Fleetingly, she wondered where Ibiza was, but at least she was keeping Fleur engaged.

'Yeah, fuck them. Will you really take me to Ibiza?'

'Promise.' But she couldn't cross her fingers behind her back this time. The young officer paced about in his perfectly creased trousers, peering into recesses as if a solution might linger there. 'What's your name, officer?' He turned to flash his ID badge again.

'No, I mean your proper name.'

He hesitated as if unsure such things were to be disclosed. 'James.'

'Take your hat and jacket off, James. I've got an idea.' Measured. She prayed he was up to playing the part of a lifetime.

'Look Fleur, James, our captain is here. He's going to take us to Ibiza.'

'But we haven't packed.'

'Yeah, I did it when you went out, we're good to go.' She beckoned the officer over; saw the quiver of his lip.

He drew a deep breath, 'Come on … Fleur … back up this ladder now, the same way you got down.' Unconvincing. They glinting in the spotlight like a circus star on a highwire. Shielding Fleur with his body, they jerkily made their way to the top of the ladder. Soft blonde hair surfaced above the concrete fortress just before she collapsed unceremoniously to the pissy-smelling ground. Anne rushed to cradle her, rocking her back and forth.

'It's okay, Fleur, it will all be okay.' Who was she trying to convince? 'No need for further action, I'm her Mental Health Worker,' she assured the shaking police officer, now flooded with adrenaline. She'd seen it before in a boy who threatened a staff member with a knife in her last children's home; it would soon settle. She flicked her ID badge toward him, judging him the type to respect anything official. 'I'll take her back to the unit now, and we'll pop into the station tomorrow. It's what we usually do.'

They both turned to a cacophony of sirens and snaking blue lights below, interrupting close examination of her 'Food Bank Volunteer' ID card.

Well, they're late to the party.

But they screamed past, making their way to someone else's drama. The buzzing in her ears eased, and she soaked up the stillness, taking a moment to breathe in Fleur's sherberty sweetness.

'Frankie. I want Frankie back,' Fleur sobbed, her thin shoulders heaving.

Who the fuck is Frankie?

Anne only knew one Frankie from their childhood, and God forbid Fleur was mixed up with that lot, or they were both for it.

'Are you okay now?' PC Wright asked, straightening his jacket. She'd forgotten he was still there.

'Thank you, James.' She liked the name James. He looked nice, all ruffled up, his hair floppy at the front, more like he should be in a boy band than in the police. She felt her cheeks warming, aware she was staring at him. 'Shouldn't you get back to work?'

'Not until I see you down safely.' And it felt good, just this once, to let someone else take control.

They waited at their bus stop, frozen, their legs pressed together for warmth. Anne fixed on the image on a poster opposite them. Banksy's 'Rose Trap' showing a rose about to be mangled in a mousetrap. She turned her back on it and put her arm protectively around Fleur, now wearing her maroon padded jacket that she'd picked up on one of her early morning foraging trips. Anne liked to forage; it was amazing what things delivery vans left lying around. She'd got some great finds for their new flat.

The lithe PC Wright waved back at them, stretching and shaking the tension free from his hands as if about to run a marathon, before joining his older, bearded colleague waiting in the patrol car, further along the bus stop. 'Any chance of giving them a lift?' His words carried on the breeze caused her to look up in hope, but she caught the older officer's, 'Grow a pair, son. 2015 and social services still can't sort it out. Sometimes I don't even bother responding to those calls.'

They stayed put as the surly driver warned James against creating unnecessary paperwork, when his rant was interrupted by the crackle of the ghost in the radio, now turned up loud. *'Lima 10. Urgent support required. Male torso ... ground disturbed by a dog walker ... SOCO securing the crime scene ...'* Anne recalled the blue stream of lights and the sirens they'd heard earlier and tried to imagine what it must feel like to be hurtling towards a dead body as the car screeched away, its blue lights turning her nails indigo. She caught the glint of fear in James' eyes; his face pinched white and serious as they screamed toward a grisly murder, which, unknown to them, was about to derail all their futures.

2

#Banksy: 'You Don't Need Planning Permission to Build

Castles in the Sky'

One week later.

Wet through and chewing on gnawed nails, she waited for Vivian to open her faded front door.

'You're not supposed to know where I live.' A mass of ginger hair atop a volcanic body peered out at Anne in the poorly lit porch. Everything about Vivian was poorly lit. The woman liked her privacy; she had good reason to.

Anne took a deep breath and 'fessed up. 'Sorry, Vivian. I followed you home after our first mentoring session.' She'd learned early that it paid to check out the people around you, to see if they were who they claimed to be - especially people in positions of so-called 'Authority'.

At first, the offer of a mentor to 'assist with her transition from the care system' had sounded too good to be true, something that would look good on her future job applications. That was before she met Vivian. Sighing at her misplaced optimism, she eyed the flaking green door that reminded her of a drug dealer's house she'd once called at for her mother. She noticed a sodden silk butterfly nestled amongst weeds in a cracked flower pot. Despondent; in need of care. It reminded her why she was there. Fleur hadn't come home for the past week.

A curling sun-faded sign: 'No riffraff' was sellotaped on the downstairs window.

What a shit hole.

'Nice place you've got here, Vivian.'

Vivian tossed back the hollow compliment with a flick of ash and continued to peruse Anne cat-like. Wary green eyes smarting with cigarette smoke warned she wasn't going to be won over that easily; that she knew insincerity when uttered. 'I thought I was no longer of use to you. You told me I was *past my sell-by date.*' Anne felt the hurt behind her mentor's words.

'I would never say anything that cruel, Vivian. I'm grateful for … for how you helped me, and I haven't replaced you with an actual person …' The slightest twitch of an eyebrow showed she had her mentor's attention. 'Fleur's gone missing.'

'Funny, there I was thinking that you two had it all sorted in your new pad. No place for outsiders.' Exactly what Anne had thought too, before Fleur's suicide attempt, and now her prolonged absence. 'I warned you that girl was trouble, that you're better off without her, but would you listen?' She hooked something from between her front teeth with a scrape of a sharp nail, examining the offending exudate before flicking it away.

Struggling not to show her disgust, Anne changed tack. 'I know you don't think much of Fleur, but she's got … issues.'

'Don't we all?' Vivian snorted dismissively, her head unnervingly still. Something at the back of Anne's mind questioned whether that was the sort of thing a mentor should say, but then Vivian didn't always respond like 'the others', the army of grey authority that all marched as one; it was her only redeeming feature.

Vivian remained contemplative, calculating. Her indecision was betrayed only by the uncontrolled movement of her drifting right pupil, the jelly-like vacillation that caught the street light. A flicker that reminded Anne of the fire in her nightmares, forcing her to submissively break eye contact, down to cerise fluffy slippers below the hem of a gaudy pink dressing gown.

Jesus, it's only 7.30 and she's ready for bed.

Anne leaned in with the slightest of submissive genuflections. Her time in the care system had gifted her little, other than the ability to work people: needy women like Vivian. 'I *really* do need your help, Vivian,' barely a whisper.

'Are you asking me as a friend, or as your mentor?' Vivian liked to know where she stood. Anne paused, searching Vivian's lardy face and wandering eye for clues.

'Cat got your tongue?'

'As … a … friend?' Vivian's eyes turned the colour of dead grass that stubbornly sticks to the sole of your trainers. Wrong answer. She'd seen this reaction before when she'd dared to tell Vivian she was terminating their mentoring contract. Her head was starting to throb.

Help me say the right things, Banksy. What would you say?

She'd left the care system with little to prepare her for life ahead. Not even in possession of her few GCSE certificates. Careless. And everything earlier had been taken by the fire. From starting with nothing, she was so close to getting the start they deserved: a nice flat and a good reference from Mrs. B at the Food Bank, where she volunteered. Next, she'd look for a paid job. But first, she needed to find Fleur, and to do that, she needed Vivian back on board.

'What sort of help?' Vivian's faltering attempt at disinterest.

'I need someone to come with me to search the places Fleur likes to go. Pubs and the like …'

'Pubs?'

Well, that pressed the right buttons.

'Wait there. I'll put something on.' The door shut in her face.

She breathed in the fetid garden smells. 'You're coming with me,' she carefully placed the damp silk butterfly in the front pouch of her recently acquired North Face backpack. 'Simon Jones' gone in the stroke of a Sharpie pen.

It was hard not to stare at Vivian's leopard skin kitten heels and hot pink velour tracksuit, clashing forcefully with her wild ginger hair. Quite unsuitable for the decaying pub in the middle of the local housing estate. 'The Hollywood' where dreams came true after a few ciders and a groping last dance.

'So, where's your local, Vivian?'

A tremble visibly rippled through her mentor's body, like Anne knew it would. She knew that to keep Vivian sweet, it paid to go along with the pretence that Vivian had friends and a vibrant social life.

'Shall we sit out here, under one of these warmers?' It seemed a prime spot with good views of everyone coming and going. She couldn't help thinking that if only she'd taken up Fleur's invitations to go out, she wouldn't feel so out of place. But she'd not felt ready, afraid that she'd always be the one to get asked for ID. Besides, she knew from experience that bad things happen when you drink.

A fleet of blue lights strobed in the distance, probably something to do with the headless body. It was the only topic of conversation at the Food Bank. 'Keep your head on ...' It was funny at first.

Vivian returned with their drinks, stamping flat footsteps in the dewy grass.

'Do you think I look eighteen, Vivian?'

'What, dressed like that?'

Shrinking into her oversized black hoodie, Anne stared morosely at her lemonade.

'You might at least wear some makeup. I can give you that makeover. Some wine?'

She accepted. Something about Vivian treating her as an equal made her feel older.

'I don't usually drink.'

'I thought that was a lie. The sort of thing you'd say to get you onto the mentoring programme.'

'I don't lie,' said Anne without even blushing.

One last visit to the rancid-smelling pub toilets where plumping and pouting girls were swigging from a bottle of vodka. Chatting inanely, they were too self-absorbed to look at the photo booth picture she was trying to bring to their attention, driving her to pocket an expensive-looking perfume abandoned on a tiled shelf. Nice. It had citrus trees on the label, a nod to the lemon-themed life she dreamed would be hers, one day. An act that didn't go unnoticed by a girl exiting her cubicle, who had been listening attentively before making her call.

Undeterred, Anne placed her list of 'Fleur's Haunts' directly under Vivian's nose; a list of places she didn't dare to go to alone. She decided to keep the new piece of information to herself.

'I know you don't think much of Fleur, but we've been right through the care system together. She was split up from her brother and sisters when I first met her ...' But Vivian's attention had wandered elsewhere; she couldn't take her eyes off a steroid-pumped man vaping large clouds into the open air. He caught Vivian's eye and winked, making her squirm.

She's flirting with him, and I'm pouring my heart out here.

'Vivian. I need your help. Fleur's gone missing. Will you help me find her?' Direct. If that didn't work, then she was stumped. Green eyes, slightly unfocused, wandered back her way.

'What makes you think she wants to be found?' Vivian certainly had a way of throwing the conversation, of saying the unexpected, and maybe that was what she needed, to think differently. She'd been in two minds whether to ask Vivian for help, but then, who else did she have? Going to the police was ruled out; they might question her about her part in the childhood fire. And she'd already told Mrs. B at the Food Bank too many lies about Fleur's whereabouts to ask for her help. But she knew enlisting Vivian came with strings attached; binding strings she'd once been brave enough to sever. Sharp nails caught the light as Vivian lit a cigarette and drained the dregs from the wine bottle. 'Maybe she's found new friends, more mature friends?'

The hair on the back of her neck tingled with inadequacy. She'd already tried not to dwell on that possibility. She fingered the crumpled note in her pocket. The note found under her door after her earlier shift at the Food Bank: 'I NOW WERE FLEUR IS. YOUVE GOT 15 DAYS TILL SHES GONE.' That was when she knew she needed help.

'There'll be a boy behind this, Fleur's always been … flighty?' Another poorly masked attempt to discredit Fleur, through smoke exhaled with all the grandeur of a wise agony aunt. She thought of Frankie. *Who the hell was Frankie?* Only Frankie McGreal came to mind, and she knew Fleur wouldn't be so stupid as to drag up all that again, disturb the bones of their long-buried secret. She needed to get to Fleur, and fast. A thick descending mist drove them to leave the pub garden, obscuring the willowy shadow following them.

'I really would appreciate your help, Vivian …' She didn't want to beg, but she knew when she was out of her depth. She couldn't possibly go to the seedy places Fleur liked to frequent with her older half-sister, Millie. There was a remote chance that Millie had left the note under her door, but she couldn't see it. Subtlety wasn't in Millie's DNA. She had reluctantly added 'Speak to Millie' to the end of her 'Fleur's Haunts' list, inexplicably pleased that she was using a pencil, easily erased if things changed. As children, Fleur and Millie lived next door to the McGreal boys, with their nicotine-haired, stubbed-out cigarette of a mother. It was all closing in on her; the McGreals, the house fire, the papercuts of her childhood.

The bus shelter rattled as vehicles sped past. A bus travelling in the opposite direction advertised a Banksy exhibition, in collaboration with War Child, *showing pieces of his art from around the world.* She felt an unexpected rush of appreciation that someone from Bristol had done so well. That he had broken free. *There is always hope …*

'It might be nice going to those places over Christmas, though.' As if answering her prayers, Vivian seemed to be on the verge of agreeing to help.

'But we'd be looking for Fleur.' She felt the need for some ground rules.

Vivian's face twisted to read: *If that's what you like to believe*, making Anne question her mentor's motivations. 'But I'm happy to help you if you help me,' her breath soured from cigarettes and alcohol.

'What do you want me to do?'

'Let me carry on being your mentor?'

Satisfied, Vivian tipsily set off for home, leaving Anne alone in the damp bus shelter. The passing lights illuminated menacing shapes in the bushes around her. She closed her eyes, tapping her foot to 'Uptown Funk', the beat still bouncing about in her head from the pub beer garden, smiling at the memory of herself and Fleur dancing wildly to that tune on the night they moved into their flat. Her bus was late. She next tried to distract herself by working out the final date of her 15 DAYS TILL SHES GONE deadline, cursing Fleur for taking their shared mobile phone with its electronic calendar.

Suddenly, a piercing light made her cover her eyes. She screamed out loud at the screech of wheels. A large, black beast of a vehicle was heading directly for her.

3

#Banksy: 'I Remember When All This Was Trees'

Unable to sleep, Anne tossed and turned. She was convinced the car had meant to hit her before swerving violently and speeding away, leaving the smell of burning rubber in the air. Too dazzled by the lights, she hadn't seen the driver or the silent slip of the informant. Thank God her bus was just behind it. Was someone out to frighten her? Well, she was terrified and was sure it had something to do with her asking around after Fleur.

Maybe she doesn't want to be found ...

Vivian's words crashed around in her skull. Was it a subtle ploy to disrupt her efforts to find Fleur? Another of Vivian's twisted mind games? She suspected Vivian was only along for the ride, the way her eyes lit up at the mention of visiting pubs. In the cold morning light, she regretted involving her mentor.

'Shit, Room, how am I going to get out of this one?' she asked, rummaging around her near-empty mini fridge for some breakfast. Anne liked to talk to her rooms; to befriend them. She'd had six in as many years. At times, they were the only witness to the sordid things that went on behind closed doors. But this one seemed special, attentive - completely deserving of the lovely lemon paint she'd bought to cover up Fleur's drunken late-night scrawling: *I fucking hate it here,* defacing their wall.

She thought she'd escaped all that. All those scribbled protests with their initials and dates from kids wanting to leave their mark on the children's homes they'd occupied. A bit like she'd heard prisoners behave. In her last residence, they'd tried to keep the place nice by erecting some high shelving on which sat the best of the shabby donated items, like the fading icing sugar doll's house. It had held her spellbound with its flowery carpets and lemon-checked curtains. Do people really get to live in houses like that? She'd stared at the lemon-painted house for hours, letting her imagination go wild, conjuring up happy, loving families, even though it strained her neck being placed up high, out of reach of inquisitive little fingers. It was the only thing she missed when she had to move on.

Looking up, she saw only the grey stains that showed through their thinly painted ceiling, spreading like the pictures of ugly cancers on the side of Fleur's cigarette packets. She finished the last of her reduced-price strawberry yoghurts, hungrily licking the dregs from the carton's stubborn recesses, the tang telling her it should have been discarded days ago. Her careful budgeting had been thrown off by the costs of looking for Fleur. Everything felt spoiled, except for Fleur's undisturbed bed.

Fuck you, Fleur, for causing all this trouble. But you'll be back when you need money, or a hug, or something.

Fighting talk, but she could feel her usual self-assurance starting to crumble. She re-read the crumpled note. FIFTEEN DAYS TILL SHES GONE. What did it mean? It felt like the ransom notes in the movies. Had Fleur been taken hostage? No, it was a warning. But who had sent it? She took down their 'Kitten for Every Month' calendar, on which she'd noted key dates such as Fleur's Social Worker visits and her Health and Beauty exam dates, which Fleur would never remember. She flicked past cute 'Snowy', December's cat, to the small grid carrying forward to 2016. Fifteen days forward took her to 3rd January. She drew a big circle around the date, taking heart from the gap bridging then and now. A whole page. Plenty of time for Fleur to show up after getting into some scrape or other, the usual contradiction of laughter and tears.

With her foraging clothes set out neatly, she relished the feel of each familiar item. Black T-shirt, dark hoodie, and a scarf to cover her face. *'Invisibility Is a Superpower'* Banksy's words, which she believed to be true. The crisp air outside the 'Youth Alive' flats caught her breath. A brittle frost coated the towering graffiti-covered tenements opposite, now temporarily housing refugees. Squelching through syrupy leaves, she crossed the park eastwards to the more affluent outskirts. The new estates where Billy once commented, 'I remember when all this was trees.' It was his favourite Banksy phrase - also tattooed along his forearm. They'd been to London to see the original artwork, and as if on a holy pilgrimage, they'd stared for ages at the words painted in the arc of a smiling face, deifying a decaying wall. It was then that Billy told her that he'd once lived in a tree. Soft sod. But it was how Anne first became aware of climate change, seeking out Banksy's messages about the need to protect the environment.

A lost, soggy purple scarf tied to a park bench warmed her heart. It was reassuring to know that there were kind people out there, wanting to reunite lost items with their rightful owners. It gave her hope. She stuffed it into the side pocket of her backpack.

Her normal route was blocked by blue tape and police vans, forcing her to divert away from the canalside waste ground where the headless body was found. The place had deteriorated since she and Billy used to fish in ponds nearby, sometimes with his little brother joining them. But that was before the ponds dried up and the flimsy council-built garages collapsed, resulting in the dumping ground it had become. A row of tents graced the utilitarian outbuildings where homeless people had settled. Many of them were immigrants; some she recognised from the Food Bank.

Careful, she traversed fly-tipped builders' debris. Ahead, two lone figures disappeared ghostlike into the mist hanging over the canal; they'd also been watching the taped-off area. Closer, she could see it was her mystery spray painter friend she sometimes met on her early forages, with his older, heavily hoodied companion who sometimes accompanied him, coaching him quietly in their art. Maybe they, too, remembered when this all used to be trees.

An Amazon van entered a nearby cul-de-sac. Early morning drop-offs for busy professional people shopping online before Christmas. Like she would in her future lemon-tinged life when she got a job and a computer. The surge of excitement at what she might find made her skin tingle. Her best find had been the Complete Artists' Drawing Set, although disappointed that it was the horse series - she understood that you can't have everything.

Here we go.

Pretending to be on her mobile phone, she waited until the delivery van departed, then sped under the cover of December darkness to pick up two small parcels left in an open porch. Stuffing them into her backpack, her deft fingers told her one of the parcels was soft and squishy, something wrapped in tissue paper.

The van made another stop at a nearby property, leaving a parcel on the front doorstep of a flatted house at the junction of Park Lane below orange illuminated bells, and a curt 'LEAVE PARCEL ON STEP' note.

Well, they bloody well deserve to get it nicked; not even a polite 'please' in their note.

With no sign of those new cameras, she furtively made her way to the doorstep, keeping to the welcome shadows gifted by the crisp December morning. The parcel was heavy. Too big for her backpack. A sound rumbled behind the door, making her jump. Locks were being unbolted. She leaped with the parcel under her arm back into the bushes, just as a pair of dark, heavily tattooed arms heaved a scantily dressed girl out of the property. Her heart missed a beat.

It's Fleur.

But although the girl had a similar mass of blond hair, her build was heavier, and the street light caught the flash of an alien nose ring. The girl stumbled along nonchalantly, turning only to give the man the middle finger before the door slammed, her face now illuminated by her mobile phone.

'Yeah, taxi for Grace. 43a Park Lane.' Spotting Anne in the bushes, she gave a small foxlike yelp, but the heavy parcel under Anne's arm drew the smile of a fellow conspirator. The girl sat on a nearby wall, yawning and scrolling through messages on her phone, her musky perfume lingering heavy in the air, leaving Anne time to slip silently away as a car pulled up.

With her backpack bulging, she almost bumped into Sasha, the new young cleaning girl with a golden plait curled around her head, clacking along in shoes that clearly didn't fit her.

'My newest recruit,' Marta, the sly-eyed caretaker, had introduced her, but the girl always kept her head down as if embarrassed. Today, on her own, the girl looked up as if she wanted to chat, but even though Anne could see she'd been crying, she didn't have the time. She needed to get to St Gabriel's church for her volunteering shift at the Food Bank. She prided herself on her punctuality.

Please come home Fleur.

The flat was so empty without her; the air hung low and rueful. She showered in their tiny, unventilated bathroom, quickly, because Billy had warned against wasting water, and brushed the steamy mirror with a squeak from her towel. 'Opposites,' they used to say. Fleur with her long blond hair contrasting with her own short, dark, wavy hair, a look she borrowed from a presenter on X Factor. But she couldn't stop thinking about the girl who'd looked so much like Fleur that morning, being so roughly thrown out of the flat by the tattooed arms. What had she done to deserve that?

Emptying out her foraging spoils, she sighed heavily. This was something she and Fleur usually did together, sharing the thrill of what she'd found for them. That was half the fun of it, like the lucky dip they used to love when the travelling fair came to their Mount Pleasant council estate every August bank holiday. Her nose detected an earthy smell. It was a small, spikey house plant. She'd find somewhere nice for it – it would look lovely in a pretty lemon plant pot. Next, her hands ran over the squishy packet, and she shook out something wrapped in tissue paper that looked like it could be a long top or a short dress. Nice, expensive-looking. The type of thing Ruth, their old social worker, used to wear. She hung it in her side of the wardrobe.

Their flat had never been so tidy, the way she'd always imagined she wanted it, like people in lemon-painted houses would keep things. But she'd been wrong. She missed the chaos and disruption that followed in Fleur's wake. Absent-mindedly, she rearranged Fleur's rainbow spectrum of nail varnishes when her eye caught Fleur's dressing table drawer. They had a rule that you didn't go through each other's things, but then Fleur didn't usually stay away this long.

Immediately, the essence of Fleur filled the room; a heady mix of cheap perfume, cherry lip gloss, and cloying hairspray. There were the remaining picture booth photos of them both pulling faces. She picked up a smart pink and white striped bag tied with a black ribbon. It was a Pandora bag – unmistakable from the hours of window shopping that used to occupy their empty evenings.

Opening the striped bag, she stared with all the wonder of having found a baby duckling in their room. The bag didn't contain jewellery, as she expected. It was something dreadful and clunky in her hands. She looked at it for a long time before her teeth started to chatter and her hands started to shake. She was holding a gun.

4

#Banksy: 'May The Police Force With You'

A buzz in the air followed the parade of officers exiting Bristol's West Grange police station, summoned for a briefing about the headless corpse.

Entering the renovated city centre headquarters, PC James Wright's skin was tingling with excitement, despite the berating comments of his older colleague Bob Lyons. 'Newfangled system. Our patch, our dirty business ...' James was uncertain how to respond when Bob oozed seething contempt at anything new; instead, he concentrated on the refurbished surroundings. Unlike Bob Lyons, he loved everything around him. The smell of fresh plaster, the crunch of new carpets, and the achievement awards adorning the walls. Hard evidence that modern policing was changing.

'Cost a bloody fortune to renovate this place. Should've invested in more bodies on the beat.'

James shrugged off Bob Lyons' cynicism, knowing that the new Artificial Intelligence algorithms and Decision-Making tools were the way forward. A career-ending conversation, as far as Bob was concerned, who detested technology almost as much as he resented new police graduates.

The refurbished room opposite them sat ready for the incoming Police Performance Team. 'Just what we were missing all along …' Ignoring his boss's sarcasm, his attention was drawn to the Force's new mission statement displayed in a rainbow arch: 'Efficient, Responsive, Respect'. Bob Lyons nudged him hard in the back, 'Oh shit, I don't believe they've called that shower in,' his head swivelling to take in the late arrival of the Regional Crime Squad. Something big was about to break.

Bob Lyons' tone hushed as their own Detective Chief Inspector Bruce Campbell took the floor. 'At least that gives us the upper hand. I've worked on complex cases before, it's good to have the home advantage.'

Stacey, DCI Campbell's PA and competent audio-visual assistant, cast a discerning look that quietened the room before pointing a remote control at an interactive screen. A stream of photos of a headless body flashed before them. The images of hideous grey-yellow flesh made James turn away, queasy. Both hands were missing from the heavy arms of the revolving torso, the severed wrists leaving exposed bone shafts protruding from frills of decaying flesh. In 3D, the images spun 360 degrees, making James' stomach contract. His biggest fear was fainting after not making it through the PM he'd observed during training.

A groan chased around the room. He wasn't on his own. His nose twitched involuntarily, almost like he'd been hit by the smell of the grotesque image in front of them. Another pull on his twitchy stomach strings.

'No fingerprints, no defining features other than …' Bruce Campbell nodded to Audio Visual whizz, Stacey. 'Our man had been frozen.' The room stayed silent. 'Yes, frozen. As in kept in a deep freeze before being delivered here.'

'Delivered here?' James whispered to Bob Lyons.

'Dumped on bloody waste ground more like.'

'Stacey?' DCI Campbell turned to the screen as his assistant clicked to zoom in on the torso's severed neck. 'Melting ice crystals,' every syllable was sandblasted in his strong Scottish accent.

'But is that so strange, sir? It's been below zero some nights lately,' braved one of the Regional officers at the back of the room. DCI Campbell exhaled. Despite his invitation to stop him as he went along, they all knew he hated being interrupted.

'Been stored and transferred in a large freezer, minus eighteen degrees minimum according to Forensics.' DCI Campbell coughed uncertainly and nodded once more to Stacey. A close-up of the man's penis filled the screen to a sharp intake of breath. James didn't get it. 'Why are we looking at the man's todger?' he whispered to Bob Lyons, who shuffled uncomfortably and hushed him to stay quiet.

'Piercings. And a Prince Albert chain. A large one …'

'So, what's the average size, sir?' another goading comment, raising a titter.

'Larger than the average bolt and chain,' DCI Campbell clarified sharply. 'That is … according to our specialist sources,' seemingly keen to dissociate himself from such knowledge. 'Not too many artists do this type of work … apparently … so we're circulating this picture as we speak.' The air hung still and heavy. 'For now, we'll identify our man as 'Albert' until we establish his real ID. White, muscular, early 30s. Some evidence of drug tracks. Probably returned to Bristol for a good reason.'

The efficient Stacey switched to reveal a tattoo on the man's chest 'Bristol City Football Club'.

'He's been sent home,' Bob Lyons muttered as the screen went blank.

'That's all we've got to go on for now,' DCI Campbell's most dismissive tone, clearly meant to discourage further questions. 'We're putting together a specialist crime team with input from Region on what will be known as Operation Cuckoo. Darren, our new Equality and Diversity lead, is preparing a press release. DS Shona Stewart will be the Senior Investigating Officer. All comms on this case must go through the SIO or Darren.' He sensed Bob's inner groan. They all knew he had been reprimanded for being obstructive during his recent diversity training.

'Oh, one more thing …' the DCI concluded. 'Albert didn't expect to exit this mortal existence just yet; the piercing was only done in the last month. Poor sod didn't get much action before he died; it takes up to eight weeks to heal.'

'Ah shit,' exclaimed Rav Shah, another of James' West Grange colleagues, against a background of sympathetic tutting.

'Usual policing duties unless told otherwise.' They were dismissed.

They were only just back at the crumbling Victorian West Grange station when James received the email. He'd been selected to be on Operation Cuckoo, to be part of the specialist crime team, shadowing DS Shona Stewart, the lead officer, whom he knew by reputation only. She was good.

'I've been invited onto the specialist team.'

'Well, whoop my arse,' grunted Bob, rising from the desk opposite James and pulling on his overcoat, thinning and shiny at the elbows. James looked up. What was that supposed to mean? He watched him pick up his phone and his cigarettes and wait for something to be spat out of the printer before leaving in a hurry, stroking his beard as he did when agitated, leaving James' 'Goodbye then …' hanging in the air.

Bob Lyons knew the young PC was watching him. Jumped up little prick. Fresh out of college and about to be thrown to the lions on a case that had Twinnie McGreal stamped all over it.

But something else was bothering him. Surely Twinnie hadn't served his time yet? As far as he knew, McGreal was still in HMP Channings Wood: Category C male prison, a fitting place for the likes of him. But if he was out, how come he hadn't picked up on his release date? He stroked his beard deep in thought; he'd have to be more vigilant. He'd missed a few things lately.

It had to be Twinnie McGreal behind the dumped headless body. Few criminals on his patch would pull off such a stunt. No doubt it was a warning meant for his twin brother and rival drug dealer Frankie McGreal, who just happened to be paying Bob handsomely for 'police privileges' - a long-standing arrangement which suited them both. And at last, Frankie answered his call.

'Yes, I've heard. Usual place? …'

Frankie McGreal, not in the mood for pleasantries, cut him off mid-sentence. Before leaving the station, Bob had printed off Twinnie's licensing conditions from the national database. The PNC confirmed his early release. The timing couldn't be worse. He'd hoped to be well retired before Twinnie got out of prison, looking to settle old scores. Back to pick up where he left off: GBH, dealing, then the security van robbery. He'd always been one greedy little bastard.

5

#Banksy: 'Follow Your Dreams - Cancelled'

'Can we talk about something other than the poor man who has been decapitated?' Mrs. B, who ran the Food Bank, was right, as usual. It was becoming the only topic of conversation, and that wasn't right in a church. The Angel Gabriel, balanced high above the altar, wore an affronted air.

They retreated to the kitchen. 'That's a nice top, Anne. Cornflower. It really brings out the blue in your eyes.' Anne's hands were stuffed into the deep pockets where she'd found a small embroidered tag declaring: '*The World's your Oyster*'. Fleetingly, she felt it really could be. That you can achieve your dreams. Then she remembered Fleur, and the gun, and the mess she was in.

'Anne – you're miles away today.' Mrs. B seemed to be waiting for a reply.

'What? ... Oh, sorry. The top was a present from my friend.' Lies seemed to trip off her tongue lately. Mrs. B nodded in approval like nice people do when they talk about having nice friends. But something was bothering Mrs. B, who seemed subdued.

'Everything okay, Mrs. B?'

The woman rested against the large industrial sink, wringing her hands. 'Not really love, I think we've got a problem.' Anne's stomach lurched. Surely, she couldn't know about Fleur going missing. Or even worse, about the gun. But Mrs. B looked away, avoiding eye contact as people do when about to discuss difficult topics.

'Things have started to go missing.'

She was flooded with relief that it wasn't to do with Fleur. 'What sort of things?'

'The donations tin has been very light these last few weeks. Improbably light.'

'Do you mean like someone's been stealing?' Mrs. B nodded, looking sadder than Anne had ever seen her. And no wonder. Who the hell would steal from a church? Anne would do anything to help Mrs. B. Not only was she the kindest person in the world, but she was also the one person who could provide her with the thing she needed most in her life, a good reference. Her passport to better things.

'Who can have taken the money?' Thinking out loud, she felt her knees buckle. Surely Mrs. B didn't suspect her of stealing?

'Oh, I don't know what to think. I'll just have to keep a closer eye on things.' They both continued with their kitchen chores, Anne increasingly miserable at the thought of her dependence on Vivian to help with her search for Fleur, who she was sure was behind the gun being placed in her drawer.

'Have you seen Vivian lately?' Mrs. B eerily seemed to read her mind.

'Yes, we've hooked up again. Something was outstanding that we needed to work on.' Mrs. B raised an eyebrow.

'I have to say I'm surprised, but your mentoring contract must be coming to an end soon?' Again, it was as if Mrs. B could pluck thoughts from her head. 'I'd like to meet her one day …'

Startled, she carelessly sliced her finger with her serrated bread knife and watched the blood seep into the fresh-smelling bread. Mrs. B couldn't possibly meet up with Vivian, who would only become resentful of their friendship, much like she was becoming sulky and withdrawn whenever she tried to talk about Fleur. Besides, she was sure to spill the beans about Fleur going missing and reveal all the cover-up lies she'd told. No, that couldn't be allowed to happen. 'Sure. I'll arrange it, Mrs. B.' Her second lie, and it was only ten o'clock.

Anne welcomed the routine of the Food Bank; the way it all ran to plan, a place where she could immerse herself in a way that didn't demand she think about other things.

'I've been working on your reference – you know, for when you're ready to move on.' As usual, Mrs. B welled up at the mention of her leaving. Anne turned awkwardly into her embrace, 'We've loved having you here, Anne.'

Briefly allowing herself to absorb the warmth of Mrs. B's hug, she breathed in her orange blossom perfume that smelled of walks in the countryside with Billy, and once again she felt the prickle of tears at thinking what life would be like with a mum like Mrs. B. 'Look at us, silly things,' Mrs. B offered her a tissue.

'And will Fleur be joining us today?' Perfect Pam, one of the nosier volunteers, asked, pausing from buttering toast, spoiling the moment, as usual.

Get lost Pam. Mind your own business for once.

'No, she's at Health and Beauty College.' Third lie. But just loud enough for Mrs. B to hear. At least that would get Fleur some brownie points and stop them from asking awkward questions, although Anne suspected Fleur hadn't attended her course for some time.

'Better there than hanging around here, getting up to mischief.' The air stilled around them. What did Pam mean? Mrs. B stiffened. Surely, they didn't suspect Fleur of taking the money? She was used to covering for Fleur, but this time everything was starting to feel different, the warning swirl in the pit of her stomach that wouldn't go away. The clock was already ticking with less than two weeks to find Fleur, and now she had a gun to worry about. And just when they were so close to getting their lives sorted. So close to moving on with their

41

life plans. Her fingers worried away at ***The World's Your Oyster*** tag.

The rest of the morning was hectic; there seemed to be kids everywhere with the schools being closed for Christmas, and more families than ever relied on help from the Food Bank. The noisy 'Walk and Talk' group arrived, ready for their morning coffee, smelling of crisp fresh air after their weekly ramble, grateful for the warmth of the church.

'We've been down by the canal,' Jonah, the leader, announced, his cheeks flushed tawny from the cold. 'You know, where the headless body was found.' It was all becoming too ghoulish, too disturbing, on top of everything else she had to worry about. She left Pam chatting to him while she busied herself looking for sugar in the cupboards under the serving counter. The sound of nails tapping above her made her look up, directly into the amused eyes of PC James Wright. 'Hello. We meet again.'

Oh, shit, what's he doing here?

'Don't worry, I haven't come to arrest you,' he seemed to have a twinkle in his eye. She gripped the counter for support. 'After that stunt you pulled about being your friend's Mental Health Worker, Fleur wasn't it, Still Waters multi-storey car park? I noticed the Food Bank logo,' he nodded at her ID badge. Her knees felt weak. Another crisis she'd kept from Mrs. B.

'Good Detective skills, PC Wright ...'

'I was in yesterday, asking about you, but you'd already left.'

Please, please don't ask to speak to Fleur.

'Anyway, how is Fleur?'

Anne thought of the hidden gun and felt her face flush.

'Is she okay now?'

'Sorry?'

'Fleur? ...'

'Yeah, sorry.'

Come on, Anne, get a grip.

'She's okay. She gets into scrapes - she's through the worst of it now. But thanks for helping out. Can I bring your coffee over?' She looked around anxiously, hoping Mrs. B wouldn't overhear.

'Good work you're doing here ... Anne Grimes.' This time, he was looking more closely at her name badge. 'Shall we start again? As you know, I'm James.' He held out his hand, but she must have looked uncertain as he pulled away. 'We've been asked to start dropping in, all part of developing good police: community relations. A sort of 'listening exercise', his keen eyes now reminding her of a baby deer. Innocent, as if he believed these things actually worked. 'A chance to pick up on any local concerns.'

Perfect Pam stopped her work to listen in.

'Like boys out on the streets spray painting?' Anne tried to deflect things, then felt disloyal to her early morning spray painting comrades. She loved how Bristol was becoming famous for its street art, especially Banksy's work, which Billy used to call their very own open-air gallery. PC Wright bent forward to take his cup of coffee, filling the air with his cinnamon-scented aftershave.

'Actually, I quite like the street art,' he said, surprising her. 'No, I'm more interested in real crime. Like what's happening to people's early morning deliveries, stuff going missing off doorsteps.' The officer's words clanged about her head, and although his lips were moving, all she could hear was the blood whooshing in her ears.

He took his drink and sat with the 'Walk and Talk' group, who quietened at his approach. But he soon engaged them in football banter, whilst remaining vigilant as to what was happening around him. Just as DS Shona Stewart had suggested he should. He was there with a single aim: to pick up whatever he could about Albert and Operation Cuckoo. 'Someone is missing a son, brother, friend,' Shona Stewart had counselled. So, he was out on community patrol, keeping all his senses open, especially after she'd hinted at a possible transfer to the new police HQ early in the new year. It paid to keep well in with DS Stewart.

Anne looked over at him, now talking to an elderly woman, deep in discussion about dog poo. There was something quite sweet about how he was listening so intently. She straightened out the crumpled 'I NOW WERE FLEUR IS' note, and as things had quietened, she started to list who might have sent it. She still hadn't discounted Millie, Fleur's half-sister, and knew she couldn't put off a visit any longer.

'See you tomorrow, Anne.' PC Wright waved as he left, talking into his radio like a grown-up police officer. She waved in a lighthearted way that hopefully masked her dismay. Why was he hanging around? Was he on to her early morning foraging? She doubted it as she was always careful to cover her tracks. And just for a moment, she allowed herself a small thrill. Taking things from doorsteps was small fry. How would he react if he knew she was hiding a gun?

Climbing the stairs to her flat, she was met with the strong smell of bleach and the sight of Brian from the neighbouring flat, scrubbing at something smeared across her front door. 'What the hell? ...'

'Sorry, Anne, I wanted to finish this before you got back and before Marta saw it.' He stopped his efforts, and they both stood back, revulsed by the washing-up bowl containing floating clots of blood and stringy animal entrails.

'Who would do this? Did you see anything?'

'No, but it must have been after Sasha had finished her cleaning,' strengthening her suspicions that his interest in Sasha was bordering on stalking the girl with the curled plaits. They scrubbed away together, she now certain there was something in the constant feeling she was being watched, ignoring his sideways glances at her. But for once, Anne was grateful for his assistance as she worked through waves of nausea. A disturbing sensation caused partly by the gory act, but also by the memories it stirred. She'd seen this before. So had Brian, during his stay in a Young Offender's prison, where anything that came to hand was smeared, usually as a warning of worse things to come.

6

#Banksy: 'Flower Thrower'

You got to Millie's place on the run-down Southbank estate via a trashed playground where slit-eyed youths with dangerous-looking dogs hung out, giving off a warning that you had strayed out of bounds. Someone had replicated Banksy's 'Flower Thrower' on a boarded-up shop front, with syringes being tossed into the air instead of flowers. It pulled at her heartstrings; she and Billy had spent ages trying to work out the romantic meaning behind the original artwork.

Rushing past, she finally reached Millie's weed-strewn path, dodging discarded cigarette butts turned mushy in the damp. There was nothing lemon about Millie's house. She knocked loudly on the partially opened front door.

Shit, this place is freezing.

'Hello,' she battled against an Oasis number blasting from the kitchen. River came toddling towards her, his cold hands outstretched to be picked up. A sour whiff of his nappy made her hold her breath and hold him at arm's length, a sodden lump hanging below the bottom of his dirty grey vest; his nose caked with dried snot. Millie came into the hall. Wobbling flesh and abundant hair, much like Fleur's, but dyed candy floss pink. Thick black roots ran like tramlines above a pair of lips tattooed on her neck.

'Fuckin' hell, you gave me the fright of me life. You're our Fleur's mate, Anne?' Then, as if she had a sixth sense, 'What trouble's she in now?' handing her a can of lager.

'It's a bit early for me. Can I have a cup of tea?'

'Over there,' she tossed a mass of pink hair toward the kettle, her mouth twisted. Anne shared her warm milky tea with River, now in his highchair – his face turned orange after his morning snack of cheesy Wotsits.

'I was hoping Fleur might be here.'

''aven't seen 'er for a couple of weeks.' Millie held a cigarette between orange fingers. 'Don't worry 'bout 'im,' noticing Anne's look of disapproval. 'I keep the doors open for the smoke to get out,' and carried on smoking, exaggeratedly, as if to make a point. 'River's been missin' 'is aunty Fleur though; likes 'er readin' to 'im.'

The back door pushed wide open, and a beanpole of a man with dark, greasy hair entered, zipping up his jeans. 'Just been for a piss,' he rubbed his hands together. 'Can't be arsed going up those bloody stairs. Pass us a beer, love.'

He screwed up dark, suspecting eyes while he sipped his beer.

'She's all right, she's our Fleur's mate.'

'You need to change that baby's arse,' his nose twitched, ratlike, as he carried on his assessment of the intruder in their kitchen.

'All right, Zane, I'll get round to it, if you're so fuckin' concerned, you do it.'

'I fuckin' will an' all.'

She followed the couple into their sparsely furnished lounge. Zane's gangly frame filled the floor while he changed River's nappy.

'Do you have any idea where Fleur might be? I need to find her. I think she might be in trouble.'

'Doesn't sound a bit like our Fleur,' Millie honked sarcastically, leading to a fit of coughing. Zane looked up, 'Last saw her with Macca.'

'God, not that shit, I've told 'er to stay away from pushers.' Millie had difficulty heaving her bulky body from the floor, shuffling to dispose of the dirty nappy.

'Think he's got a bit of a thing for her; they looked all loved up to me.'

'What's she got that'd interest 'im?' Millie asked, betraying a hint of jealousy.

'Don't know, but it all comes at a price. You get nothin' for free from the McGreals.'

Anne's breakfast hit the back of her throat. A queasy wave engulfed her, carrying the whiff of beer, dirty nappies, and trepidation. She was transported to a previous life. The McGreals. Words that confirmed her worst fears after the door-smearing incident. Surely Fleur knew more than anyone the danger she was putting them both in. 'Which one?' Her reply sounded strangled.

Zane looked up, 'What d'you mean, which one?'

'Which McGreal?'

'Shayne or Frankie …don't know, I get them all mixed up. You knew them, Millie?'

'Not much, I'd gone to live with me dad by then, but it can't be Shayne, our Fleur told me 'e's dead.'

He's dead, he's dead, he's dead; the words rebounded around Anne's head with all the force of a football being kicked by hefty boots looking for a revenge win, as flames flickered before her eyes.

Oh no, it's all coming back to haunt us. Shayne McGreal, the housefire. I need to get to Fleur, and fast. They can't ever find out what we did ...

'You all right love? You've gone a right funny colour. 'Ere, 'ave a swig of me lager,' Millie pushed the open lager can towards her. 'Looks like you've 'ad a run in with the McGreals then?' A missing girl, a gun, animal entrails. It had to be the McGreals.

Hanging on to get herself together and process everything she'd heard, she absent-mindedly helped River draw pictures on the back of old birthday cards stuffed in his toy box. She removed one, which was clearly unsuitable for a toddler. The cartoon image of a couple copulating was far too crude for the two-year-old. But it was the handwritten message that caught her eye. 'I now you think I'm a total tossa, but I'm your total tossa.' She thought of her I NOW WERE FLEUR IS message. It was the same spikey writing; the same spelling mistake. She knocked on the kitchen door.

'Zane, fancy coming to the corner shop with me? We'll take River out for some fresh air. I'll buy us some more beers while we're out.'

'All right, all right. I fuckin' well sent it.'

They diverted to the swing park where River was jumping in puddles and chasing leaves in the wind.

'So, tell me what you know.'

'Only that Grace - an old mate of mine, told me that Fleur's mixed up with Frankie McGreal.'

'Go on …'

'Well, it seems his twin brother, Twinnie McGreal has just been released from prison and he's coming for Frankie.'

'What do you mean?'

'It's all about county lines, you know, keeping to your own drug territory and all that.'

'Frankie's strayed out of line?'

'Yeah, while Twinnie was in nick. Grace said he's coming back to teach Frankie a lesson. Got them all shook up, making threats. Big threats.' Her mind flashed back to the McGreal twins, always sparring on the landing of the Mount Pleasant flats.

'How does Grace know all this?'

'She's on the game, gets to know everything. But she's always had a thing going on with Twinnie McGreal. Used to visit him in prison, feed him information about Frankie and his gang. I told the stupid cow she's playing a dangerous game getting between those two. But she doesn't care. Can't even see when someone …'

'How did you know where I lived?'

'Me and Millie went there once. Met Fleur before a party.'

'You haven't been following me, have you, Zane?'

'Fuck off, what do you think I am, some sort of weirdo?'

River started shouting excitedly for Anne to push him higher on his swing, while Zane watched, his foot hooked around the angled metal frame. Awkward, as if he had more to disclose.

'The reason I sent you that note …'

Anne paused and nodded him on, sensing his hesitation.

'Grace thinks Frankie's getting ready to make a run for it. In the new year. Heard them all talking about 3rd Jan.'

'Where to?'

'He's bought a place in Spain.'

Her legs felt wobbly, like they were about to give way. Fleur had been bleating on about Spain for ages, but she'd just thought it was a fantasy and ignored it. Maybe Fleur had been trying to tell her something all along. She suddenly needed to get home.

'Bye, River.' The child's protests mingled with the creaks of the swing in the air behind her.

Fumbling to unlock their front door, she tossed the keys on her bed and swiped up above their shared wardrobe, pulling down the biscuit tin containing their documents. She'd learned from the past that you needed to protect your valuables, especially from fire. She shook everything out on her bed. Fleur's passport was gone.

What do I do, Room? She paced the small room, scratching across worn carpet tiles before turning to the calendar again. Snowy the kitten looked sinister now, with his knowing light blue eyes. A scrawled entry caught her eye. Fleur had drawn a heart around today's date and pencilled in 'The Barge, 3 pm.' The Barge was a trendy canalside pub she frequented with her Health and Beauty course friends. 'Somewhere you can get anything,' Fleur once told her, with that cheeky wink that made her eyes crinkle and made Anne nervous.

'Bye Room. Wish me luck.' The calendar entry reminded her that the clock was ticking. She couldn't miss this opportunity and didn't feel the need to involve Vivian.

The girl behind the bar laughed when she ordered hot chocolate. 'We're not fuckin' McDonald's.' The remark attracted the attention of a noisy group sitting at a long table with pitchers of rainbow-coloured cocktails as bright as their hair and nails.

'Hey, weirdo, waiting for your girlfriend?'

Her heart sank. She knew the ringleader from school. A girl with puffy cheeks who used to remind her of a hamster; the same girl who'd started to bully Fleur until she'd stepped in.

Don't things ever change?

For an instant, she regretted not being with Vivian. She would have sorted her out.

'Watch her, she's weird,' Hamster Face played to her audience. The menace in her eyes was accentuated by the blue tinge to her lips from her cocktail, giving her the appearance of an exotic lizard.

Anne tried to ignore her and took her chance while she had their attention. 'Actually, I'm looking for Fleur Drake. It's really important. Anybody seen her?' She scanned the leering faces at the table. No response. Well, it was worth a punt even if it had all been a waste of time. But Hamster Face, now in her stride, wasn't going to let her off that easily. The girl stood as wide as she was tall, blocking her exit.

'Told you she's a lesbo ...'

Anne tried to push her aside, but the wedge of a girl wouldn't budge. There was only one thing for it. 'Isn't it time you got back to your hamster wheel?' There was a deathly hush. Hammy, like most bullies, appeared not to know how to respond to those who answered back. The girls at the long table started sniggering at the hamster reference; the ringleader turned to face them, cheeks inflated, fists clenched. Anne took her chance to leave.

'Nice one.' A girl sitting at the bar called across to her. Her heart missed a beat; she looked so much like Fleur. She recognised the girl with the big hair and the nose ring. The same girl who'd been thrown out of the flat on Park Lane the last time she'd been out foraging for parcels. She went over to her, grateful for an ally, even though it seemed odd that she was sitting alone with her drink.

The girl repeatedly checked her phone and tapped her foot on a large holdall under her bar stool, as if protecting it. The bag, emblazoned with Bristol City's red and white stripes, didn't quite suit her high-heeled boots or flimsy dress.

'You're looking for Fleur? Sit down, I'm Grace.'

The girl smiled, softening the flint edge to her chin. Then it all fell into place. This was Zane's friend who'd told him about Frankie buying a place in Spain, the same girl who liked to live dangerously by having affiliations with both of the McGreal twins. Grace looked at her levelly through heavily kohled eyes, which flicked up at the edges, giving her a surprised look. She took her time, as if used to weighing people up, sipping her cocktail in contemplation; her little finger extended.

'Don't suppose you know where I'd find her?' Anne nudged.

'No, haven't seen her.'

Anne strained to hide her disappointment. Was the girl teasing her? Grace stood up to go, drained her cocktail, and strode towards the door. She walked like the sorrel mare in her treasured Anne of Green Gables book, graceful with her chest thrust forward, brown over-the-knee suede boots clacking like hooves on the tiled floor, the holdall awkward on her slender shoulder. Then she turned and smiled her softening smile once more.

'Try The Blind Fox.'

'Where's that?'

'I'd suggest you ask Zane.'

They nodded goodbye to each other, and Anne fleetingly felt a connection, like they could be friends. She wished she'd stay and talk to her, tell her about her life, as a wave of loneliness washed over her. If she ever found Fleur, she would say 'yes' to all her suggestions to go out and enjoy their lives together, rather than being the stick in the mud. She regretted all the things she'd missed out on. But at least she had a new lead. The Blind Fox. A lot more than when she'd entered the place.

A thought flashed through her head, and she ran to the door, but was too late as Grace was heading off in a taxi which had been waiting outside for her. She was too late to ask the girl how she knew she had been speaking to Zane.

7

#Banksy: 'Rats'

'They've found Albert's head ...' The air was buzzing in West Grange police station. 'Hanging out of a box found by workmen.' PC Rav Shah paused for effect before adding, 'The rats had got to it.' The morning kitchen crew groaned, pushing away their shared plate of jam on toast. 'His nibbled head was found in Reading. Eighty miles away.'

'Ah shit, they'll want to drag the Reading police into Operation Cuckoo now. This is getting out of hand.' The veins in Bob Lyons' cheeks bulged as he spoke.

'So, what connects Bristol with Reading?' mused James.

'The fuckin' M4!' Rav's response caused them all to laugh at James' expense. But he was getting used to their taunts by now, another little humiliation that seemed to be part of his initiation to the job.

'Found by Reading Service Station. And there's also a Canterbury link ...' Rav continued, now in his stride. 'Something printed on the box. Not been released yet.'

'Someone's taking the piss,' Bob Lyons muttered, letting the door slam behind him, carrying his tea for one.

James watched Bob Lyons leave the kitchen as his phone buzzed. He took the call in the privacy of the station car park, as instructed by DS Stewart.

'You ready, James?' Shona Stewart's commanding voice rang out. 'We're meeting Henry at the mortuary. Eleven thirty. Get there for eleven and we'll squeeze in some mentoring.'

He'd kept his mentoring arrangement to himself as he was already taking enough flak from Bob Lyons and the lads for being selected to be on the specialist crime team. 'The Bumfluff team,' he'd overheard in the station kitchen. Just loud enough for him to hear.

The mortuary was in one of the outbuildings at the back of the hospital. He made sure he was early, keen to make a good impression, and had two scalding coffees waiting on the reception's fading Formica-topped table, its edges nibbled away by nervous fingers.

'Morning, James. What do you know about the Principle of Exchange?' Wow, Shona Stewart wasted no time. He was pleased she was taking this mentoring thing seriously, but her abrupt style unnerved him as dark eyes, glinting with power, bored into him. He rubbed at his temples to recall what he'd learned from his Professional Policing degree while she tapped her short, clipped nails expectantly.

'Locard stated there will always be something left behind, and there will always be something taken away from any crime scene, however minuscule.' She beamed at him as they suffered machine coffees with a tang of salt, turning to a rustle behind them.

'Well, in this case, there was certainly something left behind.' Henry joined them, taking the third plastic chair ready and waiting, her ID badge banged against the table: Dr. Henrietta Hawes, Forensic Pathologist. Spikey white-grey hair, dark eyes, nice perfume.

'Should have waited, I'd have made you a decent one,' she snubbed the offer of the machine coffee. 'It's got an identity crisis. Can't decide whether it's a coffee machine or an instant soup dispenser.' They pushed their drinks away.

'So, what have you got for us, Henry?' DS Stewart's eyes sparkled. Everything about her shone from her blazer buttons to her practical DMs. He liked his new company.

'Severed head. No ID as yet. Male in his mid-thirties. Definitely belongs to our torso.'

'How did it … become separated?' James didn't yet know this strange language of forensics.

'Not sure. Botched job, no butchering skills with this one. Amateur.' He strangely thought of Anne Boleyn - the extensive efforts made to ensure an effective decapitation.

'Judging by the tissue and bone damage, probably some type of industrial saw.'

God no, not now. His stomach full of salty coffee took a somersault.

'No hands yet?'

'Doubt we'll find them, probably fed to the pigs by now.' James clung to the side of his chair.

'You've got something else, haven't you?' Shona seemed to sense it. She'd said they'd worked together before.

'Blattodea, of German origin.' Henry looked like she was enjoying their confused look. He guessed she liked to show off her privileged knowledge and realised for the first time that they would always be one step behind Forensics. She scrolled through several pictures on her phone.

'Cockroaches?'

'Primitive winged insects. Small segment; shiny leathery encasement still intact. Being frozen helped.'

'Albert's head had also been frozen?'

'Yep, someone is going to great lengths to send us clear messages.' James felt a tingle in his veins. This was what he'd entered policing for. He already knew he wanted to become a detective, something he hoped to discuss with DS Stewart.

'Looking at the damage to the surrounding tissue, I'd guess it was put in there live.'

'Put where?' he dared.

'In Albert's ear. No wings. It's typical of females of the species. Pregnant - eggs still intact, held in oothecae … egg sacs.'

'Do they live here naturally?' took up DS Stewart, looking intrigued, while James paled.

'Mostly further South, where it's warmer. But they're not hard to get hold of; you can buy them online. They also sell them in pet shops for feeding to reptiles.' Henry munched on a custard cream dug out of the pocket of her voluminous waxed coat, more suited to hunting in the country.

James headed back to West Grange station feeling nauseous in his own skin. After his debrief with DS Stewart, he'd made a list of actions, some of which he needed to discuss with Bob Lyons. 'Keep Bob on board. He knows this patch better than anyone. He's probably already onto Albert's secrets. but he'll have his nose put out of joint that we've selected you, James. Keep close to him - keep him sweet.' It struck him as odd that she'd warned him about taking sides. When considering the challenges of policing, he'd never expected them to come from his colleagues.

'Remember, keep all senses open. Be diligent; don't leave anything concerning Operation Cuckoo lying around. Attention to detail is everything.' He already knew much of that from his policing degree, but something else bothered him. It felt like she was asking him to keep an eye on Bob Lyons.

In an out-of-town pub, Bob Lyons was meeting with amateur crook Frankie McGreal.

'So, when did Twinnie get out?' McGreal drummed his fingers on the table, sounding every bit as pissed off as he looked.

'He was released on parole six weeks ago. On license to an old address in Canterbury. That's how we've missed him.'

'It's not fucking good enough, Bob …'

Bob Lyons had never seen Frankie McGreal so agitated, chewing on nonexistent nails and checking the door every five minutes. 'But dumping a fucking dead body?'

Bob Lyons stayed quiet.

'We're getting out of here.' Frankie repeatedly rubbed his hands over his knees.

'You're leaving?'

'Just finalising everything. I've been sorting something out in Spain for a while. Didn't expect Twinnie to be out so soon, though.' His early release had taken them all by surprise.

'Don't forget you owe me, Frankie … and it goes back to the Mount Pleasant house fire.'

Frankie McGreal's slate grey eyes smirked, accentuating the meanness in his pinched face. 'You'll get what you're due, but we're not finished yet. We need you to cover our backs until we leave in the new year. Don't know what that mad bastard will do next.' They shook on it. Bob relaxed. It could still all line up nicely if he brought his retirement plans forward.

Bob Lyons might not have been a man of many words, but he prided himself on being a man of action. He needed some insurance in this changing climate and knew exactly where to get it. *Cherchez la femme.* He needed to speak to that blond-haired strumpet Grace, whom he'd locked up in the past for soliciting. These days, however, they had a mutual arrangement; from time to time, they helped each other out. But Grace was skating on thin ice this time, teaming up with Twinnie McGreal when he was in prison, while going out with Ali Kumar, one of Frankie McGreal's minders.

He was sitting outside 43a Park Lane, waiting for her to appear. It was the sort of crisp, cold morning he liked. He rolled down his window to discard the remains of his unsatisfactory breakfast batch when he noticed something odd. There was a slim, hooded figure hiding in the bushes. Slinking low in his seat, he watched the hooded person hover before stealing a large parcel left on the step.

'Cheeky little fucker …' So, there was the mystery parcel thief they'd been getting complaints about. Still, that wasn't what he was waiting for. He'd let it pass, for now. The door to the flat flung open, and Grace was unceremoniously heaved out. He smiled to himself, thinking how nothing changes, and got out of the car, taking Grace's phone from her hands. The parcel thief had disappeared into the shadows.

'Morning, Grace.'

'Oh shit. What do you want?'

'That's no way to speak to an officer of the law. Want a lift?'

'No thanks, I've just phoned for a taxi.'

'No, I think you want a lift.' He took her roughly by the elbow, ushering her across to his car.

'You on duty?'

He shook his head. 'Let's consider it a personal call.'

'Look, I'm not working. I need to get home.'

'All in good time. I'm going to treat you to a nice coffee, because I'm generous like that. I hear Twinnie McGreal's back in circulation. Now you might want to be a good girl and tell me all you know.'

8

#Banksy: 'Sorry, The Lifestyle You Ordered is Currently Out of Stock'

'Did I ever tell you about my last mentoring training session?'

Oh, please, not all that crap again.

'All about Communication. Changed my outlook on life.' Anne, wedged into a steamy corner of 'The Newt' pub, was eager to leave after another wasted visit to one of Fleur's favourite pubs. Vivian was taking her time to drain the last of her wine, wearing a look that warned they weren't leaving until she'd finished every last drop, accompanied by her drawn-out reminiscing.

'I used to work in one of the old council buildings, you know, for a temping agency.'

You don't say ...

'Loved working in the council's HR Department. Amazing what you got to know about other people's personal lives.'

Once again, Anne had to sit through a stuttering account of the council's archaic systems, 'probably still not updated - nothing ever happens quickly in public services ...' As if that was news to Anne. At the first pause for breath and the hush after the band's last tune, Anne zipped up her fleece. Her ears popped at the change in outside atmosphere as Vivian droned on, oblivious. 'You'd never believe the state of their filing systems, so easy to switch a few records around.' Anne slowed her pace to listen more closely to this new addition to Vivian's repertoire.

'I was tasked with managing the Mentor Scheme applications.'

'So, was that how you got into mentoring?'

'What do you mean by that?' Eyes flashing, the light caught her quivering pupil.

Oh, don't turn all sour on me now, Vivian. I just want to get home.

'I responded to an advert in the local paper, like everybody else. It turned out I was a natural.' Knowing what was to follow, Anne picked up her step. It was shaping up to be a long walk to the bus stop.

'Did I tell you about my training buddy?'

'The one whose name you couldn't remember?'

'Well, if you're not interested ...'

'No ... go on, tell me again.'

Vivian didn't seem to catch the exasperation in her voice, or didn't care, more like. It was as if she needed to expunge something out of her system, but these recollections of her past were becoming alarmingly frequent.

And there was I thinking mentoring was about me ...

'My buddy was called Nina, or Mina. Something foreign.'

Yeah, you couldn't be bothered getting her bloody name right.

'She had the deepest brown eyes. They threw me at first; reminded me of someone else I used to know …' Vivian fell once more into her monotonous reflections on her long past training, much of which Anne could repeat off pat.

'… She reminded me of my schoolfriend, Zita. The only real friend I ever had …' She cast Anne a disparaging look. 'Arms thin as twigs. But then she died …' Her eyes looked far away.

Anne stiffened and slowed her pace. She'd never heard this extension to the story before. Vivian was straying into new, morbid territory. Maybe the wine had lowered her guard.

'How did she die?'

'Who?'

'Your school friend, Zita.'

Vivian stopped suddenly and turned so close Anne could feel hot breath brush across her cold cheeks. 'Why are you asking me that?' Her mentor's eyes bored into her, accusing. Pupils distended like muddy puddles. 'You're just like the rest of them,' she turned away to light a cigarette.

Anne felt as if she'd been slapped across the face. She hadn't invited any of this; she was tired and wanted to get home. A jogger with a light strapped to his head ran past, twigs breaking underfoot as he ran; thankfully, breaking the tension between them.

'I've been working on something.' Vivian switched to her authoritative mentoring voice.

Oh no. What now?

'Goal setting: the cornerstone of good mentoring.'

What the hell is she talking about?

'It came to me this morning. We need to set you some goals, Anne, it's good mentoring practice.'

'What sort of goals?'

'Your life goals.' She opened both arms as if she couldn't imagine why she hadn't thought of this before.

'I've already got goals in my Care Leaver's Plan,' but Vivian was already walking off in the opposite direction. Anne boarded her bus feeling uneasy about Vivian's increasingly erratic behaviour, finding it odd that Vivian hadn't asked about Fleur all night, actively blocking any reference to her missing friend, almost as if she'd already written her off. And her sudden mood changes were more unsettling than ever. During her time in care, she'd witnessed all sorts of odd behaviour, but things felt different with Vivian. More menacing. Her increasingly scathing remarks, her inability to consider anyone else, and now these sinister recollections about her dead childhood friend.

Her reflection stared back at her through the grimy bus window. She looked pale. Exhaustion swept through her. She blinked back tears about to spill from her eyelashes, leaving her irrationally jealous of the leaves whirling in the air, having escaped from their possessive branches. How had she got into this mess?

Lying in bed, it felt like everything was collapsing around her. Where was Fleur? What had happened to their new start? She imagined the hidden words glowing through the freshly lemon-painted wall: *'I fucking hate it here;'* the very air she breathed contaminated by the menace radiating from the hidden gun. The stain of animal guts smeared on her door. How had it all gone so wrong?

She tried to sleep, but the corridor noises seemed amplified, reminding her of other footsteps that haunted her past. Footsteps in the middle of the night that used to make her too afraid to close her eyes. And questions kept floating through her head: was it Fleur who had hidden the gun? Was she alone? Only Room could say. But neither of them knew who would be coming back for it, or when. The usual morning creaks, shrieks, and slamming of doors made her heart race. She paced her room, up and down the narrow space between the two beds to the overflowing bin containing her discarded letters. She picked up her latest scribbling.

Dear Banksy, I know I'm writing more frequently than ever, but things aren't going too well here, and I don't know who to turn to. Fleur has gone missing, and I'm on a countdown to find her. I only have ten days left, and I'm starting to lose hope. I know you say 'There is Always Hope,' but I can't see a way forward. You, more than anyone, know what it's like out there on the streets and what dangers Fleur might be facing.

I've been to a few pubs with Vivian, my freaky mentor I've told you about already, but I don't think she's really interested. In fact, I think she likes Fleur being out of the way. She's becoming creepily possessive and rambling on about dark things I don't understand, as if we're lifelong friends. And I still don't know who smeared all that horrible stuff over my front door.

Also, I need to tell you that I found something terrible in Fleur's drawer. It was a gun. I know you're familiar with such things, but it's all new to me. Please help me know what to do next ...

Her new life wasn't at all how she imagined it would be.

9

#Banksy: 'A Stencilled Life'

'Could you both come into the office for a minute?'

Mrs. B looked off; her face pale, her throat blotchy. 'There is something a bit … delicate that I need to discuss with you.' The three women stood facing each other. Pamela remained starchy in her pristine apron, while Mrs. B looked to the floor, avoiding eye contact. Anne drew a deep breath. Was this about the missing donation money? She prayed Mrs. B wasn't about to get the police involved.

'I will be quick because we can't leave the tea counter unmanned for long. At eleven o'clock, we will be hosting a new group.' She stalled as if unsure how to explain things, avoiding eye contact. 'It is a newly formed group of ex-offenders.'

'Like prisoners?' wailed Pam, her hand at her mouth.

'No, Pamela; like people who have served their time for their past … offences, and are now free to live their lives back in an accepting and forgiving community.'

Go on, Mrs. B, you tell her.

But Perfect Pam was having none of it. 'Can't they find somewhere else to go?' Her stick-thin frame trembled.

'Like where Pamela? Exactly where do you think they should go? The whole idea is about rehabilitation, about reengaging with the local community. And a vital part of that community is the local church.'

Anne liked this version of Mrs. B with fire in her belly.

'Besides, they have booked a regular table at a very good rate.'

'Well, I'm not serving prisoners.'

'It was good enough for our Lord to serve prisoners … and prostitutes. Besides, I'd have thought ...' Pam looked at her with pure hatred, now shaking like a discombobulated ostrich. 'Go on, say it ...'

Well, this is interesting. What on earth does Mrs. B have on Perfect Pam?

The two women stood tense, neither willing to back down.

'If Pam's got a problem, I'll serve them today.' A glowering Pamela rebuked Anne's kind offer. 'The toys for the playgroup need a good cleaning, someone was sick in the ball pool yesterday. Maybe Pam would prefer to do that?' Pam looked morosely at her perfectly manicured nails.

The mornings were getting busier each day as they got nearer to Christmas. The small group of men who'd just entered and occupied a table by the fire exit went unnoticed.

'Four cups of tea, please, love.'

'Give us a minute to sort this toast order …' She looked up, straight into the eyes of one of the McGreal brothers. Her stomach flipped as her life flashed before her. A bully boy taking her bike from her; twin brothers fighting; a gash to the head where a boy almost lost an eye after falling on his butcher's round. The haunting memory of Shayne McGreal's terrified eyes, realising a fire was about to break out.

'Don't I know you?' his green eyes narrowed to a slit.

She turned away quickly. 'I doubt it, I've only just moved around here,' she lied in her rather good Welsh accent. Her fingers brushed against the toaster grill, making her curse.

'You need to be more careful, love.' She was trembling. How could one of the McGreal brothers be here, in her church? There was no mistaking that ginger hair and those grey-green eyes, glinting hard like slate after the rain, a deep gash slashing through one eyebrow.

She scanned the air for the Angel Gabriel, but he seemed distracted by other matters. Leaning against the counter for support, she dared to glance toward the man in his expensive Burberry raincoat, limping back to his table.

An hour later, they got up to leave. A female gesturing from the open door attracted angry glares as blasts of freezing air blew into the church. 'Twinnie, I've got a taxi waiting outside.' Anne watched the limping man leave with the young woman. Brown over-the-knee boots, masses of blond hair, still strutting like a proud horse. It was Grace. And she was with Twinnie McGreal. The same Twinnie McGreal who was behind forcing his twin Frankie to leave for Spain, according to Zane's story.

'And how are you today?' PC James Wright arrived half an hour after Twinnie McGreal and his crew had left.

Could this morning get any worse?

'Anne, have you got a minute?' Mrs. B saved the day. 'It's about Mr. Murphy. He can't come in for his food parcel; he's had a nasty fall at home. Would you be an angel and drop his food off at his flat?' She looked up at Gabriel, one angel to another, shrugging her shoulders at James.

'Looks like I'm needed. Pam will serve you.'

Mr. Murphy lived nearby, in poorly maintained sheltered accommodation built in the 1970s, according to an apologetic, faded plaque. 'Come in, the key's under the mat,' he called. That would never do; you didn't know who might be hanging around, but then she noticed the well-concealed security camera, reminding her she needed to be more careful with her foraging. Like much of her beloved Banksy's work warned, you never knew who was watching. She noticed the old man's badly bruised face.

'I know I look like a piece of prime steak,' he burst into his throaty laughter.

'Can I make you a cup of tea, Mr. Murphy?'

'Yes, please, love, but I'd be most grateful if you could take Scruff for a walk. I've usually done it well before now.'

With Mr. Murphy comfortable, she took the wire-haired terrier who lived up to his name out to College Green, in front of the magnificent Cathedral. She sat on the wide, curved bench that she and Fleur used to occupy. Few people were lingering in the cold, and as her feet grew numb, she gave up.

Back at Mr. Murphy's flat, she prepared some sandwiches for his lunch.

'Feckin' Brexit,' he cursed at the TV, nibbling at his food. His room was sparse, as if he'd outlived the desire for life's comforts. The room smelled fusty, and the winter sun bled through Mr. Murphy's curtains, eerily lighting up a picture of Our Lord in a pearly frame on his mantlepiece. It looked strangely animated; the expression pained, almost angry. Why would He look at her like that? 'He knows all the bad things you have done,' her foster father used to whisper in her ear. Did He know about the gun, or even worse, her part in the house fire?

'Feckin' tosser,' said Mr. Murphy, confusing Anne for a minute, until she realised he was talking about a shiny-faced man called David Cameron on the TV. She noticed a photograph of a family group in t-shirts and shorts, on a sandy beach, their happiness carried through the years, shining out in the grey council flat.

'That's us gang, just before we left Ireland. In Kinsale, down in the South. We used to holiday there from Cork, where we lived.' She remembered her mum once told her that her nan and grandad were from Ireland, that they'd come over to England to work on the docks, but that was all she knew. Mr. Murphy's photographs made her feel hollow, like the outline of a picture nobody had bothered to colour in. No family snaps, no sunny beach memories, as if she'd lived a stencilled life. A life in negative. Even her surname, Grimes, was false; cobbled together when they'd needed new identities after her mum had stolen stuff from a drug dealer and then grassed him up, before the big move to the Mount Pleasant estate.

She left Mr. Murphy's flat, fighting the surging feeling of abandonment, the black wash that seeped through her whenever she let her guard down, and started thinking about being abandoned by her mother.

At least things had quietened back at the church.

'So how was Mr. Murphy?'

'He's getting by. Is it okay if I go around again tomorrow to help out?'

'That's really considerate, Anne. I'll give Diana, his daughter, a ring.' Mrs. B beamed.

'So, where are you meeting Vivian today?' Her heart plummeted. She'd put her mentoring session to the back of her mind.

'In the library, in town,' her voice betrayed her misery. But at least it was far enough away from the church to prevent Vivian and Mrs. B joining forces.

'Better get off then, she doesn't sound like someone who would tolerate lateness.'

They'd met at the local library before, in the small upstairs room. Vivian seemed to like it there. It was private, and she seemed particularly taken with their flip chart. Her mentor's pout warned her she would pay for being ten minutes late.

'Sorry, Vivian, I was doing Mrs. B a favour and I ran over …' Vivian ignored her.

Please don't tell me you're in one of your sour moods, not today ...

But her mentor was preoccupied with planning their session, focused on drawing shaky columns on the wobbly Flipchart with great concentration.

'Thank you for attending this goal-setting session, Anne. You don't mind me calling you Anne, do you?'

'What else would you call me?'

Vivan smiled her thin patient smile, the one that suggested you had to make allowances for stupid people. 'It's always good practice to check, Anne. Today, we're going to talk about Self-actualisation.' She pointed at her drawing of a triangle with a stick person balancing at the top. Her blood was starting to simmer.

What the hell is she talking about? We should be out looking for Fleur, not doing this crap.

'Now tell me - what's the thing you want most in life?'

Please tell me we're not really going to do this shit.

But she played along. Like always. She had enough on her plate without upsetting Vivian. She tried to think about the things she really wanted to achieve, but couldn't shake off the image of Mr. Murphy's family, bathed in golden sunshine at the seaside. And engulfed by a wave that could no longer be held back, she started to cry.

Vivian looked aghast and left the room, telling her to pull herself together, that dealing with conflict was the one mentor training session she'd missed due to a bad stomach. She returned with a roll of toilet paper.

'Come on now, it's not that bad ...'

Anne blew her nose and held it together, and watched Vivian fill the empty flip chart columns with empty aspirations:

To take an evening dance class (with my mentor).

To take a historical tour of Canterbury (with my mentor).

To complete a Masterchef cookery course (with my mentor).

Three life goals, all squeezed into long, thin boxes by Vivian, in spikey green writing on the tilting flipchart, all of which would take another year to achieve. It seemed she had become Vivian's ticket to the things she regretted not achieving herself, a thinly veiled attempt to keep them shackled together for another year. And she had no choice but to play along with it. She waited for Vivian to leave the room, grabbed the redundant pen, and scribbled: *To get a good reference from the Food Bank,* and scrawled in capital letters at the top of the page: TO FIND FLEUR DRAKE. But resisted her most elusive aim: *To get rid of YOU.*

10

#Banksy: 'What Are You Looking At?'

PC James Wright was fiddling with a chain of paperclips, finding it hard to accept the slow pace of the murder investigation. He'd felt highly charged after being selected to be part of Operation Cuckoo, but in reality, little had changed. He'd imagined murder investigations would be action-packed, and the stalling pace was killing him. And to worsen things, Bob Lyons was giving him the most slavish of tasks, with his, 'You need to learn the basics, lad.' He was following up on Community Watch reports when, thankfully, the call from DS Stewart came through. 'There's a briefing in Police HQ this afternoon; we need to be there for 2 pm, but Henry wants to meet with us ahead of it.'

DS Shona Stewart was waiting in an upmarket café, all ethnic cushions and shutters opening to river views. Smart, with a coffee list as long as your arm. James was impressed. Henry was late. It appeared that was to be expected. 'So, what's new from your end, James?'

Disappointingly, he hadn't much to report. 'I've been doing community patrols as you suggested, at least it gets me out of the station, away from Bob Lyons' watchful eye.'

'Bob Lyons is keeping a close eye on you?'

'Yeah. Feeding me lots of menial stuff. But I did accompany him on an undercover surveillance on a flat just off Central Park - belongs to Frankie McGreal.' That caught her interest, but he didn't want to raise her hopes; there wasn't much to report.

'So, what's Bob's MO, what's he looking for, any connections with Cuckoo?' Snappy, her dark eyes glistened, expectant, catching the spark from her impressive engagement ring as she sipped her coffee. 'Why is he staking out Frankie McGreal's place?' she murmured.

'Not sure. He doesn't share much.' He was starting to think there was something odd about DS Stewart's interest in Bob Lyons' motives. His suspicions were disrupted by the whirl of an oversized, expensive-smelling waxed coat infused with Henry's pleasant spicy perfume.

'Nice place, Shona.'

'Yeah, me and Lisa like to come here.'

'Hear you're getting married next year?'

'Yes, big year for us, honeymooning in a friend's place in Antigua.'

'Say hello for me. She still on the dog squad?'

His boss nodded but switched the topic quickly, giving him the impression she didn't want him to know about her private life. 'So, what have you got for us, Henry?'

'Well, you're not going to be too happy, guys, but it's all about to switch to Canterbury.'

Shona Stewart stayed cool, tapping her fingernails hard on the glossy table. 'Go on …'

'We've identified Albert as William Reynolds. He comes with a stream of temporary addresses in Canterbury. Toxicology screening all clear, not so much as a trace of alcohol; tracking scars well healed. Seems like our man was clean.'

DS Stewart looked twitchy as if that didn't fit with what she expected to hear.

'No DNA match, and obviously no fingerprints. We got his ID from his dental records. Bruce Campbell is pulling everything together for his briefing. Thought you might appreciate the heads up before we go in.' But DS Stewart's attention seemed to have drifted.

Congregated in the HQ mini cinema, DCI Bruce Campbell strutted like a puffed-up turkey assisted by the competent Stacey. 'Result.' He paused for effect. 'What are we looking at? Or rather, *who* are we looking at?' The headless torso frames spun once more across the mini screen, 'William Reynolds. A Canterbury boy. Middle name Chaucer; it seems his family had aspirations for the lad.'

All James could think was that the last time they were there, they'd been looking at the man's penis, and it turned out his name was Willie.

'What's the link to Bristol City Football Club?' a faceless voice from the back row dared, attracting a vicious flash reminding them that DCI Campbell didn't appreciate uninvited questions.

'Got signed up for them young, had a bad injury, and got dropped.' Another groan of sympathy ran through the room. This lad had no luck.

'And the link to Reading where his head was found?'

'I'm coming to that.' Bruce Campbell barked. James smiled to himself, realising for the first time they were winding the boss up.

He then dealt the blow. 'Operation Cuckoo is transferring to Canterbury police.'

'But what about us being sent a message, the Bristol City connection?'

'If you'd kindly wait ... we're not letting that drop, our input to the specialist crime team will continue,' he nodded at DS Stewart, 'but the senior management of the case is being transferred to Canterbury from where William Reynolds hails.' Shona Stewart's shoulders relaxed beside him. Although no longer the SIO, she was to remain an integral part of the wider criminal investigation team.

'Looks like I'll be spending some time in Canterbury.'

James nodded, walking with her across the car park, head down against the beating rain. He turned in surprise as she asked, 'Fancy a pint, James? There's something I need to discuss with you.'

11

#Banksy: 'Art Should Comfort the Disturbed and Disturb the Comfortable'

'It's the small attention to detail that culminates in a successful drawing ...' Anne was suffering from her thwarted attempts to sketch the flowing mane of a Dartmoor pony, as instructed in her foraged: Complete Artists' Drawing Set. *'Close your eyes and imagine the last time you stroked a horse, let that sensation transmit to your strokes.'* But other, less tranquil signals seemed to control her charcoal-blackened, jerky fingers. And it didn't help that she'd never felt the touch of a horse, or felt *'the heat of nasally breath against your skin.'*

Her only horse-related knowledge came from her Anne of Green Gables reading book. The book from which she'd taken her new name when she and her mum had made a run for it; the book in which Mathew Cuthbert admired his beloved sorrel mare, called Belle. Other than that, it was down to the wild-eyed horses in the annual travellers' fair, chewing on the sparse grass verge beneath their Mount Pleasant council flats. Her heart wasn't in it. She couldn't shake off the thought that she only had nine days left to find Fleur.

Everything felt so pointless, and all that crying yesterday had emptied her out. But worst of all, she'd let her guard down in front of Vivian. She felt flat, like the fence flattened by an unexpected gale on Mathew Cuthbert's exposed Nova Scotia farm. She needed to write to Banksy.

'Dear Banksy, ... Sorry to be bothering you again, but I got in a right state yesterday thinking about what it would be like to have a proper family. A mum who loves me and a grandad like Mr. Murphy, and suddenly boom, I lost it. I went off like a bottle of pop. I didn't think those things bothered me anymore, but it seems they're always there. Just like the stains on these stupid carpet tiles that won't scrub away. And I'm sorry to say Fleur's still missing, and I'm running out of time and ideas.

It's hard to stay strong, Banksy, even though I know 'There is Always Hope', everything seems to be closing in on me, and I've never had to worry about shit like hoarding a gun before, lurking in the drawer like something waiting to explode. And to top it all, something from our past has cropped up, another dirty stain. A family called the McGreals from our old flats. I think they've got Fleur. What would you do, Banksy?

Transported back to the ineptly named Mount Pleasant council estate, a young Anne was scooting up and down the long, grey concrete corridors. That was before her scooter was stolen and thrown over their tenth-floor balcony. They knew it would be one of the McGreal boys, but nobody challenged that lot, especially Josie McGreal, their mother, with her paperwhite skin and nicotine-coloured hair, who fought like a tiger. There was the older boy, Shayne, who always had the police around; then the twins came next, Frankie and Twinnie (almost like they'd run out of names), who were always fighting, and then baby Jason. Strange, there was a baby she now thought for the first time, as there was never a dad around. They occupied a much bigger corner flat than the two-bed flat she, her mum, and Billy lived in. But Billy had done it up; he said they deserved nice things. She looked over at her Banksy poster: *'You're Never Too Young to Dream Big.'* It was something Billy used to say.

But Anne had learned that nothing good lasts for long. With Billy's wages and plenty of free time, things were finally looking up for Chantelle Grimes (her mum's name was taken from a country and western singer from Tennessee). 'Go and play with Fleur, I've got a friend coming round,' her mum's increasingly regular instruction while Billy was out at work.

Anne was used to being told to get out of the way. She'd wait for Fleur in the tarmac-studded playground, by the carcass of a burned-out car that became their witches' cave. And, of course, their favoured monkey bars, the totem over which their calves clamped and their school skirts billowed like sails off on another adventure.

It was during one of their upside-down monkey bar conversations that Fleur told her that her mum's new 'friend' was Shayne McGreal.

She cleared her writing paper away and left for her evening 'walk around' to see if she might spot Fleur, maybe hanging out, smoking on some street corner. But tired and cold, she gave up, the aromas drifting from the local kebab shop making her belly rumble. She pushed against the door, noting the Support Brexit sticker.

The young Turkish bloke behind the counter took her order for chips, and she briefly wondered how he felt about the sticker. He was discussing the headless corpse with his waiting customers. 'Maybe it's some gangland thing. I bet they don't think twice about decapitating someone.' He made a slicing gesture at his throat, making Anne shiver. 'Maybe it was a butcher ...' his eyes gleamed with menace. The spectre of the headless body seemed to bring out the worst in everybody. Anne was glad to leave, warming her hands on her chip wrapper, when she spotted Perfect Pam coming out of the hairdresser's opposite.

Well, she's supposed to be off sick ...

Smelling a rat, she decided to follow Pam, staying behind the well-turned-out woman who stopped occasionally to admire her hair in the festive shop windows decorated for

Christmas. Perfect Pam was someone who kept herself to herself. But Mrs. B knew something that had infuriated her. What did she know?

Pam turned quickly as if sensing someone was watching her, before doing something really strange. Digging deep into her Marks and Spencer's bag for life, she removed an envelope. Looking around carefully, she opened the top of an orange rock salt bin and dropped the envelope in. Anne waited, warming her hands on vinegar-fumed chip paper, and within a few minutes, a black hooded youth arrived, throwing his bike to one side to retrieve the envelope.

Pam progressed down the high street and, wanting to know more, Anne followed her to see where she lived. A heavy smell of whiskey hung in the cold air. A smell she knew well and detested. Their house used to stink of it after Billy went missing and Shayne McGreal moved in. *So Perfect Pam is a drinker …*

She followed the lilac-coated woman until she stopped and rang the bell of a flat above a boarded-up shop, which Fleur had once told her was a 'knocking shop'.

What's Pam doing somewhere like that?

A smart, stocky, silver-haired man came out and took Pam's arm. She followed them to The Orchid, the local Indian restaurant, where it seemed they had a reservation.

Well, that's not her husband …

Back home, she finished her chips and started looking for more references to Belle, the sorrel mare, in her Anne of Green Gables book. The book Billy taught her to read.

'God, Chantelle, you need to make more of an effort,' Billy had chastised her mum before he started reading to her. First, from the free newspaper that dropped through the door, pointing out small words, like 'died' and 'theft', the news was always bleak in those papers.

'I'm not sure who you come round here to see, me or the kid,' her mum had sulked. Then, just before he disappeared, Billy started reading to her from her proper book, the one they found on a park bench. The one that would shape her life forever: Anne of Green Gables. Something about the girl on the cover reminded her of herself; she looked a bit lost and carried a suitcase, someone else who found it difficult to settle down anywhere.

'Your Kylie's become a great reader.' Billy heaped praise on her.

Her name was Kylie Mathews, in the years before she became Anne Shirley Grimes.

She stretched on her bed and brushed her hands along the one freshly painted wall. 'A Hint of Lemon' had seemed to suit their fresh start, cover up bad things from the past – not too ambitious, but hopeful. It matched the Sunflower print she'd placed above Fleur's bed. Another great charity shop find.

Surfing through the television channels, she settled for 'A Place in the Sun.' It set her off thinking about Brexit again. Would she ever get to visit all these exotic places? She'd watched years of back episodes with her foster mother, who always talked of escaping. They watched it in secret. Her husband, Mr. Owens, liked to control what they watched. He didn't like Anne watching TV with his wife or kids and used to send her to bed early, where he would sometimes join her later. The bed where the girl before her had slept, and the girl before that. They had awards for fostering. There was nothing lemon about that house.

She looked up at the ceiling, the way she used to do when things got really bad. The stain was getting bigger, with the paint peeling around an outbreak of dirty black spots. Returning to her reading book, she swore as her twenty-pound note bookmark fell to the floor. The money that she was too superstitious to spend. Picking it up, her eyes were level with Fleur's drawer. She gingerly opened it to see things had been rearranged. With a sudden flood of panic, she knew someone had been in the flat. Pulling the drawer from its runners, she emptied the contents on her bed. No Pandora bag, no gun. Items had been taken from their room. Anne partly drew her curtains and looked out at shadows falling across the bleary street. Someone out there knew what was going on. But who?

12

#Banksy: 'Girl With A Balloon'

The jangle of bracelets announced the early morning arrival of Marta, the sly, hook-nosed caretaker with ruby red hair. If anyone might have seen something suspicious, it would be her. She was barking instructions at Sasha, the cleaning girl who looked somewhat dishevelled today. Something about her reminded Anne of the innocence in Banksy's 'Girl with a Balloon'. She and Billy had been to Waterloo in London to see it when her mum had gone on a Butlins weekend with the Bingo girls.

'Hi, ladies, I don't suppose you saw anyone in my room yesterday, only something has gone missing ...' Marta's piercing eyes warned her to think carefully, not to let her know that Fleur wasn't around. She would be sure to report them to social services.

'You accuse *me* of taking things from your room?' The affronted woman turned abruptly. Sasha, wide-eyed, took a step back and looked to the sky as if searching for something lost.

'No. Of course not, but someone has been in there - uninvited. Don't worry, maybe it was Fleur,' she backtracked. Marta squared up against her, so close that she could see the small dark hairs forming a moustache above her red lipstick;

94

icy eyes flashing with rage. 'Be very careful, Anne Grimes, I know lots about you.'

What is she talking about?

'What you do when you come back so early in the morning, always carrying a bag?' Anne froze. 'You are prostitute, out all night. I have good mind to report you.'

Anne laughed with relief, only serving to inflame Marta to the point her cheeks matched her hair. Sasha covered her mouth with her hand, her skin rough and patchy for such a young girl.

'And the other girl is always rude to me. You don't deserve nice place like this.'

'You've got it wrong, Marta, I go out early to help at the local church, with their breakfast club. If you don't believe me, come to Saint Gabriel's later, I'll be back there serving lunches.'

Marta backed off, thrown, while Sasha failed to hide her soft and dimpled smile, pleased that someone had stood up to the domineering caretaker.

'I like to help those in need. A bit like the evenings you hold here, for the refugees.' Marta stepped back as if she'd taken a blow to the stomach. Anne had no idea what went on, but she had noted the constant late-night comings and goings, the ferrying of young girls in posh cars. They parted. Sasha looked back and smiled chastely at Anne as if they'd made some sort of a pact. And Anne smiled back at the mystery girl. She watched them slope off together, Sasha with her mop slung over her shoulder, not quite the enigmatic red balloon of Anne's imagination. She'd won this battle but had started a war. Marta would be watching her every move from now on. She'd fought dirty and made an enemy. The last thing she needed.

But who has been in our room and who has taken the gun?

She found Mrs. B baking in the steamy church kitchen, her rings placed on the shelf above the worktop. For the first time, she thought of Mrs. B's husband and how strange it was that she never mentioned him.

'Will you pop in on Mr. Murphy again this morning, Anne, see how he's getting on?'

'Sure. I'll go early. I'm seeing Vivian again later.'

'You're seeing quite a bit of her recently?' said the ever-perceptive Mrs. B.

Anne sighed. 'She really seems to be into this whole goal-setting thing.'

'And what about you, Anne, how do you feel about it?'

'I'm going along with it, after all, we'll be finishing our mentoring sessions soon.'

'Does she have some sort of … exit plan? A planned end date for your mentoring?'

'No, but it's a great idea.' It really was a brilliant idea, especially if she could get Vivian to own it. She wanted to hug Mrs. B for the suggestion.

'I think it's just the thing she needs to help her move on.' Anne thought out loud.

'Don't you think it should be the other way round?' Mrs. B's caution reflected in caring eyes beneath today's pale blue eye shadow, complementing a soft baby blue cardigan.

'So, tell me about your life goals,' mused Mrs. B.

Knowing she couldn't possibly share any of her 'real' goals, she shared the one that seemed safest; the goal Vivian seemed most excited about.

'It looks like we're off to Canterbury soon.'

'I never knew you wanted to go to Canterbury.'

'I don't. But I think Vivian does.'

Anne was being her most serious, but Mrs. B laughed so hard she had to remove her glasses to dab at the tears spilling down her face. 'She sounds quite a character, Anne.'

She had wanted so much to tell Mrs. B about Fleur in that brief moment of levity, but Mrs. B was sure to get the police involved. She didn't need anyone digging into their past; Shayne McGreal dying in a house fire. Her heart pounded at the thought that Fleur could be in the hands of the younger McGreals at this very moment, at great risk of spilling their secret.

She was sure it was the McGreals' black car that had nearly run into her at the bus stop. Like they were warning her off. And they were most likely to be behind the smearing on her front door. They'd probably heard from someone in The Hollywood pub that she'd been asking about Fleur. Would she ever see her friend again? Her heart pounded as time ticked away, and she glanced up at the Angel Gabriel, who looked ready to listen. But the church was way too busy. Maybe she'd confide in him another day.

Anne left for Mr. Murphy's flat, still puzzled over who had been in their room. It must have been Fleur, but why didn't she leave her a message, or a secret sign, if she was being held against her will?

Mr. Murphy seemed uncharacteristically low, looking through a box of old photographs. 'It's my wife Bridget's birthday today,' he sighed, passing her a wedding photograph. Mr. Murphy's bride stood proudly, her dark skin standing out against pristine white snow.

She faltered, unable to hide her surprise. But time had failed to erase the happiness of the pretty brown-skinned bride wearing a wreath of spring flowers that looked so fresh, Anne imagined she could smell them.

'I met her in the butter factory where I used to make deliveries.' He gently rubbed across the photograph. 'Prettiest girl in Cork. Didn't matter where you hailed from as long as you were catholic,' making him laugh until he almost choked. She looked into his watery, fading eyes and down at his wrinkled, paper-thin hand, and resisted an urge to touch it.

Mr. Murphy took a small cross and chain out of the box.

'Here, I'd like you to have this love, you've been very kind to me. My daughter Diana doesn't want it. It used to cut into my wife's neck. It's wasted just lying there.'

His eyes wanted her to take the gift so much as he shakily clipped the chain around her neck. And she pretended, just for a minute, that Mr. Murphy was her grandad. Then she saw the angry face of our Lord glaring back at her from the mantlepiece, and she remembered the mess she was in. She felt like an imposter and quickly left Mr. Murphy's flat once satisfied that he was settled. She didn't belong there; he had his own memories, his own family. The sky had turned dark, sleety rain stinging her face, washing away yet more tears.

Back at the church, she worked on putting together some additional emergency food bags. She appreciated being alone in the storeroom with only her thoughts and stacks of 'unperishables' for company. Lately, the food bags were being distributed almost as fast as they could fill them, making her question what would happen if the food ran out? Where would people go then? Shaking out a Marks and Spencer carrier bag, a cascade of used scratch cards fell to the ground. What was going on? She straightened out a creased receipt, 'Die and Curl' - Pam's hairdresser. Were these Perfect Pam's used scratch cards? They must have cost a fortune.

13

#Banksy: 'Welcome to Hell'

Anne had been waiting for Vivian in the town library for over an hour. The weather had worsened by the time she left; rainwater dripped down the back of her fleece, making her shiver. Determined to give Vivian a piece of her mind, she passed an old man who lived opposite her mentor's house. He was bent beneath his ladder in a yellow waterproof coat like sailors wear in films. They were both soaked through, but he still managed a wave and a smile.

Knocking hard on Vivian's flaking green door, there was no answer. A scuffling from behind the door made her knock harder, determined to have it out with her mentor.

'Oh, for God's sake, come around the back,' a faint reply.

The back door creaked open to reveal Vivian, back in her cerise dressing gown. She looked terrible, making Anne stall in her rebuke.

'Vivian! Are you okay?'

Vivian squinted at her as if trying to recall who her visitor was.

'We were going to meet at the library. Remember? Work on our goals?'

Vivian remained distant, eyes darting under heavy lids before she surprised Anne by walking away as if inviting her to follow. The poor lighting made it difficult to navigate her way through towers of stacked boxes, swearing as she banged her knee painfully on one protruding like a booby trap. She followed Vivian past piles of musty-smelling newspapers standing like skyscrapers lining the poorly lit hallway.

Vivian's a hoarder?

In the sitting room, she opted for the only cleared space and sat on a hard-backed chair beside a cream-tiled fireplace, its hearth chipped like bad teeth. Vivian took a sip of her drink, which was balanced on a pile of 'Beautiful Home' magazines. Anne's eyes were drawn to a cabinet crammed with porcelain dolls; frail things with fixed, dead eyes. Vivian looked almost as fragile as if she, too, might shatter.

I can't pull out on her now, not when she's clearly not coping ...

'What are you doing here?' Vivian twisted awkwardly, making strangled knots bulge in her neck. Suddenly, Anne wasn't so sure of her mission.

'I've come to see you, haven't I? We were going to talk about my goals?' She steadied herself, not wanting her mentor to see her concern, both at the deterioration in Vivian, but also at the poor state of the house. But Vivian seemed to have drifted off, her head nodding on her chest.

'Vivian, remember our trip to Canterbury?'

She stirred, a dribble of spittle running down her chin. 'Not sure I'm up to a trip right now, they've changed my anti-depressants,' she clumsily reached out for a cigarette.

Christ, this place will go up in flames so easily …

'So, our trip to Canterbury?' she pushed until her mentor refocused and fluffed up her hair, her eyes darting disconcertingly from side to side under lazy, heavy lids before conceding. 'Maybe a trip away will do me good. We'd need to stay over …' She seemed to be thinking straight, that scheming look back in her eyes. 'Maybe a couple of nights?'

'No, Vivian, it could only be one night max. I need to be here for Fleur.' Vivian scoffed and flicked her hand as if waving away an irritating fly. 'And we will have to pick up our search as soon as we return …'

'Fleur, Fleur, Fleur.' Vivian was mocking her now, her face twisted with scorn, her movements exaggerated. 'I'm prepared to change my arrangements to get you to Canterbury, and all you can talk about is Fleur Drake.' Twisted words reflecting twisted thoughts. Vivian ran her hand along the edge of the worn fabric of the armchair as if seeking reassurance from its familiarity. They both sat quietly, the screaming silence broken only by the ticking clock.

'I haven't been away from this house for years. Maybe you're right. It might be what I need. OK, let's go.'

Oh God, it looks like we're actually going to do this thing. But why Canterbury?

Anne baulked at this change of heart. Not only had Vivian reframed the genesis of the trip, but why Canterbury? It was the last place on earth she wanted to go. The last place her mother was known to have settled.

Zane kept Anne on the doorstep, whispering conspiratorially while Millie lurked in the background. She kept one foot firmly wedged in the door.

'I've been speaking to your friend Grace, and she tells me that Frankie McGreal drinks in a pub called the Blind Fox. She said to ask Zane if I wanted to know more.'

Zane paled as the inquisitive Millie came forward. Beads of sweat broke out across his forehead, as if he'd been caught out.

'I don't know where that little slut is coming from, sending you here,' Zane said with a quick sideways glance at Millie. He sighed heavily. 'I was at the pub the other night when Grace – who keeps pestering me, by the way - told me things are really heating up between the McGreal twins. There's talk of Frankie leaving the country to set up a lap dancing club in Spain. Grace knows because they're taking some of the girls with them to get things started.'

He was confirming everything she most feared. 'Grace said to ask you about the Blind Fox,' she repeated.

He turned his head away. 'Frankie likes to drink there on Friday nights. Grace said he sometimes takes 'the kid' with him. That's what they all call Fleur.'

'Where is the Blind Fox?'

'Down in the old town. Been going for years. All the big stuff goes down there. It's a no-go area for the filth.'

Millie, who'd been listening intently, could take no more. 'So, what's this Grace like then, and how do you know so much about her?' She sparked a cigarette and an argument about Zane talking to other women.

Anne left them arguing loudly on their doorstep, armed with the information she needed and a clear plan in her head. She would get the Canterbury trip out of the way to keep Vivian on board. They would be back by Friday, just in time for a visit to the Blind Fox.

14

#Banksy: 'Think Tank'

James and DS Shona Stewart made it to his car just before the storm clouds burst.

'I thought we needed some time out. Some thinking time. Do you know The Central pub?'

James nodded. He'd been there previously, to an altercation, and the name had puzzled him because it wasn't central to anything. They entered the old pub with its beautiful tiling, a testament to the pub's past grandeur.

'Corn dealers. Moved across here from the old Corn Market.' She nodded at the wonderful motif worked into the pub tiling. It struck him that it was about the only non-work-related thing she'd ever shared with him. 'Bristol got rich on the exportation of corn. Amongst other, more unsavoury things.' He guessed she was hinting at Bristol's shameful slave trading past.

The bartender finished cleaning behind the bar, leaving a pungent blend of chemicals in the air. 'Good afternoon, DS Stewart.'

'Hi, Keith.'

The immaculate bartender nodded at the young police officer, possibly remembering him from his last visit. 'Usual, ma'am?' he deferred to her authority.

'Please.' A Jack Daniel's was poured. James was asked for his order.

'He's driving.'

'A shandy for the officer, then. I'll bring them through to the snug.'

They moved away from the regulars, sitting like fixtures under the TV with a vicious argument about Brexit raging over their heads. In the snug, she took off her expensive but understated outer jacket and shook the rain from it, remaining disconcertingly quiet.

'So, it's good news we're still involved in Operation Cuckoo.' James tried as an opener. But DS Stewart was in one of her quiet moods. She remained standing, with her fingers tracing the patterns in the fine-grained marble fireplace. He wondered why he'd been invited along if she was going to be difficult.

'Yes. It is.' She replied after what seemed an age, looking awkward for the second time that day, as if deciding whether to let him in on something, before hunkering down into the fading tapestry chair opposite him. She took a deep breath. 'Some background. When I first started here in Bristol, I worked on a case involving the McGreals.' She stayed tight-lipped, sipping on her drink. Never one for small talk.

'A strange case. Bob Lyons and I were called to a house fire on the Mount Pleasant Estate, which resulted in a fatality. The deceased was reported to be Shayne McGreal, the eldest of the McGreal brothers, assumed to have died in the house fire. Probably caused by him smoking and falling asleep ... it was concluded.' She looked intently at James, checking he was keeping up.

'Bad piece of news was Shayne McGreal. Into everything. In truth, we weren't sorry that he wouldn't be bothering us anymore.' She bit her top lip as if about to reach a point from which there would be no return. 'The funny thing was, we later got reports of Frankie McGreal helping someone out of the property just before we arrived. And our arrival was unnecessarily delayed by Bob Lyons. What do you think of that?'

'That it all felt a bit ... contrived?'

'Right,' she nodded, cupping her glass.

'So, it looked like someone got him out?' James was confused. 'And Bob Lyons had something to do with it?'

Again, she nodded, casting her eyes down to her drink, making it difficult for him to see where this was leading.

'But you said 'the deceased'. Someone died in the fire?'

She looked up and continued, measured as ever. 'The burnt body was never formally identified. It was his mother, Josie McGreal's, insistence that the deceased was her missing son, and the flat owner, Chantelle Grimes, who was his girlfriend at the time, identified him by his Irish Claddagh ring. Two close witnesses; pretty convincing.'

'What did Forensics conclude?'

'Good question, James. But nobody requested any tests. The family insisted on getting the case closed. I felt something wasn't right, and I contacted Henry. It was the first time that we worked together. I pushed hard for us to try to get DNA from the charred body. But do you know the strange thing?'

James couldn't imagine what might follow.

'We were denied permission.'

James was struggling to follow.

'Although Henry said it isn't always possible to get DNA from a badly burned body, she felt it was worth a try. We also knew we had Shayne McGreal on the system. A DNA match would have concluded everything one way or the other. I suspect there wouldn't have been a match.'

'You think it was someone else who perished in the fire?'

She nodded gravely. 'I'm sure of it.'

'Where does Bob Lyons come into this?'

'We never discussed it further. He took some leave - then just shut down on me.' That didn't come as a surprise to James. She coughed hesitantly. 'The McGreal brothers were thick as thieves at the time, and we all knew police officers were taking allegiances. It was how it worked back then. Someone on the force was helping Frankie McGreal out; he was up and coming and getting away with far too much. That *someone* got the nickname of 'The Eel'. She banged her empty glass on the table.

Nothing was adding up for James, who needed to go back a few paces.

'So, who refused to sign off the request for Forensics?' he was still mulling it over. She quietened and bit her top lip until the skin blanched. 'Bob Lyons went above us all and got the request refused, said it would be wasting valuable police resources, and it was just as the riots were sparking up, so we all got diverted.'

James sat up. What was she implying?

She paused as the smartly waistcoated Keith came in with another round of drinks.

'I knew Bob was shielding something or someone. I confronted him about it – I let him know I wasn't happy.'

'What did he say?' James understood the strength needed to confront his ill-natured boss.

'He was very influential in those days, heading for promotion. It was easy to ostracise an inexperienced female officer. And there was nothing more that could be done, the burial was imminent - the McGreals had already opened up their family plot in Central Cemetery.'

'What did you do?'

'I left. I got a transfer to detective work soon after and was glad to be out of the West Grange snake pit. I just thought you should know and understand why I've got history with Bob Lyons.' They sipped their drinks, with James processing what he'd heard.

'So, you never got to verify who died that night. Did you check for missing persons?'

'Of course, James. No misper fitted the time or the scene.'

They finished their drinks. She stayed silent, giving him some thinking time before they left, and said little as he drove her home.

'This will do, thank you. I'll walk from here.'

He looked up at the handsome pastel-painted row of Georgian terraces set high, overlooking the twinkling River Avon far below.

'I'll collect you in the morning, get you back to your car?'

'No, it's fine. Lisa will sort it.'

He whistled to himself as he drove away. What must it cost to live around here?

15

#Banksy: 'What We Do In Life Echoes In Eternity'

With eight days left to find Fleur, it felt reckless to be away overnight, especially as the Food Bank was busier than ever. But Mrs. B, almost as excited as Vivian about the Canterbury trip, insisted that she go.

'I do so love Canterbury,' she chirped. 'Make sure to visit the Cathedral and don't worry about Mr. Murphy, Pamela's dropping in on him.' Anne struggled to imagine Perfect Pam picking up Scruff's dog poo, but then Pam was turning out to be someone full of surprises.

'Bye Room,' she attempted, but couldn't break through the heavy sulkiness at her imminent departure. Vivian, at least, was perky in her flaming orange velvet trousers. She twittered inanely and pulled an unnecessarily large suitcase past the homeless people already queuing for breakfast in St. James' Church gardens, reminding Anne of how much she was needed at the Food Bank.

'Ooh, I love little breaks away,' Vivian trilled, pausing only to light a cigarette outside the coach station, coughing theatrically while Anne began to wonder what lay ahead. The last time she'd been out of Bristol was back when she and her mum did 'drop offs' with Shayne McGreal, the adults high as kites on amphetamines and adrenaline before they drove off to some town or other. Her mother's click-clacking shoes as she disappeared down alleyways to meet shady characters for a 'drop and collect'. On the way back home, they stopped at pubs, which Anne hated even more, trying to disappear into her Anne of Green Gables book to avoid the glares from the happy families about them. After, Shayne would drive them home, his free hand swigging cans of lager that her mum opened for him. They would leave her to herself while they went to bed, so rumbustious and embarrassing that she had to put her hands over her ears to block out the noise. And wonder where Billy was.

In those days, her mum didn't do hard drugs; it was only later when Shayne McGreal moved in and his mates used to stay, making the house feel like a squat. That was when Shayne started to offer her pills; 'make you feel great,' he used to say, all glassy-eyed, but she knew someone had to keep watch.

'Come on, kid, I'll teach you the ropes,' he said when her mum was out of it, and she was called upon to do the drop-offs, still stopping for drinks on the way home. She hated it, especially his fumbling when they got back. She hated everything about Shayne McGreal. Then one day he left. Everything got clean, both her mum and the house. Fleur stayed over a lot back then, especially when their mums went out to Bingo. The peaceful time before it all changed. Before the fire.

Vivian's lolling head banged against her shoulder, making her curl into herself, her forehead smearing a light grease stain on the coach window. Rocked to sleep by the momentum, she drifted back to the Mount Pleasant flats. Back to the night of the fire.

Playing out late wasn't unusual back then, while the Bingo mums were also out to play. 'Right, Fleur, let's go back for some supper, I'll make us some toast.' It was a strange night. There was a tension in the air, the sense that something big was about to happen. They had a final go on the monkey bars, everything turning fuzzy and magical under an upside-down apocalyptic sunset, before chasing up ten flights of stairs.

Panting, she swiped up at their house key on the top ledge, and they both fell into the hall giggling before a strange smell warned them someone else was in the house. She crept down the short hallway, pushed open the living room door, and stopped dead. Shayne McGreal's hulking body was sprawled over their cleaned couch; a foul stink radiated from his dirty trainers. His drug gear was laid on the table in front of him.

What is he doing back?

There was a wad of money on the table, but a stray twenty-pound note caught her eye. Creeping forward and grateful for the old threadbare carpet silencing her footsteps, she motioned for Fleur to stay back. It was hard to steady her nerves, and trembling, she reached out, careful not to knock against anything. The note was almost in her grasp when Shayne muttered something, making her heart jolt. She froze, but this was like no other game of musical statues; she would be for it if he woke up. He stilled again, spittle bubbles blowing from the corner of his drooping mouth.

Relaxing slightly, she dared to reach forward, steadying her breathing, her tongue pressed hard against her teeth in concentration. Inch by inch, she stretched forward until the note was almost at her fingertips, when, as if he had a sixth sense, his arm shot out and he grabbed at her, making her shriek. Both his smile and his breath were foul.

'Don't look so pleased to see me,' he laughed, his head lolling back like a baby.

'Who did you think it was? Silly Billy?' he laughed again. 'He's gone. You won't be seeing him again.' He coughed up phlegm, which he wiped on their new cushion cover.

Anne felt a rage consume her. What did he mean about Billy, about not seeing him again? What was he doing back here anyway, ruining things just as she'd got them straight? Filled with a raw red fury, she freed her arm, but he was already drifting away. She really wanted that twenty-pound note. It would be enough bus fare to take her far away from him.

Snoring now like the pig that he was, her eyes stung with the stale smoky smells she hated; cigarette stubs and something grey smouldering in a small glass tube over a flame. She gagged at the sight of vomit on their carpet. She didn't want to stay around to watch Shayne McGreal back in their lives, dragging her mum down again.

She crept closer, determined to take the crumpled note. Her heart beat as if fighting to escape her ribcage as she slowly but steadily reached out to take her getaway money. Then, like a snake waiting to strike at its prey, he reached out and pulled her down toward him. She saw Fleur, frozen, watching everything in the mirror above their electric fire as she punched and kicked, trying to get out of his grip.

'Ooh, looks like you're up for a fight,' he laughed, pinning her arms above her head and angling to lie on top of her. Kicking out hard, she knocked the table over.

'You little bitch …' Jumping up, he lost his balance before falling back and hitting his head hard on the corner of the solid wooden bookshelf Billy had left behind. His curses filled the air, his eyes wide with pain. Then it turned black, as it always did whenever she tried to remember beyond that moment. The lost five minutes of her life.

They walked calmly back to Fleur's flat, blue lights flashing against the embers of a fading sunset; red, orange, and a bruising purple becoming obscured by choking black smoke.

Sirens screeched out in the hot summer night, but she felt at peace. It was as if a great calmness had descended upon her. Lying on top of Fleur's narrow bed, she watched her friend sleep fitfully, her restless legs running, as always. She flicked through her Anne of Green Gables reading book, the one thing she grabbed on her way out of the smoking flat, and carefully placed the twenty-pound note between the pages. Her new bookmark.

The next day, her mother came for her. She seemed very distant and stayed silent as they got on the bus. 'Where are we going?' but she soon recognised the route back to the children's home where she'd stayed before in times of crisis; temporary respite until her mum got straight again.

'It will all be fine,' Theresa, the Senior on duty, tried to reassure her, looking in disbelief as Chantelle Grimes sashayed down the path, leaving her daughter with nothing other than the clothes she wore and a reading book. Sometimes in her dreams, her mum turns and waves at her, but in reality, she never did. That was the last time she saw her mum before Ruth, her social worker, told her she was on the fostering list. And that her mum had moved to Canterbury.

She woke to feel Vivian gently patting her arm. A light and breezy version of her mentor she'd never seen before. Storing away her haunting childhood memories, it was time to think positively and be prepared for whatever Canterbury had in store. Get it over and done with, and return to resume her search for Fleur at the Blind Fox.

The Fleece Inn was within easy walking distance of the coach station. She'd booked it all from a Yellow Pages directory on the church phone when Mrs. B wasn't around. She liked the sound of The Fleece Inn. It reminded her of a film she'd watched with Billy: Jason and the Argonauts. She thought of sharing this with Vivian, but resisted; she liked to keep Billy to herself.

Vivian was checking them in while flirting overtly with the young hotel manager, making Anne turn away, cheeks burning with embarrassment. She flicked through a rack of tourist leaflets and free newspapers, noticing a smartly dressed woman waiting patiently to register. She looked strangely out of place against the old pub's flock wallpaper and musty carpets.

'Can I help you?' the manager asked, glad to be rid of Vivian.

'Yes. I'd like to book in. The name's Stewart.'

Of course, Anne had no idea that it was James Wright's boss there on semi-official business; Shona Stewart was a semi-official type of person.

Their room looked out over the street where people were busy Christmas shopping. She thought how much Fleur would love all this, or maybe she wouldn't – she hardly knew Fleur these days. It was as if she were slipping away from her. Like some ethereal Will o' the Wisp sprite hovering just beyond her fingertips, teasing her. Her stuttering thoughts were broken by Vivian humming in the bathroom. Her heart sank. What were they doing here? What did Vivian want from this visit? She thumbed through the free paper, 'The Kentish News'. 'There's a Christmas market,' she called to Vivian, who was fussily touching up her make-up in the bathroom mirror.

'Great. We'll have a drink in the bar first, then we'll find it.'

Anne questioned the wisdom of Vivian drinking so early in the day, but she would go along with whatever her mentor wanted, at least for now. Down in the bar, she ordered a hot chocolate. 'At least one of us made an effort,' Vivian's castigating comment on Anne's fleecy jacket and jeans.

'I've only brought practical things with me,' she shrugged.

'You don't say. It's almost like you don't want to be here.'

She watched Vivian sidle up to a man, all skin and bone, bent over his pint.

'No work on today, Mike?' The bartender seemed to know him well.

'Nothing fuckin' doin' in this weather,' the ghoul replied.

Vivian tutted sympathetically at his meteorological misfortune, whilst Anne, still smarting from her mentor's cutting remarks, found a seat tucked away in an alcove, beating herself up for not thinking more about what clothes she might need.

'Nice fire,' said the smart woman from reception, with her gleaming hair and sparkling engagement ring. She looked even more out of place in the dull lounge. 'Last-minute booking,' the woman said as if reading her thoughts, scrunching her nose. 'Still, who doesn't love an open fire?' Anne nodded uncertainly.

'Shitty weather. Too cold for bricklaying ...' Vivian repeated Mike the ghoul's misfortune authoritatively to an unimpressed Anne, the smart onlooker, turning away to work on her open PC.

'So, what shall we do first?' Vivan asked, downing her wine and bubbling with excitement.

'I'm not really bothered ...'

'Oh, come on, Annie, don't be like that.'

Don't fucking call me Annie, you know I hate it.

'I'll take you on a walking tour of my old haunts,' Vivian waved her arms about theatrically, drawing the attention of Shona Stewart, now snapping closed her computer and putting on her smart, sharply tailored raincoat.

'Well, I'd like to go to the Cathedral,' she conceded, thinking of Mrs. B and how she'd be keen to hear all about it when she got back.

'Okay, if you really want to - if that's your thing,' making Anne wonder exactly why they'd come to one of Britain's most ancient cities if Vivian didn't like old places. Why was she here?

'See you tonight then, my lovely?' Skeletal Mike called over in a thick West Country accent as he creaked out of the bar, making Anne suspect Vivian had arranged to meet up with him later. 'Oh, what's that face for Annie,' she mocked, her hideous bottom lip sticking out, pulling at Anne's chin. The smart woman winced as she passed them.

'Let's just go. Now.' Humiliation stung Anne's cheeks pink.

Clouds heavy with snow hovered above the hotel, and Anne, grateful for her warm fleece, zipped up against the cold blast. They headed in the direction of the Christmas market while DS Stewart quietly slipped out of the rear of the hotel, where her lift was waiting. Twinnie McGreal, in his Burberry checked cap, was waving from his car. He was a man used to using rear entrances – the main reason he had booked the Fleece Hotel. They needed to be inconspicuous.

'Everything okay, Boss?'

DS Shona Stewart nodded. 'Thought I'd come down and deal with things myself.' She was never one for small talk.

The Christmas market soon lifted Anne's spirits with the sweet smell of spiced mulled wine and the tinny Christmas songs hanging in the air. This was the type of Christmas scene she'd longed for as a child, when Christmas always landed with disappointment. Vivian, also in the Christmas spirit, was on her second glass of mulled wine when, suddenly, it occurred to Anne that her mum might have visited this market. She started to examine people's faces more closely. But couldn't imagine Christmas markets being her mum's thing.

Vivian, quite a spectacle in her wide orange velvet trousers now accessorized with a jaunty purple jacket and matching beret, was staring into the depths of a wishing well beneath a huge Christmas tree in the open courtyard. The falling snow left white splotches on her heavily mascaraed eyelashes. She dropped a coin into the wishing well, leaving Anne wondering what she'd wished for. She knew so little about Vivian's life but guessed she'd also had her traumas – the things that clung to you like ugly warts.

'Look, there's a walking tour, let's jump on the back and listen,' said Anne excitedly. The stocky tour guide strode ahead in a heavy wool coat and a fur hat with flaps, which made her look Russian. 'Rasputin,' joked Anne, but Vivan chose not to respond. Then something quite magical happened.

'Saint Gabriel's chapel is in the crypt of the Cathedral ...' She could hardly believe her ears, so they had an Angel Gabriel here too? She looked around for Vivian to tell her about this connection to home, but her velveted mentor stayed sullen on a low wall, sulking like a naughty child on a school trip.

'Look, Annie, you finish your precious tour if you must, I've got other things to do. I'll see you back at the Fleece later.'

Enraptured by the tour guide's knowledge, Anne waved Vivian off as the tour group snaked past DS Shona Stewart and Twinnie McGreal sitting in a private booth in The Purple Olive cocktail bar. 'Overpriced and overrated,' Twinnie would describe the bar later to his pals in the reptile shop he was funding, but he expected this was the type of place Shona Stewart was used to.

'I've been fielding calls from a very concerned wife.' Said Shona Stewart, straight as an arrow. 'I think I've managed to gain the woman's confidence. She's invited me round.'

'You sure it's William Reynolds' wife?'

'Yeah. Well, his partner more like. Calls herself Iris Reynolds, but there's no record of a marriage. At least not to her. Said I'd go around and see her in person. She's talking about going to the papers, and your name's cropped up. She needs quietening for both our sakes.'

'I've got plenty of ways to shut her up,' he smirked in a way Shona Stewart found juvenile.

'Don't think that's the best idea you've ever had. Look, the headless body case is losing momentum. Don't do anything else daft. I'll make sure the case goes cold, but only if you keep a lid on things.'

He sulked, knowing she was right, and called over for more cocktails.

'We don't need to worry, I've got enough on her. She's been remanded for handling in the past, and there's other stuff I can bring up.'

'Knew I could count on you, Boss.' He sipped his second Martini espresso. His guilty pleasure. After all, it was Happy Hour.

16

#Banksy: 'Not Everyone Will Understand Your Journey,
That's okay, You're Here to Live Your Life, Not Make
Everyone Understand'

Anne entered Canterbury Cathedral's magnificent Christ
Church Gate looking for St. Gabriel's chapel. The air was filled
with mystical, haunting music floating high above her; music
fit for angels. She descended stone steps worn smooth and
shiny by the passing centuries, to the ancient chapel with its
low, vaulted ceiling. Her attention was immediately captured
by a stunningly beautiful painting: 'The Annunciation'. The
Virgin Mary, bathed in gold, looked adoringly at the infant
Jesus, and in that moment, Anne pined for such love. How
could a mother give her child away so easily? Had she been
unlovable in some way? The question that had haunted her all
her young life.

She looked to the Angel Gabriel for answers, but this
Gabriel seemed quite different from the angel in her church.
He looked more aloof than her gentle, ever-present Gabriel;
this one looked grand, distracted, like he needed to be
somewhere else. She was startled at someone speaking behind
her, and for a minute, dreaded 'the voices' returning. But this
was not a place for demons; it was one of the caretakers waiting

to pull a plaited silken rope across the entrance. It was time for the small chapel to close.

Stopping at the Cathedral bookstore, she bought a small poster depicting one of the beautiful chapel paintings, thinking Mr. Murphy might like it, and lit a candle for Fleur before reluctantly leaving. It had snowed heavily outside, presenting a perfect Christmas card scene, and near their hotel, she saw Vivian exiting a vintage clothes shop. Her bright velvet clothes stood out against the blinding white background. She turned at Anne's call, a long piece of mottled fur topped with a small fox's head swung around her neck.

'Like it?'

It's the most disgusting thing I've ever seen in my life.

'It's very ... unique, Vivian, very you.'

'Come on, let's go and get some drinkies before dinner,' and taking her by surprise, her mentor linked her by the arm.

'You seem very much at home here, Vivian?' Hot chocolate warmed her hands; her back turned away from the hearth and the crackling flames.

'I studied here when I was younger ... but only briefly.' Vivian had a faraway look in her eyes. Under the golden evening lights, she looked softer, almost pretty, as the fire played with the highlights in her ginger hair.

'What did you study?' But Vivian was now distracted as cadaveric Mike had returned to occupy his seat at the bar.

'Look who's here. No, don't stare, he might see us looking,' Vivian was preening much like a teenager at her first dance.

'Drinks, ladies? Maybe a Snowball?' He'd smartened up a bit; his overpowering chemical aftershave reached them from the bar.

Must fancy his chances ...

Vivian lapped up the attention, giggling so much that Anne left them to it until a clumsy knocking on the door disturbed her reading of The Kentish News. Vivian stumbled into the room, her cheeks a mottled pink. 'Time for your makeover, Annie ...'

What the ...

But her mentor wasn't for backing down. She handed Anne a frothy Snowball drink in a glass imprinted with a tiny prancing reindeer, ignoring her rising protestations. 'I'm going to start by straightening your hair for you,' in a tone that suggested it was best to give in. Next came the bulging makeup bag. 'There, what do you think?' Vivian, self-satisfied with her efforts, stood back as Anne viewed her transformation in the pockmarked mirror. Her lips and cheeks were well-defined; her eyes turned deep and dreamy with mascara and kohl eyeliner. For an instant, she saw her mum reflecting back at her.

Vivian added a vintage Hermes silk scarf from her full suitcase, its luxurious pearliness accentuated her dark complexion perfectly. She liked what she saw and started to look forward to their evening out together, before Vivian, devoid of all sensitivity, delivered the blow.

'I invited Mike to join us for something to eat, you never know, he might even pay; he seems loaded.'

Anne had enjoyed the past hour, listening to Vivian instruct her in the art of applying makeup. But, as usual, her mentor had gone and spoiled things. She downed her Snowball in one, then waited until Vivian was in the shower and helped herself to some of the opened wine Vivian had dragged along in her bulging suitcase.

'We're meeting Mike down in the bar at seven,' Vivian called from the bathroom, completely oblivious to Anne growing quiet, withdrawing into herself.

'I think you two should go out on your own. You don't want me spoiling your fun.'

'Oh, come on, Annie, don't be like that.'

She defiantly downed more wine, and maybe it was the alcohol, or the strong desire to get away from Vivian, that she suddenly knew with great clarity what she intended to do.

'There's somewhere I want to go tonight anyway, so maybe things have worked out for the best.'

Vivian didn't put up any resistance. 'Where are you off to then?' peeping around the bathroom door with a flimsy towel around her head above ballooning, livid, mottled breasts.

'I'm just going to check out something I saw advertised this afternoon. A Banksy exhibition,' she lied.

'Ooh nice.' Quickly followed by: 'What time do you think you will be back?'

Shite, she's planning on bringing Bones back to our room.

'Not sure, about midnight?'

'That's fine by me, you go and have some fun.'

As if I need your permission to do anything.

And she gulped more of Vivian's wine, partly in protest, but mostly for Dutch courage.

Mike whistled when she joined him at the bar. Vivian, still upstairs, was taking an age to get ready. 'Do you fancy going out somewhere special?' He put his arm around her waist. She leaned into him, close. She needed some information.

'Is there anywhere around here where I could get some drugs?' she whispered into Mike's ear.

'Oh, I definitely like the sound of that - the Pilgrim Bar is where all the students go, you can get whatever you want there. I'll take you.'

Anne recalled the bar by the river. She'd seen it on her illicit afternoon tour with Rasputin. She felt Mike's hand stray to her knee, the uninvited warmth through her jeans, and shuddered. 'Ready when you are,' he looked at her lustily.

Creep. He's almost old enough to be my father.

And Anne knew how to deal with creeps. Bending forward, she accidentally knocked his pint over, soaking him. 'Bloody hell, look what you've gone and done, I can't go anywhere now.'

'Ooh, ever so sorry.' And she left, leaving Mike and the newly arrived Vivian fawning over him, enjoying patting his trousers dry.

Making her way through the dimly lit lanes, she tried to work out how she felt. Apprehensive about what she was setting out to do, but quietly determined to see it through. She thought of the last time she'd seen her mum. The day she clacked away, leaving her at the children's home, still wearing the previous night's Bingo clothes. Anne had started crying, with the staff doing their best to comfort her. 'Your mum will be back soon,' said Theresa, despite the doubt Anne read in her face. But it wasn't her mum she was crying for, it was Fleur. Who would look out for her now?

Not long after, Fleur came to stay there too. For a short break, when her mum went into hospital and ended up staying for over a year, splitting them up only when Anne was placed with her foster family, the Owens. Ruth was their social worker then and came to take Anne from the Owens' when the placement broke down and Mr. Owens, whom Anne preferred to call 'Dickhead', had to go into hospital for treatment for minor burns. Somehow, he'd got trapped in his garage, and a small fire had broken out.

She now knew exactly what she would say to her mum. 'Why didn't you come back for me all those years ago?'

17

#Banksy: 'Warning Sign'

DS Stewart sat on the leatherette couch in Iris Reynold's small but tidy, terraced house. A vanilla-scented candle was burning on the mantlepiece. It was neater than Shona Stewart expected. She took it as a warning sign; she didn't like it when things didn't go to plan.

The teary, stringy-haired woman with large grey brown eyes sat opposite her. She had a prematurely lined face that told a million sad stories, but she also had a bit of an edge to her, making DS Stewart choose her words carefully. However she played things, she wasn't in for an easy ride.

'I'm afraid I can now confirm that the man in our mortuary is William Chaucer Reynolds.'

Iris Reynolds burst into tears, wiping her nose on the sleeve of her sweatshirt. Her mascara was running down her cheeks. 'I knew it. Really. Deep down.' She blew her nose loudly on a tissue that Shona Stewart handed her. 'All those questions the police asked about his work patterns and the vehicles he drove for Jacksons Haulage. I blame that bastard Twinnie McGreal; he had a real hold over him. I've told the police about him. Is that why you're here?' she sniffed.

Shona Stewart didn't react, preferring to see how things played out.

'I still can't believe Will is dead. He'd been working all hours, saving for us to buy our own place. Left Jacksons, got a good job in security. He'd turned a corner.' Her jutted chin was testament to her belief that her errant partner had gone straight.

Shona Stewart didn't flinch, although she was irked to hear of William Reynolds' redemptive ways - it didn't help her case. And she could tell from Iris' tone that the woman wasn't for backing down. Good job she'd come prepared.

'When did you last see Mr. Reynolds, Iris?'

'A few weeks ago. I knew something was wrong; he's never been away this long before. He's not phoned me or left any messages. He might not have been the sharpest tool in the box, but he always provided for us.'

'Us?'

Iris stood up, lit a cigarette, and fetched a photograph of herself and a toddler.

'Lovely child. How long ago was this taken?'

'About ten years ago. She lives with her dad.'

'Mr. Reynolds isn't the child's father?' But DS Stewart already knew that. Iris shook her head, eyes full of remorse. 'No, but he's always looked after her like his own. Our Maddie. Will's made sure she has everything she needs.'

DS Stewart rose to replace the photograph on the bookshelf, noticing a near-empty blister pack of Temazepam.

'Can I see him?' Iris sniffed.

'You can, but we do have a definitive ID from his dental records, and I'm afraid it might be very distressing for you.'

She sobbed harder.

'Also, you'd need to come to Bristol.' She had no intention of Iris Reynolds poking her nose into things; she was there with the single intention of making sure the woman didn't cause any further trouble. Iris lit another cigarette, and Shona noticed she wasn't wearing a wedding ring.

'Are you Mr. Reynolds' next of kin?'

'No ...' Shona Stewart already knew he hadn't got divorced from his ex-wife, who ran a B&B in Weymouth. She shook her head, implying that it wouldn't be straightforward for the distraught woman to see Albert's body.

'Can I make us more tea?'

Iris nodded at the kind officer who seemed to understand her predicament.

'You're not from 'round here?' Iris snuffled.

'No, but I've been working on the case from the Bristol end, where Mr. Reynolds' body was recovered.'

'There's something not right ...'

Here we go, thought Shona Stewart.

'Will told me he'd never go back to Bristol, he hated everything about the place after the football club let him go. Anyway, how would he have got there? His car's still here. He'd have told me if he had a big job on.'

'People do strange things for strange reasons.'

'Not Will. He was keeping his nose clean. Looking out for something new after all those hand-to-mouth driving jobs. Best thing he ever did moving on from Jacksons … they're the meat packers he used to work for, but it was all temporary, no contract or anything.'

The meat packers that trafficked much more than meat, thought DS Stewart, whilst smiling sympathetically. William Reynolds was far from the saint Iris was making him out to be.

'It's all down to that bastard Twinnie McGreal. Always getting Will to do his dirty work for him. Will's lived in fear of him ever since the Group 4 shooting, when the money went missing.'

Shona Stewart didn't need all that business being dragged up and placed her cup down on the glass table with a clatter that surprised them both.

'Would you like to make a formal complaint against Mr. McGreal?' She took out her notepad. The woman looked uncertain, shaken at the sudden change in tone. 'I can assure you that I can look into everything you have raised. But Iris, I hope you don't mind me bringing it up, but you've had a previous conviction for handling stolen goods and lying to the police?'

Iris turned ashen. 'How do you know about that?'

'It's just that it makes you an unreliable witness. People have short memories, and I'm only here to act in your best interests.'

'I don't know what you mean?'

Shona Stewart took out a small bag of white powder from her bag and placed it under the cushion nearest to her while Iris was looking for more cigarettes. 'If you help me, Iris, I will help you.' She'd done her homework. Iris Reynold's daughter had been removed from her care, and following numerous safeguarding conferences, only minimal supervised contact was allowed due to her mother's continued Class A drug dependencies.

'I'm clean ...'

'Doesn't look like it to me.' She pulled out the condemning plastic bag from under the cushion and raised an eyebrow.

'You bitch!' cried Iris. 'You fucking bitch ...'

18

#Banksy: 'No Loitering'

The Pilgrim Bar was easy to find in its prominent location on the riverbank. It looked lovely with long, twinkling ropes of Christmas lights reflecting on the river. The noise got louder along with the strong whiff of cannabis, its pungent weedy smell lingering in the heavy winter air. Anne shivered, partly due to the cold crispness but also in anticipation of what she might be walking into.

She caught her reflection in the mirror behind the bar and was pleased to see that she looked older and more sophisticated than many of the girls around her. Waiting at the quieter end of the long bar, adorned with sketches of the characters from the Canterbury Tales, the efficient blue-haired bartender came to serve her.

'What can I get you, mate?'

'A bottle of lager, please.' It seemed everyone was swigging out of lager bottles.

'There you go.'

'Is there anywhere I can get something a bit harder?'

'Bouncers on the door, mate.'

'Thanks.'

She stood back and watched a pumped-up tattooed bouncer handing over small packages to over-eager students.

'What do you want?'

She took a deep breath. 'Don't suppose you know anyone called Chantelle?' What were the chances of anyone knowing her mum? It was such a long shot. But she knew her mum would be where the drug scene was, and there couldn't be that many Chantelles in Canterbury, surely? The bouncer looked her over suspiciously, then turned to his older bald workmate, busy chatting up some very young, underdressed girls.

'Someone here asking about Chantelle.'

'Who's asking?'

So, they do know her. What did creepy Mike say? It's the type of place where you can get anything. What are you up to now, mum?

Her heart was racing. 'I'm Kylie, her daughter.'

The bald man came over and took a long look at her. What was she inviting here? 'I'll call Guy.' He made a call on his handset before a tall, smartly dressed man came out and asked if he could help her. He also looked her over with interest. 'Well, you're Chantelle's kid all right. Wait here, I'll give her a ring.'

She waited outside, nervously downing her drink, her heart pounding as her breath turned to small puffy clouds in the cold night air.

'I've been asked to take you to Chantelle's place if you would care to follow me.' Guy had the air of someone who was used to being in control. He reminded her of that posh boxer, Chris … someone. Her thoughts were scrambled.

'I'm not sure,' she started to back off.

'Don't worry,' said the gravelly-voiced Guy. 'It is only ten minutes away.'

She took a deep breath, put her empty lager bottle in her shoulder bag for insurance, and followed him. Her legs were trembling.

They drove off, following the river to the outskirts of the city, where Guy turned up a long driveway. A large mansion-like house came into view, surrounded by gently falling snow, its roof hidden by a low-hanging winter fog. An enormous Christmas tree dwarfed a planter, twinkling with tasteful pale pink lights. Everything was so silent after the noisy pub, it made her ears buzz. Guy had a key and took her through to a lavishly decorated room. A woman's room with its beige and pink decor. It was centred with a huge fireplace above which was a portrait of an attractive, slim woman in a peacock blue evening gown. She stared in disbelief, as if at her reflection, before she realised she was staring at her mother.

'Nice, isn't it? Had it done to mark my birthday. A present to me, from me, you might say.' The smell of cigarettes hit the back of her head before the waves carrying the familiar resonance of her mother's deep voice, a little more refined than it used to be. She turned to see her mother dressed in a long peach silk dressing gown, with tumbling dark hair. Older, but still the same trim frame, a little rounder now, the scrawniness gone, but she could still see the hard lines around her mother's painted mouth, still there in real life, although airbrushed out of the dominating portrait.

'I'm surprised you agreed to see me.' Anne sounded stronger than she felt.

'Knew you'd turn up someday, thought we might as well get it over and done with.'

Her mother was looking her up and down as if making an assessment.

'Nice scarf,' she sniffed. 'Well, you didn't turn out too bad after all,' her voice flat, devoid of any emotion, just like she remembered.

Anne picked up a photograph of two small girls sitting on a pony, yellow polka dot ribbons in their hair, and a girl probably in her early twenties holding the reins. She was annoyed that her hand was trembling.

'These your stepkids, then?'

'No, cheeky bitch, they're mine, Charlotte and Rosie, twins. They're your little sisters.'

They didn't look much like her or her mum, all freckles and long strawberry blonde hair.

'I've got sisters?' Anne took a step back, the words knocking her off balance. 'Who's the other girl holding the reins?'

'She's your older sister, Katherine, named after your grandmother Kitty. I went back for her.'

Anne closed her eyes as she struggled to work it out. She'd had an older sister all the time. And one that looked very much like her.

There's a complete fucking family here that I knew nothing about.

'She was in care from little, never could cope with her when I was young. Felt a bit bad about it when I got all this and went back to get her.' It took a minute to sink in.

'You went back for her and left me? I never even knew I had an older sister.'

Guy came into the room and asked if anyone would like a drink.

'Piss off,' spat her mother, 'we're catching up.'

'Thought about coming for you, but you'd drag up too much of the past. Anyway, you'd been fostered by then, the social worker said you were happy enough.'

'You didn't even bother to check? Never crossed your mind I might be in the hands of an abusive fucker of a foster dad?' Anne's voice was rising, becoming unsteady.

Her mum didn't flinch. 'I knew you'd get by, Kylie. You always had it about you. People liked you.'

She's thinking of Billy; she was punishing me because he liked spending time with me ... her own child.

'So, I went back for Katherine. Anyway, you'd already had my best years, time she got some.' Her mother took the photograph from her hands. 'You do look like Katherine, though. We all ended up with Kitty's eyes, the making of us.'

'Kitty, my ... grandmother?' Questions spoken through a jealous pang that her older sister had something that directly connected her to the past. It was just a name, but it was more than she had. She felt faint.

'Your grandma, back in Ireland, had Spanish roots she used to tell us, something about sailors settling there after a shipwreck.' Her mother replaced the photograph carefully on the mantlepiece as if it might be contaminated by her touch. Anne sat down, trying to still the stars flashing before her eyes.

'Should make more of your ... assets ... Kylie.'

'Is that how you got all this?'

'Ways and means, Kylie, ways and means.' She walked over to put out her cigarette and sat on the sofa next to her, forcing her to stand up and her mother to sigh.

'How's that kid Fleur? Used to like her, but she had a terrible mother.'

Like you were Mother Teresa?

Anne forged on through her dizziness, feeling the need to strike back.

'Fleur's gone missing. Think she's gone off with one of the McGreals, you might remember them, people always seemed to go missing when they were around?'

Her mum stood up, then abruptly sat down again. It had hit her like a wrecking ball. The desired effect. 'Guy, more ciggies,' she barked before Guy came in with a smart art deco cigarette box and lit her mother a cigarette with an oversized ornate lighter.

'Go now.' She dismissed him, and he bowed ever so slightly, casting his eyes in her direction as if checking she was okay. But Chantelle Grimes was rattled.

Her mother took a long drag, then turned to look Anne sternly in the eye, causing an excited thrill to surge through her body; she'd unsettled her mother's Alice in Wonderland existence.

'I'm warning you, Kylie, don't you bring any of that shit down here. I'm respected around here, moved on from those vermin.'

'That includes me, does it?' squaring up to her mother, who backed away from her.

'You always had a strange side to you, even as a kid. Used to frighten me sometimes.'

'Maybe that's because I was constantly getting you out of scrapes, like when I had to sort out …'

'Enough, Kylie,' her mother spat at her. 'She's ready to go back,' she shouted to Guy, who must have been waiting outside the door listening to everything.

'Have a happy life, mum. You and my sisters,' but her mother had turned her back on her. She wanted her to turn around, to say she was sorry, but she was gone. Before she knew what she was doing, she pocketed a small egg-shaped clock while Guy fetched her jacket. She needed to take something with her … anything.

Guy coursed a long road around the back of the house, giving a full view of the ample grounds and snow-covered paddocks beyond. They passed a work yard with a fleet of trucks neatly lined up with smart red livery: 'Jacksons Logistics.' Slowly, they made their way back to The Fleece to see bony Mike stumbling out of the hotel entrance. She ignored him and waved Guy off with the impression that they shared something; both orbiting on the edge of Chantelle's self-obsessed universe.

'See *you* did alright, earn a bit, did you, my lovely? You should've told me you were on the game. I'd have paid plenty.'

Anne didn't bother to respond. In the bar, she ordered a brandy and Coke, catching her image in the mirror. It hurt that she looked so much like her mum. She prayed that the similarities stopped there. Her nerves were starting to jangle, that nervous, out-of-control feeling that she feared. Still, the brandy tasted good, warming; she could see why people on the telly always poured a brandy for shock. Exhausted, she went upstairs to their room, passing the smart woman with the bobbed haircut and shiny DMs checking out.

'You'll still have to pay for the full night.'

'Not a problem. Just finished my work earlier than expected.'

'Hope to see you back again soon.'

'I very much doubt it.'

It confirmed Anne's impression that she was used to nicer things in life.

The next morning, they breakfasted in silence. She sensed Vivian was succumbing to one of her dark moods.

'So, how did it go with Mike?'

'Never mind Mike. Why should I tell you anything when you have so many secrets?'

'What are you talking about, Vivian?'

Surely she can't know about my mum?

They moved outside so that Vivan could have a cigarette.

'Mike told me you went out searching for drugs.' Vivian censured her; slit eyes, lids heavy, warding off a cloud of cigarette smoke. Anne laughed until her sides hurt.

'Well, I'm glad you're amused, but we don't tolerate drug taking, us mentors. It's just not ... allowed.'

She steadied herself; the last thing she needed was for Vivian to turn all righteous. Sighing, she confessed, 'I went out to try to find my mum, I knew she'd settled here, in Canterbury, and I knew she'd be connected to the drug scene.'

Vivan looked at her disbelievingly.

'Mike put me on to a place called the Pilgrim Bar.'

'God, I can't believe that place is still going, it's where I once met someone ... I grew very close to.'

Anne felt shocked at this unexpected revelation.

'And was your mum at the Pilgrim Bar?' They both tracked a cloud of cigarette smoke floating in the cold air.

'No, but I think she runs it. I was driven out to her place by someone called Guy who looked like Chris Eubank, you know, the boxer?'

Vivian raised her eyebrows as if she'd gone a step too far.

'Well, he took me to her mansion with a huge pink Christmas tree. My mum has twin girls and ponies, and there was a portrait of her above the fire ...'

Vivian broke into a coughing fit and laughed until last night's mascara ran down her face. 'You expect me to believe all that?'

Anne hadn't thought how incredulous it all sounded and started laughing herself.

'You should be writing fiction, Annie. Alright, so you don't want me to know where you went, but just promise me you didn't do any drugs.'

'I promise. I've seen what that does to people, believe me, drugs aren't for me.'

'Are you talking about Fleur?'

Anne nodded. But she hadn't been, she'd been thinking about Shayne McGreal burning in a house fire.

'I prefer not to take risks,' said Anne as they walked up the stairs to collect their things from their room. 'Speaking of risks, I hope you used a condom last night.'

Vivian's left eye twitched, and the colour drained from her cheeks.

God, don't old people know anything?

'You going to see Mike again?'

'We're going to keep in touch; time I got a mobile phone. Mike gave me his number.' Vivian seemed to shudder with pleasure just at the mention of his name, leaving Anne to think that her mentor had enjoyed quite a night. She opened the creaking window wide in an attempt to free the lusty smells lingering in their overheated room.

The walk across town was sombre, with both women engaged in private thoughts under snow-laden yellowish-grey clouds. One last stroll along the riverbank to end their trip and clear their heads.

'Vivian, there's something I've been wanting to ask you. Did you get what you wanted out of this trip?'

'Sort of. I got to visit my old college, to remember the happy times with John.'

'The boy you were talking about earlier?'

She looked away.

'Is that where you went when I was at the Cathedral?' Vivian thrust her hands into her coat pockets. A little fox's head nestled under her chin.

'What did you study at college?'

'Art and Design. I used to be good at it, I used to paint a lot.'

That seemed almost as incredulous as her mother's ownership of ponies. 'Is that where you met John?' Again, she nodded but stayed quiet.

'Did you finish your course?'

'No, I fell in love and got pregnant.' Anne gasped at the unexpectedness of it.

'What happened?'

'My mother made me leave.'

It's all come back round to mothers and babies ...

'Would you come with me? I want to see if the house is still there?'

'Your student house?'

'No, the maternity home where the nuns took my baby from me.'

She followed her mentor, carefully stepping over a decomposing duck's bony carcass. Black beady eyes in a snapped head. Probably attacked by a rat or a fox.

'Kent House.' The fading name was struck through with a stabbing crucifix. Vivian stood statue-like as if weighed down by bad memories, her arms wrapped around her, keeping out more than the cold. 'Nobody told me I couldn't keep my baby, they didn't even let me see him.' Sobs racked her body. 'My mother insisted I go back home, and I never had any further contact with Canterbury, until now.'

'What about the baby's dad?'

'John didn't know anything about it. My mother saw to that. Maybe I shouldn't have told you all this.'

Anne took her hand.

'We all have secrets, Vivian,' and, caught off guard, she unburdened herself by sharing her own secret. Shayne

McGreal and her blacked out memories of the housefire, explaining why it was more important than ever to get back and find Fleur, and what might happen to them if the McGreal brothers ever found out the truth.

It had been an emotional trip for both of them. They were both damaged by past events. She thought of all the crappy things that had been revealed about mothers and motherhood as they walked back to the hotel to collect their luggage, leaving only footprints in the snow to show they'd ever been there. Vivian picked up a fallen pine cone, which she gently caressed in her pocket.

In their silence, they both thought about the truths left behind them. The tapestry of their respective lives, where the trusty weave had somehow split, warped, and frayed beyond repair.

'It's a good job we've found each other,' Vivian said, squeezing her arm possessively. And as they neared Bristol, Anne wondered why she had let down her guard and told Vivian her secret about the Mount Pleasant house fire. Every sinew told her Vivian would use it against her; use it to keep them bound together. But for now, she needed Vivian on board if she was to find Fleur. Although she sensed more strongly than ever that finding Fleur was the last of Vivian's intentions.

19

#Banksy: 'Fallen Angel'

'Hello Room.'

The air hung as stale and turgid as her mood. She unpacked lethargically, wanting so much for Fleur to be there; to tell her about finding her mum and her newly discovered sisters. But things were already fading into a dream. Her eye caught the official-looking letter that was waiting on the mat. It was addressed to 'Miss Fleur Drake' and a quick scan revealed it was from Fleur's new social worker, Polly Morton, who wanted to meet up as soon as possible, 'ideally before the New Year.' She needed to think of something. She couldn't afford for the authorities to come around, asking questions.

Next morning, she trudged through snow thick as marzipan to St. Gabriel's church. 'Mrs. B ...' She stilled in the silence. No Mrs. B, no Radio 4, what was going on?

'In here.' A thin, echoey voice drifted from the interview room. 'Sit down, Anne.' The woman looked tired, as washed out as the tea towel draped across her shoulder, stirring tea in the large metal teapot. Who else were they expecting?

'Is everything okay, Mrs. B?'

'I'm sorry, love, I'm a bit upset. Mr. Murphy died at the weekend.'

Anne's throat tightened at the thought of the old man she liked to think of as her grandad. And she hadn't been there for him. They sat in a claustrophobic silence broken only by the scraping of the metal spoon against the sides of the big teapot. Anne focused on Mrs. B's arthritic knuckles bulging over the top of her scratched wedding ring.

'How did he die?' She managed after an age.

Please, please stop that scratching. And why the large teapot?

Mrs. B stayed silent, only looking up to greet her expected guests.

'It was his heart,' announced Mr. Murphy's daughter, Diana, the strict-looking one she recognised from his photographs.

'But I have a few questions if you don't mind.'

Shit, what's PC Wright doing here?

Her stomach lurched. So that's what Mrs. B had set up, and still she wouldn't meet her eye. Her scrambled brain struggled to work out exactly which of her crimes he wanted to question her about.

Up close, Diana looked very much like her dark-skinned mother, who had worked in the butter factory. 'I wanted to personally say thank you for being so kind to my father, we really appreciated it.' Anne's breathing steadied, but her respite was short.

'There's just something puzzling us,' interjected PC Wright, looking the most serious she'd ever seen him.

'Someone has been using Mr. Murphy's credit card while he's been ill, housebound.'

Mrs. B coughed nervously. So that was what this was all about. But it wasn't hard for Anne to look genuinely astonished as she had no idea who it could be. Then she realised. It must be Perfect Pam, she was the only other person with access to Mr. Murphy's flat. She thought of the missing church funds and Pam's stash of scratch cards, it had to be her.

'I don't suppose you know anything about it?' James pushed, looking directly at her.

'No,' she said honestly. Although she had her suspicions, she wasn't about to share them with an overbearing police officer. 'What's been bought on it?' she asked, searching for clues.

'Purchases that lead us to suspect a female is using it. Online orders of perfumes and high-value accessories.'

'It's been blocked now,' said Diana, but we just hope nothing else has been taken. Then she suddenly stopped, gasped with her hand to her mouth.

'That's my mother's cross and chain,' she said, pointing at Anne's neck. Anne reddened and felt dizzy. There was too much happening.

'Are you sure?' asked James. 'Anne?' Mrs. B shuffled uncomfortably in her chair.

'Mr. Murphy gave it to me.' But she could see they didn't believe her. She tried hard to remember what he'd told her as Diana stood up, distressed, every inch of her accusing.

'Sit down, please, Diana, let's hear what Anne has to say.' At least James stayed objective.

'Anne, what made you think Mr. Murphy wanted you to have the jewellery?' James took command, with a slightly softer tone to his questioning.

'We've all had a hard life, but we never stooped to stealing things,' wailed Diana.

'He said it belonged to his wife, Bridget; he met her at the butter factory. I saw her wedding photograph with her lovely flowers in the snow. I was surprised he had married someone from a different background ... Yes, but it was okay because she was a catholic, he said.' She scrambled desperately for more facts, anything that would make them believe her.

Diana smiled the faintest of smiles, as if she'd heard that story many times before.

'He said it had cut into her skin once, so he didn't want her to wear it, and you didn't want it ...'

Diana's face crumpled. 'I'm so sorry I doubted you, Anne. My father obviously enjoyed your company very much to share all that. It's just that I'm so upset about everything, and we might have to get Scruff put down.' She sobbed and blew her nose simultaneously.

'Oh no,' Anne cried out, 'you can't do that. I'll take him. I love dogs.'

'That would be so helpful,' said Diana, looking in a way that Anne knew there was no turning back.

'But are you allowed animals in your accommodation?' asked the sensible Mrs. B, now returned to her usual attentiveness.

'No, but I think I know someone who'll love him.'

20

#Banksy: 'Laugh Now, But One Day We'll Be in Charge'

'I bought something nice for Mr. Murphy,' she said before Mrs. B's guests left, her cheeks reddening as they perused the religious print bought in Canterbury; her gift now feeling insignificant. 'Would you like it, Diana?'

'Lovely gesture but wasted on me, we had way too much religion stuffed down our throats as kids.'

'Maybe we will get it framed with a small tribute to Mr. Murphy. Hang it over there under the Angel himself?' Mrs. B had the best suggestions. Although Anne knew deep down that things would never be the same between them again, after the earlier glimmer of distrust behind the older woman's eyes.

'I'm off then,' said James. 'Might pop in later for a cup of tea. Need to ask around about that credit card.' He always seemed to be sniffing around lately. But at least she was off the hook. For now.

Anne steadied herself by setting out the crockery ahead of the lunch rush. She tried not to think too much about Mr. Murphy. Maybe it was safer not to get attached to anyone, so nobody could hurt you. She thought Fleur was a bit like that, kicking out at anyone who got too close—another reason why Anne always needed to be there for her.

She looked up at the Angel Gabriel.

What a morning ...

Mrs. B allowed her to use the church phone to call Polly Morton, Fleur's new social worker. But a tired voice told her she was out of luck. 'Sorry, Polly has finished for the Christmas holiday. I'm Sandra, covering for the Christmas break. Can I take a message?'

'Yes, it's Fleur Drake here,' she whispered. 'Polly has written asking to meet up. Can I get back to her mid-January? It's just that I'm going away soon with a friend's family.'

'Oh, anywhere nice?' asked Sandra, sounding like she'd rather be anywhere else than covering the emergency calls over the Christmas break.

'Yes, we're going skiing.' The lies flowed.

'Ooh, lovely. I'll pass the message on. Have you got a contact number?'

'Oh, I think Polly already has it.'

'I really do need to take a number, Polly insists.'

Anne reeled off the church phone number, switching two of the numbers in the process. 'Thanks ever so much,' Sandra sounded relieved that she'd followed protocol, 'and remember not to break anything.'

Anne paused, not understanding.

'On your skiing trip ...'

Like I'd like to break your neck.

'Come in, Pamela. Anything wrong?' Mrs. B called to the woman lingering in the corridor. Anne had been filling her in on the Canterbury trip.

'That young policeman is in the church hall asking questions about a missing credit card. He wants to speak to you next, Anne. Pity Fleur's not here to talk to him. Where is she, by the way?'

Anne froze, caught off guard.

'Oh, Fleur's just busy. Christmas is a demanding time for the beauty industry.' Mrs. B nodded in agreement. Taking her turn to catch Perfect Pam off guard, she continued, 'By the way, Pam, I saw you going into The Orchid restaurant the other night. I love Indian food; would you recommend it?' and enjoyed the freshly-coiffed woman's spluttering departure.

After her shift, she made her way to Millie and Zane's house with a sorrowful Scruff trailing behind on his lead.

'Shite, what 'ave you got there?' asked the candy floss haired Millie, stubbing out a cigarette on the slushy path. River came running to them, gurgling, delighted with the dog.

'Do you think you would be able to look after him? His owner has just died, and he'll get put down if we don't do anything.' Suddenly, Anne was overwhelmed at the realisation that Mr. Murphy had passed away; she hadn't had time to let it sink in before now.

Keep it together, please don't lose it here

'What's going on?' asked Zane, arriving from the shop with fresh beers.

'She wants us to take that raggy-arsed thing over there.'

'Bloody love dogs I do,' said Zane.

'I've got a bit of money to start you off with dog food, and I can always bring stuff from the Food Bank to help out. They all squealed as Scruff cocked his leg on the side of a chair before Zane picked him up and threw him into the backyard. He seemed very comfortable with handling dogs.

'I'm thinking of going to the Blind Fox tonight,' she shared confidentially while Millie was out of the room, picking her moment carefully to avoid trouble like last time.

'Well, just be careful. Some big shit goes on in that place, there's a real edge to everything now, with the dead body turning up and everything.'

The rain had eased off by the time she got back to her flat. She put Fleur's official letter safely away in their biscuit tin. There was something good about seeing Fleur's name on paper. Something concrete that she found comforting, that confirmed Fleur belonged with her, at their address. There was a knock on the door. She froze. What now?

'Everything all right?' she asked the pale youngster, who, with his dyed black hair and black ankle-length coat, looked like the Grim Reaper. It was Brian who had helped her clear the animal mess smeared on her door. When they first moved in, breaking all confidentiality, Marta the caretaker, had told them that he'd come from a young offender's prison and he had 'dirty habits'. She and Fleur had spent ages trying to guess what Brian's dirty habits could be. 'Brian the Wanker', Fleur had concluded to Anne's shock. Although he did seem to fit his new nickname, or BTW, as Anne preferred to call him.

'You seen anything of that kid Sasha lately?' Through his jittery awkwardness, she could see he was worried.

'No, not since last week. Why?'

'Oh, I've just been keeping an eye out for her.'

'More like you fancy her.' She regretted her words instantly. She'd touched a nerve.

'Jesus, Anne. She's just a kid. Something's not right there. I think she's in trouble. Don't want her to disappear, like the last cleaning girl …'

'I'll let you know if I see her,' she cut him short. Brian was clearly paranoid, probably smoking too much weed. Besides, she had enough to worry about, as the tune playing on her radio reminded her. 'The Twelve Days of Christmas' served only to remind her that time was running out.

21

#Banksy: 'A Lot of People Never Use Their Initiative, Because Nobody Told Them to'

'The Blind Fox? Never heard of it.' Vivian's eyes were green and eager, failing to betray her rising excitement as she kept Anne waiting in her porch.

'Well, will you come with me, or not?' Anne was finding her mentor's game-playing tiring.

'What time did you say?'

'Look, if you don't want to come …'

'I think I can change things around if it's *that* important …' exhaled Vivian, fluffing up her hair, not chancing Anne to retract the offer.

'I could even give you some more make-up tips, like we did at The Fleece? Make you look older? … and we could go for something to eat first?'

Anne nodded reluctantly, aware that it would clear out the last of her finances, but she needed to keep Vivian on board. Besides, she had a strong feeling in her gut that they were going to find Fleur this time, then it would be goodbye, Vivian. Forever.

Hardly able to touch her food, they left to catch the bus for the Blind Fox situated in the Old Town district. She caught their reflections in the steamy bus window. What would people take them for? Certainly not mother and daughter. They didn't look much like sisters, either; perhaps they would be taken for work colleagues? Anne's legs were turning to jelly with every stop. She had no idea what lay ahead.

'Vivian, if anyone asks, shall we say we work together? I suppose we do, in a way.' Vivian looked quizzically at Anne, never one for planning ahead.

'Use your imagination, Anne. We are obviously flight attendants on our night off!'

'No. No, we're not,' dismissed Anne curtly. 'This isn't a game, Vivian, we're here on business.' They walked along the busy avenue to the Old Town in silence. Anne asked, 'Just out of interest, Vivian, as my mentor, what do you think I might be good at in the future?' But Vivian struggled to respond.

At least make something up, you must have seen some promise in me ...

With her confidence draining like the channels of gushing water in the roadside gutter, she hunched down into her sweater.

'Don't you just love going out?' said Vivian, impervious to Anne's unease, just as the orange fizzy sign of the 'Blind Fox' came into view. Vivian's step quickened. Trembling, Anne followed. She had come too far to turn back now.

Anne insisted on occupying a table at the back of the pub, satisfied that they could blend into the background, yet get a good view of the bar.

'Nice place this. I haven't been out dancing for ages.' Vivian returned from the bar with two glasses of wine, which Anne needed to make last all night. Fortified by the alcohol, she felt brave enough to go exploring in the busy pub toilets. There was no sign of Fleur, but it was still early. She doubled back to a small side bar where a few men were huddled, a blond-haired lad in a vest blocked her way with a look that told her to stay clear. She skirted the length of the main bar, her boots sticking to the gluey residue on the pub floor. The music was getting louder, and people were cramming onto the dance floor to Slade's grating 'It's Christmas ...' classic anthem. She felt the vibrations run up and down her spine and picked up a blue drink left behind by one of the dancers – it tasted of bubble gum. No wonder Fleur loved them so much.

On her return, two blokes were sitting at their table. One in a shirt that was soaked through, the other, round-faced with braided hair in heavy dreadlocks. He wore a denim jacket with lots of badges pinned on it, and begrudgingly returned her smile.

'You've been an age,' Vivian chastised, fluffing up her hair. 'Meet Steve and Rasta Dave.'

Steve gestured for them to share his bottle of wine, making Vivian tremble with pleasure before leading him to the dance floor, her missile-like breasts clearing the way. They returned with another bottle of wine. Vivian whispered to her, in her mentoring voice, 'Always try to get your drinks bought for you.' Nearly jumping out of her skin, she turned at a hand placed on her shoulder. It was Zane, grinning inanely. Boy, did he need some dental work.

'Well, if it isn't Cinderella.' He looked her up and down approvingly. 'Any sign of Fleur?'

'No, but it's still early for Fleur. Have you seen anything?'

'No, but Grace has just come in.'

She followed his gaze to the blonde-haired girl waving at them from the bar. Anne recognised her from the Barge and her brief appearance at the Food Bank.

'Did you say she was … a prostitute?' She whispered into his ear, against the background din.

'All the girls over there are prossies.' He pointed as she pushed his arm down, not wanting to draw their attention. 'They sit in that corner waiting for someone to buy them a drink.' Anne felt nauseous. Some of the girls were much younger than herself. She could imagine Fleur being part of that group; flattered by the supposed friendships, the attention of older men, the money, and now the thrilling prospect of visiting Spain. Fleur, always desperate for adventure, would find this so seductive.

Steve and Rasta Dave got up to leave, leaving their wine in a bucket, presumably for them to finish. Anne poured a glass for Zane. 'Millie not here then?'

'We're not joined at the fucking hip, you know, we do our own thing,' he was eyeing the women on the dancefloor.

'Millie goes out with the girls then?'

'Don't be daft, she's got River to look after.'

Grace interrupted them, a mass of blond hair, strutting in her signature long suede boots, sidling up close to Zane.

'You made it then …'

The looks between Zane and Grace seemed over-friendly, making her wonder if there was more to their friendship. Zane brushed his fingers against Grace's cheek. She looked a bit out of it, her eyes wild, reminding her of how Fleur used to get.

'Hi Grace, don't suppose you've seen Fleur tonight?' She didn't want to interrupt them, but needed to know.

'No, she'd only be here if Frankie was in, even then he doesn't always bring her, you know.' She took Zane's drink from his hand and finished it off.

'Is Frankie likely to come in tonight then?'

'How would I know? Might do, might not. His mate Ali's in – him over there, he shares a flat with Frankie on Park Lane. She pointed to a smartly dressed Asian bloke; his back to them as he spoke to Rasta Dave, whose pin badges were catching the disco lights. Anne knew Park Lane well. It was one of her best foraging roads. The one where she'd first met Grace after she was roughly thrown out onto the street.

'Ready, girls?' a short, silver-haired man in a suit called over. Anne recognised him immediately. It was Perfect Pam's escort who accompanied her to The Orchid restaurant.

What are they doing hanging around with him? He's old enough to be their father.

'Looks like we're off, flat as a witch's tit in here. Sammi's taking us down to the docks to see what's in.' Grace kissed Zane on the neck and whispered something Anne couldn't catch before whistling over to three or four girls who grabbed coats and umbrellas and followed Grace outside in a whirlwind of hairspray.

'Zane, I've got a plan,' she said quietly as Zane drained their wine bottle while Vivian gyrated on the dance floor with Steve. 'Let's wait and follow Ali, Frankie McGreal's flatmate, wherever they go next might lead us to Fleur.'

'You're fucking mad, you. Get us a lager and I'll think about it.'

The disco lights dimmed, and Anne sourced a redundant bottle of lager from the bar counter for Zane. Vivian returned looking sheepish. 'Steve has invited me back to his for … a nightcap. But I told him that I'm with you. He said you can come too?'

'Oh, that's okay, Vivian, you go, I'm good here. Just wait a minute, though.' She disappeared in the direction of the pub toilets and returned with a packet of condoms, which were being given out free in a festive public health campaign. She handed them over secretively. The pub was emptying. The staff were brusque, wanting to get home. Anne saw Ali and the others make their way to the door and helped herself to the five-pound tip they'd left on the bar.

'Quick, they're leaving.'

Outside, they watched them get into a large black beast of a vehicle, which looked very much like the one that had frightened her at the bus stop. She and Zane got into one of the taxis queuing outside the Blind Fox, exactly as Zane said there would be.

'Follow that car.'

'You for real?' the taxi driver asked Anne.

'Yeah, we're following it to a party – just not sure of the exact address.'

'On to it,' said the taxi driver while Zane whistled quietly.

'And I thought Fleur was the mad one around here. Look, I'm off as soon as we stop. I don't want to get mixed up with whatever Fleur might be into, okay?'

'Right.' It wasn't a problem. She just needed to see where they were going. But, disappointedly, they returned to the Park Lane flat. The taxi pulled up a little way behind the parked Beast, and Anne paid the driver with the last of her money. She'd be walking home.

Standing in the shadows, they watched the ground-floor lights being flicked on. Anne already knew this house, with its illuminated bells, where she had stolen a heavy parcel of camera parts a few weeks before. Had she really been so close to where Fleur was staying? Maybe she'd been drawn to this flat by some secret pull from Fleur? Crazy early morning thoughts born out of alcohol and adrenaline.

'What are you going to do now?' asked Zane, sparking up his vape, which danced arcs, like fireflies in the dark.

'Go home and come back in the morning.'

'Fuckin' mad you are,' he mumbled as he made off, shivering with the cold.

Anne left in the opposite direction, mentally planning her next move, completely unaware of two police officers on a stakeout of the house, sitting in the dark with their car lights switched off. Officers Bob Lyons and James Wright sat in a strained atmosphere. James had been surprised to be asked to accompany Bob Lyons on his continuing surveillance of Frankie McGreal's flat. But Bob sat resolute, as closed as a barn door, refusing to share any background information with him. Still, it was exciting - exactly the sort of stuff Shona Stewart would want to be kept informed of.

Except not much was happening. A small group had just returned, probably been on a Christmas night out. Bob got out of the car to pee in the bushes when James noticed something that made him sit up and take notice. He squinted hard at the lone figure. Is that really you, Anne Grimes?

The following morning, Anne rose early and made her way back to the Park Lane flat, carrying the parcel of computer parts in her backpack. She saw Grace still wearing last night's clothes, leaving the flat, looking like she hadn't slept all night. They walked a little way along the road together.

'What are you doing here?' Grace asked snappily. She had a nasty graze on her face.

'I told you, I'm looking for Fleur.'

'I'd stay away from that lot if I were you.'

'What were you doing there?' Anne asked sheepishly.

'Me and Ali get it together sometimes …' Anne thought of the tattooed arms evicting her from the property a couple of weeks earlier.

'Was Fleur in there?'

'No. She's staying with Frankie at his other place.' Anne couldn't hide her disappointment.

'Where's that then?'

'An old place they call the Big House, on the outskirts of town, in the grounds of the Old Infirmary.' She knew it. Billy had once taken her there to pick blackberries that had stained her lips and fingers.

'Has he got another flat there?'

'No, he owns the place. Has his parties there.'

'What parties?'

'Fuck off, don't you know anything? Fleur always went to his parties, that's how they got together.' Another insight into the secret life of Miss Fleur Drake.

'How d'you get an invite?'

'Come with me, I'll get you in. A bus picks us up in Harbourside Lane, 6.30 pm every other Friday. The next big one is New Year's Eve. Word has it it's the last one before they leave.'

'Will Fleur definitely be there?'

'I expect so, it's Frankie's last big bash …'

With less than a week to find Fleur, Anne couldn't afford any more wrong turns.

'Don't miss it, we'll make loads, but be careful, it's easy getting in - but not always easy getting out.' Grace slung her bag over her shoulder and trounced off, leaving a trail of strawberry vaping cloud in the air.

Walking up the steps of 43a, Anne's heart felt like it could bounce right out of her ribcage. She pressed the illuminated bell, her finger shaking.

'What fuckin' time do you call this?' Ali appeared, tussled in boxer shorts with his arms wrapped around his upper body against the biting wind.

'Sorry, but this got delivered to my house by mistake. I think it's for you.'

He took the parcel and mumbled something before slamming the door. But she had the evidence she'd been looking for; the maroon padded jacket she'd picked up on one of her foraging trips was hanging up on a peg in the hall. The first sign that she was getting close to finding Fleur.

22

#B 'Fragile Silence'

DS Shona Stewart entered the smart riverfront café where James was waiting for her. Catching her breath, she stopped to check her sports watch. 'Not bad, shaved almost two minutes off my PB.' She ran capable fingers through her shiny hair, barely ruffled after her run. '10k. And much of it uphill,' she added unnecessarily. James was already impressed. At times, though, he was finding her smugness to be grating.

'Anything new for me?' Straight to the point. She smelled of heat, and there was a gleam of sweat on her skin as she removed her coordinated running jacket and dropped onto the chair.

'Well, we're still watching Frankie McGreal's flat in town.' He fleetingly recalled Anne Grimes hanging around the property, but preferred to keep that to himself.

His boss raised a questioning eyebrow.

'What's Bob playing at? Is the surveillance connected to Operation Cuckoo?'

But James couldn't answer, knowing he'd be the last person to be let in on Bob Lyons' motives. He updated her on the mundane details of the flat's occupants. She waved away the insignificance of it and shrugged into a fragile silence.

'Stick with it anyway. Bob's got good instincts. He's watching Frankie McGreal's place for a reason. We just need to know what that reason is.' She cracked her knuckles in a way that made him shudder. She'd had her nails done. Red with silver stars, uncharacteristically frivolous.

'So, he never briefs you on what he's looking for?'

He thought of the tension between them and shook his head. He'd hoped she wouldn't ask that. 'Do you push him?' A hint of irritation peppered her question. 'We need to know exactly what his interest is, James.' She tapped her nails on the polished wooden tabletop. 'Just a thought - but maybe he invites you along to get to hear what you might know. Bob Lyons is a player. Be careful what you might reveal, James.'

That threw him. What did he know that the older police officer didn't?

She went to refill her skinny latte when her phone vibrated on the tabletop. It stopped briefly before vibrating again. Someone wanted to contact her. He glanced down, and the name 'Cockie' flashed across the screen. Should he attract her attention? Probably not, she was almost at the front of the queue. The phone beeped as a message came through. He looked up again at the back of his boss' head and gingerly turned the phone toward him. He noticed the word 'Frankie' just before the message disappeared. He tried to steady his hands. Were these messages about Frankie McGreal?

The phone vibrated again, and this time he nudged it toward the edge of the table as a second message came through, aware that he had seconds before it would disappear. Once again, it was from 'Cockie', but he could only catch something about: '*The Farm*'. He nudged the phone back to its original position, bending as if to tie a stray shoelace. While Shona Stewart, irritated at the tardiness of the young serving girl, caught her young officer's reflection in the gleaming, spurting coffee machine. Her brow wrinkled. Had her young mentee just been reading her phone messages?

'So how long has it been since you were based in Bristol?' he tried to break the uneasy silence, to decipher his boss' intractable expression that was starting to unsettle him.

'I started out in West Grange station,' she sighed heavily before reluctantly offering more. 'I worked under Bob Lyons, as you know, until the Shayne McGreal incident. Bob used to be a real character, well-known all over the patch.' She winced at her skinny coffee, still too hot. 'Old school, but still well respected.' She surprised James at this level of regard for her old adversary.

'We were next thrown together after I'd left and moved into Detective work. It was my first big bust as a senior detective, and of course, it had to involve the McGreal twins. They were venturing into new ground, security van robbery.' Casually picking up her phone, she scrolled through her messages, forcing him to look away.

'I didn't think the McGreal twins could stand each other.'

'Thick as thieves, literally, back then,' she smiled, enjoying her joke. Her voice lowered, making him lean in closer. 'Frankie McGreal was always the small guy – the runner, never really had the brains to plan anything big, but was happy to go along with whatever Twinnie wanted. And Twinnie wanted to go big, to surpass even his big brother Shayne, who used to be the godfather of the family.'

'The one who died in the fire?'

She nodded but pulled a face that asked, 'If that's what you'd like to believe.' Opening a sachet of brown sugar, she sprinkled the smallest amount over her coffee. 'Twinnie McGreal started expanding eastwards, using his links in Reading and Canterbury. Ambitious. But we were on to him, watching his every move.' She licked some sugar from her top lip and paused; a sign she was about to disclose something big.

'I was working with Bob Lyons after a tip-off about an imminent Group 4 security van hijacking on the A roads between Reading and Bristol. It was our big chance to get that bastard Twinnie McGreal once and for all. The van was followed to Reading, then we took over at the agreed point.' She crunched appreciatively on a rogue sugar granule.

'The hijack went ahead as planned. Turned out to be a total cock up, at least on our side. Twinnie's boys jumped the van - in the middle of nowhere, of course - brandishing guns and shooting randomly. The van driver quickly caved in, but they didn't expect the second person, the security guard, to put up such a fight. He did eventually open the van, but then he collapsed after being hit by a stray bullet. Twinnie's lot grabbed what they could and got off smartish. We might have stood a chance to overpower them, but Bob Lyons wouldn't budge. He said we needed to see to the injured security guard and wait for the armed police to arrive.'

'Did the security guard survive?'

'Taken to hospital and thankfully pulled through. He clearly wasn't in on it.'

'But you think the driver was?'

'We discovered that the van driver had previously worked for Twinnie McGreal - let's say they had history. Worked out perfectly for Twinnie; an old contact now working as a driver for a security firm. But it all fell apart when the driver's phone showed up incriminating stuff, implicating Twinnie McGreal. Don't think the driver meant it to be found; he was just a bit thick. Lost his job over it.'

'And that's what Twinnie McGreal was doing time for in HMP Channing Wood?'

'Yeah. Pity he didn't get longer. Should have done, but he pleaded guilty and with the best criminal defence team on his side, he got six years.'

'And he thought the driver had grassed on him?'

'Yep, and guess who the security van driver was?'

He stalled before it came to him. 'William Reynolds.'

She nodded. 'Our very own Albert. Our Cuckoo. A sacrificial lamb sent home as a warning to Frankie as soon as Twinnie got out of prison. I had McGreal in for questioning when I was in Canterbury last week. Smug bastard. He knows we haven't got a single thing to pin it on him.'

But something still didn't figure for James. 'But what gripe has he got with Frankie?'

'Well, apart from Frankie dealing on his patch while he was in prison, it all goes back to the night of the security van heist.'

James still didn't get it.

'A lot more money went missing during the robbery than was recovered.'

She enjoyed his confusion, taking her time before delivering the hand grenade.

'The night of the robbery, all our attention was on the guard who was shot. It was mayhem. Twinnie's lot got away, trying to run us over as they left. Local blue lights arrived, then armed police, ambulances, and of course, the van had to be secured.'

She shook her head at the memory. 'It was a shambles, and in the middle of all the chaos, the rest of the money went missing.'

'How much?'

'150k.'

He whistled air through his teeth.

'We were all investigated, but the IOPC never concluded anything. The CCTV was out on the van; William Reynolds had already seen to that. The robbery was in the middle of nowhere, and our dashcam turned out to be faulty. No witnesses, no evidence other than the driver's phone. The IOPC found some irregularities in our paperwork, along with our 'poor state of readiness'. We got a right bollocking but were cleared back to work.'

'Nobody ever got to the bottom of where the original tip-off about the robbery came from?'

'No. It was anonymous. Unofficially, we all started to talk about 'The Eel' again, the slippery character behind it all - someone made a lot of money that night. Someone in the police close to one of the McGreal clan.'

James knew she was talking about Bob Lyons.

It had worked. She'd diverted his attention. Away from Cockie. Away from his careless messages about The Farm.

23

#Banksy: 'The Scar of Bethlehem'

Christmas Day, and Anne was awake early.

Where are you, Fleur? What are you doing this cold Christmas morning?

Back in her foraging gear, she set her mind on doing something positive. She decided to go looking for last-minute parcel drop-offs while simultaneously keeping an eye open for Fleur. She passed the Park Lane flat, but could see from a distance that there were no lights on and the curtains were open. The place was deserted.

Continuing to the affluent East Parkside area, she passed a boarded-up Children's Centre bearing a sorry 'For Sale' sign. But someone was busy at work. It was her spray-painting friend, finishing a mural showing Santa being pulled by a Mercedes-Benz on the hoarding covering the rundown Children's Centre. She waved, giving him the thumbs up, and in a lighter mood, progressed to the smarter area where tall gates fronted long drives. Something bright atop a gatepost caught her eye. A yellow woolly bobble hat, something a walker would wear. It felt like a good omen, and zipping it into her backpack, the warning shout came too late, as the cyclist veered into her, sending her flying off her feet.

'Use your bell next time,' she called, exasperated at her clothes soaked in dirty, melting slush.

'Anne?' A thin voice escaped from the heavy hood of a thick jacket.

'PC Wright?' she uttered in disbelief.

'I'm really sorry, Anne. I've been out looking for the parcel thief. I thought the Christmas rush might have tempted them.'

A lame explanation on his part; his main interest had been surveying Frankie McGreal's Park Lane property and the surrounding area, in the hope of finding something useful to report back to Shona Stewart. 'Anyway, what are you doing out so early?'

Anne thought quickly. 'I'm going to get some dog food and take it over to a friend looking after Scruff, you remember … Mr. Murphy's dog?' Her eyes started to mist as they did whenever she thought of her old friend. 'Needed to get it done early before I go to church. Anyway, what are *you* doing out on a *bike* in this weather?'

He looked sheepish. 'Stuff's been going missing from doorsteps. The boss thought it best to use the station's bike.' Not a complete lie.

'On Christmas morning? They're taking the piss.'

The look that scudded across James' face confirmed that he'd already considered that as a possibility. He remounted his bicycle.

'What shop are you going to?'

'The all-night shop on Church Road.'

They forged ahead together, Anne thinking how close she'd come to getting caught out. The bicycle ploy was very clever; she would never have expected a police officer to be about on Christmas morning, least of all on a bike.

In the over-bright shop, Anne looked at his side profile caught in the light between night and early morning, his hood was down, revealing his well-cut blond hair falling floppy at the front. He turned and looked at her, and she was startled by his clear, light brown eyes framed with long, fawn-like eyelashes.

'Fancy a polo mint?' he smiled at her; the first time she'd seen him smile in an off-duty, natural way. He was good-looking. She felt jumpy, making it hard to concentrate on her purchases: the cheapest tin of dog food, a bottle of milk, and some reduced-priced chocolate for River.

'That's one pound eighty.' The turbaned shopkeeper rang the till. She stalled; she didn't have enough money.

'I'm sure your boyfriend can chip in,' the shopkeeper winked. They both mumbled, explaining they weren't together 'in that way', laughing self-consciously.

'Thanks for the loan, I'll pay you back.'

'No worry, after all, I did knock you over. Nice hat,' he commented as she pulled out the yellow bobble hat to pack away her purchases, struggling to remember how it had got there.

'I wear it sometimes with my hiking group,' she lied, caught off guard.

'I like hiking too.' It didn't surprise her. She guessed from his athletic physique that he was sporty. They travelled the short distance to Millie's house, with her walking on the pavement while he struggled to cycle slowly to keep to her pace and avoid buildups of ice and slush. He stood astride his bike by the curbside as she deposited her goodies on Millie's front step.

'Does the dog like milk?' he enquired using his best policing skills.

'No, it's for River, their toddler.'

'River?' he screwed his face in a judgemental way.

'Yeah, River, got a problem with that?' she replied curtly, suddenly feeling inexplicably protective towards Millie and her dysfunctional family.

'There's more to you than meets the eye, Anne Grimes.' She liked his soft smile and his approving tone, but felt worried that he was getting to know too much about her. In the early morning light, she noticed some silver scarring due to acne around his ears; a boy playing at being an officer of the law.

On return to her flat, she picked up an irregularly shaped parcel bearing her name and address, and stood looking at it with all the shock of having found a baby goat outside her door. It was the only legitimate parcel she'd ever received. Puzzled, she knocked on BTW's door. 'Do you know anything about this, Brian?' He'd know if anyone did; he always seemed to be on the lookout lately, smoking his funny stuff in the open air or looking for Sasha out of the large window at the top of their bleak breezeblock stairway.

'Shit, Anne, what time do you call this?' he yawned, making her duck to dodge his offensive breath. 'No, I didn't see anything. Although I did hear a posh bird talking on a phone earlier. Gone by the time I'd finished my piss.'

None the wiser, she placed the parcel on her bed: 'Miss Anne Grimes' written neatly in purple felt tip. She was good at guessing parcels, but this one was such a strange shape. Tearing at the packaging, something scratchy poked out, revealing green protruding branches. It was a small Christmas tree with '*Have a lovely Christmas*' handwritten on a brown label tied to its peak. She plugged it in, admiring the pink lights. It lit up the lacklustre room, touching something deep in her core. It was Christmas morning, and someone had been kind enough to remember her. The feeling took her back to the best Christmases, when she was young and was allowed to choose a present from the Argos catalogue, with Billy's help.

She hummed carols, which Room, also lifted by the charm of the surprise gift, seemed to appreciate. She placed her eclectic foraging finds ready for wrapping, enjoying festive songs on her small radio, a Ninja Turtle-themed early find.

Some heavily scented candles were perfect for Mrs. B, and for Fleur, she wrapped the best of her finished drawings of grazing Dartmoor ponies, which, she had to admit, were quite good. A Top Gear Annual was all that remained unattributed and unwrapped. But who'd want that? Standing back with a steaming cup of tea, she felt a rush of love for what she'd created.

The Christmas morning church service came with an overpowering smell of old people in mothballed clothes; a far cry from the well-heeled, packed-out churches on 'Songs of Praise'. Looking around, she felt a surge of disappointment. There was nothing special or mystical as Reverend Paul preached about the Angel Gabriel and the significance of their church's namesake at Christmas time.

'The Angel Gabriel carries God's power; he is God's strength.'

Well, they could have made more of an effort for him, at least got some fairy lights or something ...

'Angels are perfect spiritual beings. In fact, Gabriel only appears in the bible three times, all in situations of the 'news bearer'. The third occasion, of course, when he speaks to Mary to announce the news that she will bear God's son, the very occasion we are celebrating today.' Somehow she'd forgotten about all that.

The bespectacled Reverend quietened; a few echoey coughs being his only accompaniment. She looked over at the print she'd brought back from Canterbury Cathedral, complete with a few words provided by Mr. Murphy's daughter, Diana, and was suddenly aware of a warm tingle radiating across her shoulders. She was flooded with a sense of belonging. But the spell was soon broken when they were invited to turn and greet those around them. The old man behind her dabbed at his dripping nose with a damp tissue before holding out his hand in welcome, which she reluctantly shook. It was Christmas after all.

She went to give Mrs. B the Marks and Spencer candles and heard her light, tinkling laughter from behind her office door. Something made her stop and knock, even though the door was ajar. Reverend Paul was sitting on the corner of the desk, with Mrs. B sitting directly in front of him. The strong smell of alcohol hit her nostrils. They both stopped abruptly like she'd disturbed something special.

'Come in, Anne, it's good to see you here this morning.' Reverend Paul recovered quickly and stood up. 'We have this tradition where Janice and I have a small Christmas drink to celebrate the work of the passing year. It's my little thank you.'

Mrs. B's name is Janice?

It didn't sound right coming from Reverend Paul; it sounded too ... familiar. Mrs. B blushed slightly, or maybe it was the rosy makeup. Her unsettlingly bright lipstick matched her Christmas jumper, detracting from her naturalness; the usual pastel softness that Anne loved so much about Mrs. B.

'And I've got something here for you too.' Mrs. B lifted a well-wrapped present from one of the desk drawers. 'I hope you might find this useful. Go on, open it.' It was a Mary Berry cookbook. 'I thought we might work our way through some of the recipes; develop your baking skills?' Mrs. B had a real twinkle in her eye; maybe it was whatever they were drinking, but Anne didn't mind; this book held the promise of them spending time together on quiet mornings before the church got busy. Anne felt tearful; it was a lovely, thoughtful gift. Typical of Mrs. B, who claimed to love the candles but gushed concern that the present had cost Anne too much money.

'I always save a bit from my benefits for special occasions,' she didn't dare look up at Angel Gabriel, overseer of all things in the church, not today of all days. Returning to the church hall, she heard someone talking in the Quiet Room.

'I don't know if I can get away tomorrow, my son can't be left alone, with this tag thing ... Yes, I'm considering the job offer. I'll let you know …' She waited for the call to finish and brushed past Perfect Pam, who looked flustered, aware she might have been overheard. 'Enjoy listening to other people's conversations, do we?' She flounced past Anne in her lilac coat.

Perfect Pam has a son who is on a tag? Well, well.

Back in the church hall, Reverend Paul was shaking hands with someone whose back was turned to her.

No, it can't be.

James Wright. Who looked more pleased to see her than she was to see him. She shuddered at his Christmas jumper – a reindeer with a flashing red nose.

'Present from your gran?'

'I thought everyone would be wearing them today.' His cheeks reddened, accentuating his soft dimples. 'So, what are you doing for the rest of the day?' he changed the subject.

'Just back to my flat. The usual, PJ's and a Christmas film.'

'Santa bring you some new pyjamas then?' his cheeks flushed even redder as if he thought his remark was a bit too personal. He rushed on.

'You and Fleur doing a big Christmas dinner then?'

'No, she's eating with her family, she'll be back later.' She avoided meeting his eye. 'What about you? Have you got a nice Christmas dinner to go back to?'

'No. Too much bother for one.' He paused for a moment. 'Just say if you don't fancy it, but I'm going for a McDonald's, would you like to come?'

It was exactly what Anne fancied; she was ravenous, and there was next to no food in the flat except for some out-of-date bits and pieces from last week's Food Bank. She took one last glance at the Angel Gabriel, looking down from above, peaceful. His work done for another year.

'I checked this one was open. McDonald's has a specific Christmas rota, the one by the Park never opens on bank holidays, while the one in town seems to be open twenty-four-seven.' He looked pleased with his panegyric knowledge of McDonald's opening times, opening the car door for her. 'Pays to know, we use them a lot on night duty,' he coughed, catching her bemused expression. He knew his attention to detail wasn't for everyone; the station sergeant positively bristled the last time he shared his knowledge of train timetables. Still, it was his diligence that had got him a distinction in his policing degree.

'What are you having?'

Anne pointed at a large poster stating: 'We are Reindeer Ready'. 'Well, you're in the right place with that jumper,' she giggled, but he didn't seem to appreciate the joke. Anne ordered for them both, insisting on paying, but they both knew she didn't have much money.

'You get them next time,' he said, and she felt her heart make a little jump. She was being bought burgers by someone who was hinting at doing it again.

Shame, oh shame, this someone is a police officer.

She looked at his fawn-like eyelashes and his light brown eyes flecked with gold. Although he was attractive, there was something babyish about him, something he still had to grow into. He looked up at her over his burger, and she was suddenly irrationally pleased that she'd decided to wear Fleur's mascara to the Christmas church service.

'What?' he attempted through a mouthful of burger.

'Oh, nothing, it's just that you remind me of someone.'

'Who?' he asked playfully, wiping sauce from his chin with a paper napkin.

'Bambi!' she exclaimed, 'especially in that jumper.'

He looked taken aback, crestfallen, and seemed to sink in on himself. He'd heard his station Sergeant once joke, 'not even shaving yet,' and then there were the bumfluff remarks. She'd hit a nerve, and she knew it.

Oh God, I've upset him now. Maybe he was expecting me to say some footballer or someone famous. Still, if he can't take a joke, that's his problem.

'Anyway, how's your burger?' she tried to rescue the situation.

'Fills a gap.' Brusque. He stood up to buy milkshakes.

'Let me get these,' Anne tried, but he shook his head.

'My treat, better than eating alone.'

'And I thought it was my special appeal.' Then, for some inexplicable reason, she blushed. They finished their drinks in silence. Her Bambi remark had irked him; spoiled something nice. She tried to go back a few steps. 'So how come you came to church today?'

'Found myself at a bit of a loose end, so I thought I'd come along, with it being Christmas and all that.' Not a complete untruth on his part, but he kept his ulterior motive of trying to establish Anne's links to the McGreals to himself. It would make good intel for Shona Stewart. He turned as a group of rowdy youths entered, clumsily knocking his drink over with his elbow.

'Shit.'

'Ooh, PC Wright, you just swore.'

'Well, even police officers are human, you know. I locked one of them up recently, nasty piece of work ...' he dropped his head, and mopped up the creamy mess with a napkin too flimsy for the sticky mess. 'We're just out there trying to do a good job.'

'Tell me one thing you've done this week that you're proud of.' For some reason, she felt like baiting him; he was, after all, easy prey.

'Well, I helped get a cat down from a tree,' his self-effacing reply.

With his cleaning up finished, he turned to face her directly. 'Actually, I was on special ops last week - undercover surveillance. Might be something big.'

'Get lost, all you do is sit in warm cars and take turns to sleep all night.' She immediately regretted her remarkable gift for delivering retorts with a sledgehammer. But he was in his stride - there were things he wanted to know.

He looked at her directly. 'We've been watching a property in Park Lane.' He noted her hesitation. Her eyes lowered to her milkshake. 'You'd be surprised at just what we get to see. Especially at 2 am on a Saturday...' Now he'd lit the fuse, he sat back, studying her reaction.

Remaining cool, she sipped her milkshake. 'Never had a late night out yourself then?'

'Looked like you were having a good time.' There was an edge to his comment.

'Call that surveillance or spying on me?' Her words sounded too harsh. After all, he'd just bought her lunch. 'So, see anything interesting on your … surveillance PC Wright?'

suddenly realising this was worth pursuing, as he might have seen Fleur.

'No. Not much apart from a party of revellers returning from a night out.'

She was disappointed; he was confirming what she suspected, that Fleur wasn't staying at the Park Lane flat.

'Go anywhere nice then?'

'I went to a place called the Blind Fox, if you must know.'

He nearly choked on what was left of his milkshake. '*You* went to the Blind Fox?'

'Yeah, just me and my … friend, Vivian.'

'I expect you know it's a place frequented by criminals, then?' He waited for her reaction, but she wasn't taking the bait. 'You're playing with fire going to places like that, Anne,' he warned her. 'And it wasn't Vivian I saw you with in Park Lane, was it?' his eyes lowered to downplay his interest.

'Once a copper ...' but it was clear she wasn't prepared to share any more with him.

'Anne,' he turned serious, 'Have you any idea what goes down in that place?'

'A bit,' she answered, pleased that she once again had his full attention. She looked down at her hands, trying to hide her bitten nails. 'We went there to meet up with Fleur. To catch up before she left for Christmas, but we must have missed each other.' Not a complete lie. 'Anyway, it's a good place to dance.'

'Well, I'd highly recommend you find another.'

'Yes, Dad,' mockingly shaking her head, pleased that she'd rattled his sanctimonious cage. They finished their meals in silence, and he scrunched up their wrappers like he was wringing a bird's neck, everything binned along with any chance of friendly conversation. She refused his offer of a lift, preferring to walk home.

Leaning against his car door, he watched her walk away, rattling his car keys and feeling a little rattled himself. The conundrum that was Anne Grimes became a misty blur in the rain.

The rain quickly turned to sleet, and she regretted leaving James and his warm car behind. Looking into softly illuminated houses, she imagined families preparing for their lavish Christmas dinners. Why had she been so argumentative when he'd been kind enough to buy her a Christmas burger? What had got into her? Okay, he'd surprised her by knowing where she was last Friday night, but he didn't know much more than that: stuff like her best friend was probably being held against her will by a drug dealer whose brother had died as a result of her actions. A rustling behind her made her turn abruptly, and for a moment, she hoped it might be James, but nobody was there.

Her thoughts drifted to Fleur and the secret they had kept for so long, and then the voices started, as they often did when she tried to recall the details of that fateful night. It hadn't happened in ages, but they were there now, mocking her. Worse still, it worried her that she couldn't shake the feeling that somebody was following her. Was she going mad?

Her eye caught a lone bird soaring up to roost in the tenement block of flats now occupied by refugees - the top shrouded by low cloud. Not so many lights on up there, the occasional sad-looking window decorated with a Christmas tree.

I fucking hate Christmas.

Nearing her flat, her heart quickened at a shape emerging from the mist. Someone was sitting on the front steps. Their mobile phone illuminated a mass of hair studded with tiny beads of condensation, glimmering jewel-like. She gasped. It was Fleur; returned home for Christmas.

24

#Banksy: 'Forgive Us Our Trespassing'

Running now, she slowed as the shape unfolded before her, and a figure much stockier than Fleur got to their feet. A mass of dark, wavy hair lapped the collar of a heavy winter coat. Her heavy breathing stalled as the silhouetted person slowly turned from their phone to look at her. The woman, dressed in her long coat and winter boots, was familiar. Rasputin came to mind. But it was a different ghost from Canterbury trespassing on her territory, someone she knew only from an image in a photograph, holding the reins of a pony on which sat a pair of identical twins.

'Hello Anne, I'm Katherine. I've come to wish you a Happy Christmas.' Her arm was extended awkwardly, unsteady under an oversized bag. Anne suddenly felt faint, with no idea what to say. What was her older sister doing here?

The last time she'd felt like this was when she shook the hands of her foster parents, the Owens. They'd laughed at her formality, making her feel embarrassed. It would have been better for all of them if it had stopped there and then, if everyone had kept to their own boundaries. Would this turn out the same?

'What do you want?' Her voice sounded strangled, maybe a little too unfriendly. She didn't know how to play this.

'A cup of tea would be nice? I'm freezing.' Katherine attempted a smile, biting her bottom lip, exposing perfect white teeth in the dim light, but Anne could sense her nervousness. Flooded with embarrassment at the size of her flat, she invited Katherine inside, mindful of the mansion her sisters lived in. She felt eternally grateful that she'd finished painting the 'Hint of Lemon' wall, burying the dreadful words beneath it. A Hint of Lemon seemed perfect; nothing pretentious that someone like her sister would see right through, but her attempt at something better, something offering just enough of a welcome on such a dull day.

Room also seemed to share her surprise, as Katherine's expensive perfume filled the air. Anne swiped away her writing paper, not wanting her sister to see her latest letter to Banksy. Katherine stayed standing, pointing to the Sunflower print on Fleur's wall. 'I've seen this painting in Amsterdam ...' then quietened as if maybe that was a bit 'show-offish,' But Anne was too preoccupied with making tea and trying to work out why her sister was there. To break the awkward silence, she turned on the TV: a carol concert from York Cathedral, and they both stared at the TV as if entranced.

'I like York.' Katherine's words split the mystified air.

Of course you do. I bet you've been everywhere, seen everything.

The side profile of her sister was startlingly familiar; the same thick, dark, wavy hair and a deep worry line on her brow that they shared, but Katherine was heavier-boned than herself and her mother. Someone who struggled with her weight, she guessed.

'I expect you're wondering why I'm here?' her voice sounded deep and gravelly, older than she'd expected. Posh. But certain words and inflections gave her Bristol background away. Her mother hadn't managed to wipe it all clean. 'Do you share with someone else?' Katherine nodded toward the second of the single beds while Anne perched awkwardly on the edge of hers.

'Yes. With Fleur, but she's away for the holidays.'

'Skiing?'

Anne smiled. Where else would one be at this time of year?

'How did you know where to find me?'

'My … our mum had your address in the back of her diary. She has all her personal bits and pieces in there, I know where she hides everything,' she smiled a familiar smile.

'So, did your mum tell you about me?'

'Not exactly. I overheard some of your conversation that night, though, especially just before you left. It got a bit … loud?' She fidgeted with the sleeve of her cashmere jumper, pulling it down over her thumb. 'Guy told me the rest.' Anne recalled Guy with his smart waistcoat, the driver who reminded her of Chris Eubank.

'I'm on my way to stay with a friend from university. Mum is in our place in Antigua for Christmas. Went earlier than usual, said she needed to get away from something about to kick off. Guy is driving me.'

'Is he waiting outside?'

'No, he's gone for something to eat. He's coming back for me at 5 pm.'

Their conversation was rudely interrupted by music loud enough to make the walls vibrate.

'What's that?' Katherine asked wide-eyed.

'It's just Brian the Wanker from next door, playing up as usual.' The look on her sister's face made her smile, spilling into laughter until their tears fell, relieving the tension.

'I hope you don't mind me saying, but you sounded just like Mum when you said that.' And just for a second, Anne felt a bolt of warmth.

'So, you get to have your own driver?' curling her feet beneath her. The still, companionable air showed that Room, too, was interested.

'Well, mum goes missing from time to time and I get left to look after the kids, well, look after everything really. Kids, ponies, the house, the bills. I need Guy's help.'

'Makes you sound like some sort of slave or something.'

'It has felt like that at times, especially when I was younger, when I first had to go back. I used to try to run away, try to get back to my lovely foster family. We still keep in touch, although Mum would go mad if she knew.' Then she quietened as if she might have said too much. Anne flicked to another channel, to an odd-looking man prancing around with a turkey on his head, making them both laugh.

'So where did you say you're staying tonight?'

'Guy is driving me over to my friend Chris' house. We're at uni together.'

'Wow, you're at university. You must have got all the brains. What are you studying?'

'Animal Science at Canterbury Christ Church. Not sure where it will lead. I'd love to be a horse vet. That's also what Chris wants to do.'

'Where does Chris live?'

'On a farm overlooking Weston-super-Mare. Mum doesn't like me going there, she'd prefer me to stay at home, but Guy won't say anything, like he won't say anything about me coming here.'

'Sounds like you two are thick as thieves?'

'We sort of look after each other. Mum can be a bit … unpredictable? There was the time when the outbuildings got firebombed in the middle of the night. You never quite know what's going to happen next.' A disturbed look clouded her face, suggesting she felt uncomfortable, disloyal even, discussing their mother's antics as she twisted a heavy gold ring around her forefinger.

'Didn't you want to live away, go to a different uni away from home?'

'Yes, of course, but mum would never allow it. Besides it would all come crashing down if I weren't there, and then there's the twins Charlotte and Rosie, who would look after them?'

'Sounds like you're trapped.'

'Feels like it at times. But then mum goes away pretty regularly, leaving me behind now that I'm old enough, so I do get some space. It's not all that bad, really.'

I bet it's not, living in a mansion with ponies and a driver.

'I just needed to come when I heard about you. I had no idea about you, Anne. I actually came earlier, then lost my nerve and left.'

'Of course. You left the Christmas tree!' They both looked over at the tree with its pink lights.

'Have you had your Christmas dinner?' Her sister scanned the room as if looking for evidence, her eyes finding Anne's sketches.

'Ooh, these are really good, Anne. You understand horses.'

She kept it to herself that she'd only ever seen one at a bank holiday fair and had to draw from her imagination, and clues from her Anne of Green Gables book.

'Not really, but I can sense the inner restlessness, the ripple of muscle that wants to break free.' Then Anne realised she'd been using Fleur as her muse. All that repressed energy.

'So have you eaten?' her sister probed.

'Yes, I was taken out earlier by a friend, James. We went to a country pub.' It sounded better than McDonald's.

'Ooh, that sounds lovely,' but Katherine was distracted, now looking at the postcards of Canterbury Cathedral and the small St Gabriel's chapel, Blue-Tacked to the wall. Katherine devoured the out-of-date pastries Anne served up, pushing aside some stale cocktail sausages with her fork.

'I'm vegetarian. So would you be if you saw some of the things in our meat factory.'

'You own a factory?'

'Part own it. Mum's into all sorts of business ventures, but everything's up the wall with Brexit looming.' She recalled the Jacksons Haulage yard in the grounds of her mother's property.

'Who is Jackson?'

'No idea.' A look passed between them that suggested she didn't ask her mother questions.

'How long have you lived here, and why did you change your name from Kylie to Anne?'

Jeez, do all sisters have so many annoying questions?

She plumped up the pillows on Fleur's bed for Katherine to make herself comfortable, stretching out opposite on her own bed.

'Mum had to do a runner. I was very young. She upset some drug dealers before we came to Bristol, stole some of their gear, and sold it on. She had to come into school and drag me out of class. We lived in a sort of hostel out of town for a while, where some social workers and special police officers helped us, because Mum helped them. Then we had to move well away and take on new names. Eventually, we got a nice flat on the Mount Pleasant estate. We were settled for a while until mum's boyfriend Billy disappeared and there was a fire … and I ended up back in care.' Katherine sat stock still, absorbing all this new information. Furrowed concentration lines creased her brow.

'I was fostered in Bristol too, lived there until I was fifteen, then one day, mum and a social worker came along and she took me back to Canterbury. I cried and cried for weeks. Over time, I settled down, then the twins came along, and I sort of got a family again. But I never trust what she might do next. I always try to stay one step ahead. Guy helps with that.'

'Who's the twin's dad?'

'She just got pregnant, said it was a 'one-nighter'. She likes to party. Her 'social set' she calls them.'

'So, what's in your bag?' Anne's turn to ask questions.

'My overnight stuff for staying at Chris' house, and I hope you don't mind, but I have brought some things of mine that I don't use anymore. Nice things,' she added quickly. 'Too nice to throw away, really.'

Anne watched as her big sister took a scarf and some perfume from a lovely designer handbag. Anne didn't own a bag other than her going-out bag and her backpack. Were these things really for her? Next, Katherine pulled out a short purple leather jacket. It was lovely. 'Go on, try it on,' urged Katherine, and Anne didn't need much persuading. It was a little on the big side, but she loved it immediately.

'Doesn't fit me anymore, but I wore it to death, wore it everywhere. Can't bear to throw it out. It looks great on you,' her eyes pleaded for Anne to take it.

'I feel terrible, I haven't got anything for you.'

'Could I have one of these sketches?'

'Of course. I've done more.' They went through her sketchbook together, and she selected one with two horses running in the mist.

'I'll buy you something special when I get a paying job.' She told her sister all about the Food Bank, her volunteering, and Vivian, her needy mentor.

'Tell me about James …'

'He's a police officer.' And it felt good that she was hinting that he was her boyfriend. Then Katherine's mobile phone rang. 'Oh, it's Guy. He's outside,' she sounded disappointed. 'Quick, give me your mobile number and we'll keep in touch.'

'I haven't got a phone. Fleur has taken our shared phone with her.' Anne's skin tingled with embarrassment. Everybody her age had a mobile phone.

'Here, take this one. I can get a new one. I'm always losing things. It will just give Mum one more thing to moan about.' She spoke quickly, as she expertly tapped at her phone, wiping things from its memory.

'I can't take that. What will you do without a phone?'

'I'll get another one with my Christmas money. Don't worry about the costs on that one. Remember, I pay all the bills.' She winked, then wrote down the new passcode, leaving Anne impressed with her technical ability. She bent over and hugged her younger sister with all her might. 'I'm so glad I've found you, Anne. Let's never let each other go.'

'Thanks for all this stuff, it's … awesome.' A new word for Anne, but it seemed to fit in Katherine's world.

'Have a good time at Chris' farm.'

'Oh, I will, he's a great laugh.'

'Chris is a boy?'

'No, Chris is a man,' she winked mischievously. 'He's my boyfriend, but never, ever tell Mum.'

She left hurriedly, leaving Anne suffused in an unfamiliar warmth. She had a sister. Lovely, smart, generous Katherine, and they were already keeping secrets from their mum.

Guy waved as they departed, narrowly missing a smart saloon car driving out of the car park from the flats opposite. Although it was foggy, she could make out that Sasha was sitting alone in the back of the large car. She was wearing a ridiculous low-cut red velvet dress trimmed with white fur. The driver was Sammi, the smartly dressed man with the silver suit who had escorted Grace and the girls away from the Blind Fox. Perfect Pam's escort.

BTW's front door was open, but his room was empty. She wanted to tell him she'd solved the Christmas tree mystery and to pass the Top Gear book on to him.

'Brian?' she called.

No reply. Surely, he wouldn't have gone out and left his door open. A noise led her to the landing on the stairs, where Brian was half hanging out of the corridor window, soaking wet above the waist. He turned and put a finger to his lips, beckoning her to follow him downstairs. Keeping to the shadows of their building, he stopped and pointed over to two people huddled together in the doorway of the adjacent block, silhouetted by an outdoor light. It was Marta, a triangle in a rainproof poncho, topped with ruby-red bobbed hair. But she couldn't make out the second person. Marta seemed to be taking bundles from a holdall on the ground. Brian pulled her back into the shadows as a car flashed past, briefly illuminating everything like spotlights exposing players on a stage. It was Sammi, returning in the large limousine, but no sign of Sasha.

Anne's heart was banging about in her ribcage. Voices were raised. It went on for several minutes. Angry words were muffled in the biting wind. Brian put his finger to his lips and pushed her into a door recess as an external security light was set off by Marta's skulking companion. Their transaction was completed.

There was something familiar about the dark, hooded figure, the holdall slung over his shoulder slowing him down and making his limp more pronounced than ever. She sucked in her breath. It was Twinnie McGreal. And she'd like to bet it was the same red and white striped holdall that Grace had been carrying in the trendy canal-side pub where she'd stood up to 'Hammy Hamster'.

She gasped to see Brian videoing everything on his phone, covering its glow with the crook of his arm. 'Smile for the camera,' he instructed playfully, making her swipe at him, fearful he'd be seen. He laughed even more at her instruction to 'stick your camera up your arse,' and carried on filming as

Marta departed in the opposite direction, over towards the block of tenement flats where Sammi's limousine had pulled up. Another shadowy figure was leaving from the front of their building. 'Did you see that?' But Brian wasn't going to be distracted from his filming: 'Plenty of funny stuff going on around here lately ... we're being watched from all sides.'

She stayed in the shadows, trying to make sense of everything, the blood pulsing in her ears, far enough away from BTW; too much nervous energy, and not enough deodorant. But what had they just witnessed? What was Twinnie McGreal doing outside their apartment block on Christmas night, and who else had been watching?

'What do you think they were up to?' Back in BTW's room, she refused the grimy towel he offered her, along with a swig from his half-empty bottle of cheap vodka.

'Don't know. But I've got loads on 'Not so Smarter-Marta.' Gesturing around him, she could see his large PC, some neatly laid-out camera gear, and a stack of printed-off photos of shadowy figures. 'Been filming her for ages; I've even filmed her on her 'funny nights' over at the refugee's place. She has a couple of rooms where I thought they were preparing things for a Christmas fancy-dress party. Lots of girls parading about, half-dressed, coming and going in posh cars.

'Have you ever seen Fleur with them?' Maybe Fleur was closer to home than she'd previously thought. Maybe the Frankie McGreal thing was a red herring.

'Fleur? No, fuckin' 'ell Fleur can look after herself, it's the young kids like Sasha I'm worried about.'

'Why are you so concerned?'

'I saw them all being dressed up in Christmas outfits. You know, kinky stuff. Then it came to me. They're not going to any party; those girls are the Christmas presents being rolled out at everyone else's parties.' She recalled the velveted Sasha in the back of Sammi's limousine and felt a wave of nausea.

'What do you mean?' Although she suspected she knew.

'They're prostituting those young girls, and Marta's at the heart of it all.'

25

#Banksy: 'Choose Your Weapon'

Five days left and still no sign of Fleur.

Running out of ideas, she knew it all hinged on Fleur being at Frankie McGreal's New Year's Eve party. For the second day running, she took the bus to the Old Infirmary, walked through the overgrown grounds concealing the 'Big House' where the party was to be held. The House sat squat in darkness, its heavy wooden shutters firmly closed to the outside world. She could only wait and pray that the New Year party was still going ahead and that Fleur would be there.

Her bus flashed past a poster of Banksy's 'Choose Your Weapon' stencil, portraying fighting dogs as youths' new weapons. The violent images made her shudder; they brought back memories of the hidden gun and a new rush of fear about the danger in Fleur's world. It felt like a warning.

'There's a message for you on the answer phone.' Mrs. B sounded as surprised as she was. She played back the crackled sound of Vivian's voice inviting her to an impromptu 'end-of-year' mentoring session. 'We have some unfinished business.' Even Mrs. B thought that sounded ominous.

'Why would she want to see you so urgently?' the older woman asked, back in pale pink lipstick and a reassuringly soft, baby pink jumper.

'I'm not sure, but Vivian doesn't hold all the cards. The only unfinished business I have in mind is to finish our mentoring contract. But I need to convince Vivian that it is her idea.'

'Excellent. I think the woman is taking liberties.' Strong words for the kind-hearted Mrs. B: 'Let me know if I can help.'

Gearing up for a difficult meeting, Anne needed to decide on her strategy; how to persuade Vivian to suggest they might 'cut the ties.' It was just a shame they were meeting at Vivian's house; she always felt safer on neutral territory.

'Is everything okay, Vivian?' Her mentor's appearance threw her off balance; her eyes were red and puffy. She'd been crying.

'I expect you've been too busy to think about me,' strangled words caught in a croak at the back of her throat.

She's trying to play the jilted card, but I'm having none of it ...

'I've been busy working over the Christmas holidays, Vivian. People depend on us for their food, you know.' Vivian pouted like a chastised child. 'And I've been out looking for Fleur. Anyway, the last time we were out at the Blind Fox, *you* abandoned *me* for that Steve bloke. Remember?'

Vivian stilled, as if trying to recall events, and lit a cigarette. Anne held steady, determined not to be sidetracked from her mission.

'I see you've been busy, people coming and going in big cars,' through exhaled smoke, a spiteful glint slicing her pupils.

Anne froze. 'Have you been spying on me, Vivian?'

'Have you been spying on me, Vivian?' her mentor mimicked in a chilling singsong voice.

Struggling to repress her disgust, Anne stayed cool, aware more than ever that it was time to finish the deteriorating relationship, when Vivian stopped abruptly and turned toward her. There was a menace in Vivian's demeanour that reminded her of a boy from her past who liked to threaten the younger children by flicking a lighter in their faces. She stood very still.

'No such luxury as Christmas visitors for me …' Vivian slumped back against the porch wall, drawing heavily on her cigarette. Anne could smell alcohol on her breath. 'No return calls from Mike or that user Steve. I bought a phone especially so they could contact me. Tried leaving them messages, but the bastards must have given me the wrong numbers.' Anne didn't know what to say. She was probably right. Vivian started to sob, her shoulders heaving before escalating into a loud wail.

'Nobody understands me like you, Anne. Thank you for coming to see me.' Had she forgotten that she'd been summoned there? She needed to finish this quickly.

'I only want to cuddle up with someone at Christmas. What do I need to do to make men like me?' she pouted.

Anne shuffled awkwardly, her cheeks burning.

'Why do the men in my life always let me down, Annie? What am I doing wrong?' Her wailing now drifted into the air. Fighting the strong desire to walk away, she handed her mentor a crumpled tissue from her jacket pocket. A scratching noise came from behind the door.

'What was that?'

She followed Vivian down her hallway and into the cold sitting room. She needed Vivian to settle before broaching the topic of finishing their mentoring. They sat in a heavy silence only broken by the clock ticking and Vivian's diminishing snuffling.

'Do you have any goals in your life, Vivian? Some New Year's resolutions, maybe? Something positive to work on?' Mentor speak - part of her strategy.

'I'm supposed to say things like that ...' Vivian snapped back, rubbing her knuckles into her palms as she prattled on about being let down by men.

Anne was starting to despair. Why was she taking all this crap? She clearly wasn't going to get anywhere with Vivian in this mood.

'Sorry, Vivian, have to go. I promised to help Mrs. B with some baking for the Scouts' New Year's Eve party.'

Vivian sniggered and stood up, lifting some papers from the mantlepiece. 'Your end-of-mentoring progress report.' Anne's heart lifted; this might be the ideal opportunity to bring things to a close.

'You've completed it? Great - can I see?' but Vivian whisked it away.

'Thought I might like to discuss it with your precious Mrs. Barlow first.' The final and most dreaded of threats. She couldn't possibly let Vivian reveal all the lies she'd told. She was trapped, and they both knew it. Vivian smiled, her profile hideous in the harsh half-light. 'So, what are you doing on New Year's Eve?'

Oh no, she's not coming with me.

The scratching sound came louder from the kitchen. 'Ignore it, it's just the cat.'

'I never knew you had a cat.'

'There's lots about me that you don't know, but we still have plenty of time ...'

Vivian went to the kitchen, where the meowing grew louder, followed by a horrendous commotion and the slamming of a cupboard door. Anne took her chance to get closer to the front door, ready to leave. Vivian returned without the cat but with angry red scratches down her arm.

'Maybe we could go for a drink? Just the one? Try some of those places Fleur used to visit?'

'Oh, I've already made arrangements to go out.' Anne managed to get to the door without mentioning the New Year's Eve party. 'Bye, Vivian. Happy New Year.' She had already formed her own New Year's resolution: *I'm never coming back here again.*

She stopped at the mini supermarket to top up on essentials, and on her return to the flat, was mortified to find an official-looking woman waiting for her. With her many-bangled arm extended, she smiled a stiff little smile. 'Hello, I'm Polly Morton. You must be Fleur.'

Oh God, the new social worker must have decided to drop in.

She took a deep breath; could she get away with pretending to be Fleur? The flowery-coated woman didn't have any case notes with her, just a small jute bag and a notebook with butterflies on the cover. She knew the type.

'Hello Miss Morton, yes, I'm Fleur Drake, pleased to meet you.' Polly Morton, more used to abuse than such pleasantries, tilted her head with a surprised, 'Call me Polly.'

Anne busied herself making them tea, wondering how far she could take this, grateful that she'd stopped for fresh milk on her way home. 'Here is my Care Leaver's Plan,' she handed over the file, which she always made Fleur keep up to date. Polly Morton started making notes and signing sections in the Care Plan. 'We're nearly at the end of this, you're turning eighteen soon, aren't you?' Anne sensed this was a courtesy call, probably a last tick in a box before Fleur's eighteenth birthday, when the contact would cease.

'Yes, I'll be eighteen in a few weeks. I'll be going out with the girls from my course.'

'And how is college going? Health and Beauty, isn't it?' casting a doubtful eye over Anne's appearance.

'Yeah, we've been experimenting with hair dying this term. I'm never the same color twice these days. You should see me with my make-up on, I look completely different!' She smiled sweetly, offering Polly Morton a biscuit from an out-of-date packet from the Food Bank. 'We're still on our Christmas break. I've just been out walking my friend's dog, Scruff. I do it as a favour for them.' Polly scribbled more notes. 'So, how are you managing financially?'

'Oh, very well. Me and Anne are good at budgeting. And 'cos she works at the local Food Bank, we never go hungry.' More scribbling. 'It is so good to finally meet you, Polly, but I do miss my old social worker, Ruth. She was with me for several years. She helped me and Anne get this flat together, even helped us get our passports, and she arranged for Anne to have a brilliant mentor.'

'Are you expecting Anne back soon? I'd like to meet her.'

'No, she's working extra hours at the Food Bank. Sometimes I help out - when I'm not at college.'

'And how about the goals in your 'Forwards Plan' … sorry, I haven't got a copy with me today …'

What a surprise, you social workers never have the right paperwork. Get your own flowery life in order …

'There's a copy at the back of that file. Not much left to do, other than finish my course and then move on and get a salon job. The Plan will be complete when I turn eighteen.'

'Will you and Anne be staying together?'

'Most likely ...' more note scribbling.

'That's all good then. Can I use your bathroom?'

'Sure.' Anne expected this; a subtle but predictable way of checking for anything untoward or illegal. But no worries on that front. She had nothing to hide.

The file was signed off, and Polly Morton finished the remaining biscuits before leaving, commenting that it would be good to have more Fleur Drakes on her books. Nice girls. Proof that the care system wasn't all bad.

Mrs. B was busy rolling out trays of sausage rolls for the Scouts' New Year's Eve party, listening to a carol concert on Radio 4. 'I always drop in on my neighbour, we will have a small tipple at midnight. How about you, Anne?'

'I'm going to a party. It's in the Big House, over in the grounds of the Old Infirmary.' Her stomach turned somersaults each time she thought about the night ahead. It was her final chance to find Fleur before she left for Spain in two days.

She pushed a trolley laden with festive food into the main body of the church and closed her eyes to soak up the peaceful atmosphere and calm her taut nerves. A shadow passed between columns on the wall opposite, making her catch her breath. She chastised herself; she was over-imagining a lot of things lately. She started humming to calm herself, knowing nobody had access to the church except herself and Mrs. B. But now she was certain she could hear footsteps on the wooden floor.

'Hello ...' no reply. 'Who's there?' Sharper. A shuffling sound startled her, making her spin around.

'Is that you, Pam?' The only other person she could think it might be.

Hysterical laughter filled the vacuous church hall, and she jumped as Vivian emerged from the shadows. 'Vivian. You terrified me!' Her mentor laughed louder, even more echoey and demonic in the hallowed space.

Anne steadied herself against the serving counter. 'I didn't hear you come in …'

'Yes, Mrs. B, no Mrs. B,' back in her childish taunting voice. Had she been listening to their kitchen conversation?

Please tell me you haven't come to speak to Mrs. B …

She needed to get Vivian out of there, and fast. Vivian was now leaning over the counter, whispering so close to her ear that she could smell her sour breath. 'We've unfinished business, Annie.' She waved her progress report in Anne's face.

'Look, I'll make us both a coffee and we can sit in the summer house, you can have a cigarette out there.' Praying she sounded calmer than she felt, she went to get the keys, taking Mrs. B a hot drink. 'You stay in there, Mrs. B. I'm almost set up. I'm sure you've got loads to catch up on.'

She carried their coffees outside to find Vivian mumbling about 'commitments and loyalty'. Anne wondered how long her mentor planned to stay; she needed to be on the minibus to the New Year's Eve party by 6.30 pm. Then she noticed something strange. Her mentor was wearing odd boots. She suppressed the urge to giggle at the mismatched footwear. Vivian was in the darkest of moods.

Smoking in jerking, agitated movements, Vivian stubbed out her lipstick-stained cigarette on a small camping table, her unbrushed hair gathered up in a scrunchy band, her eye makeup smudged. She looked rough as hell, staring at her untouched coffee.

'I don't suppose you've remembered it's my birthday?'

Anne looked up, surprised. 'I don't think you've actually told me that before, Vivian.'

Her mentor sat in her faux leopard skin coat and odd boots, toying with a sugar sachet, her sausage-like fingers massaging it harder and harder until the contents spilled out over the small table. Was that what this was all about? Was it really her mentor's birthday? She didn't know what to believe anymore. She hadn't seen any cards when she'd been at her house earlier. Maybe that was why she'd been so fretful, so moody. Nobody had remembered her birthday. Thrown off guard, Anne started to feel sorry for her.

'Well, Happy Birthday. Maybe we can celebrate some other time, after all the New Year's celebrations?'

Vivian's glare made her draw back, glad she was sitting by the exit to the garden, a trick she'd learned long ago. She cowered slightly as Vivian stood up, straightened her coat, and departed. She had been holding her breath and exhaled slowly at her mentor's egress. No progress report, no Happy New Year greeting; just her odd boots resounding unevenly on the paving, now turning frosty.

Back in the church, she looked up at the Angel Gabriel, softly illuminated. It had been a difficult year; maybe the next one would be more settled. He appeared to have one eyebrow raised as if in doubt.

No, I'm not inviting her to the party. She's not coming with me. I've got to find Fleur, and I don't need Vivian's interference.

'Say something?' asked Mrs. B. 'Go on, you get yourself off, you've got your party to go to, and ... Happy New Year.' Mrs. B reached out to hug her, and tears sprang to Anne's eyes. It was only a matter of time before Vivian spoiled everything between them. She had to find Fleur, then she could tell Mrs. B everything and move on.

'Enjoy your party. And Anne ... be careful.' Mrs. B was a woman of great foresight.

26

#*Banksy: 'The Girl with The Pierced Eardrum'*

There was no sign of Grace at the Harbourside pickup point, where revellers were gathering ahead of the New Year fireworks display. A 'Get Brexit Done' banner was pushed into Anne's face by a profusely tattooed man with bulging eyes, one of an army of protesting Brexiteers clashing with party goers adorned with ridiculous luminous halos. She elbowed her way through the frenzy until she finally saw the straggling line of vaping girls under their strawberry cloud, and the battered minibus that would take her to Fleur. Exactly as Grace had described.

The feeling that someone was watching her made her turn. A pair of eyes shone out of a large spray-painted silhouette. Haunted eyes that implored, 'You don't belong with them. Turn back.' She'd forgotten about this piece of Banksy's artwork, hidden from view like much that went on in these backstreets. 'A skit on a famous Dutch painting,' Billy had once told her, admiringly. The eyes of the girl looking out from under a scarf bound around her head seemed to search for something beyond the crowds. Had those knowing eyes ever seen Fleur standing in this same queue?

Uneasy, she pulled her purple leather jacket around her; the comforting perfume ingrained in the soft hide grounded her, along with Fleur's sensible ankle boots, good for poor weather and good if she needed to run. She had no idea what she was letting herself in for; she just had to get on that minibus.

'Hiya Rudi,' a barely dressed youngster shouted to a gaunt man who stood talking to the driver, who pinched her bum as she boarded. The girl was one of Grace's crowd who worked from the Blind Fox. The girls were preparing themselves, popping pills, and swigging alcohol.

But where was Grace? Her passport to getting on the minibus. Her passport to finding Fleur. An arm was placed in front of her. 'Not seen you before?' Rudi's sinewy barrier stayed firm, making her heart race.

'No, I was going to make my own way there, but then my lift went tits-up. Grace said to tell Rudi that she'd sent me.' Her fingers were crossed behind her back.

'You know Grace?'

'Yeah, we work together down at the docks.' That seemed to satisfy Rudi, his judging, feral, pale blue eyes sizing her up and down. He nodded her on board. Opting for a seat at the back, she looked out at the silhouette on the wall, the warning eyes following her with a new sense of urgency. She still had time to get off the minibus. She knew this lift came with unspoken conditions. But time was running out. It was too late to turn back now.

Her phone buzzed. *Happy New Year's Eve, Luv, Katherine xx.* It was just the confidence boost she needed, and turning away from the burning eyes in the portrait, she tried to contact Fleur on the mobile number they used to share. Surely, she would expect a call on New Year's Eve. But once again, it was dead.

She used the silence her earplugs brought her to think about what she would do once they arrived. What trouble lay ahead? Her heart raced as the minibus sped out of town. There was no turning back now. She knew the route, out beyond houses to fields, the minibus carrying its precious human cargo towards the site of the Old Infirmary, to Frankie McGreal's Big House.

Rudi and the driver spoke in a foreign language; arrangements for only them to know, and the air clouded over as the two girls in front started vaping. The girls to the side of her lit up a joint, clouding her mind with the pungent smells; a mix between something from the country and school bike sheds. A sudden flashback to her mum's flat in Mount Pleasant, with Shayne McGreal and his mates off their heads on the stuff. She hated it. Skunk, they used to call it. Was that what a real skunk would smell like? She still wasn't sure.

'Pass it 'round, Ellie,' a girl at the front shouted back to a pretty girl ferreting her way through a small bag of multi-coloured pills, undecided on her recreational cocktail.

'Want some speed?' she asked as if she was dishing out Smarties.

'Yeah, cool,' Anne stashed some of the pills in her jacket pocket.

'You can pay me later.' Words spoken harshly for such a pretty face, as if she needed Anne to know she was in the girl's debt. 'We should earn a bomb tonight, a purple-haired girl called over. Won't be able to walk straight though ...' Pretty Ellie laughed, but not in a way that felt humorous, making her stomach plummet, reminding her this trip came with conditions.

The vaping girls were getting louder, and Ellie started walking up and down the bus pretending she was on a catwalk, her eyes glassy like they were somewhere else. The same way Fleur's used to get. She was now passing around a bottle of vodka, swigging great gulps between takers.

'Hey, don't forget us at the front,' called back Rudi, taking the bottle and patting Ellie's bum as she turned around. 'Save some of that for me,' but he wasn't talking about the vodka. He gulped greedily, wiping his mouth on his sleeve before passing it on for the driver to swig from, while Ellie laughed and wriggled.

Images of the drug runs with Shayne McGreal flooded her brain. The rising volume that used to stoke her apprehension.

His behavior, turning increasingly reckless and uninhibited as he and her mum imbibed whatever was going.

God, what am I doing? Why am I getting into all this shit again?

But she knew if she were to save Fleur and get their lives back on track, then she had to go through with it.

The minibus ground to a screech on the drive of the Big House, which was secluded in extensive grounds. Two men emerged from the shadows and thumbed Rudi and the driver to pass what had once been a grand place with a winding set of steps leading up to a fortress of a front door. Derelict outhouses to the side spilled out old furniture. Light flooded into the garden from window shutters now peeled back. Good for shutting things out, even better for shutting things in.

Bloody hell, Frankie McGreal must be loaded ...

They disembarked, with Ellie stumbling off the bus already high on pills. The girls in the know went over to a table laden with drinks before making their way upstairs. She held back, needing to take a good look around. With any luck, she might spot Fleur and not have to follow them.

'Where's the bog?' she asked a girl pouring drinks in a white apron who looked about fifteen.

'Over there. I'd go now, when it gets busy, everyone has to piss outside.'

'I'm looking for my mate Fleur. She said she'd meet me here.' But the girl looked at her blankly. Downing her wine in one gulp, she helped herself to a second glass and made her way through to the large, wood-panelled entrance hall lined with staring portraits of dead people. The toilet was well concealed behind a carved wooden door.

Oh My God, there's a chandelier in the bathroom ...

She exhaled loudly as the lights split and sparkled around her. Satisfied with her hair and makeup, she left the safety of the bathroom just as a jabbering assemblage arrived. She followed a preening gaggle into a large room with the furniture moved back to clear a dance floor. A large poster of Banksy's DJ'ing 'Gorilla in a Pink Mask' was illuminated by strobe lights, synchronized blinking to the booming music. It was a painting she'd never liked; she'd felt too sorry for the sad-eyed gorilla. A large, cheesy disco ball with tiny mirrors threw off lights above bodies lurking in the darker edges of the room. The DJ was grinding behind a heavy table with clawed legs. She turned away from the hunted look in the gorilla's eyes, which seemed to follow her around the room.

The French windows opened out to a back lawn where bodies were huddled in groups beneath reeking clouds of smoke. People were sitting on the patio furniture, breathing over glass apparatus, bulbous pipes like the ones in her old school chemistry lab. On a table, just inside the main room, a set of brass antique scales was set up, topped with an old-fashioned sailing ship. A lithe man dressed in a skeleton costume was building small mountains of white powder, which he scooped with a silver spoon, measuring and distributing bliss and abandonment while taking money, which he stored in a protesting drawer of the proud antique desk.

The music was getting louder; it felt like a festival. The keen early dancers were making the wooden floor bounce with the vibrations. Techno dance music, 'acid house', the type Fleur loved to listen to. She walked around smiling like she was having fun, but there was no sign of Fleur. The traffic on the stairs was getting busier. Girls were taking their drinks upstairs, some accompanied by men.

A blast of air from the open doors hit her. A girl made directly for her. 'Want anything? Uppers, downers?'

'No, I'm good thanks,' flashing her pills from her pocket to a satisfied nod.

From the patio, people were laughing at those peeing in nearby bushes. Staying in the shadows, she tried to assess how many rooms there were. The size of the building was daunting, but she wasn't leaving without searching every nook and cranny. Whatever it took.

A noisy group of newcomers arrived from a side entrance. It was Grace linking Ali, Frankie McGreal's flatmate, and trailing behind them was the smartly dressed Sammi, Perfect

Pam's friend. Her head was spinning. What was he doing here? Grace looked upset, trying to pull away from Ali.

'I told you to get upstairs.'

'But I didn't think I'd be working tonight, I thought I'd be with you …'

'Later. Earn some fuckin' money first. The lads will be looking for some action.' Grace picked up a drink and took herself upstairs, stopping for a short dance first. Defiant.

Knowing she needed to search upstairs, she reluctantly headed for the grand staircase. A commotion on the dance floor made her look back. She hung over the banister to see what the fuss was about and stopped dead in her tracks to see Vivian in her orange velvet trouser suit and wild ginger hair doing her signature writhing dance.

'Someone's brought their mum,' laughed a very young girl. 'Great mover though.' It appeared Vivian was a hit as she was clapped off the dance floor.

Oh fuck. She must have overheard my conversation with Mrs. B in the church kitchen. I told her it was the Big House in the grounds of the Old Infirmary, enough for a taxi driver to work with.

It was going to be a long night.

A pinch at her elbow made her yelp as she felt the bones scrape together.

'Shouldn't you be upstairs?' It was the driver's escort, Rudi.

'Yeah, all right, I was waiting for Grace.' Feisty.

'Well, she's already upstairs. I suggest you get your arse into action and quick.'

'All right, I'm going,' she spat back. Her heart was bumping against her ribs. Her head told her to find an excuse, to run, but she knew she had to stay. She had come so far; she was close, she could feel it in the air around her. This was exactly where Fleur would want to be.

On a turn in the grand staircase, she saw a screened-off area below, which looked like a mini cinema where naked girls were dancing on a screen. There was a sign: Private Party. Ali and Rasta Dave, with his dreadlocks swinging, were part of a select group watching something that had switched to sordid scenes. A chill filled the space between her shoulder blades; this was turning very seedy. Dear God, Fleur, where are you?

She passed portraits of men, imperious in their grandiose suits and chains of office, adorning the grand staircase.

All men, getting just what they want.

Rudi's patience was running short. 'In there,' he pushed her roughly into an empty bedroom, the dishevelled bedcovers making it clear the bed had already been used. A heavily embroidered red curtain was slung across the window, giving the room a sleazy cast. The beat of the music filled the air, rising from the patio, making the windows vibrate. Her stomach twitched its warning. She felt sick with fear. She put her ear against the solid door but could only hear the hubbub from downstairs. Laughter, people enjoying themselves. She gingerly turned the handle, needing to get out to look for Fleur.

'Where d'you think you're going?' Rudi's deep voice resonated around the hall.

'To the fuckin' bathroom, where do you think?' He pointed to a room at the end of a long corridor with deer's heads protruding high, startled eyes peering out from tartan wallpaper. Most of the doors were closed to outsiders, and she strained to hear what was going on behind them. The last door before the bathroom was slightly ajar. There were people in there. She peeped in to see Ellie flat out on the bed in just her bra with a large man heaving over her. Her stomach jolted. It was revolting. Ellie was out of it. Pretty, shapely Ellie, who had given her the pills on the bus and paraded like a fashion model. Her heart stalled. It was obscene. She heard another man's voice in the room.

Dear God, please don't let someone be watching them.

The second man was Ali. She caught her breath. He was filming everything on his mobile phone; maybe that was what they had switched to watching downstairs. She just about made it to the bathroom, which she noticed had no locks, before she threw up. Patting water over her face, she banged her head against the cold tiles. Memories of a young girl pinned down on a hard bed flooded her head. Memories she had spent years trying to shut away. Her foster father holding her down, a young, thin body beneath a large hand over her mouth, while she tensed her body against the pain, kept her eyes screwed tight, and took her mind to nicer places. That was when she started talking to her Room, the only witness to what was happening. The young girl who could never feel clean again, sitting on a different bathroom floor, banging her head against different cold tiles. But it was the same violation.

'Are you ready, or do I have to come in there and get you?' Rudi was more impatient than ever.

She came out popping some of the pills that Ellie had given her on the minibus.

'Just gearing up ...' she smiled, flicking her hair, dreading her return to the red-tinged room; knowing she had to hold it together if she was to find Fleur.

It seemed an age that she waited in that room, not knowing what was in store for her, not daring to go outside to face Rudi, her prison guard. The pills started to work, making her feel dreamy. Pulling back the curtain, she looked down onto the garden where people were dancing; a wild throbbing mass, and she longed to be down there with them. Vivian was on the edge of a frosty lawn, dancing by herself, a bottle of wine in her hand. She tried to shout down, but the words wouldn't form.

She tried to open the window, but it was nailed shut; besides, her hands didn't seem to work as they should. Stumbling around the room, nothing seemed to stay still with everything swirling about her. The music reached her, making her desperate to dance like nothing else mattered.

Waving her arms around, she took off her jacket. Feeling overheated, there was sweat running down her face, collecting between her breasts, but she carried on dancing. Nothing to think about but the music, the beat rattling the windows, the throbbing floorboards under her feet. She took off her boots and turned as the door opened and Rudi came in with another man. He appeared to be shouting at her, something distorted and echoey, which made her giggle. Then it all went dark as Rudi punched her in the face.

How long had she been out cold? Sitting up on the big double bed, she was shivering, her arms wrapped around her partly dressed body. The red curtain was back in place, shutting her in. Her face hurt. She needed to go to the toilet urgently. Pulling on her jacket, she soaked up the smell of her sister's perfume and dared to look out of the bedroom door. Thankfully, no sign of Rudi.

What has just happened to me?

In the bathroom, she patted cold water on her swollen nose. Her top lip was sore. Congealed blood, like a pink snail trail, ran down the side of her face. She looked in her bag and gingerly touched up her makeup. Her phone had been taken. But at least she was thinking more clearly now. There was a hush down below, then the New Year's Eve countdown, five, four, three… followed by loud banging and shouting.

What the hell?

Chaos was breaking out. It was all kicking off with bodies scurrying to safety. Her instinct was to run, but her clearing mind told her this could be her big chance to explore further, to find Fleur. Gently opening doors, she worked systematically along the corridor. Noises told her some rooms were still in use. In the closest room, there were entangled bodies too engaged to notice her. Next, a couple of rumpled rooms that had served their purpose. Moving stealthily to the partly open door of the end room, she scanned across several writhing bodies, shouts for her to 'come on in.' But no sign of Fleur. Scurrying past the room where she'd seen Ellie earlier, she found a couple of locked rooms, leaving one last door to try. Gingerly, she pushed on the door to see a man standing at the foot of a bed where two girls dressed in school uniforms lolled, looking bored, almost grateful that she'd disturbed the sordid scene, while the portly man turned and cursed, 'piss off, this is private.'

Plenty going on, but no Fleur. She needed to check out downstairs, beyond the hallway, into the closed rooms beyond the screened 'Private Party' area, to act fast before Rudi found she was missing. Pushing against bodies gathered on the stairs, the music suddenly stopped. Overhead lights were being switched on. The mood was turning sour. Beams of light flashed from torches, piercing discreet recesses, flushing couples out. Disgruntled youths were being ushered in from the garden. A dog started barking. It was all so disorientating that she had to hold onto the banister for support.

A group of masked men was shouting and wielding weapons above their heads, parting the way through protesting bodies. The intruders were turning over tables, smashing glasses and bottles. Her head was spinning. What was going on? Was the house being burgled?

She felt herself being roughly spun around.

Oh no, no, it's Rudi ... come to take me back upstairs

She struck out, but it wasn't Rudi; the man was too slim, too tall. She tried to break free from his vice-like grip on her wrists.

'Stay still, Anne, it's a police raid.'

'James?'

He whispered softly into her ear. 'Say nothing. We've been waiting for Twinnie McGreal's crowd to arrive. They're down there, turning the place over. Whatever you do, don't go down.'

She looked at him bleary-eyed.

He grasped her wrists harder as she tried to pull away.

'Stay still, Anne, I'm working undercover.'

One of the bouncers rushed past, pressing them together on the stairs and nearly knocking her off balance. She clung to James, who turned his head into her so as not to be recognised by a second man rushing up behind. It felt as if he was nuzzling into her neck, and she liked the comfort of it.

'Thanks for that, Anne. That's Twinnie McGreal's lot. We've had a tip-off - tonight's the night Twinnie is coming to stake out his ground.' She felt disappointed, used. She had liked his closeness, but it was clear he was using her as a decoy.

'Ouch,' she said, rubbing her face, making James look closely at her.

'What happened to your face?'

'Oh, it's a long story, but someone punched me.'

'Someone punched you? What are you doing at the rave, Anne?' She hadn't realised it was a rave until then, and just for a moment felt a small thrill at this rite of passage. He looked confused. 'And what were you doing upstairs?' She hung her head; she didn't know where to start.

'Are you hurt? Anne, look at me … in any other way?' he asked urgently. She didn't get to reply as several more men rushed past them.

He swore and grabbed her as she stumbled and fell into him, their faces touching. She reached to cover his exposed face from the intruders, and he awkwardly turned to her. She thought he was about to kiss her and brushed her lips against his, gently. It felt warm, safe. Before she realised it, she was kissing him, exploring his mouth with her tongue. The men hurtled past, and they pulled apart. It was hard to say who was most surprised. She, by her uninvited actions, or James, who, in the heat of the moment, had responded by kissing her back. He held her at a distance to examine her more closely. 'Are you sure you're okay, Anne?' Tender words, stirring something deep in her core that she'd never felt before. Her emotions were turning somersaults. A buzz from his jacket collar made him pull away.

'Gotta go.' He pulled away gently, talking in a whisper to something buried deep in his jacket collar before telling her, 'Both McGreal brothers are in here somewhere, Anne. It's going to get nasty. Get out now. We're looking for firearms.'

'But I can't leave until I find Fleur.' She looked away from his intense gaze, from his soft lips. 'She's been missing for ages.'

He pushed her away from him. 'But I thought you said you'd been with Fleur over Christmas?'

'Yeah, well, I lied,' her lips pouting.

'I think you've got some explaining to do. I'll come to the Food Bank on Tuesday. Now get out.' She felt his urgency.

'Okay, but you owe me a favour. There's a guy here called Ali, he's close to Frankie McGreal. There's horrible stuff on his phone. Will you find it and destroy it?' But he wasn't listening as he let her arm go to follow a stream of people shouting and barging their way up the stairs.

Downstairs, she heard rattling gunshots coming from above. *Dear Banksy, please keep James safe,* she prayed to herself, ignoring his concerns for her own safety. She couldn't leave without checking the downstairs rooms. The cordoned-off cinema area was abandoned, glasses left half full. People were complaining angrily as armed police with dogs blocked the front exits. A heavy internal door in front of her was locked, leaving her with nowhere to go other than through the side door the catering staff had used earlier.

Outside, she checked the perimeter path around the house, ablaze with all of the rooms now harshly illuminated, but there were no other external doors. The room with the red curtains was still there, a testament that she hadn't dreamt up her assault, but she couldn't think about what might have gone on in there, not now.

A splintering sound pierced the air. More gunshots from the house. A door burst open from one of the disused stable blocks, and a large black 4 by 4 vehicle sped off down a back lane. It was The Beast from the Blind Fox, but with the registration plates removed. She jumped back into the shadows to see a man with piled-up dreadlocks driving, and another tall man with a shaved head sat in the back. Frankie McGreal. As it sped off, she saw the top of a girl's bleached head ducked down low. It was Fleur. She was too late.

On the main drive, she passed blue lights, partygoers being cautioned and handcuffed. Ahead of her, a hunched, hooded figure was also leaving in a hurry. The figure turned back and gave her the thumbs up. It was her mystery morning spray painter; what was he doing there? Then she heard a familiar voice shouting into the face of an unamused police officer and went to help.

'Take her home, she needs her beauty sleep, that one.'

'Vivian, come with me …' They hurried down the tree-lined drive together.

'I've been looking for you all night,' Vivian scolded. 'But what a night. Thanks for inviting me, Anne. Where would I be without you?' And after all she'd been through, it was the warped possessiveness of Vivian's arm heavy on her shoulder that sent icy shivers down her spine.

27

#Banksy: 'Well Hung Lover'

New Year's Day, 2016.

Anne is trapped in a fiery red room where a clawed monster is chasing her. She blinks her way back to consciousness and can't think why her nose hurts before the events of the previous night hit her like a lightning bolt. She'd been assaulted.

And she'd been so close to finding Fleur. One day to go, but she was in a worse mess than ever. Her thoughts were on a reel: the image of Fleur's head being pushed down by Frankie McGreal in the back of the speeding black Beast; herself being pushed down on a bed in a sordid red room. She knew what she had to do.

After showering away the clinging reminders of the previous night, she dressed in her dreariest, warmest clothes. It was a risk whether the Women's Clinic on the other side of town would be open on New Year's Day. She'd been taken to a similar clinic by her foster mother; their secret. She remembered staring up at one of Banky's most iconic pieces of artwork on the outside of the building. Jane Owens, her foster mum, had tried to shield her from the sexually explicit artwork above them, from the obvious attributes of the 'Well Hung Lover', making her cover her eyes against the sexual undertones. They were good at hiding things, the Owens family. Jane Owens had silently booked her into the Brook Clinic for her to be put on the contraceptive pill to help with 'bad period pains'.

They were nice there. She thought they knew, but nobody asked the right questions. Then her foster mum took her back to school, like everything was normal, before the angry tears started. Her English teacher noticed, and even took her to one side, but again she never asked the right questions. How could Anne explain? She didn't know the words to describe what was happening to her. That was when the whispering voices started.

The clinic had switched venues to a smarter part of town, but it still had the same antiseptic smell. 'Take a seat here, Doctor Cynthia will call you through.' A humming fish tank emitted a flickering neon light as she stared at the out-of-date magazine that somehow appeared on her knee.

'Come in, Anne,' said Doctor Cynthia, an older black woman whose grey-speckled, bird's nest hair placed her beyond retirement age. 'Have you visited us before?'

Anne hesitated.

'It's quite all right if you prefer not to tell us. We don't keep any records here and we certainly don't ever share information,' the older woman said, studying her puffy face. After some routine medical questions, she gave her a small box. 'Take two pills as soon as possible. These work by stopping the release of an egg; they also prevent sperm from passing through the cervix, thereby preventing pregnancy.' She was making it easy, being factual and offering hard scientific facts in place of judgements.

'You might get some side effects of nausea or abdominal pain, nothing that some paracetamol won't fix.' Then she turned and asked the directest of questions. 'Have you been assaulted, Anne?' She maintained steady eye contact. 'I can refer you for support, you know, it often helps.'

Anne shook her head, thanked the doctor, and left with a handful of leaflets. It was still early, and with everything closed for the bank holiday, she made her way to St. Gabriel's church. Mrs. B had said something about spending a few hours in the church over the holiday period in case anyone needed an emergency food parcel. Suddenly, she longed for the comforting presence of Mrs. B. Maybe she'd even tell her all that had happened, that things were starting to get out of control. She had one day left to find Fleur, and she was no nearer. She longed to feel Mrs. B's arms around her, to snuggle into her fluffy jumper.

It was quiet as she entered the church. Flicking on the kitchen lights, she took her emergency contraception pills with gulps of icy tap water, then made her way into the main church hall where symphonic music was playing softly. Drawn towards the melodic tune, she stopped abruptly. Mrs. B and

Reverend Paul were dancing, holding each other so close that Mrs. B's head was resting on his shoulder. She had her eyes closed.

Anne felt dizzy, needing to hold the side of the altar for support. Looking up at the Angel Gabriel, she saw a tear trickle down his pale, immute face. She stayed still for what seemed an eternity, trying to make sense of everything. The music continued, and she turned and left as quietly as she'd entered, completely unnoticed by the embracing couple. She felt cheated out of her hug and the confession she'd finally been ready to make.

Her world was fracturing about her. She'd messed up. For all she knew, Frankie McGreal could already be on his way to Spain. Maybe she was already too late.

28

#Banksy: 'Keep Your Coins, I Want Change'

PC Wright didn't need to be in West Grange police station on New Year's Day, but he had little else to do. Besides, he wanted to tie up all the paperwork while everything was fresh in his mind. He couldn't sit still; drumming his fingers, tapping his feet. He was buzzing at the first serious arrests he'd ever made. Shona Stewart was coming in later for the debrief, and he couldn't wait to tell her everything. Although they hadn't caught the McGreals, they'd arrested those closest to Frankie McGreal, along with one of Twinnie's axe-wielding henchmen.

He'd played a key part in the team that had arrested hardened criminals, and it felt good to be changing things for the better. 'Miscreants,' his station sergeant described them before they'd charged the gang with possessing and supplying Class A drugs. Crack cocaine, ecstasy, heroin, crystal meth, the lot. And a thorough house search by the dog squad had sniffed out the weapons they were looking for. He felt jubilant helping to get that lot off the streets of Bristol. His first real policing success.

'Happy New Year!' Detective Chief Inspector Bruce Campbell swept through the office with a box of Scottish shortbread to celebrate. Darren from Communications was on his heels, ready to prepare a press release.

James, stretched in his computer chair, was thinking about the night before. He couldn't stop thinking about Anne - what had she been doing at the rave? Upstairs, of all places, and she never explained how she'd come by her injuries. Maybe he needed to ask her if she wanted to press charges against anyone. He felt a sense of outrage that anyone could hurt her, but she didn't help herself. How come she kept turning up in the dodgiest of places?

'Enjoy it while it lasts, kid,' Bob Lyons launched across the office. Bob was like a bear with a sore paw, confined to desk duties; his only chase was chasing criminal records while a harassment complaint against him was being investigated. James could feel his animosity radiate across the room. 'One arrest and you look like a dog with two dicks. Wait till you've put in forty years, then you can sit back and celebrate, son.' James ignored him, casting occasional glances over to the jaded, overweight police officer. It was hard to think he was once well-respected. Could Bob Lyons really be the Eel, the mastermind who protected Frankie McGreal and got away with £150k from the botched security van robbery?

But his thoughts kept returning to Anne. How did she keep getting into such scrapes? What was she doing at the rave anyway? She'd told him she'd been lying all along about Fleur.

Should he believe a word she said? Yet there was a lot to like about her. The way she'd helped Mr. Murphy, helped Millie and River, and the church work she did every day at the Food Bank. His mind wandered back to the kiss. Again.

It was very unprofessional of him to be caught like that, but what choice did he have? She started it and seemed to enjoy it until he pulled away. It had driven him mad all night. It was only a kiss.

'See Frankie McGreal got away,' the grizzly bear boomed over with more than a hint of gratification. He didn't respond. That bit hurt the most. Frankie McGreal and his driver had escaped. No trace of them, but then they didn't know what vehicle they were looking for: escaped by some back lane while everyone was in a tussle at the front of the property.

He scoured more CCTV coverage taken from the police vans. There was Anne again, walking away from the building with the grainy image of an accompanying female. Maybe she'd seen something; he'd have to ask her. He re-ran it. He liked looking at Anne. There was something stoic about her. She stood erect, like she was ready to take the world on. At least Anne wasn't upstairs when the other girls were cautioned. He preferred not to think about what they'd found upstairs; they were leaving that with the WPCs.

'Nice work, babe,' Jolene, a blue-haired Community Police Officer with strangely exaggerated lips, came and sat opposite him. 'Should have called me, I'd have accompanied you, treated you to some rave action,' winking suggestively at him. Jolene was good at her job; highly rated at West Grange, but a little too eager to 'please' - anything to further her career, it was rumoured. 'I finish at one, fancy a drink, PC Wright?'

'Everywhere's closed, Jolene, it's New Year's Day.' Ignoring her protests, he continued correcting a statement on his computer.

'I meant at my place,' she stretched over and stroked his knee under the table. 'Turns me on, all this action, how 'bout you?' He felt a surge of panic. Arresting hardened criminals didn't faze him one bit, but Jolene and her persistence scared him to death.

'OK, let's piece things together,' DCI Bruce Campbell came to his rescue, shouting above the general din in his penetrating Scottish accent. 'Incident room, everyone who was there last night.'

'Oh well, bye babe. For now …' purred through bright red lips that he was relieved to leave behind. He gathered his papers and followed a small group squeezing into the adjacent briefing room.

'So, guys and gals, what did we get? Some firearms that aren't on the streets any longer.' DCI Campbell pointed to photographs of several weapons pinned to the board to his side.

'Nothing registered, nothing traceable of course.' He rested on his pointing stick as if about to join a New Year shooting party. 'Good drugs haul, all logged and secured as we speak.' He coughed. 'Found some nasty goings on in the brothel upstairs, but so far everyone's declaring it was all consensual, no money passing hands. The underage lassies are in the good hands of our specialist WPCs.' James winced. Was this confirming his worst suspicions about Anne?

'A lot of young girls, most of them still in care. Said they were picked up in town by someone called Rudi.' He pointed to a grainy picture of a battered minibus. Picked this up on CCTV from one of our vans. We need to track him down. This is the white minibus they use to ferry the girls around in. We're sweeping it now, but the girls are saying they came willingly. They've been voluntarily fingerprinted and will be followed up, if they don't go missing in the meantime. It'll be the usual personal safety lecture for them.' He shook his head. Bruce Campbell knew the dangers. He had daughters of his own. He quickly moved to the next board.

'We arrested a twenty-eight-year-old accomplice, a man of Asian origin known as Ali Kumar, although 'Computer Bob' has found a whole list of AKAs for him.' There was a sneer at the mention of Bob, now confined to desk duty. 'Kumar inhabits a flat on the edge of Central Park owned by Frankie

McGreal. Young PC Wright here has recently been on surveillance of the property. Care to fill us in?'

James felt his heart race, then plummet. There was nothing to report. They all looked at him expectantly. 'Well, not much going on, sir. It's been very quiet at the flat, 43a Park Lane. No suspicious activity. Occasionally, they go out … mostly to a local called the Blind Fox. Girls come and go. Lots of deliveries…' his voice trailed.

'Any sign of dealing from the property?'

He shook his head. 'Ali Kumar goes out mostly at night – sometimes collected by Frankie McGreal and another of his drivers, who we've identified as David Ocasio. A man with dreadlocks who likes to wear badges on his clothes.'

'What? Those wee badges kiddies wear?' Bruce Campbell screwed his face and made additions to his board. James thought of the times Bob Lyons had left him in the surveillance vehicle, instructing him to stay in the car. Why hadn't he pushed Bob, been more inquisitive? 'Policing is all about curiosity,' Shona Stewart had counselled him, tapping her nose. But Bob Lyons quickly shut down whenever he asked any questions.

DCI Campbell returned to his rogue's gallery. 'We're interviewing Kumar later today, leaving him to stew for a bit first, see if he spills anything. Got the tech guys and gals looking at his phone. Early feedback is that there's some incriminating stuff on it, certainly enough to hold him a bit longer. Forensics are out dusting Kumar's flat. We need some links to those firearms.' James remembered Anne's pleas for him to destroy Ali Kumar's phone. Were there pictures of her on it? DCI Campbell moved to the photographs of the McGreal twins, each with their 'known connections' listed below them. 'Firstly, Frankie McGreal, but as PC Wright has confirmed, we've seen nothing of him at Park Lane. Keeps himself to himself. Gets other people to do his dirty work for him.'

'He's been staying at his other property, known as the Big House,' Rav Shah interjected, to the annoyance of Bruce Campbell. 'Did you see that fuckin' place? Sauna, tennis court, the lot. Know where I'd rather be.' Bruce Campbell straightened his contorted face before continuing, 'David Ocasio / Badge / The Driver. Elusive to say the least…'

Shona Stewart slipped in and sat beside James. 'Missed much?' He shook his head. Bruce Campbell turned to a series of screenshots and smiled. 'But we did get this. The new D-Cam speed camera on Hawthorne Road. Picked this vehicle up in the locality, doing 80 in a 40 limit at 01.35 am - the same time we were making arrests at the front of the property. We've got this digital image of the driver. It's a bit blurred, but it's the best we've got on Dave Ocasio. There's a man with a shaved head and a blonde-haired female in the back. No plates, but that timing and that car, I'd put my money on it being

Frankie McGreal making his break. We're waiting for more CCTV footage to see if we can track their journey, but as we know, it's New Year's Day and the trackers are a tad busy.'

James wondered whether the female passenger was Fleur. It corroborated Anne's story. If so, she'd been very close to finding her. Did Fleur go voluntarily with Frankie McGreal? What was going on there? Was that all that Anne was doing at the rave? But who had hurt her and why? His head was swimming with questions.

Shona Stewart took the floor. 'So, on a broader note, what do we know about the link up with Twinnie McGreal and Operation Cuckoo?' She pointed to his mug shot and listed known contacts. 'These men crashed the rave last night. A sort of 'frightener' we think. It appears Frankie McGreal has made a hasty exit.'

'Locked him up more than once,' Rav groaned as DS Stewart pointed once more to Twinnie McGreal's profile; the ginger-haired man with a deep gash running through his eyebrow.

'Michael Jackson McGreal, otherwise known as Twinnie,' Shona Stewart continued. 'Not long out of prison, HMP Channings Wood, Cat C for his part in planning the robbery of a Group 4 van, where the driver got shot. Other previous for lowlife stuff: violence, dealing, intimidation. But it appears he's out with bigger ambitions. Probably made some useful contacts in nick. We know he's been travelling back and forward between here and Canterbury, from where he's out on license. We've got records from probation to show that he gets … assistance with his travel costs.' A gasp ran around the room.

'It's all legit. Turned over a new leaf in prison, apparently, got early release and now runs sessions for ex-offenders. Including one back here that meets in our very own St Gabriel's church.' James felt glued to his chair, the colour rushing to his cheeks following the black look that said they'd be discussing this later. How had this slipped under his radar? St. Gabriel's church, another link to Anne Grimes …

'Seems PC Wright has good policing instincts – he's been doing community liaison at St. Gabriel's, sniffing around letting him know we're on to him.' James was flooded with gratitude towards Shona Stewart for her manipulation of the truth. She looked directly at him, but he couldn't interpret her expression.

'Shit, it's like he's recruiting locally?' interjected Rav.

DS Stewart cut him short. 'Let's stick with what we do know, for now. He's putting the squeeze on Frankie, sufficient to make him and his crew take flight. The girls have told our specialist WPC sex worker that Frankie McGreal might be on his way to southern Spain already. Some of the girls are planning to follow him out, to work for him in a lap-dancing bar he's setting up. That's why they're saying nothing. They're staying loyal to him.'

James sat up alert. Did that mean Fleur would be going to Spain too? Did Anne know?

'So. Back to Frankie McGreal,' DCI Bruce Campbell took up. The New Year rave was his goodbye bash, but he got out just before we made our entrance,' he paused briefly. 'Almost like he'd got a tip-off about our raid … it has been suggested.'

Someone whistled from the back of the room. Could he really have been tipped off? DS Stewart looked directly at James, and he understood fully why she had been complimentary about him in front of the DCI. She needed him to keep an eye on Bob Lyons. The slippery Eel.

'Our priority remains to lock up these two. The McGreal Twins: top of the food chain. They're causing havoc on our bloody patch, and I want it stopped. We're leaving Twinnie McGreal to Canterbury police with DS Stewart acting as liaison, but I want Frankie McGreal before he fucks off to Spain.' They were dismissed. You didn't ask questions when DCI Campbell used that sort of language. Although one thing had become clearer than ever to James: help Anne to find Fleur, and that would lead him directly to Frankie McGreal. But for now, he needed to keep Anne's possible involvement to himself. He didn't want to implicate her in anything until he knew more. She was already in enough trouble.

'I know it was difficult to hear some of that stuff without prior warning, but sometimes things just move that fast, James.' The chilly outside air took his breath away. They were standing by her car. He was grateful she'd got him out of a tight spot, but he still felt she could have briefed him first; that he was the victim of a weird power play enjoyed by Shona Stewart.

'Sorry I didn't pick up on the St. Gabriel's stuff, ma'am, but I do have a good contact there.'

'Sounds good. Squeeze that contact for all it's worth.' James blushed unaccountably before returning to his desk, his previous jubilation sapped. He'd missed something right under his nose. He shuddered at a piece of paper left on his keyboard. The imprint of bright red lips and a mobile phone number. He'd need to have a word with Jolene; she was getting out of hand. He tossed the note into his waste paper bin, already planning his next move. He needed to speak to Anne.

Bob Lyons' desk was deserted; probably out on one of his many cigarette breaks. James entered search criteria for 'Anne Grimes' on Bob's advanced National Police Records system, which he often left open. He waited, but nothing turned up, so at least she had a clean record. He remembered she'd told him she lived in some Youth-style accommodation. What was it called? Back at his own desk, he ran through maps of the Elm Grove district where he knew she lived. There it was - the 'Youth Alive' accommodation. Whistling, he gathered up his keys.

29

#Banksy: 'Love is in The Air'

It was hard to fight off images of Reverend Paul and Mrs. B's intimate dancing. Was there nobody left to trust? Firstly, clingy Vivian was spiralling out of control with her erratic behaviour, and now Mrs. B had let her down just as she'd decided to confide in her. She retched more yellow-green bile into the waste paper basket by the side of her bed.

A tear trickled down her nose, reminding her of the Angel Gabriel's tears. The lump in her throat hurt as if her grief had become stuck there. Why did all the adults in her life let her down? And now she'd have to leave her job at the Food Bank, just as things were working out. Her losses mounted before her eyes as she brushed away a tsunami of tears, life's salty disappointments. She reached up for her Anne of Green Gables book, the twenty-pound note floating down reminded her of where it all went wrong. Where were her Marilla and Mathew? Where were the people who would love her and care for her no matter what?

'Go away.' She called out at the whispering coming from behind her door.

Please don't let the voices start again ...

She put her hands over her ears. But the voices were getting louder, making her pull her soggy pillow around her ears. 'Go away, go away,' her fists in tight balls.

'Anne, it's only me, I've come to see if you're all right.' It was James.

'Go away, I'm not feeling very well, I think I've got the ... flu.'

'Don't be daft, Anne, let me in. I've got some news about Frankie McGreal on the run to Spain.' He knew he shouldn't have said that, but he needed to speak to her, whatever it took.

'Wait a minute.' She hurriedly splashed cold water on her face and dabbed damp toilet paper across her puffy eyes. 'How did you get in?'

'Someone was coming out as I arrived ... Good God, Anne, you look terrible, are you okay?'

'Well, I wasn't exactly expecting company. How do you know where I live?'

'I'm a police officer, Anne. I can find these things out.'

'Spying again?' But she couldn't hide the defeat in her voice. Not up for a fight, she sank back onto her bed.

'I was concerned about you. I wanted to check you were okay.' There was more than a hint of truth behind his words, more than he'd realised. Maybe the questioning could wait until later. She looked in a bad way.

Out of uniform, James was back in the tracksuit that he'd worn when she'd kissed him at the rave. She breathed in his cinnamon aftershave as he bent to remove his shoes. Nobody had ever done that in their flat before, ever. His socks were very white, maybe a Christmas present.

'It's a bit ... dark in here, saving on your bills?' he smiled.

She brushed past him to switch on the small bedside lamp with its gentle golden glow. Their hands brushed together, and she felt a spark of electricity.

He hesitated as to where to sit, settling for the stool pushed under the small dressing table. In its mirror, she saw her thumbs hooked into the sleeves of her jumper, pulled tight across her chest. She looked frozen, balanced stiffly on the edge of the bed. He picked up the framed picture of Katherine and raised an eyebrow, his light brown eyes illuminated almost golden in the soft lamplight, beneath those curling lashes.

'It's my older sister, Katherine.' She didn't say anymore; let him into the rabbit holes of her past life.

'Katherine Grimes,' he said out loud.

'Katherine Mathews. Different dads.' Then it struck her, maybe they had the same dad.

'Pretty girl. She looks like you.' Her heart missed a beat. Was he saying he thought she was pretty? She unfolded her arms, resisting the urge to bite her nails.

'How is your face?'

'Oh, it's okay. A bit sore but the swelling is going down.'

'Good.'

God, this is awkward. What does he want?

'You said you had some news about Frankie McGreal?'

'Yeah, we've arrested Ali Kumar for possession and distribution of drugs, but a good solicitor could probably get him off.

'His phone? ...'

'Our tech people are going through it as we speak.' She winced. 'Don't worry, I'll make sure everything stays confidential, but it's hard evidence; we have to use it. Is there anything ... of you on it?' It was a hard question to ask, but he had to know. She shook her head, but in reality, she didn't know. The thought of others watching Ellie in that room made her head woozy. It was like a second assault on her.

'There's incriminating stuff in his flat too, but whether it will be enough to hold him or not, I don't know.'

She started to feel like she was burning up.

'Are you sure you're okay, Anne?'

'Yeah, I took some tablets. I think they're having an effect on me.'

'Tablets?'

She couldn't stand this any longer. It was becoming claustrophobic, as if the walls were closing in on her. 'Yeah, painkillers for my nose. Fancy a walk?'

She was grateful for the outdoor space, which made it easier to talk. But was James someone she could confide in? Could she tell him what really happened at the rave? She wouldn't know where to start, or end, for that matter; there was so much going on. Maybe she would just answer his questions; see where that led them.

'Do you fancy something to eat?'

She nodded. She hadn't eaten anything substantial in days. They got in his car, still immaculately clean inside. 'Do you think we could go past Frankie McGreal's place, just to make sure they're not back there, maybe packing up …?'

'Sure, as long as you feel you're up to it.' They drove up the familiar winding path, but the stout house was dark and still. The shutters were back in place. No signs of life other than a police car and a 'Scientific Forensics' van stationed outside the front door.

They drove in silence back into the centre of town.

They stalled at traffic lights opposite one of Banksy's best-known installations: 'The Mild, Mild West', showing three policemen backing off as a large teddy bear aimed a Molotov cocktail at them.

'What's it saying?'

'Some sort of protest against police trying to stop illegal raves.' Her views had changed since her recent experience; she didn't care if she never went to another rave as long as she lived.

'You know a lot about Banksy ...' he strained to look up as they waited for traffic lights to change at a triangular junction just outside the city centre.

'Billy, my mum's ex, used to take me to see Banksy's work. He loved it.' She seemed to drift somewhere far away until they reached their destination, a tiny restaurant in a row of shops tucked away along Bristol's celebrated Christmas Steps. A few shops in the ancient row were open, hoping to tempt visitors in. He pushed at a door that magically revealed a room much bigger than the tiny bevelled windows suggested. Holding the narrow door open for her, she had to duck, immersed in his aftershave; botanical and something sharp – possibly lemon.

'This is nice.'

'Yeah, I sometimes catch up with people here.' She wondered who he meant by people. They took the table of a couple just departing.

'I like that jacket,' he nodded admiringly.

'My sister gave it to me.'

'Katherine?'

'Good recall, PC Wright.'

'So where does Katherine live?'

'You ask a lot of questions ...' Then she decided there was no harm in telling him more. 'In Canterbury. She lives with my mum and her younger twin sisters.'

'You've got three sisters?' he exhaled loudly. She still couldn't believe it herself.

'Anyway, how about you? Any brothers or sisters?'

'No, just me.' Somehow, she wasn't surprised; he looked like an only child: cosseted.

'Why weren't you at home with your family over Christmas?'

'My mum has met someone new and I thought I'd give them some space. Anyway, this is my first Christmas in my new place and I didn't want to be running back to Bath to be fed.'

'You come from Bath, very posh. So did your mum and dad get divorced?'

'You ask a lot of questions, Anne Grimes.' They both laughed.

'No, my dad died when I was eleven. Hard at the time, but you get over it. My dad was in the police force. He was attacked trying to help a lad who'd been set on. Ended up on life support with terrible head injuries.' Then Anne knew why James had become a policeman and felt guilty for her jibes. James stared at the menu as if not knowing why on earth he had just told Anne his life story. It was something he preferred to keep to himself.

He ordered them beef stew and dumplings, laughing that Anne had never tasted dumplings before, and watched amused as she dunked thick, crusty bread into her stew. She ate like she hadn't seen food in days, despite her sore face. He liked that about her. The few girls he had taken out for meals had appetites of birds, pecking at their food.

'So, do you get to see Katherine often?'

'No, we've only just met each other. She was sitting on my doorstep when I got back home on Christmas Day - after we'd been to McDonald's?' He thought back to their less-than-satisfying burger meal. It seemed like ages ago. A lot had happened to both of them in the last few weeks.

'The day you told me you were going home to Fleur?'

She reddened. 'I couldn't tell anyone she'd gone missing. Don't want to get the authorities involved. We're only in the flat on the condition that we stay out of trouble, at least until she's eighteen.'

'You carry a lot on those shoulders of yours, Anne.' He reached out both hands across the table, extending long, capable fingers. He knew a lot about protecting someone; he'd carried their load after his dad had died and his mum had fallen apart.

She thought he was reaching out to touch her hand, but his hands stayed splayed on the table. Although disappointed, it pleased her that he paid attention to his grooming.

'This place is licensed. Fancy a glass of wine?'

They took their drinks to a well-worn leather sofa with ethnic throws and some rare winter sunshine, which split into shafts illuminating motes floating in the air. She didn't feel at all out of place, not like she usually did when mingling with those who led more privileged lives, needing to steal something to address her deficits.

'Do you come here often?' They both laughed at her question.

'You trying to pick me up, Anne Grimes?' They both blushed.

'Kylie Mathews actually.' Then she immediately regretted it. Angry that she'd let her guard down so easily.

'Want to talk about it?' And she spent the next hour telling James about her mother having to change their names, about being left in the children's home, and then about her trip to Canterbury, where they were reunited. He sat back, looking straight ahead as she talked. She felt like a train, talking faster, letting off steam. He whistled.

'Well, I didn't see that coming. Now I see why you and Fleur are so close, why you need to find her.'

'She's all I've ever had. At least until Katherine came along.' He took her hand and massaged it gently, absentmindedly. Then his phone rang.

'I'm really sorry, Anne, but I need to get you back. They think they've found more footage of who was driving McGreal's car.'

'Do you mean Rasta Dave? With the dreadlocks and badges on his jacket?' He looked at her, amazed.

'Did you see the car?'

'Yeah, I think it's the same one I've seen at the Blind Fox. It had plates then. MC FU2.'

'Good God, Anne, we've been trying to trace that car all night. The plates had been removed. I don't suppose you've ever come across anyone called Rudi?'

'Yeah, I'll tell you all about him on our way back. If you tell me what you know about them leaving for Spain.' And for the first time, she had the faintest glimmer of hope that they might, together, work things out. That maybe she'd found someone she could trust.

30

#Banksy: 'If You Don't Mask You Don't Get'

Bob Lyons was like a cat on hot bricks. He hadn't worked so many hours since he'd started on the force. But then there was a lot to sort out, and time was running out. Frankie McGreal was about to move on, but he wasn't getting away without paying his dues; Bob's long-awaited pension top-up. He breathed in the cold air, stinging his fragile nostrils, inflamed by too many years of cigarette smoke. He was waiting for that little shit Rasta Dave. Disrespectful. Never on time.

He'd finished his shift and doubled back to a lane close to Frankie's Big House, careful to check he wasn't being followed. You never knew who was watching. Least of all that impressionable little shit James Wright. All qualifications and jumping as high as Shona Stewart instructed him to. He made his way past the shuttered house to the Old Infirmary's disused car park and waited until a battered Volvo pulled up. Smart move.

'Bet that's cheaper on your insurance.'

Dave Ocasio shrugged. 'Got it at the auction. Frankie had to get rid of anything incriminating. Fresh start and all that.'

'Frankie not with you then?'

'Already on their way south, taking the night ferry.'

'You not going with them?'

'I'm tying up loose ends, driving a car over later.'

'I sincerely hope I'm one of those loose ends,' he offered Dave a cigarette.

They both knew he was about to be well rewarded for tipping off Frankie about the police raid on New Year's Eve.

Dave still couldn't believe Frankie went ahead with the rave. One last bash, a final two fingers before he left for Spain. Arrogant sod, it nearly backfired on all of them. It certainly had on Ali Kumar, who'd been arrested, just as Dave Ocasio had arranged. There was no love lost between them.

'So, how are we going to do this?' Bob was keen to close business and get on his way.

'The usual.' Dave gestured to the boot of the car, feeling some regret at breaking off his long-term relationship with Bob Lyons. It was good to know your back was covered.

Bob had a greedy gleam in his eye at the thought of his payoff.

'You're not the only ones moving on.'

Dave looked up, surprised. He couldn't imagine Bob Lyons doing anything else. He'd been the local copper for most of his life.

'I'm off to Australia. To see my son and grandkids. Who knows, I might never come back. Do some fishing, grow some roses.'

'I didn't know you had a family, Bob.'

'Yeah, well out of the way, made all this easier for me. No Achilles' heel, you might say.' They sat quietly as old acquaintances do. Thinking about families. Easy with the silence.

'Remember the first time you arrested me?' Dave took another cigarette.

'Soliciting. Around Temple Mead Station toilets.' They both smiled. Bob had picked him up in a sorry state, probably no more than fifteen, living on the streets. He'd helped him with hostel accommodation; looked out for him. It was Dave who'd introduced him to Frankie McGreal back in the early days. That was when Bob Lyons decided to back Frankie and give him a leg up to get established in the criminal world. He needed an insider in the rapidly changing drug scene, and Frankie McGreal was his safest bet.

But his twin brother Twinnie was always going to spoil things. He got Frankie involved in things way out of his depth, then dropped him like a sack of potatoes. He knew both brothers well. He was probably the only family outsider who knew Twinnie's nickname of 'Cockie,' short for cockroach. Some twisted sign of affection.

'I hear you're all setting up in Marbella. I've got a forwarding address.'

'You're fucking with me. Nobody's got that address.' Dave Ocasio spat over his shoulder, his poorly tethered dreadlocks swinging free.

'You should have told Grace to keep stum,' the police officer lied, more to see Dave's reaction, but also to keep some last shred of insurance.

'Grace gave you Frankie's new address?'

Bob Lyons looked into the distance. Russian roulette. He knew Grace had the address, but she certainly wasn't telling him, no matter how hard he'd pushed. Loyalty amongst thieves; he admired her for it.

Rasta Dave returned from the back of the car with a large stuffed envelope.

'Frankie sorted it before he went. A bit extra to show his appreciation.' They shook hands.

'Nice doing business with you, Dave.' Bob never said things he didn't mean.

31

#Banksy: 'Nobody Ever Listened To Me, Until They Didn't Know Who I Was ...'

The 3rd of January crept under her door like any other gloomy winter's day, except that this was the day beyond which Anne had no future. All remained calm; no drama; the biggest anti-climax of her life. And things stayed like that until later in the day when the banging on the door started.

She rushed to answer it, hoping it might be Fleur. Changed her mind about going away.

'Sorry, Anne, he just pushed past me, bloody pig.'

She was surprised to see James, with BTW oily-skinned and agitated, hovering over his shoulder. James was back in uniform, looking more formal than ever. He didn't react to Brian. The stern look on his face indicated this wasn't a social call.

'You here about Sasha?' twitchy Brian questioned.

James turned and shut the door in BTW's face.

'Is everything okay, James?'

He averted his eyes from her worried gaze. 'Anne, I think you'd better sit down.'

Sitting on her bed, she saw the whole sorry story unfold in the dressing table mirror over his shoulder. Two people acting out a scene from one of her soaps.

'A body's been found near Park Lane.'

She watched in the mirror as a girl who looked like her, put her hand to her mouth.

'It's a young female. About sixteen or seventeen from the first reports. Blonde hair.' He put his hand on her shoulder. She felt its warmth through her T-shirt.

'I know that you've been looking for Fleur ...'

'No, no, no,' she saw the reflection in the mirror cry out, turning her face into the police officer's shoulder.

'Let's get your coat. I think we need to go and see Millie.' He checked she had her keys, like they always do on TV dramas, before he led her away, his arm around her shoulder. A facile attempt to shield her from what lay ahead. BTW looked down suspiciously from his window as they got into the patrol car. He took a picture with his phone, just in case. A shadowy figure in the bushes went unnoticed.

'What happened to her?' she gulped. She didn't want to know, yet was desperate for details.

'Look, I don't know much more, Anne, but we need to identify the body, and I know you have informed me of a missing person who ... fits the same description.' Anne looked down at her hands, shaking, her nails ragged after recent events. It was as if she weren't present, like she was observing someone else acting her part, someone who hadn't learned their lines.

'We need Millie to come along to identify her. Unless you know of any other next of kin?' Anne shook her head. 'Is there a mother about we might contact?' She looked away. There were never mothers about when you needed them, not for the likes of her or Fleur. There was the new social worker, but Anne knew that would open a whole different can of worms after the lies she'd told Polly Morton.

She suddenly felt very alone. Very afraid of what was about to happen.

He paused before delivering the body blow.

'I need to tell you ... the female was wearing a maroon padded jacket. It sounds very much like the one Fleur was wearing when I helped her down from the multi-storey car park.'

They could hear Zane and Millie arguing before they reached the front door.

'You've fucking taken my money.'

'We need to eat Zane.'

'You went out with the girls more like ...'

'Yeah, rich comin' from you who 'ardly comes 'ome these days.' They both fell silent as they saw a uniformed police officer and Anne Grimes standing in their hall.

'What the f...?'

James gently nudged Anne forward.

'Millie … a girl's body has been found, we need to go and identify it.'

Millie looked stunned before yelping, 'Fleur? No, no, no…' After some gentle encouragement from herself and Zane, she went upstairs sobbing, 'I need to put something decent on.'

'Where's River?' asked Anne.

'He's asleep on the couch.' Scruff and River were curled together amidst discarded KitKat wrappers. She hoped Scruff hadn't eaten the chocolate, but now wasn't the time to query it. Millie joined them, surprising them with her shocking pink lipstick.

'Fleur bought it for me, she used to say it suited me.'

Anne suspected it was one from a collection she'd stolen for Fleur from Debenhams, and shuddered at the thought of her past life, how she would steal anything they needed. Maybe this was what they called retribution. God's way of saying enough is enough.

'You look lovely love, just lovely. Now go on. Do what you've got to do. Don't worry about us, I'll put River to bed.' It was the most caring thing Anne had ever heard Zane say. He sounded so tender.

'Read him a story?'

His shooting look told them that Millie had pushed it a bit far. Anne tried to brace herself for what lay ahead. 'Thanks for comin' with me.' Millie held her hand so tight that her rings dug into her flesh. Anne knew from her blanched skin that it should be hurting, but she couldn't feel a thing.

They left the window looking into the haunting white room, clinical smells clinging to their nostrils, with Millie crying and clutching at her arm. James looked over from the waiting room. He'd wanted to be with Anne, to comfort her. Instead, he had PCSO Jolene Whittaker with her enlarged red lips by his side.

'Asked if I could come along ... never seen a dead body before,' she whispered in his ear.

He ignored her inane comments and stood apart from her as the distressed women exited the room, Anne shook her head.

'Looks like it's not her then?' Jolene's eyes were wide with speculation.

He continued to ignore her, wanting to get to Anne, ashen and shaking. He wanted to take her home. To comfort her.

'Strange, there was no ID on the body. Not even a mobile phone.'

'Not everyone wants to be identified,' replied James.

Jolene needed to think about that. It didn't sound like any young person she knew. Finally, they were ready to leave. Anne was first to speak. 'I know who she is ...' They all

stopped and looked at her. 'It's someone called Grace. She …
works … worked from the Blind Fox.'

James looked questioningly at her.

She couldn't bring herself to tell them anymore, not yet.
About lovely, vivacious Grace, who worked as a prostitute.
That she hung out between the two McGreal brothers and their
cronies.

'She works from the Blind Fox?'

She nodded, but he didn't push for more. They all knew
what lay behind her carefully chosen words. 'What, that girl
Grace - who my Zane knows?' Millie asked, her eyes
somewhere else, clamouring to remember what she could
about the girl she'd never met but had been jealous of.

'Do you know her full name, Anne?'

She shook her head, ashamed she couldn't dignify the girl
with a surname.

'Get those details to Gabby, our sex worker liaison; she
knows all the girls,' he said to a wide-eyed Jolene who looked
as if she was enjoying herself far too much. He avoided Anne's
eye contact - how come she knew so much about the girls who
frequented the Blind Fox? His mind was racing, trying to piece
it all together.

'The hooker's a looker,' whispered Jolene into James's ear
as they followed the sisters out. Furious at her soulless words,
he strode ahead, letting the door swing in her face.

'You can make your own way back from here.' He left the startled Jolene standing silhouetted against the harsh outside light of the mortuary, hidden out of sight from the hospital mainstream footfall, as they always are.

Anne felt numb. A numbness she hadn't felt in years, and it frightened her more than what she had just witnessed. Her throat felt strangled, her swallowing uncoordinated. She opened the car window, waiting for the voices to start.

'Are you okay?' A question not deserving of an answer.

Millie sobbed quietly, once again clutching Anne for support. They dropped her back with the anxiously waiting Zane.

'It wasn't Fleur, love. It was your friend, Grace.' They embraced on the doorstep, and Anne could see the sorrow carved deep into Zane's brow. The news had hit him hard.

James took Anne's keys from her trembling hands and opened her door for her. Room's concern was palpable in the tense air. 'Cup of tea?'

She nodded. 'Plenty of sugar. Please. Don't you need to get back to work?'

'No, I finished at five.'

'But that was way before you got here.'

'Yeah, I just needed to know you were okay.'

She collapsed on her bed and finally let herself weep. He sat on the floor beside her, gently rubbing her hand, and the tears flowed. She cried for Grace, for Fleur, for the girls who would be going out to work on the streets, or being coerced into sex that night. For her Hint of Lemon life turning a dirty, muddy brown.

All cried out, she sat up and rubbed her nose on her sleeve.

'I feel terrible. I was so glad when it wasn't Fleur, but then I also knew Grace. It's almost as if I was making a judgment that one girl's life is worth more than another's …' James held her in the stillness of the sad room.   She wanted so much to tell him everything, to answer all of those unasked questions about the rave and the Blind Fox and everything else in her life, but how could she possibly tell him that she and Fleur had walked away as a man burned to death? That they'd caused the death of Shayne McGreal. The single fact that would prevent her from ever letting her get too close to him.

Outside, Marta watched, eagle-eyed and alert, looking at the police car. Why was there a policeman on her premises? Whatever the reason, she wasn't happy. The last thing she needed was the police poking their corrupt noses into things, especially when she and Twinnie were about to start up 'The Farm' - their next business venture. They were already paying that stuck-up bitch Shona Stewart enough.

32

#Banksy: 'Ruined Landscape'

Memories of Anne's previous life loomed at the bottom of a great black hole where Grace morphed grotesquely into a version of Fleur, swirling in the unyielding pit. James suggested she talk to a bereavement officer he rated, and she briefly considered it, but didn't have much faith in crap like that; best saved for people who really needed it. She needed to deal with things her way.

Crossing town, she waited for Bristol Museum to open. Hours later, balanced on a thin ledge, she clasped her hands on her knee and carefully studied the statue of Banksy's 'Paint Pot Angel' which had drifted in and out of her dreams all night. She recalled the time Billy had taken her to see it. It had disturbed her, and as she closed her eyes, she could feel his reassuring hand in hers and hear the awe in his voice.

'What's it about, Billy?' She'd had to turn away from the innocent-looking angel defiled by a bucket of paint placed over its head, like a hood blinding it with streams of paint dripping down its body, blood-like.

'Life isn't always what you expect,' he'd said. 'It makes you think about the things we covet.' But she'd not understood his words, remaining disappointed at spoiling the full magnificence of the angel who had literally become 'defaced'.

But now she understood. Completely. She felt the outrage and unfairness in a life that fails to deliver. The façade. Maybe Billy already suspected her mum was playing around with Shayne McGreal, always lingering in the background. She thought of Fleur's '*I fucking hate it here*' message, which she'd ignored and brushed over; of Grace appearing to be in control yet suffering the ultimate fate. Was everything a façade? Where did her truth lie now? Fleur had gone; Mrs. B's actions would inevitably separate them. What was left? She thought of the sentiment that had pulled her through so much in the past few years. *There is Always Hope* … She had truly believed that, but what did she hope for now? What was she living for?

Then it hit her with great clarity. It was time to move on. 'Thanks, Banksy.' She gently stroked the hem of the angel's robe, and with a renewed desire to take something positive from the chaos surrounding her, she made her way to another angel, one whose tears had flowed at the misplaced actions of others.

She knocked gingerly on Mrs. B's office door, not knowing how she would react to the woman's façade of 'decency'. Frank, the new church caretaker, creaked down the corridor, rocking as he walked. Something to do with years at sea, he'd told them. 'She's not here, love, she's gone to meet someone. A pressing appointment,' he drawled in his strong West Country accent, somehow reassuring, but his eyes were tired, washed-out as if he'd seen too many things. Although it was hard to hide her disappointment, she sorted, cleaned, served, and chatted with increased vigour. Even the Angel Gabriel carried a new air of optimism, freed from his scaffolding after the leaky roof repair; no more angelic tears, she smiled at her stupid misunderstanding. Her heart felt light. She, too, would be repaired. After the shift, she returned the church keys to Mrs. B's office as usual. An opened envelope lay in the drawer. She saw Vivian's spiky handwriting: *'Private'*. Her heart pumped hard. Why was Vivian writing to Mrs. Barlow?

With a pressing appointment of her own to attend, she rushed to the local police station, averting her gaze to a depressing flutter of EU flags hanging limp and damp, as if they'd already given up hope.

Nothing serious, they'd said, but it might be useful if she could provide an informal statement, to add to what they already knew about Grace's life. Her confidence wavered at the thought of entering a police station, but soon settled at the welcome handshake of a friendly-looking WPC who escorted her into the 'Relatives Room,' with its well-worn chairs and sun-faded silk flowers.

'Hi Anne, I'm WPC Gabby McArdle; I'm dealing with the sad death of Grace Hill.' So, they had her surname. Where was her family in all this? Why hadn't they looked after her better?

Then she thought of her own family and understood how things go adrift.

'Can you start by telling me how you knew Grace?' She liked Gabby McArdle, with her no-fuss hairstyle and well-clipped nails with moon-shaped cuticles. She looked in control of things, filling her with gratitude that there were people like Gabby out there working with young, vulnerable girls on the street. Although it hadn't done Grace much good.

'Well, we weren't close friends or anything, but she was a kind person; looked after the girls at the Blind Fox.' She desperately wanted to make the best of what she knew about the risk-taking Grace.

'Do you frequent the Blind Fox, Anne?' intelligent brown eyes under an upturned eyebrow.

'Not really. I went there once with my mentor.'

'You have a mentor?'

'Yeah, it was a condition of my leaving care and moving into the Youth Alive flats.'

That, for some reason, seemed to interest WPC Gabby. 'Do you mind if I take some notes?'

'No, of course not.'

Be careful, Anne ...

'And you go out drinking with your mentor?'

'Only because it was her birthday. She wanted to celebrate.' She was lying already.

'And she took you to the Blind Fox?' The officer blinked several times as if encouraging an explanation out of her. Anne nodded. Gabby McArdle switched tack.

'Did you ever see Grace hanging around the Youth Alive flats, Anne?'

'No.'

Gabby McArdle made notes, giving Anne welcome space to breathe and recalibrate.

'Have you ever seen anything around your flats that might concern you?' she continued.

'No.' This was a strange line of questioning.

'Oh, it's just that we do visit there from time to time.' She thought of BTW and his cannabis-smoking friends; she'd have to warn him.

'When did you last see Grace?'

'It was at a New Year's rave. And before that, I'd seen her getting thrown out of someone's flat.'

'And where was that, Anne?'

'It was Flat 43a on Park Lane.' She remembered it well - when Ali had thrown Grace out of the flat. The flat where she saw her maroon padded jacket hanging up. The one Grace must have taken.

'That's near where we found Grace's body. We've been to that flat, but guess what? Cleared out. They'd left in a hurry. Looks like they'd had some real parties there though.' Anne's heart drummed a dance out of step. Should she tell Gabby McArdle about Fleur? But the officer had already moved on.

'Did you know the previous Park Lane residents, Anne?'

'Not really.' Anne answered honestly, eyes steady. 'But I did see them at the New Year's rave.'

'Tell me about the rave.'

Her heart was fluttering, bird-like in her rib cage. This was getting too close to home. Gabby McArdle was looking at her intensely; a mix of interest and concern stirred in her pupils.

'How did Grace seem at the rave?'

She gave a gilded account of Grace arriving with Ali, making it sound romantic, out of respect for Grace.

'Well, that's about all I think. Thanks for coming in. I just wanted to build up a fuller picture of Grace's lifestyle. You've corroborated what we already knew or suspected.' Anne didn't know what that meant, but was pleased to be getting out of the interview room, which was becoming claustrophobic.

'Oh, I've got a package for you to take, but you need to sign for it.' Anne must have looked confused.

'Your phone - from the police raid? PC Wright insisted I have it ready for you to collect.' She wanted to ask about Ali's phone, whether they'd seen the images of Ellie from that terrible night, but the urge to leave was stronger.

'Thanks for coming in, Anne, and remember I'm here for you or any of the other girls if you ever want to sound anything out.'

God, she thinks I'm a sex worker.

But then what was she supposed to think? She had hung out at some very seedy places. They were about to leave the room when Gabby stopped and faced her directly. 'How come you ended up identifying the body, Anne? If, as you say, you didn't know Grace that well?'

'We thought it might have been someone else.'

'Someone else is missing?'

'No. She's back now.' Another lie. To a smart police officer.

Shit, why did I say that? Maybe Gabby McArdle could help me.

But a memory of Banksy's 'Lying to the Police is Never Wrong' slogan helped her settle her nerves, to stick with her story.

'I don't remember speaking to you when we interviewed the other girls after the rave?'

'No, I'd left early.'

'We didn't get your fingerprints then?'

'No.'

'Would you mind if I took them now? It's voluntary. I've found it useful to have the girls on file. You never know when

…' she trailed off. They both knew what she meant. Anne had no reason not to have her fingerprints taken. Gabby McArdle seemed like a good person, and she was glad she was there for people who genuinely needed her help.

'How did Grace die?' The one thing she still didn't know.

'We're pretty certain it was an overdose. Such a waste of a young life. Seems she was very upset about something.' She looked genuinely regretful.

Gabby McArdle waved goodbye, watching her rush out into the cold wind, flooded with a strong feeling that all was not well with Anne Grimes. She was glad she'd got her prints. After all these years, she knew a girl who was hiding something when she met one.

In a café not far from the community police station, two women were having a coffee. One in a bottle green velvet coat and matching beret. The other, more pedestrian, was wearing peach lipstick and a practical raincoat. They didn't appear to have much in common but were heavily engaged in conversation. Their shared topic was Anne Grimes.

Mrs. B was wary of the velveted Vivian after all she'd heard from Anne, but it made sense for them to get together to discuss Anne's prospects, as suggested in the letter left on her desk. And, maybe she could do Anne a favour by questioning Vivian's plans to end the mentoring.

But something was worrying her about Vivian. She seemed overly excited. Jittery - already on her third cup of coffee. Besides which, an elderly gentleman was clearly trying to catch her attention, but maybe he was mistaking her for someone else. He seemed to be calling her Ffion.

Vivian ignored him and carried on.

'I think that man wants to talk to you.'

'Ignore him. He's the local paedophile.'

Mrs. B turned away, shocked, as Vivian returned to the purpose of her invitation. 'It's with a weighty heart that I have to let you know I'm not prepared to sign off Anne's progress report.' Mrs. B had almost expected this. Another of Anne's mentor's delaying tactics. She could see what Anne was up against.

'But Anne has made exceptional progress, Vivian. She's had to deal with a lot in her life. I've found her an asset to our small team at the Food Bank. I even trust her to run things when I'm not around.'

Vivian quietened, the lids of her eyes falling heavily as if veiling her grief about the situation.

'Bye, Ffion.' The older gentleman called over. It appeared he'd been seeking permission to put up a 'Missing Cat' poster. He didn't look much like a paedophile, but then Mrs. B often wondered what one would look like. Vivian ignored him and raised her eyes to the ceiling as if in despair.

'So did you want to discuss anything else?' It was all getting a little too theatrical for the sensible Mrs. Barlow.

'Have you noticed any change in Anne lately?' Vivian probed.

'Not really …' But Janice Barlow had noticed Anne's fluctuating moods, especially since Christmas.

'I have it on good authority that she is taking drugs. Hard drugs,' continued Vivian, undeterred.

Mrs. B thought of the New Year's Eve rave. Wasn't that where people went to 'do' drugs? She thought of the missing church money and the accusations of Mr. Murphy's daughter. The small creeping suspicion was growing into an ugly succubus. Could there be something in what Vivian was saying?

33

#Banksy: 'The Original Rat'

James sensed Shona Stewart's sudden reluctance to enter the pub, which was surprising as it was her impromptu suggestion to update him on her most recent trip to Canterbury.

'I'll bring them through,' Keith, the smart waistcoated bartender, called over as they made their way to the Central's snug with the impressive marble fireplace.

'It's all coming together,' Shona Stewart eventually said with a self-reassuring smooth down of her skirt. 'We've established evidence that Twinnie McGreal has known Albert, or William Reynolds as we now know him, for several years.'

This was big news for James, who was becoming frustrated at the case's slow progress. Operation Cuckoo had seemed to stall, allowing time for Bob Lyons to allocate him menial tasks such as checking ASBOs and following up on missing pets. DS Stewart took a measured sip of her Jack Daniels. 'Twinnie McGreal has shares in a meat factory based in Canterbury. They make regular trips to factories in Europe. William Reynolds has worked at the factory in both portering and driving jobs for McGreal. Two rats, together from the start.'

'So ... Albert worked for Twinnie McGreal?'

Her nod suggested he needn't be so rudimentary.

'Part of his disposable workforce, you might say,' he noticed she liked to smile at her own jokes.

'But why has Twinnie been seen back in Bristol? Surely, he'd want to distance himself from William Reynold's decapitated body?'

'Well, the official reason was to run his ex-offending rehab programme, but I suspect it's been about power playing; putting pressure on Frankie to make sure he'd scared him off good and proper.'

'So, he can reclaim his old stomping ground.'

His boss nodded. 'And it looks as if there's a new business venture.' She'd decided to let him in on the latest development, the reason she'd brought him to the pub. To disclose just enough to keep him loyal to her.

'Dealing?'

She looked at him as if he'd missed something crucial. What had he missed?

'Canterbury police have been watching the meat factory for some time. It seems they're not fussy about what or who they ferry back and forth in their refrigerated lorries.' James felt repulsion surge through his veins.

'People trafficking?'

She smoothed her shiny bobbed hair. He'd got there at last.

'They traffick people over here, lie low for a while, then move them on. We're stepping up surveillance at the Elm

Grove refugees' tenements. We've established a tentative link.'

He thought of Anne. She lived opposite those buildings.

'Might be a long job. I've drafted in some help from outside Bristol, and I don't want Bob Lyons getting involved. Keep your eyes on him, James, don't let him in on what I've told you.'

He nodded but had no idea of how he would do that. Bob Lyons would smell a rat at a hundred yards.

'Good. That's clear then.'

They finished their drinks in silence, James more confused than ever.

After Shona Stewart's departure, James texted Anne his excuses as to why he wouldn't be seeing her for a while. He couldn't afford to mess this up by having personal business interfering with a forthcoming surveillance. It was getting too messy. He felt a pang of guilt knowing how hard she'd been hit with losing Fleur, compounded by Grace's death. But he needed to keep some distance. If only for her own safety.

34

#Banksy: 'If you get tired, learn to rest, not to quit'

Anne was making her way to Millie's house. She needed company, and Millie and River were the closest thing to family she had, at least in Bristol. She hoped she might still play some part in the toddler's life.

'Maybe it's time we went to the police?' said Millie, looking more tussled than usual. 'I mean, that could 'ave been our Fleur lyin' dead in that morgue.' Pale and drawn, it appeared that sleep had also been eluding Millie. But going to the police was the last thing Anne wanted.

'No need, Millie - James and I are working together on it, and he's not like other police officers; he's decent. He's working on a couple of leads as we speak.' Not a complete lie, she prayed it would appease the restless Millie. And it seemed to have worked, with Millie now more interested in her relationship with James than searching for her missing half-sister.

'I thought there was somethin' between you two. Go on then, do tell all.' And for some reason, Anne felt relieved to share the times they had spent together, starting with him saving Fleur from falling from the multi-storey car park. It felt good talking about him to another female, and Millie was a good listener.

'So, our Fleur brought you two together then?' It was a novel way of looking at things, but she was probably right. Throughout their chat, Anne felt herself warming towards James, owning her feelings for him. Her phone buzzed. A text from James. Her heart raced; she'd save it for later.

Zane came downstairs, yawning with bad breath, just as she was leaving.

'They fucked off to Spain then,' he whispered, looking deflated.

He seemed listless, deeply affected by Grace's death, devoid of his usual nervous energy. She reached out to touch his hand. They'd all been through too much. Millie caught her gesture out of the corner of her eye.

'Get your own fuckin' fella.' All sisterly closeness dissipating along with any hope that they might stay friends.

Her thoughts were all over the place as she walked home, still looking over her shoulder; sure that she was being followed. She brushed away tears after reading James' 'distancing' text, familiar waves of rejection washing over her. BTW was leaning against a sidewall, smoking in a haze of herby-smelling weed.

'Everything okay?'

She brushed past him, trying to hide her tears, then remembered her conversation with Gabby McArdle.

'Be careful smoking that stuff out here, Brian, the police are watching the flats.'

'Old news, kid.' What did he mean?

'Surprised they're not out there now. Spotted them ages ago, and you need to be careful, that crafty pig who you like has joined them. Nosey porkers, all of them,' he spat over his shoulder.

'James?'

'I bet he's not told you he's on some sort of surveillance - he was here last night.'

'What do you mean? Watching our flats?'

'They park over there.' He nodded to the refugees' tenements, where Marta had her office. Her head was spinning. Was it James who had been following her all this time?

'Good morning, Mrs. B.'

But the older woman wearing the palest pink lipstick and baby pink cardigan turned her head away.

Is everyone finding me repulsive today? ...

But she needed to be calm, stay in control until she could get what she needed and move on.

'Anne, please close the door. There is something rather distressing that I need to discuss with you.' She felt her knees weaken. Had Mrs. B found out about Fleur?

The older woman averted her gaze. 'It has been brought to my attention that you … might be taking drugs.'

Her heart squeezed in her ribcage, a cry caught at the back of her throat. Vivian. She could not believe the depths she would sink to, to stop her from moving on; to keep her pinned to her side.

'That lying bitch!' Anne couldn't help herself.

'Anne!' declared Mrs. B, covering her mouth, now convinced it must be the drugs talking.

'Please just give me my reference and I will be on my way.'

'I don't think you've understood Anne. It is my responsibility to look after you, to help keep you from harm and the evils of temptation all around us.'

She felt injustice stab at her heart at the scheming of Vivian. Mrs. B had tears in her eyes. 'If you let me in, we can work on it; turn things around, Anne.'

But she'd taken enough. 'Who are *you* to lecture *me*, Mrs. B? You're no saint!' Anne, vitriolic, saw Mrs. B shrink back, trembling at what she might know. 'I'm not hanging around here any longer. I resign!'

Mrs. B stood to prevent her from leaving.

'You think you're so clever, so smug. Well, you don't know anything about me. You have no idea who the real me is. Sort your own crappy life out!' The injustice of everything multiplied to a thousand daggers piercing Anne's already bruised heart.

Zane was waiting on the doorstep of her flat, his discarded vape packaging on the path.

'Put that in the bin, don't treat *my* place like a shithole.'

He bent down and picked it up. He looked brittle.

'Sorry Anne. Have you got a few minutes? I need to talk to you, away from Millie.'

His eyes were bleary. 'It's hard to hold it together, to be honest.' He rubbed the back of his hand across his streaming nose. 'Grace and I were close, like really close. I always tried to look out for her, but she was a stubborn little cow. I think I loved her.' His voice cracked as he wiped a blob of snot on the sleeve of his denim jacket, pausing to observe it. 'Came to bring you this. Grace was all excited because she thought she was going to Spain with them all. She thought I might ... like ... join her at some point.' He handed over a scrappy piece of paper.

Would you really have gone off to Spain and left Millie and River?

'Here, take it. I'm pretty sure it's where Fleur will be. It's Frankie McGreal's new address in Marbella; she found it in Ali's flat. McGreal was planning to fly out several girls from the Blind Fox. He's setting up a lap dancing club out there, then at the last minute, he dropped Grace. It was like he'd found out something bad about her, singled her out. He caused her fuckin' death.'

The whole thing sounded just like the McGreals: empty promises for desperate people. How could Frankie McGreal promise something so exciting and then snatch it away? And what did he find out about Grace? That she'd visited Twinnie in prison, or that she'd been stupid enough to help him during his trips back to Bristol? Grace lived on the edge. Was this the price to pay for stepping out of line? Fleur would be next if she ever spilled their secret.

'It's Grace's funeral next week. You going?' He looked almost transparent, with loose skin hanging from his pocked cheekbones.

She looked at the scrap of paper in her hands, its jagged edges torn roughly from River's colouring book. The Villa Florentina. It sounded so exotic, so inviting, but so out of her reach. Then she thought of her last letter to Banksy, when she'd been asking for his counsel, and she knew exactly what she was going to do.

'Sorry, Zane, I won't be here for the funeral.'

He shook his head in disbelief, his eyes narrow and accusing.

'You've got to. We all need to be there for Grace.'

'No, there's someone still living who needs me more. I'm going to Spain.'

Pocketing the small clock she'd lifted from her mother's house, she took the bus across town to the pawn brokers where she'd been before with her mum. With no idea what the clock was worth, the sharpness of the dealer's jaundiced features, matching his sharp intake of breath, spoke volumes about the clock's credentials.

'I've pawned it before, at the shop by my dad's house, so I know how much it's worth,' she lied. He looked disappointed that she might know its value as he started counting out notes. Lots of them. She walked away with one hundred and fifty pounds in her hand and her receipt. Only enough for a one-way ticket, but enough to get her moving. It was easy to book everything on her new phone, despite Room's sulkiness.

The early bus to Bristol airport was on time, and she climbed aboard clutching her stuffed backpack. She was off to Spain, and she wasn't coming home without Fleur.

35

#Banksy: 'Exit Through the Gift Shop'

The Villa Florentina sparkled in the late afternoon sun, offering Frankie McGreal the perfect refuge from his mad bastard of a twin brother and his threats to kill him.

Maria, one of his house team, greeted him home with a cocktail. The usual, margaritas with limes picked fresh from the garden. 'Line them up - Dave's just parking the car.' He stretched and thumbed through his mail before it was tossed into the large wrought iron fire grate.

'Fleur, come and have a drink …' No reply. She must be in the basement gym. Some fucking welcome home.

He'd worked hard to put his stamp on the place. Only he and Rasta Dave knew he'd been setting it up for months using local agents. Tasteful pieces ordered from local artists adorned the white rustic walls. He wished he'd made the move years ago.

'Fleur, get your arse down here …'

Dave returned, wearing his hair plaited in new, more elaborate braids since the move, and slunk into his usual seat by the large window facing the garden. 'So, what did you think of the Bar Bianco?' He licked salt from his lips through the citrus-sour bite of his margarita.

'About the best we've seen so far. Those small outhouses would make ideal accommodation when the girls come out.'

'Not much for them to do though.'

'Just how I like it, Dave. Don't want them mixing with the locals. They're here to do a job. We just need to sort out the owners. I'm relying on you and Spike for that. Make them a reasonable offer, make sure we get their clients, then get some incriminating photos.' Frankie McGreal had big plans. New year, new start.

'Fleur will be glad to have the girls over here. She's looking bored,' Dave Ocasio scrolled through his phone.

'Yeah, all this fucking luxury and she still isn't happy.'

Dave smiled to himself - he liked to drop Fleur in it.

'Fleur, you joining us or what?' Frankie shouted up from the bottom of the winding marble staircase, towering over a huge vase of birds of paradise on an antique marble table. The Villa Florentina. He loved everything about it. He struck gold with the previous owner being persuaded to sell it for a song. A shout reached them from the top of the stairs.

'Mr. Frankie, come quick,' Maria shouted down, interrupted from turning back the beds.

'It's Mr. Spike. I think he's died, and there's a letter.'

'What the fuck ...' He took the stairs two at a time. What had happened to Spike, Fleur's bodyguard? Had they been broken into? He stood over Spike, slumped in the corridor. The man was out cold. Drunk, slobber running down his face.

'Where's Fleur?' he kicked hard at the dazed man.

'She's in there, taking a nap,' he slurred, disoriented.

Frankie slapped him hard across his face, dragging him up by his t-shirt.

'Does it look like she's in there?'

'… the cocktails …' stuttered Spike, everything becoming clear. Fleur had drugged him. He was for it. Then the punches started.

Frankie didn't know what was going on. Where could she be? Why would she leave? He looked around the room. His briefcase was open on the bed. He hadn't bothered to lock it, becoming sloppy since the move. But then there was nothing in there that he didn't mind Fleur seeing. The Valentine's cards they'd sent each other were scattered over the porcelain-tiled floor. What had spooked her?

He shuffled through other papers, contracts, property deeds, and receipts in an incomprehensible language. A sharp pain stabbed in his chest as he realised her passport was missing. He'd kept it bound to his, along with a wad of euros; their quick getaway money. There was something about binding them together that had felt symbolic, like she was his. Until now.

He flicked through some letters poking out from under a pillow. Letters from his mother. He panicked. What was in them? He was going to tell her that his mum was about to follow them out, that he was buying a nice little place nearby for her.

'Maria, you said there was a letter for me?' He took it downstairs. He needed a stiff whiskey. The little cow had really pulled the rug from under him this time. His hands shook as he read her looped, babyish writing.

Sorry babe, I needed to do it this way 'cos I knew you'd never let me go. I'm going back to Bristol. Don't try to follow me, too many people are after you. I won't be gone long. There's something urgent I need to tell Anne, and you have taken my phone, so there's no other way. Anyway, this is something so big, I have to do it face-to-face. I love you babe, and I'll be back as soon as I've done what I need to do. Lol xxx.'

He turned away from Dave. He didn't want his driver to see him with tears in his eyes. He flung his crystal whiskey glass into the ornately tiled fireplace, its peaty aroma filled the room. He wanted to wring Fleur's neck. Surely she knew what danger she was putting them all in by going back home.

'Pack a bag, Dave. You're going back to Bristol. I want Fleur here with me. She knows too much.'

Fleur had executed a plan. She'd taken control of a situation for the first time in her young life. She'd used her stashed-away 'insurance money' for her getaway, the one useful thing she'd learned from her mother. After reading the letters from Josie McGreal, she knew she had to act.

It was easy collecting an assortment of pills; they were left freely about the place, and she waited until Frankie and Rasta Dave were away for the full day, somewhere unpronounceable out of town, where they were looking to buy a bar.

After waving the lads off, with her insides feeling like jelly, she had got to work crushing up the tablets. Spike downed his coffee with a very generous Spanish brandy: Soberano, a 5-year-old, the best. He always started drinking early when Frankie was away. It hadn't taken long for her cocktail of crushed pills to take effect.

Carefully stepping over Spike, slumped outside her dressing room, she had taken a taxi from the shopping plaza where they always parked up. The first outbound plane with available seats was going to London, but that didn't matter; she would easily catch a train back to Bristol. Her stomach twitched like plucked strings, but a pina colada and some airport shopping helped her settle. Exiting via the airport gift shop, she boarded the Ryanair flight with premium vodka for Zane and Millie, some Chanel No 5 for Anne, and a teddy for

River. She was on her way home, hardly daring to believe it had been so easy.

But life was about to play one of its spiteful tricks. As her plane took to the air, her lifelong friend and partner in crime, Anne Grimes, was waiting at baggage collection on the other side of Malaga airport, clutching a scrunched piece of paper. 'The Villa Florentina.' Wearing her cut-off jeans and a determined look on her face, she was heading out to find Fleur.

36

#Banksy: 'Season's Greetings'

The dense London traffic was starting to irritate Fleur, waiting at the back of a long taxi queue in drizzly rain that soaked through her unseasonal clothes. She was trying to work out how it took longer to get from London to Bristol than it had taken to travel from Spain. It didn't make sense.

Finally, the cab turned the corner into the grey car park behind the drab Youth Alive block. She couldn't wait to see Anne's face when she shared her earth-shattering news. But something was wrong. People were shouting at each other outside their flat.

'I want to know where Sasha is. What have you done with her?'

'You are crazy. Loco. You are accusing *me* of something?' Marta, with her hawk nose, was fronting up to Brian the Wanker.

'I know you're up to something, Marta. I've got hard evidence.'

What was going on? Nothing ever happened at their place, and nobody ever challenged the spiteful Marta. You got kicked out if you did.

The air stilled as the sparring partners gawped at bronzed Fleur Drake in her soggy summer dress, teetering on silver high-heeled shoes, revealing perfectly manicured toenails. Her redundant sunglasses still perched on her head gave her the air of an out-of-work film star gracing her humble roots. BTW stepped aside to let her pass, before the ruby-haired Marta stormed off, casting a scowl at Fleur in her new designer clothes.

'Decided to come back then?' She ignored him but let him carry her case upstairs.

'Thought you'd gone the same way as the other girls.'

She cast him a sideward glance. 'I haven't got the faintest idea what you're talking about, Brian, and guess what? I don't give a flying fuck.' She guessed he'd been smoking his weed.

Now he was prattling on about someone called Sasha. '… gone missing,' like she cared. She couldn't remember the girl. She fumbled to open the door, her frozen hands shaking, excited at the reception she would get when Anne saw her and she revealed what she knew. But Brian wouldn't shut up.

'Piss off, Brian.'

Undeterred, he followed her in. She looked around, her heart sinking as she realised the flat was empty. Silent. She'd come all this way and now had to wait a bit longer. Anne would be at the Food Bank or somewhere else doing her usual good things. She picked up a new calendar left on Anne's bed. A reduced-price Banksy calendar with a boy playing in snow on the front cover. However, it was obvious that the snow was ash from a burning bin. It made her wince. She'd never understand how Anne loved the dreary street artist so much. She'd been pleased to leave all that messy graffiti behind.

Brian the Wanker was now in her face, still prattling on about girls going missing. Just what was he on? She looked about for a drink. It would be cocktail time at Frankie's. God, why didn't Anne keep any drinks in the flat? What was she, a child? Tempted to open the premium vodka, she decided to save it for later, for her Welcome Home celebrations with Millie.

Her eye caught a framed photo of a girl who looked very much like Anne. What was going on? Her heart contracted as a wave of jealousy swept over her. Who was the girl in the photograph taking pride of place on their dressing table?

'It's Katherine,' said Brian, over her shoulder. She picked up a purple leather jacket arranged across Anne's bed. 'That was Katherine's, too.'

Had someone else moved into their flat? She felt angry. This wasn't the homecoming she'd expected. And Brian was still going on about Marta and someone called Sasha.

'Shut the fuck up,' she spat at him. It worked. He stopped midsentence as if she'd slapped him across the face. But he held the winning card.

'I don't suppose you want to know about Anne going away then?'

'What do you mean, Anne's gone away?'

'Look around you, Fleur. Isn't it obvious nobody slept here last night? Saw her leaving with her backpack. I'm telling you strange things are going on around here, and Marta and McGreal have something to do with it.'

'McGreal? ... But Frankie's in Spain?'

'No, he's not, he's here doing deals with Marta.'

'You must mean Twinnie McGreal. What's he been doing around here?'

'McGreal and Marta have been doing deals. I think she grooms girls for him before moving them on. They supply them for parties and stuff, and this older geezer drives them around in a limo.'

But Fleur wasn't listening.

'I tried to warn Anne,' Brian said, gaining speed. 'She was with me when we saw Marta and McGreal together.'

'Brian, listen to me. Twinnie McGreal is living in Canterbury. Everybody knows that. He can't travel around the country willy-nilly; he's still on licence.'

She scrutinised BTW closely; he was becoming increasingly agitated.

'And Anne's been seeing some copper, been watching our flats, he has. Filth.' Followed by his obligatory glob of spit. She'd been prepared to hear him out until that point. But now he'd blown it. Anne would never go out with a copper.

'Have you been on the draw, Brian?' She walked him backward towards the front door. He sounded crazed, delusional; she'd seen it before with some of Frankie's mates who overdid the cannabis.

'They're watching our flats, probably out there now.' He advised her to draw the blinds.

'Look, Brian, I need to see my sister and my nephew, but I'm around if you need help.' He looked at her, astonished, not used to this caring side of Fleur. Off his guard, she gave him a final push out of the door. 'And Brian, stay off the weed for a bit?'

She'd forgotten how far it was to Millie's house. Her sandals were soaked through by the time she got there. But she couldn't help running up Millie's path strewn with cigarette ends in the way hers was strewn with pine needles. Millie was upstairs with River. She peeked playfully around the bedroom door.

'Yoo hoo, guess who?!' But Millie carried on with her nappy changing. 'Millie, it's me, I'm back!' Her sister ignored her. 'Anne?' the toddler shouted, excited, pulling himself up.

She couldn't believe what she was hearing. Had Anne been hanging around with her sister and her nephew? Then a scruffy dog started to growl at her as she tried to pick River up. How come everything had changed?

'Can't keep them two apart.' Millie pushed the growling dog aside with her foot. They all tumbled downstairs, and Millie opened a new pack of Zane's lagers. Everything appeared to be the same, yet to Fleur, it felt like the earth had shifted on its axis. You'd think she'd never been away, the reception she was getting. She got down on the floor, trying to win River over, but he played with his battered fire truck, which was making a terrible din. She tried to tempt him with the expensive teddy she'd bought for him, which the scruffy dog seemed to appreciate more, in an amorous way.

'So, Anne's been coming around here then?'

'Yeah, she's been worried sick about you, just fuckin' off, nobody knowin' where you were. Out of 'er mind with worry she was, especially when she knew you were with Frankie McGreal.' Millie's voice was getting higher and tinnier as she spoke, but Fleur could only feel the sting of jealousy that Anne and her sister had been hanging out together. And Millie hadn't even commented on her lovely new clothes or her glowing suntan. Things weren't at all how she'd imagined they would be. But much worse was in store to spoil her prodigal homecoming.

'Did you 'ear about the dead girl, Grace?' Millie refreshed their lagers before telling her about Grace's overdose and how she and Anne had identified her in the mortuary. Fleur couldn't take it all in. Grace was dead? Did Frankie know about this? Had he been keeping it from her? Now, even Grace had let her down.

'Looked like she was carved out of stone, she did. So peaceful.'

'But why did they ask you to identify her? You didn't know her?'

'Cos we fuckin' well thought it was *you*. She was wearin' your fuckin' coat.'

That made them both cry. Millie was crying genuine tears for Grace, for what they'd all been through. Fleur cried because everything had changed so much. Millie went to put her arm around her sister, but Fleur pulled away from stale armpits.

'She 'adn't suffered any pain ...' Millie was trying to think of comforting things to say, but her efforts were lost on Fleur, now realising she wouldn't get the homecoming party she'd expected.

'I put it all down to Frankie McGreal,' Millie admonished, lighting another cigarette. 'Tellin' 'er she wouldn't be goin' out to Spain.'

'What do you mean? We're just not ready for the girls yet. Grace would definitely have been coming, she is … was … my mate, and Frankie would do whatever I asked him to.'

'Then why 'aven't you been in touch with us? I bet 'e's taken your phone off ya. Wake up, Fleur, it's like 'e's 'oldin' you prisoner out there.' There was more than a sting of truth in her sister's words, which hurt. But she wasn't having her sister, well, her half-sister actually, talking about her Frankie like that.

'Comin' 'ere in yer posh shoes and fancy clothes.' So that was it. Her sister was jealous. Nobody understood what they had between them. They were all jealous that she'd found love and escaped all this shit.

Things were heating up. 'Seems like Anne's got her foot in the door here anyway, like you didn't even bother to miss me. Especially River.' Fleur's throat tugged at her words. 'You always used to think Anne was a stuck-up little cow.'

'You're the only cow 'round 'ere, Fleur, and a selfish cow at that,' Millie spat.

'Selfish cow, selfish cow,' repeated River. Then a full-scale row broke out, and as usual, all the old stuff was dredged up. Life hadn't turned out as they'd hoped. Millie wanted Zane there to help her deal with everything. Fleur wanted to be back with Frankie, but she needed to speak to Anne first. Then she would go back to Spain and never return. Too much had changed to keep her in Bristol. She'd only come back to put things right. All this way for, well, nothing frankly. Her sister wasn't pleased to see her; River didn't want her; he wouldn't even look at his new teddy, which the dog was now trying to shag. And Anne was nowhere to be found. Another can of lager and any lingering inhibitions were sent flying.

'You shouldn't smoke around children, Millie, it's not good for River.'

'Like you're a fuckin' authority on bringin' up children ...' Millie closed the door so River wouldn't hear. She had a few things to say to her half-sister and, fuelled with the tingle of excitement that she was in the right, she was about to put her cow of a younger sister back in her place once and for all.

'Been worried sick about you, that girl 'as. Thought you were both goin' to lose the flat, then where would she be?'

'What do you mean, where would *she* be?'

'She's been lookin' everywhere for you Fleur, while you've been livin' the 'igh life with shithead.'

'Don't call him that. I love him and he loves me.'

'You wouldn't know love if it shat on you from above, not like me and Zane. Look at the 'ome we've made.' Candy floss hair tossed free.

'And you wouldn't believe 'ow supportive 'e was when I 'ad to go and identify a dead girl we thought might be YOU.'

That hurt. Fleur wasn't taking that lying down. 'Don't know what you're all stressing about. Zane knew I'd been seeing Frankie McGreal, you all did.'

'Yeah, and that's why we were all worried, 'angin' around with a drug dealer.'

Reverting to throwing whatever ammunition she had to hand, Fleur should have thought twice before launching her gift-wrapped hand grenade. 'You think you've got it so good, well you should know that Zane's been dickin' Grace for years behind your back.'

Millie slapped her sister so hard that her hand hurt. She pushed Fleur to the door and, for once, closed it firmly. She turned up the TV so River wouldn't hear her sobbing in the kitchen. And worst of all, they were all out of beers; her selfish half-sister had drunk them all.

She paced the kitchen, her mind working overtime. Zane had been so upset at Grace's death. Deep down, she knew there was something between them; she'd known it for some time, kept it buried until Fleur turned up and spoiled everything. Like she always did.

'Fuck off you little slut,' Millie's final words to Fleur, rebounded around the quiet, damp road. But it wasn't her own words she was hearing, it was their mum's.

With her face stinging and tears blurring her path, Fleur felt lost, like a child whose friends hadn't turned up for her party. It wasn't supposed to be like this. She was rocked by the news of Grace's death. Were they to blame for leaving so quickly?

Everyone knew how much those girls wanted a way out; maybe Grace would still be alive if she'd just paid more attention to what was going on. Hadn't been such a self-centred airhead - Frankie's pet name for her.

She sobbed out loud. Why did she always have to spoil things? She regretted telling Millie about Zane; after all, they'd been together for years. Why did she do those things - break everything good, and where was Anne? She sat shivering on the curved bench on College Green in the Cathedral grounds, somewhere she and Anne always used to make for.

Shivering in her unsuitable clothing, she ran through the possible places Anne could be in the small, claustrophobic world in which she existed. The church was ruled out as Anne never worked Saturdays. But there was one place she hadn't tried. An icicle tickled her spine. But Fleur, not attuned to her internal warning system, put it down to the cold and left the damp, curved bench for Vivian's house.

37

#Banksy: 'Better Out than In'

The bald, bronzed headed taxi driver seemed eager to recommend his cousin Jorge's hotel close to Marbella Marina.

'Okay, the Hotel Summer Breeze it is then,' and in the gentlest of breezes, they left the bustling airport behind them. The aroma of grilled fish followed the car as it sped through a tangle of back streets. Anne was pleased with the small hotel situated just off the promenade, which was sun-faded but inviting with abundant red geraniums in aqua blue pots.

After unpacking, she took her complimentary orange juice out to the pool and thought about Mrs. B opening up the church, her skin tingling at the betrayal of the adults left behind. First, Mrs. B and Reverend Paul, then Vivian and her spiteful letter. Was there nobody to trust? But maybe she shouldn't have said those awful things to Mrs. B. Maybe some things weren't better out than in.

A bright blue damselfly hovered at the pool edge, its beady eyes assessing her before it dipped lazily into the water. She longed to take a swim but hadn't owned a costume since her first children's home. Sipping her juice, she recalled her journey out to Spain. She still couldn't believe how easy it had been, making her wonder why people would vote to lose such freedoms. It felt unfair that others might be closing down a world she had hardly got to enjoy. Although even to the point she boarded the plane, she was certain she would be turned back.

But she had made it, and along the way, she'd learned lots of new things; not least that a timetable is a timetable whether you're taking the bus, train, or plane. It was quite a revelation. Closing her eyes, she felt the sun warm on her skin. She'd never done anything so grown-up. But now, with no idea what to do next, she started to make a list. Firstly, find Villa Florentina and see if I can spot Fleur. Secondly, … she thought hard, but nothing came to mind. If Fleur was being held against her will, how would she free her and get them both home safely?

Wearing her new sunglasses, found at the Currency Exchange Bureau, she set off to find the Villa Florentina. She clutched her simple map drawn by Jorge, Hotel Summer Breeze's attentive concierge, who'd stutteringly advised: 'Not far to walk. About twenty minutes.' Satisfied that she'd left enough of a trail, in case she ran into trouble, she headed away from the town, to the detached houses lining the outskirts of the main resort like a string of expensive pearls.

The villa, situated just off the main road, was older than she'd imagined. It was traditionally built, like the nicer houses featured on 'A Place in the Sun'. It radiated soft golden rays in the afternoon light, and all around was quiet, making it hard to imagine Fleur living there.

She occupied a seat in a café just along from the villa, attracted by the strong smell of coffee lingering in the air. Opposite, the villa's heavy wrought iron gates displayed a picture of a guard dog. They were shut tight, and she dared to stray near as the late afternoon shadows grew longer and softer. But beyond, there was no sign of life. Tempted to rifle through the ornate mailbox, she stalled in case of hidden cameras. For now, she was content enough to have found her bearings and resolved to return early next morning.

'I don't suppose you have a lost property box, Jorge? I've forgotten to bring my swimming costume.' The beaming concierge disappeared into a back room, returning with a basket of swimwear, inflatables, and towels.

'Gracias.' A new word she'd picked up in the café.

The lights softly bounced about the still pool, holding the last of the evening warmth. This was a million miles away from the crowded council swimming baths of her childhood.

Thank you, Pool. She'd made a new friend.

'Bye, Anna,' Jorge called as she left the following morning.

'I'm off to the Villa Florentina again, see you later,' she refreshed her breadcrumb trail. He nodded, officious, busily sorting through piles of papers under a creaking fan.

Dusting away crispy overnight pine needles, she settled back at her favourite table with fresh coffee and a newspaper with headlines she didn't understand. David Cameron's shiny face glared out from the front page. Brexit - again. 'Feckin' tosser,' she smiled at the memory of Mr. Murphy's words, feeling a connection that he must also have been a 'remainer'. Sniffing her strong coffee before each sip, she felt like someone well-travelled; 'European'. And the print of Van Gogh's Sunflowers hanging on the white-washed wall (the same as the one she'd hung by Fleur's bed) made the world feel a small place. Mr. Murphy was right, 'feck Brexit.'

She liked this place where people strolled past, chatting loudly on their mobile phones, calling fondly to each other. Where kittens tumbled and chased something jumping in the long, parched grass adjacent to the café.

Just before lunchtime, a car with blacked-out windows turned into the drive and stalled, waiting for the gates of the Villa Florentina to open. The driver's window was rolled down. Rasta Dave was at the wheel. Her heart jumped. So, they were here. She listened hard for barking dogs, but thankfully heard nothing. Her heart raced. It was about to start.

She left the money for her coffee plus a tip in the jar on the counter as she'd seen others do, and cautiously crossed the dusty road, releasing a wonderful scent of pine that reminded her of Sasha with her cleaning bucket. She froze as the still air was sullied with the noise of doors slamming and loud shouting, making her take cover in some scratchy bushes. She didn't like what she was hearing. The shouting was turning nasty. Was Fleur in there amongst that racket?

She edged closer for a better view but couldn't see anything beyond the bushes and exotic palms in the villa's garden. Gingerly, she made her way to the rear of the property and jumped back at the approach of Rasta Dave, still wearing his cap with the pin badges, returning after parking the car, his fists clenched as if ready for a fight.

Climbing onto the boundary wall, she cursed at the impracticality of her cut-down jeans, scraping her knees on the brickwork. But it was worth it for the improved view through the luscious planting, across to the shaded patio windows where a man with a sun-bronzed, shaved head and goatee beard was making all the noise. Frankie McGreal. And he appeared to be repeatedly punching a man who was rolling on the floor. What was going on?

She remembered the punch in the face from Rudi and felt the pain of the man. Should she call the police? But she didn't know the number. Besides, it would blow her cover. Where was Fleur in the middle of all this? Surely everyone in the house could hear what was going on. Maybe she was used to keeping out of the way, or worse still, locked up somewhere.

Then she had a new thought; this could be the perfect time to get into the house, to act while everyone was distracted by the fight. She said a quick prayer and knew that at least Jorge knew where she was, if she didn't make it out of there.

Balanced on the wall, she circumnavigated the rear of the house, slowly crawling toward a brick utility room where she would get a better view of the back of the house. She straddled across to an adjoining wall butted against the villa's thickly plastered outer walls, and reached up to its brick toppers to steady her balance. But the weathered brick came loose, causing her to fall back, grabbing out at the beautiful purple trailing plant tumbling down from a balcony above. Bougainvillea, the ultimate burglar deterrent. Its spiked thorns tore open the skin on her palms. 'Shit, shit, shit,' she cursed, as she let go of the tumbling tendrils, leaving her to fall awkwardly, several feet to the ground with a soft thud.

A manicured grass border cushioned her fall. She lay frozen with fear. All stayed quiet except the tick-tick of the sprinkler system creating small rainbows all around her. Inelegantly, she had made it into the inner, lawned perimeter of the house. She leaned back against the shadowed external wall to regain her composure under the shade of towering cypress trees.

Crawling along below window height, she reached the small utility room and slowly pulled herself up to look through the patio doors. The bouncing glare from the sun made it difficult to make things out. A movement from inside startled her, before she screamed out loud at the face of someone staring back at her from within. The door slid open, and a pair of strong arms grabbed her by the throat before she could turn and run.

Her eyes adjusted to the dark interior, and she quickly scoured the room for any sign of Fleur. But there was nothing. She'd blown it.

'Let her go, you fuckin' moron before you strangle her …'

'Well, I don't know who she is. She could be staking us out.'

'Look at her, does she look like the filth?' Silence.

She wished the stars would clear so she could get her vision back and focus on what was going on.

'So, who the fuck is she, Frankie?' asked Rasta Dave. 'Wait, I know her. She was with some crazy woman at the Blind Fox. The one who was all over Steve.' He peered at her closely, as if she were an alien species. 'What's she doing here?'

'No idea. But what's more worrying is how she found us. The men looked at each other, then back at her, obviously thrown by her arrival. Frankie McGreal grabbed her by the shoulders and stared hard in her face. As if searching for clues.

'Lookin' for your mate love? Well, you're too fuckin' late.'

She sensed his bile, felt his spit on her cheek, but was too afraid to turn away from his flinty eyes. She tensed. Why was she too late? What had they done with Fleur?

'You on your own?' She nodded. He pushed her down into a hard chair, staying so close to her face that she saw the stubble on his chin and smelled the alcohol on his breath. She expected him to hit her and braced herself for the pain of it. Instead, he kept looking deep into her eyes, like some deranged caged animal. Then he laughed. He laughed until tears streamed down his face.

'You all right, Frankie mate?' A third man entered the room, ready to help out if needed. But Frankie kept on laughing, and she watched disgusted as the third man dragged a floppy body across the floor towards a pantry. A cold room for storing perishables: she knew this from her Anne of Green Gables book.

Frankie McGreal paced the room. He looked unhinged.

'What'll I do about him?' The third man asked.

'Let him stew for a bit, Spike, then deliver him back to his lot. That's what he gets for trying to back out of a deal.'

She avoided all eye contact, not wanting to know what was going on. Under her bowed head, she got a glimpse of Frankie

McGreal's profile and was struck by the likeness between him and Twinnie. But close up, she could see that Frankie had softer features, large grey-green eyes, and good skin accentuated by his tanned, shaved head. She could see what Fleur saw in him. He turned back toward her as if he were reading her thoughts.

'Soft cow – Fleur's gone home looking for YOU.' Inscrutable, he seemed to like shouting in people's faces. His demonic laughing started once again until he held his sides against the splitting pain. Spike was also now laughing, at her expense, she suspected. What were they saying? Fleur had gone home? By herself?

'Seems she'd rather be home with you than living it up here with me. You've always been my competition, Anne Grimes, or is it Kylie Mathews?' She shrank back into herself. How come he knew so much about her? Just how much had Fleur shared with him? If he knew about her part in the house fire, then she was dead meat.

'Who is she?' asked Dave.

'Some snotty little kid who lived on our floor at the Mount Pleasant flats. Mad cow of a mother, always sniffing around our Shayne, wouldn't leave him alone.' Anne stilled at the mention of Shayne McGreal, keeping her eyes lowered.

'Fleur never stopped talking about you; Anne this and Anne that … always wondering what you were up to.'

'She'll come back once she knows we've got her,' Spike grabbed her roughly by the arm. He pushed her roughly up the stairs and held open the door of Fleur's dressing room.

'Your new accommodation, make the most of it.' He locked the door firmly.

'Don't let this one escape, if that's not too much to ask, shithead,' Frankie shouted up the stairs to Spike, whose face was still swollen from the pasting he'd received after Fleur had left. He'd been stupid, he knew. But he would keep a closer watch this time.

The sheer luxury of the place was mind-blowing. Fleur had certainly been treated to the best of things. Why would she choose to leave all this behind? The temptation to steal something was strong; maybe some of those luxurious bath products. But Spike had taken her backpack. She smarted at the thought she'd been so close to finding Fleur. She felt cheated. All this way and she was none the wiser. Washing away the dried blood from her fall, the reddened water swirled disturbingly.

She browsed through some cards stacked on a bedside table: Valentine cards. The message inside Frankie McGreal's was spine-tinglingly tender, making her feel she was intruding. She placed it back carefully. Two things surprised her. Firstly, that Fleur had been with Frankie for almost a year, and secondly, something in his eyes earlier had squeezed at her heart. He genuinely seemed to be missing Fleur. Could he really love her? His Valentine message suggested as much, and he'd certainly been treating her to a life of luxury in this most opulent of prisons. She held her head in her hands. Had she got it all badly wrong?

38

#Banksy: 'Cardinal Sin'

'Dave, I've booked you on the 6 pm Eurostar.' Frankie dealt the blow quickly. 'We all know you haven't got the stomach for the ferry,' stifling a smirk. Dave Ocasio hated Frankie mocking his seasickness, along with his many other weaknesses. He had no option but to take the train. And if Fleur wasn't so amenable to returning to Spain with him, at least he'd have a car and a boot.

'What about her upstairs?'

'Leave her to me. Call it collateral damage.'

Rasta Dave remained petulant. He didn't want to go back to the UK with all the dangers it presented, and all because of that stupid cow. He never knew what Frankie saw in Fleur, buying her all that stuff. He'd been Frankie's mate as long as he could remember, covered up some real shit for him, and this was how he got repaid. Still, what Frankie wanted, Frankie got. Shame it wasn't him.

He put on his jacket before leaving.

'And don't be so obvious with those stupid badges. The police will be all over them after the rave.'

That hurt the most. He thought Frankie liked his look; his prize badges from when they saw reggae bands together all those years ago. The time he knew he was falling in love with

Frankie McGreal. Though he never made his move, it was enough just to watch him sleep in the cheap rooms they shared back then. But Ali Kumar was on to him. That's why he'd tipped off that bent copper Bob Lyons about the rave and got Ali banged up. He didn't want him in Spain with them spoiling things. But that was before he had to return to Bristol; he'd have to watch his back.

He set off early while the villa was still sleepy, loaded his Pet Shop Boy CDs – another of his guilty secrets and started to think of his game plan. He had a rough idea where Fleur and Anne lived from Frankie's directions, but first, he would make things work in his favour for once and spend some time in Bristol's low-key gay bars. After all, he'd lived like a monk since they'd moved to Spain.

The journey was long but uneventful, and after a shower, he walked into The Follies nightclub.

'Well, if it's not Julio Iglesias!'

'Fuck off, Simon, and get me a Black Russian.' He liked Simon, the straight-talking manager. He took no messing; he was a bit like Frankie in that respect, but was more amenable to his advances.

All partied out, it was time to find Fleur. Tired and irritable, he waited outside the Youth Alive flats, but it didn't look like anyone was home. He made his way slowly to the address of her older sister, who lived on his old housing estate, taking in everything around him. The slit-eyed youths and the creeping sense of decay. He had grown up close by, when it hadn't been easy concealing his sexuality, constantly getting into fights. Then he hooked up with Frankie and did things he never thought he was capable of, desperate to prove his manliness.

Outside Millie's house, he could hear an almighty row kicking off.

'Fuck off, you little slut,' before the front door slammed behind Fleur.

It hadn't taken Fleur long to find her feet. He couldn't believe his luck. This was going to be easier than he thought. The imperious Fleur stormed out, turned, and put two fingers up to her sister's house. Proud little bitch with her head held high, in that way he hated. Like she was better than the rest of them. Dressed like she was off to the beach, what was she thinking?

His trip was proving to be easier than he'd thought. But why was the older sister calling Fleur a little slut? Had she been seeing other blokes? He needed to know more. In the warmth of his car, he followed her discreetly. It would be great to report back to Frankie that she was disloyal; that she'd been seeing someone else. That would be the end of Fleur Drake. Frankie hated betrayal above everything else, especially when somebody knew so much about his plans. Maybe this would make him see reason. It might even be enough for Frankie to ask him to finish her off. And left to his own devices, he probably would.

39

#Banksy: 'Rats with Sunglasses'

'The boss asked if you want some magazines to read?' Spike, in his Nike tracksuit, warily placed a basket inside her bedroom. Vogue, Red, Harper's Bazaar; expensive. Anne chose Country Life; the landscape and ponies reminded her of another citadel, her mother's house in Canterbury.

She made her way to the pool under Spike's attentive watch behind his reflective Ray-Ban sunglasses, looking for possible escape routes as she had no doubt Fleur would have done before her. She picked a fresh lemon from an overhanging branch, dug a trench with her nail, and breathed in the zesty aroma. The juice trickled down her wrist, the tingling on her tongue keeping her senses sharp. Occupying a sun lounger close to the pool's edge, she trailed her hands in the water, creating concentric circles that seemed to reflect her predicament. What did they plan to do with her? Drown her in the pool? Would they take her somewhere and shoot her? Where would they bury her body? She imagined the scraping of a spade through pine-scented soil, before falling into a restless sleep.

Later that evening, a noise outside her door disturbed her. Spike's Adidas sliders were slapping on the tiles. She ran to wedge a chair under the doorknob. A trick that had worked for her in the past.

Oh God, this is it, they're going to finish me off.

'Frankie wants to know if you'd like to have dinner with him.'

Thrown, she breathed deeply before accepting the invitation. Wearing a loose-fitting dress from Fleur's extensive wardrobe and some sparkly flip-flops, she ventured downstairs to face whatever lay ahead.

Frankie McGreal, sporting ubiquitous Ray-Bans, whistled as she entered the plush dining room adorned with its tasteful furnishings. She looked around her. 'You like it? I'm trying to make a good home for us, for me and Fleur. We've had fun picking up nice things.' Anne doubted Fleur had much to do with choosing what she could see around her. It was far too sophisticated, like something from the lemon-tinged homes in the magazines she'd been browsing earlier.

'I asked the chef to knock up some paella, thought you might like a taste of Spain.'

She'd never tasted anything like it, and Frankie laughed as she accepted a second helping, her stomach growling. She hadn't eaten anything substantial for days.

'Can't understand why she's gone off. I'm hoping you might be able to help me with that one. His eyes were fierce, demanding of explanations. She'd been hoping for the same thing from him and had nothing new to offer, other than to suggest that maybe Fleur wasn't happy being cooped up, held prisoner in this gilded cage.

'Maybe she wanted a bit more freedom, it's a bit lonely here if you're out most of the time. Has she got any friends here?'

'No, but the girls are coming out soon. I'm closing a deal on a nightclub. Fleur knew all that; she just had to wait a bit longer - seemed okay with it.' They finished a delicious lemon tarte, and took their drinks outside to the terrace, Anne keeping the news of Grace to herself. She hadn't known what to expect when setting off for Spain, but she certainly hadn't expected this.

'Fuckin' miss her like crazy, the place isn't the same without her.'

She sat back and they laughed at Fleur's 'shenanigans' as he called them. 'I told her all along; I'm taking care of you. Wanted to protect her from herself ... until she was eighteen. Then she'd get her own set of keys and could do what she liked.'

'Why eighteen?'

'Well, call me old-fashioned, but it's a big birthday, always was in our family.'

'But Fleur was eighteen last week ...'

He paused from swirling his brandy. 'Why didn't she tell me? We'd have had one hell of a party.'

'Maybe she didn't want to be freed ...'

'So why would she run away?' They both quietened to their thoughts, the silence broken only by the ceiling fan and the odd cicada clicks from the woods. The hoot of an owl felt ominous, like a warning not to get too comfortable in the company of this notorious gangster. A shiver ran down her spine.

'Someone walk over your grave?' She averted her eyes, not wanting to think about graves.

'Come on, let's finish these off inside.'

He sat on the lavish settee opposite her, by a shelf of photographs of the loving couple in polished frames. 'Spike says she was going through my things, and my mum's letters seemed to spook her.'

'Your mum's still alive?'

'Shit, Anne, she's only in her fifties. Granted, she's had a bloody hard life, but now she's ready to follow us out here.'

'She's coming out to Spain?'

'Yeah, one of the main reasons we set up here. I like to ... well, look after her. Need to get her out before all this Brexit shit hits the fan. Spoil her a bit after the crap life she's had.'

Anne thought how lovely it must be to be spoilt by someone, for someone to want to care for you. Why, oh why would Fleur turn her back on all this? 'Can I see the letters?'

He sat in the background, taking calls on his phone while she sorted through the large manila envelope containing Josie

McGreal's letters. Careful, rounded words; someone who took pride in her writing, not a bit like she imagined from what she remembered of the ramshackle Mount Pleasant flat.

'Always liked to write, my mum. A bit old-fashioned like that, she loves reading too. Got her English O-level at night school.'

Anne didn't know what was hardest to believe, that she was sitting on a bed beside Frankie McGreal or that his mum had gone to night school. She systematically scanned some of the letters but could sense that Frankie was growing impatient.

'Fuck this. Spike, stick them all on the fire - along with all that legal stuff.' The blood drained from her head. If he burned the letters, she'd never know why Fleur had left. They returned downstairs, where Spike was carrying a basket of logs for the fire. Her heart was beating fast; she needed to read those letters. Perched awkwardly on a small leather fireside stool, she pretended to flick through a local newspaper, watching the letters curl and burn out of the corner of her eye.

'Could I have a coffee refill, please, Frankie?'

'What did your last slave die of?' he chided before going to make fresh coffee. Spike was surfing through the TV channels, and with her pulse pounding in her ears, she reached over to try to rescue the last letters from the pile.

'What the fuck are you doing?' Frankie bellowed, making her freeze, trying quickly to think of an explanation, but relief flooded as she saw he was talking to Spike. 'Turn that fucking thing off, we're going to listen to music.' She sat in despair as the last of the letters went up in flames.

'Well, you know her best. What made her run?'

She had nothing to offer. 'Maybe it was knowing your mum was coming out here? Fleur was never big on mums.' He scrutinised her with one eye scrunched, then returned to his phone messages, saying nothing for what felt like an eternity.

'Yeah, maybe you're right. Could never see her getting along with my mum. Too much alike,' he laughed quietly to himself in that sinister way that set her nerves tingling.

'Do you think Fleur might be in danger if anyone finds out she's back in Bristol?'

'Too fucking right. They're all after me and mine.'

'You're talking about Twinnie?' She didn't know how far to push this.

'Yeah, he's off the scale. Gone nuts.' He rolled something between cigarette papers. Deft fingers that meant business.

'Yeah, I've met him.'

He stopped, left eye scrunched once more. 'Didn't think he'd be in your social circle.'

'No, I met him in church.'

'Fuckin' hell, don't tell me he's seen the light,' head thrown back, his demented laugh filled the echoey room once more.

'It was at the Food Bank at St. Gabriel's church, where I volunteer. He's started up a group for ex-offenders.' Frankie laughed harder than ever, in a way that made her blood curdle. He looked capable of doing bad things when he laughed like that.

'He'll be recruiting. Getting people to do his dirty work for him. Gets on by intimidating people, does Twinnie. Always been the same.' He threw the end of his rolled joint into the embers of the fire.

'Remember when he worked at the butcher's and liked to threaten all the kids with the shit he brought home?' She avoided his eye contact. Could it have been Twinnie McGreal who defaced her front door? She prayed he didn't know where she lived.

'That was what made him go bad, working with all that blood and guts.' He stopped suddenly. 'I hope you don't think I'm into the new sort of crap Twinnie's into now?'

'Like what?'

'People trafficking,' he spat between puffs on his joint.

Hard, cold words tinged with disgust. 'They bring people over in lorries. Sometimes kids, then move them on. He works from a place in Canterbury. I thought he'd stay down there when he was released, but the little fucker seems to be setting something up in Bristol.' But she'd stopped listening.

'Where do they traffic people to?' Her thoughts turned to Sasha with her pretty features and long plaited hair.

'Anywhere people will pay for them. Twinnie's got Polish connections; he's been out there a couple of times. Even asked if I needed any help with girls for my parties,' he stopped short as if maybe he'd revealed too much about himself. But Anne was already making further connections between Twinnie McGreal and Marta and the red-striped holdall full of money.

She thought of BTW, who they all thought was paranoid with his concerns for the transient cleaning girls, certain he was onto something. Now it all made sense - the police surveillance around their property, Gabby McArdle's questioning about her accommodation. She thought of Fleur returning to their flat, walking into more danger than she could ever guess. She dared to look him directly in the eye: 'Frankie, I need to go back to make sure Fleur's safe. I could talk to her, persuade her to come back here. I think Twinnie knows where we live. Can I warn Fleur? Did she take her phone with her?'

'No. She didn't have one.' Curt. No attempt to explain why Fleur was prevented from having a phone. He held her stare, but she could see he was considering her suggestion.

'You fucking with me?'

'No. I can find out what spooked her, then persuade her to come back.'

His face was inscrutable, a knife-like edge to his steely eyes, reminding her of just who she was dealing with. She breathed deeply to steady her nerves before he started laughing again. The glint of a gold tooth reflected in the mirror opposite her. Frankie McGreal, Janus-like; two shaved heads laughing maniacally.

'You're striking a deal with *me*?' he whispered low, so close to her face that his breath brushed her cheek, making her back away. 'Well, I'd already decided you were going back. Especially if it means you can persuade that stubborn little cow to come back here. I can't see Dave persuading her any time soon; those two never got on.'

'You're going back then?' Spike asked later, with a hint of envy.

'Yeah, how about you? When will you next go back home?'

'No saying. Especially after the threats we were getting. We were all afraid of getting firebombed in the middle of the night.'

She thought of her sister's words about how her mum's place had once been firebombed. Another Canterbury link. Surely her mum couldn't be mixed up with the McGreals again? 'Don't bring all that shit down here,' she'd warned her, but she obviously had dodgy contacts keeping her in that luxurious lifestyle. Had she kept old friendships going? She thought of the Jacksons' fleet of lorries on the land at the back of her mother's house and the twins with their long strawberry-blonde hair. About the way twins run in families. Surely not?

Before she left, Frankie McGreal handed her a wallet stuffed with cash and a small gift-wrapped parcel. 'I bought this for Fleur.' He handed over the present. 'I was going to give it to her on her eighteenth birthday, along with her key.' He looked sheepish. 'The dosh will cover your flight and give something small to your Food Bank. The rest can get Fleur back here. Want me to call you a cab?'

'No, it's all right, thanks.' She wanted to get out before he changed his mind.

He opened the front door to a pulse of blue flashing lights. There were two vehicles: a local police car with a Guardia police officer standing aside, waiting for a younger man to exit his hired car. She looked more closely.

'James?'

'Buenas Noches, Officer, would you like to come in?' Frankie offered politely, while the Guardia officer looked on, confused. James confirmed that Anne was the person he was looking for, the one he'd presumed was in great danger. The Guardia returned to his flashing car, cursing the stupid English and something about Brexit under his breath.

Turning on her heels, she started walking towards the town.

'Anne, wait, I've come to help you find Fleur.'

'She's gone home, James. Back to see me,' she said, enjoying the confused expression on his face. She waved goodbye to Frankie McGreal. 'I'll get Fleur to call you as soon as possible.'

Her shoulders felt lighter. She'd escaped. With a spring in her step, she picked up her pace toward her hotel, ignoring James' pleas for her to get into his hired car. But, deep down, she was pleased that he'd travelled all this way to find her.

His car pulled up slightly ahead of her, and James walked toward her, looking cool in his short-sleeved Fred Perry shirt and pressed shorts. He brushed his hair back with his palms, as he did when agitated.

'Anne, get in.'

She lifted her eyebrows.

'Okay, *please* get in, we need to talk.' She acquiesced. Partly because she'd seen that determined look before, and also because it was difficult walking on the dusty, uneven path in flip-flops.

He followed her directions to the hotel.

'At least let me buy you a drink and explain why I had to sever our …'

'Hola, Anna,' Jorge called over, relaxed now that his missing guest had returned. She had found herself a boyfriend. They took their drinks out to a table by the gently lit pool.

Hello Pool, I made it back after all ...

'So, how did you find out where I was?'

'Zane gave me the address. He was very cut up about Grace, and really worried about you leaving for Spain. He ... sort of hinted there was history between you and the McGreals.' He looked at her sideways, as if trying to understand her past and the company she kept. But he'd bide his time; Anne was already reacting like a coiled snake ready to strike at the least thing.

'Zane photographed the address of the Villa Florentina on his phone.' James rushed on. 'Quite clever really.'

'What, for a loser like Zane?' He looked taken aback.

Quietened, they sipped their drinks before her mood smoothed and she opened up about her time in the villa; about how she was starting to feel that Fleur might actually be happy with Frankie McGreal.

But he'd long stopped listening to her. In the pale moonlight shimmering on the pool, his thoughts reverted to their first complicated kiss at the rave and to the time he'd comforted her after Grace's death. He looked deep into her eyes, indigo under the pool lights, at the new freckles scattered across her nose and her perfectly bow-shaped lips. And, once again, she surprised him by making the first move and kissing him softly. He cupped her face in the palms of his hands and returned her kisses. She tasted of salt and lemons.

The night was so warm they pushed back the bed sheets and opened the window for air, filling the room with the scent of the pine trees below and the strumming of a folk song from a neighbouring bar. Haunting tunes of love and loss. They kissed and caressed each other's bodies deep into the night. For Anne, it was a delicious departure from the thrusting, lustful, uninvited pain of the past, now erased by this gentle experience. They were making love. For James, it was tender and wonderful.

'Thank you, Anne.'

Nobody had ever said anything so caring to her. She'd never imagined lovemaking could be like this. Responsive, consensual, and safe. They lay on top of the covers with their hands entwined. But the soft air was bruised by his phone ringing. The maggot in a sweet apple.

'It's work.' She nodded that he should take the call.

'They're about to move some young people we've been tracking. I need to get back tomorrow for a briefing.'

She was disappointed that the moment had to end, but deep down, she knew that they had to go back. She longed to know what Fleur had to tell her, what she hadn't been able to find out. So much had changed since the start of her journey.

A spare seat was available on James' flight. The passengers settled, and she read an extensive article on Banksy's global profile in the airline magazine while he snoozed. His latest artwork was in the Calais Jungle camp: 'The Son of a Migrant from Syria', where Steve Jobs was painted as a migrant with a sack over his shoulder and a computer in his hand. The irony made her smile, but the deeper messaging about the restricted movement of people reminded her of the urgency to get home.

After one last lingering kiss, James drove off, and she rushed up the stairs to their flat. BTW was there as usual, watching out of the first-floor side window. He wanted to talk, but she was too excited about seeing Fleur. He was prattling on about a new, even younger cleaning girl.

'Sorry, Brian, we'll talk later - I need to catch up with Fleur first.'

'She's not here.' It hit her like a sledgehammer.

'What d'you mean she's not here?' catching her breath.

'She was here, all suntanned and rude as ever …' He looked as if he'd been stung by a wasp. 'Hung around for a bit, but you know Fleur. Got fed up waiting and left.'

She got fed up and left?

Anne was beyond disappointed that she'd have to wait a bit longer, but BTW seemed reluctant to leave. Then she remembered the reason for James having to return so abruptly.

'By the way, you know my mate, James?'

He looked blank.

'The copper. Well, he'll be coming around here later. I told him about Sasha going missing, he's coming for more details, he thinks you're onto something.'

'I know I'm onto something, but I didn't want to share it with the pigs.'

'They're here to protect us, Brian,' surprising herself at how much her viewpoint had changed lately. But Brian's expression remained unconvinced. 'I've got to go, Brian. But speak to James; he's okay.'

She needed to get to Millie's. She just knew that Fleur would be with River.

Millie could hardly speak for crying. Fleur had been and gone, leaving a trail of misery behind her. She'd hardly been home two minutes, yet had caused maximum destruction in her sister's house. As she listened to Millie, she thought that sometimes she could hate Fleur and wondered just what Frankie McGreal saw in her. Maybe Fleur didn't deserve *him*.

She made hot, sweet drinks as Millie poured out her long-held suspicions about Zane and Grace. She'd confronted him about it, but of course, he'd denied everything. Anne felt a pang of guilt as she knew something had been going on between them.

'I've thrown him out.' She blew her nose into a soggy tissue. 'Shitty bastard.'

'Ditty dastard,' repeated River, playing with his truck. Anne put the TV on to distract him while they talked.

'Where will he go?'

'Probably got a string of 'em, all waitin' to take 'im in. Well, they're welcome to 'im. River and me will do fine on our own.' Then she sobbed harder as she told Anne something that nobody else knew, patting her stomach. River came and rubbed his head against his mum's knees as she stroked the toddler's hair and speculated about life on her own with two demanding children.

Millie slipped out 'for some fresh air,' whilst Anne played with River. Where could Fleur have gone? She was starting to feel panic rising for the girl who seemed to have alienated everyone around her. Fleur would regret spoiling things for Millie. She'd done this all her life; struck out at those she loved most, then suffered pain and anguish at the hurt she caused. But where was she? Brian said he would phone her if she returned, but her phone stayed silent.

Maybe she could get Fleur to put things right between Millie and Zane before she went back to Spain, say she'd got it wrong. Anything to get them back together. Those kids needed parents around them. But she had to find Fleur first.

'Did Aunty Fleur come to see you, River?' At first, the toddler ignored her. She rolled the child's fire truck backwards and forwards, and he fetched a ginger-haired, moth-eaten Barbie doll, which he ran over with the fire truck.

'That's Fleur's old doll, never could get rid of it. They were playing with it together last time she was 'ere,' said Millie, observing from the doorway.

'What, running it over violently?' They both smiled.

'Ginger troll.'

'What did you just say, River?'

He repeated it. And Anne knew exactly where Fleur had gone.

Fleur was having no luck at Vivian's house, shouting through the letter box and knocking until her knuckles hurt. A light was switched on upstairs. Standing back, she looked up at the windows, trying to work out what was going on. The house looked boarded up from the inside as if someone had papered over the windows. Everything about it was as weird as the ginger troll that lived there.

Empty and miserable, she started to walk away when the door creaked open behind her. Vivian looked even more hideous than she remembered. 'Come in. I'm expecting Anne at any minute.' The door closed behind her, and she had trouble adjusting her eyes in the dark, shadowy hall. There was a noxious fug in the air, a mixture of rotting food and something much worse, a tang that lingered at the back of her nose. She retched; it was enough to make anyone throw up.

'When will Anne be coming? ...' She followed Vivian along the shadowy hallway until she disappeared into the kitchen. Brushing past a tower of musty books standing guard like shrouded figures, something squishy under her foot made her yell out loud. With her heart pounding, she picked up something small and furry. She fingered the repulsive object, then screamed loudly at the remains of a dead mouse, small bones like needles falling through her fingers. 'I was just preparing something special for Annie. I expect she'll be around any minute.'

The door creaked open behind her. Struggling to turn around in the restricted space, she saw the shadow of something rushing towards her. A sharp blow to the back of her head. A spurt of blood across stacked cardboard boxes, as if abstractedly flicked with paint. Her last random memories before she slumped to the filthy floor.

Outside, stalking Dave Ocasio was bored waiting around in his car. Fleur had been in there for ages. Who lived in the dump of a house with weird papered-over windows anyway? He'd give her another half an hour. There was a 'special' on at The Club that he didn't want to miss. He twitched all over at the thought of it. He'd be back first thing, maybe catch her with someone else. Get the evidence he needed to convince Frankie she was nothing more than a little tramp.

Spruced up, he bounced down the lane to The Follies Club. '*Society gets the Kind of Vandalism it Deserves*', a slogan spray-painted on a nearby wall. He liked it. Clever. But tonight, there was only one thought on his mind. Simon. It was probably his last night, and he was out for some fun.

40

#Banksy: 'Wall and Piece'

At first, James didn't know what to make of Anne's neighbour, Brian, and his rambling concerns about missing girls. Their stilted conversation exposed his deep distrust of everyone in positions of authority. He suspected Brian was displaying symptoms of paranoia; he'd attended a police seminar on it once.

Looking around, there were, however, encouraging signs of organisation in Brian's life amidst stacks of printed photographs. His camera gear was neatly spread out on his small Ikea dining table alongside a single knife, fork, and spoon. Under the table stood stacks of old black and white DVDs. It appeared he looked after the things he appreciated, which was to his credit. The sparse room was painted white with just one poster, Banksy's 'One Nation Under CCTV'– the irony in the picture was not lost on James: a youth spray-painting anti-surveillance messages while being tracked by a camera.

'Can you talk me through what you think is happening around here, what made you start taking all these pictures?'

James was surprised by Brian's coherent account of why he was concerned about young girls vanishing. At first, he was reluctant to share names, dates, and sightings that he'd recorded systematically, but he soon loosened up. He seemed particularly concerned about a young girl called Sasha. James started taking notes. Brian showed him some of the video footage on his PC. There was a lot of it. Time was pressing, and with some coaxing, he agreed to forward it to James' work computer.

'I see you like collecting DVDs?' he said on his way out.

'Yeah, nobody wants them anymore, I pick them up for nothing, gives me something to do.'

'Are you into all that old stuff then?'

'It's our heritage, man. I used to study film and media...' Brian trailed off, as if remembering a different life.

Back in his car, James thought about how often the police come into contact with people with mental health problems. At first, it had surprised him how criminality seemed to befall the most vulnerable in society. He thought of Brian alone in his flat, clearly displaying signs of persecution. But then they did have the flats opposite under surveillance. Wouldn't that make anyone suspicious?

'Mad, bad or sad,' Bob Lyons had once told him. 'It's easy, lad, just stick to that.'

But James believed that people were much more complicated. For now, he'd remain open-minded about Brian and see what his video clips had to show. At least he'd gained his trust sufficient to forward his filming to him.

He shared his thoughts about Brian with DS Stewart at their afternoon meeting at the smart café with the river views. She was back from Canterbury for a few days but seemed tetchy and distant.

'Sounds like a very unreliable witness.' She curtly dismissed him and his thoughts about surveillance culture, draining her coffee. She stood up, ready to leave. He was confused. They hadn't been there long, and she was already getting ready to go. He hardly saw her these days.

'I hear you took some annual leave?'

'Yeah, Bob Lyons cleared it.'

'Clear it with me next time. I need to know your whereabouts.' She was in a foul mood.

'But you were in Canterbury, ma'am ...'

'No excuses, James, you report to me and me only. Don't forget that.'

What would she say if she found out he'd been to Spain and met Frankie McGreal since they last met? But he wasn't prepared to drop Anne or Fleur in it. You never knew how Shona Stewart would react, even if it might earn him some Brownie points. And, if he was honest, it felt good to keep something from his tightly sprung boss. Just for now.

Bruised, he returned to West Grange station ready to start sorting through Brian's video clips. He waved goodbye to Bob Lyons, who left with a begrudged grunt, before becoming immersed in his viewing, when a loud honking from outside his office made it impossible to concentrate. A youth in a black jacket and yellow bandana was sitting astride an electric bike, backing into the shadows whenever anybody passed, resuming his annoying honking when all was clear.

Frustrated, James went out to see what was going on. The excitable youngster jumped on his e-bike, beckoning for him to follow.

'Look, go home, it's late ...' he sighed. The last thing he needed was a spat with a local youth.

'There's something you need to see,' the young man replied, pulling down the yellow bandana covering his mouth. What was up with this kid? James reluctantly watched the youngster now weaving dangerously across the dual carriageway as if to hold his attention.

'What the? ...' About to pack up for the day anyway, he got into his car. The boy on the bike was heading towards the heavily graffiti-covered Stokes Croft area, where he stopped abruptly, casting his bike down on a triangular patch of grass where several roads converged. James, following, pulled up behind him. Animated, the youth jumped up and down, pointing to something just visible above his head. It was

Banksy's iconic 'Mild Mild West' art piece, the same one he and Anne had admired recently. The hooded youth put his thumb up and grinned before disappearing down a narrow alleyway.

A strong smell of fresh paint reached his nostrils, making James wonder whether the boy had defaced the infamous art installation. But why would he direct a police officer to his crime? Standing back, he looked up at the painting, which looked the same as before. Puzzled, he spotted discarded containers left on the triangular piece of grass where the boy's bike had stood. 'Short Lasting Watercolour Paint'. He looked more closely and could see some subtle additions that had been made to the original painting. He took out his phone, needing to act quickly as the semi-permanent paint was already starting to streak as the rain began.

Back in his car, he expanded the images, and the new additions jumped straight from the screen, slightly richer in intensity than the original paint. One of the spray-painted policemen now carried a bag of money, and there was a fresh addition of a banner stating: 'Animal Farm. Lions Sleep While Mothers Weep. 5.2.2016.' The final addition was a swarm of small insects surrounding one of the policemen.

Today was the 1st of February, 2016. What was the significance of the messaging dated a few days into the future? He drove away, the painting now returned to its original state.

He needed to speak to Anne, who knew more than most about Banksy's work, especially this iconic piece she'd loved ever since visiting it with someone from her childhood called Billy.

Locking the heavy church door after her late shift, Anne was surprised to see James waiting outside for her. It had been a good shift; things were settling down between her and Mrs. B, and she was hopeful of finally getting her reference. She got in James' car, and he showed her his pictures. She was as puzzled as he was. 'You mean the paint just washed away?' she asked in disbelief. He nodded, sharing her incredulity, 'almost as if it never happened.'

'Animal Farm,' she pondered. 'We did that at school, all the animals ended up fighting and jostling for position.'

'What about the slogan - Lions Sleep While Mothers Weep? Does that mean anything to you, Anne?'

'No idea. The Mild Mild West painting is an objection to police overreacting to raves and parties. Billy told me it was about fighting back.' Anne remained mystified, but something was starting to make sense to James.

'But why are mothers weeping? That's creepy,' she grimaced.

He described the youth on the bike and his yellow bandana. Her pupils widened, turning fluid in the semi-darkness. 'I think I know him, James.' He was describing her mystery spray

painter. 'I see someone just like him early mornings when …
I'm out and about.' Then she gushed, 'I last saw him lurking
around Orwell Crescent, sitting on a wall like he was watching
someone.'

'Orwell Crescent, 5th February. It's a warning. Something's
about to happen.'

'What about the insects?' She looked at the expanded
picture on his phone.

'I'm not sure, but I think they're cockroaches …'

Then it all fell into place. He felt the same rush of
satisfaction as the first time he completed his Rubik's cube as
a teenager. He reached out, clumsy in the confined space, and
hugged her. 'Anne Grimes – you are a star! Fancy a drink?'

'No, I can't,' she replied reluctantly. I need to check if
Fleur's back. We still haven't caught up yet.' The darkened flat
loomed above them.

'Doesn't look like she's in. Come on, let's go for a drink.'

'I can't, James. I really need to find her. The only place I
haven't tried is my mentor's house. River said something that
made me think she might have gone there looking for me.'
Disappointed, he followed her directions. She planted a soft
kiss on his cheek before getting out of the car, too excited at
the thought of seeing Fleur to hear his warning for her to be
careful.

41

#Banksy: 'Take the Money and Run'

'Can I take you for a pint, Bob?'

Bob Lyons couldn't have looked more surprised if James had crept up and run off with his packed lunch.

They drove in silence to the pub with its grassed beer garden and an archway of bare thorny stems that showed the promise of summertime roses. He'd chosen carefully, knowing Bob Lyons loved roses. Roses and cricket seemed to be the sum of Bob's pleasantries.

'So, what's this all about?' Bob eyed him with a hint of respect after taking such decisive action.

'Look, Bob, we all know Operation Cuckoo is stalling. We still don't have anything substantial to connect Albert's murder with Twinnie McGreal. I think you know more than you're letting on.' James held his breath. They both knew he was probing to see what the experienced officer knew. 'He's pissing about with us - on our own patch, boss. What are we missing?' Carefully rehearsed words - but his confidence was slipping.

Bob mulled it over sullenly. It had been a long time since anyone had asked him for his opinion. Somehow, he'd become the laughingstock of the station. The kid had guts inviting him out, pushing him for information. The sort of thing he used to do. He sipped his beer. Why not help him out? He'd had his payoff; what did he have to lose?

James listened attentively as Bob Lyons hunched forward as if about to share something confidential. 'I knew it was going to turn nasty the day Albert's headless body turned up, and then all that cockroach business.' The hulking man shook his head in disgust.

'The cockroach was a reference to Twinnie McGreal, wasn't it?' James held his breath while Bob stared at the frothy topping on his beer. It seemed the young rookie knew more than he suspected.

'Only people close to Twinnie McGreal get to call him Cockie, short for Cockroach – an old family nickname.' That confirmed James' suspicions about the Cockie messages on DS Stewart's phone and the meaning behind the youth's spray painting. But James needed more.

The older officer looked him directly in the eye. 'When I first started out, I used to bloody love this job. Was good at it, you know.' He stroked his beard, removing wisps of beer froth. 'I'd always sided with Frankie McGreal. Small-time crook, easy to handle, you scratch my back …' He raised a bushy eyebrow as if to check James was following him.

'It started to veer out of control the night I helped him get Shayne, his older brother, out of a housefire. They wanted to make it look like he'd died in the fire to avoid an imminent arrest; he was due to go down for several years. Frankie needed my help. They got him out, but there was no one more surprised than me when someone else's charred remains showed up. I was dropped right in it, and your friend, Shona Stewart, was on to me.'

'So, who died in the housefire?' The one question that had been niggling away at him ever since hearing Shona Stewart's corroborating account.

Bob hung his head. 'No idea. I didn't have anything to do with that bit. Nor did Frankie, that much was clear. It was all Twinnie McGreal's doing, twisted little bastard, thinking it gave him some hold over all of us. That's when the McGreal twins started to split away from each other.'

'And you never found out who died?' Bob shook his head and swirled his empty glass, indicating a refill was required.

'Why weren't any DNA tests done after the fire?' James asked on his return, forcing Bob to look away.

'I was afraid my role in it all would be exposed. Anyway, the body was too badly burned; we didn't have the advanced stuff we have now. I checked for weeks, but nobody was reported missing. I could see it might all go quiet, especially as we were all diverted to the summer rioting. The worst decision of my career, and I'm not proud of it. But, if I'm honest, it suited us all to assume it was Shayne McGreal who died and was now off the scene.' He held his large hands open in a 'take it or leave it' gesture. So, Bob Lyons was guilty of assisting Frankie McGreal just as Shona Stewart had told him. But why was he revealing so much? It wasn't putting him in a good light.

'Everything went quiet after that, and we all got on with our business. Then, a couple of years later, Dave Ocasio, Frankie McGreal's driver, tipped me off about a Group 4 Security van heist Twinnie was going to pull off. Seemed a great chance to get back at the conniving little bastard. But he'd invited Frankie along for the ride. Dave thought Frankie was lined up to be the fall guy if anything went wrong - Frankie being a bit thick, would never have seen that coming in a million years.'

'He was being set up by his twin brother?'

Bob Lyons nodded. 'Twinnie was getting too big for his boots with all of these bigger and riskier jobs. He'd moved across to Canterbury by then, followed someone over there, but still couldn't leave things to settle here. Just couldn't let things be. Dave Ocasio could see Frankie McGreal was getting out of his depth and came to me. Dragged up all the stuff about the house fire to blackmail me. I had no option but to help, but my arm didn't need much twisting.

'So, he tipped you off so you could catch Twinnie out?'

Bob Lyons quietened while a young Goth couple hovered, looking for a seat. One glare from him and they moved elsewhere. Bob wasn't one for diversity. 'I made sure I was the first responder on duty the night of the Group 4 robbery, working with a young officer, WPC Lisa Burns. Quiet girl, thought she wouldn't give me much trouble.'

James shot up, nearly spilling his shandy. Shona Stewart had said she was with Bob Lyons on the night of the robbery.

'Things went haywire that night. Of course, Twinnie didn't show up, just his sidekicks. Then the security guard got shot by one of Twinnie's lot. Nasty injury, but thank God he survived.' James could see by Bob's trembling hand how badly it had affected him. 'No arrests made. Everyone got away, I ended up with a bollocking and a recommendation for some shitty retraining, and Frankie got out of it in one piece. But that wasn't the end of it. A lot of money went missing that night. I could never prove it, but I knew it was Lisa Burns. Seems I underestimated her abilities. She avoided me like the plague after that; moved into dog handling.'

'Was DS Stewart involved?'

Bob stiffened. 'Only in that she's Lisa Burns' fiancé.'

'She wasn't there with you that night?'

'No, she'd moved on by then. Quickly promoted to Detective Sergeant and transferred to Canterbury. Can't say I missed her much. Would trample on anyone to get a promotion.'

'And Twinnie served time for the robbery?'

'Yeah, I made sure of that. He got six years for it. Twinnie knew we'd had a tip-off, but didn't know it was Dave Ocasio. He blamed Frankie. Luckily, there was enough on the van driver's phone to put Twinnie away. But now he's out and looking for revenge.'

'And Albert, William Reynolds, that is, was the security van driver?' James just needed to double-check he'd understood everything correctly. Bob downed his pint, leaving James grateful for putting him straight, but feeling naive that he'd been so easily duped by Shona Stewart.

'Time to go, son. I'm only telling you all this because I won't be around much longer. Already discussed it with the boss. I'm taking the rest of my leave and not coming back. Off to Australia. Call it early retirement.'

'Can I just show you this?' Bob Lyons whistled as he looked at the Mild Mild West images on James' phone.

'Haven't got a clue about any of that.'

But things were falling into place nicely for James. 'One last favour? Will you approve a trip down to Canterbury for me? It's all to do with Operation Cuckoo. I need to confirm something.'

James was waiting for DS Shona Stewart in their usual upmarket riverside café. Iris Reynolds had told him everything he needed to know, handing over the bag of cocaine DS Stewart had planted in her house.

Shona Stewart, home for the weekend, had been excited to hear about Bob Lyons' early retirement, wanting to know more. With his heart racing, James tried to ignore the concealed wire digging uncomfortably into his shoulder blade.

'The force will be a better place without the likes of Bob Lyons.' She celebrated by buying them both a slice of chocolate gateau. Putting on her coat, she explained she needed to hurry, as she was home to finalise wedding arrangements. She turned and slumped into her chair as if in slow motion as James dropped the bombshell.

'I hear something big is about to kick off in Orwell Crescent.' He played with his cake fork.

She stayed cool. 'Who have you been talking to, James?'

'I'll share that later, ma'am, but I want in on anything to do with The Farm.' It was a huge gamble, but he was holding all the cards. He had her prints on the cocaine bag along with Iris Reynold's statement, but given Iris' past, he needed more. The rapid pulse ticking at her temple showed her turmoil. She bit her top lip and tapped her nails on the tabletop in irritation.

'I told Twinnie it was too soon to set up a bloody cannabis farm, right under everyone's noses.' He had her. He hadn't mentioned anything specific about a cannabis farm; he had only been working on assumptions. But she'd just confirmed it.

'Stupid sod trying something like that when he's still on licence. He needs to lie low - at least until I close the Reynolds case down.'

His heart was beating out of control, but he breathed evenly. 'I've also been looking into the Group 4 robbery that put Twinnie away. I know Lisa Burns was there that night, not you, ma'am. I also know about your intimidation of Iris Reynolds.' He enjoyed seeing his cool boss squirm.

'You've been talking to Bob Lyons,' she smirked. 'Well, nobody will believe that bent old bastard. I've got enough to put him behind bars for years,' a vitriolic shake of her gleaming bobbed hair, as if confirming her self-righteousness. Her turn to gloat.

'Shame he's already left for Australia then.'

The look of astonishment was worth waiting for.

'Look, James, I don't know where this is leading, but Twinnie will make a lot of money out of this cannabis farm, and I can do as you ask and work you in on a share. I just need to talk to Twinnie first.' She reached for her phone. He held his breath - she mustn't make that call.

Time stalled as she fumbled in her bag, the long seconds on the café's enormous clock ticked away. James' hands were shaking. If necessary, he was prepared to take the phone from her forcefully. He was saved as the café doors burst open and DS Ryan Fletcher from Canterbury police approached and cautioned Shona Stewart for suspected corruption and interfering with an ongoing investigation. The shamed officer was escorted away.

Planning for 5th February was complete. Meticulous. Each of them knew their role and the high stakes if things fouled up. After a select briefing, it became clear that the cannabis farm was intended to be the 'front of house' operation of a much seedier business venture. The Bristol base of an international people trafficking ring conveniently providing free labour to harvest the cannabis.

James, partnered with Jolene Whittaker, had been instructed to watch her carefully, with her still new to the job and being 'a bit on the enthusiastic side'. Things remained strained between them after her insensitive comments at the mortuary. They sat in an awkward silence, patiently waiting at the entrance to Orwell Crescent, a cul-de-sac just off the Bristol ring road; houses seemingly like any other behind suburban net curtains.

'I'm sorry about what I said at the morgue.' She broke the tension. 'It's just that sometimes I don't know how to handle things, my emotions get the better of me.' James appreciated her honesty, but now wasn't the time for a heart-to-heart.

'Let's just stay focused on the job, Jolene.' She offered him a conciliatory sherbert lemon, just as their radio buzzed to warn of the approach of a smartly dressed couple. A silver-haired, short Asian man and his elegant female partner in a pale lilac coat. Jolene photographed them. 'Do you think they are the owners?' James shrugged, although there was something familiar about the woman.

'How much do you think that house is worth?' she broke his concentration.

'Half a million?' James knew a thing or two about house prices since he'd started saving to buy his own flat.

'Who's funding that then?' That was the thing about Jolene: she might be a rough diamond, but she had an inquisitive brain. She asked the right questions. It made him think about the people who pulled the strings of the minions. People like the McGreals. People like Shona Stewart, now being questioned in the Embankment HQ. They'd managed to arrest her before she had a chance to warn off Twinnie McGreal, also held in an undisclosed high-security facility just outside Canterbury.

'Pouncing Tiger!' The call came through. It was about to start. An innocuous grey van pulled up ahead, driven by a man in a dark hooded jacket with a Rolling Stones motif. His companion, also hooded and wearing a mask, jumped out, and they started ushering a sorry huddle of stumbling, blindfolded youngsters into a respectable-looking property. Even from where they held their station, James could tell some of them were very young.

Then all hell broke loose as they slipped into their designated roles. Regional police blazed in using unmarked police cars to block off the cul-de-sac, just as a larger van pulled up, discharging armed officers to position themselves on either side of the front door.

They knocked hard, shouting through the letterbox, attempting legal entry before the door-battering equipment was brought into action. Two officers, one described admiringly later by Jolene as being built 'like a brick shit house', rammed the door until it splintered. An armed procession followed. James and Jolene watched from their post at the end of the cul-de-sac, where they were diverting traffic to the main road, ready to raise the alarm in the case of any new arrivals.

'All clear.' The call came to stand down. They returned to their vehicle as four hooded men, and the smart couple they'd seen previously were handcuffed before being securely belted into the back of the large police response van. Everything was being filmed by body cams and a wide-angle mobile roof camera.

The well-coiffed woman, head down, looked like a rabbit frozen in car headlights. It came to him – it was the older volunteer, Pam, from Anne's church. He left his station to inform the Inspector in charge of the raid and turned sharply at the sound of panicked shouting.

'Take cover, he's got a shooter …' There was movement from a large polytunnel behind a high-walled side garden. A ruby-haired woman exited at the rear, bent low in red boots, followed closely by the masked escort, about to escape into an alleyway.

Instinct took over, and James started to run after them. He chased them down the narrow alleyway, stopping only at the ricocheting thud. It took a few long seconds before he felt the sharp pain in his chest, the force of it knocking him flying between dirty bins. His breath was forced from his body as the world turned black.

More shots, faint now; distant, woozy. A sea of shocked faces looked down on him. Hushed words, 'Hold on, son, you'll pull through.' The last thing he saw was the stricken face of a young man in a yellow bandana standing on the alley wall. But this time the youth wasn't grinning.

42

#Banksy: 'Peace Dove'

James was floating in and out of consciousness. He tried to reach for a dove that had been soaring through the air. Finally, within grasp, it settled on some bleeping hospital equipment. He woke with a jolt, catching the doctor's attention.

'A severe case of winding and a broken rib,' the yawning Emergency Room consultant was telling a gowned nurse. 'Welcome back!' she said to James. 'You've done well. Your ECG showed some dysrhythmia, so we shocked you. Can't say I'm surprised after the blow you took to your diaphragm.'

It all flashed back before his eyes. The cannabis farm, Orwell Crescent, the ricochet of the gunshot. 'Thanks, Doctor.' He attempted shakily to get out of his bed.

'Whoa, you'll need to rest up. We need to make sure there's no internal bleeding. Bloody good job you were wearing a protective body vest. It's saved your life.' Her bleep rang and she and the nurse rushed to attend to another emergency.

'Dr. Carson said I can go as soon as I feel up to it,' he lied an hour later to a harassed nursing assistant, who shrugged and helped him take his painkillers and get into his uniform. Outside the hospital, he gingerly got into a taxi, which took him back to West Grange police station.

'James, you're supposed to be in hospital!' but he ignored Jolene's protests, wanting to see what had happened in his absence. Jolene had been busy. 'Needed to do something to keep my mind from …' She had concerned tears in her eyes, which she hastily brushed away. He felt touched and grateful to sit down as she brought him up to speed.

'Two of them got away. The bloke who shot you and a woman called Marta Bartosz. Polish, key holder, and caretaker at the Elm Grove residential complex. Resided there for the past twelve years.' Her diligence was impressive, but she had more: 'Bartosz brought her heavy weights over from Poland with her, and it looks like one of the younger escorts is ready to spill the beans. Also Polish, he's here illegally on an expired student visa. He's holding out for deportation with no sentence.' James recalled the confusion as the woman in the red boots made a run for it. Clever. She'd waited for the shooting to start, then got away in a rat run of back alleyways.

They worked quietly alongside each other, Jolene working through dashcam footage while James, following up on the Elm Grove lead, continued to browse through Brian's extensive stock of video clips. Jolene fussed over him with coffees and a stack of biscuits when he found what he'd been looking for. A ruby-haired woman was handing money over to Twinnie McGreal, whom he recognized from DCI Campbell's mugshots. Although it would take a bit of enhancement to prove it was him, he knew he'd found the link between Marta Bartosz and Twinnie McGreal. 'Wait 'till the boss sees this. We've got him!'

But James wasn't listening to the excitable Jolene. Immersed in the video footage was a clip of Anne swiping Brian's camera away from her face, and threatening him, 'Stick that camera up your arse ...' he couldn't help laughing, but then noticed something odd. He re-ran the series of clips several times.

An older woman could be seen lurking in the background. Wild ginger hair, leopard skin coat. She reappeared throughout several weeks of footage, waiting in the same secluded spot, watching Anne's flat. Then he spotted her in a different frame, trailing behind Anne on her way to the bus stop. Anne had a stalker, and what's more, he thought he recognised her.

He needed to warn Anne, but there was just one last thing to do. Topping up his painkillers, he asked Jolene to drive him over to Mr. Griffiths' house. He'd been there previously when the disaffected Bob Lyons had him following up trivial Neighbourhood Watch cases.

It took an age for Mr. Griffiths to answer his door. The stiff old man smiled, recognising the young police officer, his eyes red and watery as if he'd been napping. 'Have you found my cat?'

'No, sir, I need some more information.'

Impressed, Mr. Griffiths invited James in, ready to retell the story of Arthur the missing cat, while Jolene waited for him outside. 'So, Mr. Griffiths, who does that house in the corner belong to?' James was sure that was where he'd seen Anne's ginger-haired stalker the last time he visited.

'It's Lilian Parry's house. But she died years ago. It's passed on to her daughter, Vivian, now. Lil and I were very close, once. She was the reason I came to work here in the first place. We left the valleys and came here for jobs in the cigarette factory, like most of the lads from the closed pits.' James was fastidiously taking notes.

'She had to move to get away from the publicity. Chased out she was.'

James looked up. 'What do you mean? What did she have to run from?'

'When her daughter got out ...'

'Got out of where?'

'Some sort of prison, up north, far from here; the only place they took kids like that. Lilian was always a bit afraid of her daughter, liked the freedom when young Vivian was locked away. It was a hell of a shock when she came out, and she had to look after her again.' He started coughing so badly that James helped him to his armchair, gritting his teeth against the pain in his bruised chest.

'Did you two ever, well, live together?'

'No, no,' Mr. Griffiths blew his nose. 'It was enough to just be around for them. Besides, Lil wasn't one for settling down.' He paused. 'But there were things that weren't right in that house.'

'Like what?' James asked, sure he was on to something.

'Well, Lilian was very strict. She was very hard on the child, especially after what happened ... used to say she had the devil in her. Hated her daughter's flaming ginger hair. She used to ...' he stalled as if he still couldn't believe the mother's actions. 'She used to dye it. In the end, it got so damaged that it fell out. I think Lilian was pleased that the girl went bald. Like she deserved it.'

'So, she wears a wig now?' The old man nodded, sadness etched around his eyes.

'Did Vivian always live in that house?'

'No, she went away to some college in Canterbury. A bit of an artist. Very good by all accounts. But that didn't last long; she never finished her course.'

'Why?'

'She couldn't look after herself, according to Lil. Ffion was never the same after she came back. Turned sort of hostile towards everyone.' He could see the old man was getting tired, his mind was starting to drift.

'Ffion? Who was Ffion, Mr. Griffiths?'

'Oh, that was Vivian's real name. Lil changed it to something not so recognisable, after her coming out.'

'What did she do to be locked away?' But Mr. Griffiths was finding it hard to concentrate.

'Oh, it's all old news now, son. I don't want to be dredging it all up again. Now back to my Arthur.'

'Sorry, who's Arthur?'

Mr. Griffiths scowled at him; hadn't he been listening to anything? 'My cat.'

They sat together while the old man sipped his tea, and he tried to process everything he'd learned about Vivian Parry, previously known as Ffion, and her abusive mother. He was getting his things together, but he had one last question. 'Was Parry always their surname?'

'No, before that they were Hughes; Lil's maiden name.'

'Ffion Hughes … Before she became Vivian Parry.'

They stood on the doorstep looking over at the dimly lit house. 'What's with the windows?'

'Must be clearing it out. Don't bloody fancy that job. Hoarders. Vivian, and her mother before her.' He seemed to suddenly take a turn for the worse, his breathing laboured, making his thin shoulders heave with the effort. Jolene called for an ambulance and they waited for the ambulance to arrive, promising to visit him in the hospital.

'You'll still keep an eye out for Arthur?' he called from his stretcher.

James nodded sincerely. He most certainly would be keeping an eye on what was going on around Mr. Griffiths' house.

43

#Banksy: 'Get Out While You Can'

James rechecked his phone; still no word from Anne. She'd obviously found Fleur, and they were catching up. He chided himself for being impatient; she'd get in touch when she was ready. He needed to concentrate and review the muddle of notes spanning decades that he'd taken at Mr. Griffiths' house. He ran a quick computer search on Vivian Parry; nothing came up. It was as if the woman never existed.

According to Mr. Griffiths, Vivian had suffered a very disturbed childhood, but what exactly had she done to be incarcerated so far away from home? And why was the name Ffion Hughes vaguely familiar to him? He didn't have to wait long until a stream of newspaper clippings from 1981 filled his screen.

30th July, 1981.

'While the world watched enraptured at the Royal wedding of Lady Diana Spencer and Prince Charles, in a suburb of Caerphilly, a young girl was brutally murdered.'

'The body of the murdered girl, Zita Singh, aged 6, was found beneath a tree. Two inquisitive children

raised the alarm ... items of clothing, including the girl's trainers were missing.'

2nd August, 1981

'Zita Singh had recently started at the local school where she was reported to be a 'bright and popular pupil,' reports Detective Charles Crocker, who is leading on the case. He is not ruling out an accomplice to young Zita Singh's murder. An appeal is out for decent-minded people to come forward with any information that might lead to an arrest. The school will remain closed as a mark of respect. Banks of flowers have been piling up at the school entrance ...'

4th August, 1981

'Last night, young Zita Singh's parents made an emotional appeal for anyone who might be withholding information about their murdered daughter to come forward. They described their little girl as 'an angel taken too soon.' Neighbours on the local estate have joined in the extensive police search for anything that might help with the case. Police are asking onlookers to stay away from the area.'

5ᵗʰ August, 1981

'The mother of Ffion Hughes, a school friend of Zita Singh, took her daughter to St. Paul's police station after finding Zita's blood-stained ribbons and trainers under her daughter's bed. The Hughes' house has been sealed for forensic investigation, and entry in and around their property has been restricted ...'

Brian, looking all spruced up, was on his way out as James pulled up outside Anne's flat. 'Heard you've got them all banged up?'

'Yeah, thanks to your video footage, Brian. I'll be around to see where we go next with it all, I expect you'll be needed to make a statement to help us with our enquiries …'

BTW scowled, helping the police wasn't on his itinerary.

'Where are you off to?'

'Going to see Sasha. They're holding them in a so-called place of safety. Some detention centre, as if she hasn't been through enough. I'm taking her some chocolates and thought I'd do some filming,' he winked as he flashed a small video camera secreted in a pocket in his coat lining. In a different world, Brian would have made a great investigative journalist.

'Look, Brian, I need to speak to Anne urgently.'

'Not here, mate. Still not back. They're both missing now.'

He made for Millie's house.

'Fuckin' 'ell, is everyone out lookin' for Anne Grimes? Well, she's not 'ere.'

'What does *he* want?' asked Zane, looking suspiciously from behind the door. 'Look, if it's anything to do with that cannabis raid, I had nothing to do with it.'

James ignored his implied involvement, which he would normally be straight onto, but not today. 'I'm looking for Anne or Fleur; I expect they'll be together, but they're not at their place.'

'Come in, we don't want the whole fuckin' world to know the filth's at our door.'

James had parked the police car further down the road as he knew his presence would be noted, but it was harder to conceal his uniform.

'Don't know where either of 'em are. They can both piss off as far as we're concerned, comin' 'ere tellin' lies,' placing her arms around Zane's waist. 'Fleur said some terrible things about 'im and the dead girl, Grace. Obviously not true.' She patted her stomach, leaving James confused.

'So, you've no idea where they might be?'

'No, but River seemed to know where Fleur was off to. Kept goin' on about a ginger troll, couldn't shut him up all night, soft sod,' squeezing Zane's narrow waist lovingly.

James handed over the chocolate he'd bought for River and raced towards the Parry house. Had he delivered Anne directly into the hands of a convicted murderer?

Fleur stirred. Her head hurt. She reached up to feel her hair matted with blood, stuck to the side of her face. She tried to reach higher to investigate the wound on her head, but her wrist snagged on something. She was chained to a radiator, old-fashioned, like they used to have in school. Her mouth was bone dry. She saw Anne's leg protruding from the side of an armchair.

'Anne ...' Her voice was little more than a croak, her vision blurred. Then she smelled it, the acrid smell of smoke. 'Anne, wake up!' Why was Anne unconscious? Had she been drugged? Where was Vivian? 'Vivian, help us. I can smell smoke. We'll do whatever you want. Just help us. Please ...'

A booming voice filled the room. 'Too late for that. You killed Zita Singh. Zita, my friend with the pretty ribbons.' The woman looked deranged. Eyes wild under heavy, sagging lids, clearly mixing them up with someone else.

'Who's Zita Singh?'

'Oh, very clever, as if you don't know.' You both killed her and left me to take the blame. She started a hideous childhood chant, 'Fooled me once, you won't fool me twice,' while pacing about the room. 'You planted her shoes in our house when everybody was at the street party for the Royal wedding. Nobody believed me after that. You knew that I had epilepsy and had blackouts. They would never believe anything a crazy kid said. I was the last to cuddle her.' She turned her palms upwards, rubbing hard, as if trying to wipe away blood stains.

'Vivian, I don't know what you're talking about. Who has been murdered?'

Out of the corner of her eye, she could see that Anne was starting to stir.

'Then everyone left me. Even my mum didn't come to see me, just left me there, miles and miles from home.' Vivian started to cry. She heaved short, breathy sobs like a child with a grazed knee after a playground fall. Fleur felt herself drifting, her head too heavy to keep erect.

'Please let me go, Vivian. We can work this out … together,' she barely managed.

'STOP TRYING TO TRICK ME,' she yelled in Fleur's face as the young girl gasped at the hideous sight of Vivian's wig starting to slip.

She crashed past Fleur. 'I need a cigarette,' and her footsteps reverberated on the hall stairs before everything went quiet.

'Anne, wake up. I've come back to tell you something really important.' But there was no response.

'Come on, Anne, I need you to wake up for me.'

Anne's leg twitched, ever so slightly. She was getting through to her; she just had to stay awake and fight her drowsiness. Swirls of smoke drifted in from the hallway. She pulled hard against the radiator, but those old houses were built to last. The radiator was solid. 'ANNE,' she screamed as the smell of smoke became stronger.

She tried to shuffle towards her friend, to get a foot hooked under the bar of a wooden fireside chair, hoping it would topple and wake Anne. But the pain shooting up her calf was unbearable. 'Anne, Anne, wake up,' she shouted until her throat was hoarse. Her nostrils picked up something putrid above her head, the stench becoming so strong she had to turn her face into her shoulder. Squinting up, she screamed at the sight of two glazed eyes. An emaciated cat, fallen into its last sleep on a tattered cushion. She shouted until she had nothing left.

Outside, Rasta Dave was in his car snoozing after a sordid last night in The Dungeon, one of The Follies' more select locked rooms. Simon had joined him for a night he'd lived his whole life for. He jumped, startling himself, aroused by the erotic flashbacks, and wound down his window for some fresh air. What was going on behind the creepy green door? He was sure he just heard someone screaming.

44

#Banksy: 'Flying Copper'

Under his blue light, James sped across town to Vivian Parry's house, where he was sure he would find both of the missing girls. He didn't wait to call it in. His instincts told him to just get there. Fast.

Racing up the overgrown path, the pain from his chest was blinding. He held his arm over his face against thick smoke billowing from a cracked upstairs window. The front door wouldn't budge to his pained attempts, so he raced around to the back and kicked in the rotting external door, adrenaline now blocking his pain.

He was in, but God, the place stank. There were plates stacked high, and a green, decaying chicken carcass on the draining board. With his arm over his mouth, he raced down the densely packed hallway, following the sound of shouting. It was Fleur, her hair matted with blood. He chilled at the sight of the chain tethering her to a radiator.

'It's okay, Fleur, I'll get you out. Where's Anne?'

'Over there, she's out cold. Vivian said something about tablets ...'

His heart banged at the sight of Anne's body slumped between a chair and a tiled fireplace, his eyes smarting with the descending clouds of black smoke. Quickly, he closed the internal doors, hoping it might give them some time, but the crashing sounds upstairs told him that he had to be quick. He rapidly assessed Anne; there didn't seem to be any obvious injuries, just some dried vomit on her fleecy jacket. He shook her by the shoulders.

'James?' she responded drowsily. 'Why are you here?'

'Thank God. Stay down on the floor, see if you can crawl outside.' He needed to free Fleur.

'Fleur,' she cried out, not understanding why her friend was secured to the radiator, before violent coughing spasms gripped her. 'Vivian, she put something in my drink …' she gasped between breaths.

'Get outside, Anne. Now! I'll come for you when I've freed Fleur.'

Back in the kitchen, he dampened an old tea towel to cover his nose and mouth. His bruised chest made it difficult to bend, but he returned with a hammer found under the sink.

'What's going on?' A man appeared from the back door. James turned, grateful for some help. Rasta Dave, now wide awake, couldn't believe his eyes. Fleur was slumped against a radiator. She looked in a bad way. Had all this happened while he was asleep outside in the car? Frankie would kill him if he ever got to know. He returned to the yard to fetch the iron bar propping up the back gate. 'I saw the flames from outside, I've phoned for the fire brigade,' he lied. Whatever was about to happen, he had to get out without bringing attention to himself or Fleur.

Dave pushed his long dreadlocks aside and wielded the heavy bar with heft. Their combined efforts broke the stubborn radiator bracket, causing the whole thing to crash from the wall with a hissing spurt of water.

Outside, James ran to assist Anne, who lay suspiciously silent, roused only by intermittent coughing spasms. She was murmuring a single word over and over: 'Retribution,' until she went quiet, making him panic. Lying still, her skin appeared translucent, and there was a blue tinge to her lips. He shook her firmly before starting CPR, praying the emergency services would arrive soon. 'How long did they say …?' he turned, but his mystery assistant had gone. He looked around dazed. Fleur had gone too. An engine started up, but he couldn't leave Anne. As the car sped off, he recalled the long dreadlocks and a jacket adorned with badges resting on the back window ledge. Fleur had been abducted by David Ocasio, Frankie McGreal's driver, from right under his nose.

45

#Banksy: 'The Antics Roadshow'

Dave swore at the loud banging coming from the boot of his car. The bitch was making a terrible din. He'd hoped she wouldn't pull through, make things easier for everyone. But that wasn't in Fleur's DNA. He was in deep shit, although maybe all was not lost, if only he could find a way to finish the job off himself. Frankie need not know about the fire; assume she'd come home and decided not to return. He could easily make up something about her disappearing into the night with another bloke. All he needed was somewhere quiet to finish her off, and he knew just the place.

He needed to be quick; that copper would have called it in by now. He drove through back streets to The Follies, knowing Simon would help him. The Dungeon would be the perfect place; deserted in the daytime. He could sort things there, dump her body, torch the car, then start making his way back to Spain. After all, he'd done similar things before.

Simon Pope, yawning whilst watering his cactus collection in his flat above The Follies Club, noticed movement on his CCTV monitor. Why was Dave Ocasio dragging a girl into the doorway of the club he managed? He didn't need this sort of shit. He rewound the camera and wiped the film before disabling it. Made one quick call on his mobile before he dashed down to Dave, banging loudly on the door below.

'Don't ask any fucking questions, Simon, I'm taking her downstairs to the Dungeon.'

'She doesn't look your type, darling,' raising one well-plucked eyebrow. He lit them both a cigarette; Dave looked like he needed one.

'Help me put her in the cage until I decide what to do with her. I need a drink.'

Fleur, woozy after inhaling so much smoke, her lungs raw with all the coughing, felt as if her head was about to explode. She was coming to, trying to work out why Rasta Dave was there. And why was he acting like this? So was Simon.

'What's she done, Dave?'

'Stole something from me.'

'I haven't stolen anything ...' she stuttered.

'Shut up,' he kicked hard against the cage.

'Pass me that bottle of vodka,' he barked at Simon.

He wedged Fleur's head between his chest and the side of the metal cage and tried to prise her mouth open. She reacted by biting him hard.

'You little bitch,' he slapped her across the face. 'Sit on her,' he ordered Simon, pushing the vodka bottle against her gritted teeth. Then they both stopped dead as the door flung open and Ali Kumar entered.

'Hello, Dave. Nice to see you again.'

The regional ANPR alert soon picked up the green Seat parked close to the Follies gay club. PC Rav Shah arrived to find Fleur enjoying a drink with the manager, Simon Pope. Surprised, she denied that she'd been abducted; said that she'd willingly accompanied Dave Ocasio for a drink. 'PC Wright must have got confused – after all, he had just saved us from a house fire.' She was convincing with her sweet smile, swathed in Simon's silk dressing gown, her hair bound up in a towel.

'So … where is David Ocasio now? A warrant is out for his arrest.'

'Sorry, you've just missed him.' He left with an old friend who, no, she didn't recognise.

Simon went along with her story, and although he was happy for the police to take his CCTV footage, unfortunately, the camera was only set at night.

Fleur didn't rate Dave's chances at the hands of Ali Kumar, not after the dirty double cross when he'd grassed Ali up, leading to his arrest before they left for Spain.

'I thought Ali was banged up?' she asked Simon after PC Shah left, more confused than ever.

'Out on bail. Ali comes in here quite often.'

'Well, I never.'

He refilled their glasses. 'I like your style, Fleur Drake. Fancy working for me?'

'No thanks, Simon. Nice offer, but there's someone I need to get back to.'

Anne's mind was drifting. One minute, she was trailing her hand in a warm pool with sunbeams dancing on the surface, studied by a damsel fly with beady eyes. Then she was up high, looking down on a grey, mottled girl on a mortuary trolley - in the corner, a decomposing cat. She knew she had to stay by the poolside; stay with the warmth and the light, but an over-riding sense of guilt gripped her, preventing her from surfacing.

'It's unusual for a young patient not to have responded by now,' the ICU doctor told James. We've tried to de-intubate her twice, but she's struggling to breathe independently. Her records show she's had chronic childhood asthma, probably the result of damp housing or excessive indoor smoking. Her scarred lungs are causing the complications.' James had been by her bedside for two days, caressing her hand with a recording of Spanish guitar music playing gently in the background.

'Seems like I'm going to have to wait for my interview,' Gabby McArdle called from her vigil at the doorway. He wished she'd go away, but she had good reason to be there.

Anne's fingerprints had been picked up on one of the guns seized at the rave. James waited for her to take a break.

'Quick, I think you're clear for now,' he said, ushering Fleur into the cramped hospital side room. 'I'll watch out for Gabby McArdle in the corridor. When you're done, I'll be ready to drop you at the airport.'

Anne heard it all and smelled the new sherberty aroma waft around the sterile room. Although she was finding it impossible to break through this thing the doctors called 'an induced coma', she was forewarned of anyone entering her room by her enhanced senses. She tried in vain to muster every bit of willpower, but nothing broke her inner turmoil and the powerful chemicals keeping her dormant. All the same, it felt good to hear Fleur's voice and know she was safe.

Fleur sounded shocked. Hesitant, for once. 'Oh, Anne … I'm so sorry I got you into all this mess ...' The room quietened as she heard Fleur pour some water and the rustle of Get-Well cards being scanned; her mocking snort at James' collection of Spanish Guitar CDs. 'I need to make it quick, Anne, a police woman is hanging about waiting for you to come around, and she's a right rottweiler. I'm flying back tonight. I need to get back to Frankie before word gets out that I'm over here. There are plenty of people who would like to see me off,' her tinkling laugh filled the room. But Anne sensed her underlying concern. She was now munching on the grapes that Millie had inadvisably brought in, making Anne smile inwardly. Then she delivered the bombshell.

'I came back to tell you that Shayne McGreal survived the house fire all those years ago. He's living in Ireland and plans to stay there, so we are free to live our lives now. No more guilty looking over our shoulders. I've written it all in a letter left in our biscuit tin for when you get home.' Every sinew in Anne's body strained to break free at this earth-shattering news, desperate to know more. That must have been what Fleur had read in Josie McGreal's letters. Fleur prattled on, 'It also means you're free to see James, who, by the way, I think is perfect for you. He's told me all about the two of you staying over in Spain and hinted that you're more than just friends. He's certainly looking out for you, and he's saved both our lives.' It's like he's our ... hero.' The darkness was lifting. Anne needed to tell Fleur to grow up, to stop looking for heroes, but could only listen in her induced state. But there was more earth-shattering news to follow.

'I also wanted to be the one to tell you that Vivian died in the fire at her house. I'm not sorry, not one bit. But I know you always see the best in people, and I expect you'll take it hard.' The sound of nails being scratched through her long ponytail made Anne's skin crawl, as it always did.

'I've been reading some of your letters to Banksy - about your trip to Canterbury and finding your mum and new sisters, and I hope you don't mind me saying, but I think it's time you grew up and moved on from this whole Banksy thing. You don't need anyone else; we'll always be there for each other, and you can come out to Spain any time. I'd appreciate the company. You've always been the yin to my yang ...'

James knocked. 'The ICU doctor's coming - it's time we went.'

Fleur bent and kissed Anne gently on her clammy cheek before following James out of the room, clutching the last of Millie's grapes. 'She's not going to need these anytime soon ...' narrowly missing the tear trickling down Anne's face.

In the car, James asked how Anne's fingerprints had come to be on a gun seized during the raid at Frankie McGreal's Big House. Fleur looked at him, horrified, suddenly recalling the gun she'd hidden in their flat. 'Quick - record me on your phone – I'll explain it all.' And a full account followed of how she'd hidden the gun without Anne's knowledge. A plausible enough explanation; factual enough to shift the focus from Anne onto herself and Frankie McGreal.

'I'm also sorry that I made you look bad, James – when I said I left Vivian's house willingly with Rasta Dave, you know, after the fire ...' Fleur's phone interrupted her apology.

'It's Frankie … again. I should never have given him my new number …' She switched his message to speakerphone: 'Fuckin' hell, Fleur, what's going on? Is Dave with you? he isn't answering my calls …' She swiped the phone off and nibbled at her nails.

'Are you sure you want to go back to him? I can try to help you out here, if you stay?'

She waved him away, already thinking up ways to win Frankie over.

'Oh, talking of Frankie, I nearly forgot.' He pulled up outside the airport Departures Hall and handed over a gift-wrapped package. 'Anne brought this back from Spain for you. It's from Frankie, for your eighteenth birthday.' Two sets of keys fell into her lap, one for the Villa Florentina, the other bound with a shop label: *Your future nail bar, Hun xxx.* Keys to her own business.

She hugged James goodbye, leaving him wondering how Fleur Drake always seemed to land on her feet, as her sparkly sundress disappeared into the hubbub of the airport crowd. He pulled off, thinking it strange how trouble always seemed to follow Fleur. Or was it the other way round?

46

#Banksy: 'Follow Your Dreams'

'Are we sitting comfortably, guys and gals?' DCI Bruce Campbell was all set for his briefing. James scanned the room: no Bob Lyons and no DS Shona Stewart; the start of a new era. Jolene waved before clumsily barging across limbs to sit next to him, her blue, backcombed hair stacked high. 'Well, well, who'd have thought it, rushing into a house fire to save those girls?' He blushed, shushing her to be quiet, but Jolene wasn't being put off that easily. 'Wasn't one of them that girl Anne, who identified the overdose at the mortuary?'

'You mean the girl who sadly died of an overdose, Jolene?'

DCI Bruce Campbell coughed theatrically. 'As usual, please feel free to interrupt ...' setting off muffled sniggers. 'As you are aware, several arrests were made at Orwell Crescent. The forensic team is in there now giving it a thorough going over.' He banged his stick on the picture of a hook-nosed woman with ruby-red hair. 'Marta Bartosz. Got away. We've since received her police record through Interpol. One interesting woman, operating here under our very noses. Reported missing from Warsaw twelve years ago following a high-profile trafficking case. Seems she switched names and switched operations to Bristol.' He paused to show his contempt, turning his attention to Twinnie McGreal's profile picture.

'Bartosz quickly fell in with our friend McGreal. A marriage made in hell. She recruited the heavyweights from Poland, while he provided the transport from his Canterbury-based meat packaging company. They preyed on vulnerable, wee youngsters, who had left their families in search of a job and a better life for themselves.'

'Any of them talking, boss?' Rav Shah's query was met with derision. 'A little patience, please ...' He continued. 'We're hopeful that one of the Polish escorts we've arrested might do a deal with us, but nothing so far. Nothing from the young people who have been trafficked either, before you ask ... They've been taken to a detention centre for their safety.'

James thought of Brian visiting Sasha, then he remembered Perfect Pam.

'What about the respectable couple fronting the whole thing?'

DCI Campbell drew breath between gritted teeth. 'I'm coming to them, PC Wright ...' shoulders now squared against further interruptions, he continued. 'In fact, the only person talking to us *is* your lady – Mrs. Pamela Huntingdon.' He pointed to her profile picture, where she stared out like a startled rabbit. 'Seems she had been rather naively employed by an admiring Sammi Rashid, supposedly as a house manager. She's spilling the beans because she needs to get home to look after her son and make sure he complies with his tag conditions. A woman out of her depth,' he said, with more than a hint of sympathy. 'She was being blackmailed by a gang that used her son as a drug runner. She also coughed up to petty theft from the local church.' James was certain she'd also taken Mr. Griffiths' credit card to buy expensive products to sell on, but now wasn't the time.

'With no option other than to take up Sammi Rashid's offer, she'd agreed to pose as his wife. Together, they'd provided good cover as a respectable suburban couple. Sufficient to prevent the neighbours in Orwell Crescent from becoming suspicious. Good day's work, everyone, but especially by PC Wright and Jolene. Their diligent attention to the video footage from a young occupant at Elm Grove is proof of the links between Twinnie McGreal and Marta Bartosz.' He paused. 'Their efforts also reveal high-level corruption by one of our senior officers, currently under investigation by the IOPC.' They all knew he was referring to DS Shona Stewart, but there were to be no further questions. His tone indicated they were being dismissed.

'How are you doing, Mr. Griffiths?'

The old man sat beside his hospital bed, lost in the folds of an oversized dressing gown. 'Come and sit down, son,' he patted the bedspread.

James hated delivering bad news, but wanted to be the one to tell Mr. Griffiths about Vivian Parry's death. 'And I'm very sorry to have to tell you this, but it looks like Arthur had got himself shut in somehow.' Mr. Griffiths didn't need to know his cat had been stolen and starved to death. The old man quietened, rubbing his dressing gown cord between his fingers. 'Never was a lucky house. I always thought Lil and I might settle down one day. But she never seemed to develop proper attachments to anyone.'

'Not even her daughter?'

'Least of all her. Wicked to her she was, always thought I might be able to help on that front, but they both shut me out.' He dabbed at his eyes. 'She had a sad life, that child. Cruel. With everyone blaming her for something she didn't do.'

'What do you mean? She was sentenced for killing Zita Singh. I've been through the records. I've read all the court reports.'

'I've got proof she didn't do it.'

'What?'

The watery-eyed man sighed heavily and told him everything as if unburdening a great load. 'Lilian received a letter from someone called Cerys Williams, dying of cancer in prison in Scotland. It's all in the letter. A confession from Williams saying that she killed Zita Singh and framed Ffion, who you know as Vivian, for the murder.'

'Did Lilian ever tell Vivian about the letter?'

'No, she sat on it all these years.' He dabbed at his streaming eyes. 'Could be stubborn like that, felt it gave her some hold over her daughter. She was a difficult woman, was Lil. Beautiful but difficult.' He wiped his eyes with a tissue handed to him by James. 'I tried hard to get a chance to tell Vivian after Lil passed, but the girl would have nothing to do with me. I've tried to speak to her over the years, but she closed the door on me well before her mother died. Always called me a nosey parker. I gave up in the end, almost started to feel she didn't deserve to know.' His words caught in his throat, his face crumpled. 'I kept the letter safe for her all this time. And now she will never know.'

47

Lemon Lives

June 2016.

One last glance in the hotel mirror. Anne smoothed down her flowery summer dress; her skin radiant against Vivian's pearlised Hermes scarf. In the background, the TV was airing a news report on Banksy's mural of the blue EU star motif, which had appeared at Dover Port. The reporter stood beneath a blank wall, where 'Brexiteers' had whitewashed over it during the night. It brought back memories of her painting over Fleur's protest, 'I fucking hate it here', all those months ago. It seemed like a lifetime away. But painting over things didn't put things right. She knew that now. One last mirror check, and she headed for the commemoration ceremony.

After the short but tasteful outdoor eulogy, Dr. Henrietta Hawes came to join her. James released her hand at the woman's approach.

'Well, that closes that mystery down. Billy Hodges, RIP.' Although her manner was habitually abrupt, Anne couldn't thank Henry enough for going the extra mile to help them identify Billy's remains. The hotel terrace overlooked the Clifton suspension bridge, and the river Avon twinkled in the midday sunshine below, making Henry's dark clothes look heavy and out of place. Anne breathed in the perfume around her. Rambling roses and honeysuckle. She couldn't imagine anywhere more beautiful. It was such a shame she never got to share it with Billy.

James, now chatting to the Celebrant, caught her glance. His clear brown eyes creased into their secret smile. They had been seeing a lot of each other after the arrest of Twinnie McGreal and the winding down of Operation Cuckoo, as much as possible between his shifts and her new work hours. Mrs. B had encouraged her to apply for the job: 'Go on, Anne, you were born to be a youth support worker,' and armed with a glowing reference, she had nailed it.

The light was dusky as she entered the small hotel function room and picked up the framed photograph of Billy that James had found in some newspaper archives. The only one she'd ever seen, but she clearly remembered his beloved T-shirt adorned with a peace sign.

'Sounds like he was a very decent man.' Henry stood behind her.

'Yes, he was very kind to everyone and everything. Thanks for not giving up on the DNA.'

'It's not always possible in the case of badly charred bones, but techniques are improving all the time. Fortunately, we obtained a good enough sample from the exhumation. Although the Super took a bit of convincing to sign it off, thankfully, it turned out to be worth it. He eventually caved in, knowing the police wouldn't come out well with all the local press interest around the McGreal arrest and Shona Stewart's corrupt part in it all.'

'I never knew Billy had a police record; it came as a bit of a shock.'

'Hmm,' Henry was distracted, surveying the trays of leftover food. 'Seems he was part of an environmental group; liked to live in trees. He caused damage sufficient to slow down the construction of a proposed power plant. Quite a political thorn in the side at the time. It also explained how Billy's free lifestyle prevented him from being reported missing. Pity, though, once he went back to living rough, he was an easy target for the McGreal clan, making it easy to switch bodies and get Shayne McGreal out of the smoking flat. An arrest warrant has been issued, but McGreal's probably living it up on the continent with Frankie.' Her attention was drawn to the arrival of a tray of fresh pastries, leaving Anne to think it best not to disclose that Shayne McGreal was living in Ireland. Maybe she'd tell James. Sometime.

The Humanist Celebrant had managed to capture Billy's free spirit perfectly. Her wording struck just the right balance; humorous yet respectful, leaving Anne finally at peace with her loss. She turned at a flash of someone wearing a yellow bandana exiting the hotel car park. It was Sparrow, her early morning spray painter friend, who had made it after all.

Another free spirit, but today without his ethereal spray-painting mentor. She was pleased he'd been there to mark Billy's life, especially after coming forward to provide a DNA sample following a press shout-out, then surprising them all with an overnight mural on the wall of the decaying St Gabriel's church. She'd noticed the beautifully spray-painted art piece as she carefully locked up her new bicycle, the crowd around her muttering something about it being a Banksy. But she knew it was the work of Sparrow, leaving a perfect memorial to his eco-warrior brother, Billy, on the anniversary of his fortieth birthday.

'Care to dance, Anne Shirley Grimes?' She clung to James on the dance floor of the cliff-top hotel, which opened up to the balmy terrace overlooking the river below. Her treat. She could afford it now, with her new job.

'Bye, Room.' But Room remained sullen, unimpressed that Anne hardly seemed to be home for long these days. 'I'll bring you back something nice.'

'Cool scarf,' the airport check-out attendant cast an appreciative look, orange-painted nails briefly suspended from his checking of Anne's documents.

'Thanks, it's Hermes. A close friend gave it to me.' It still hurt to think of Vivian's death, especially after finding out about her damaged childhood and being framed for such a hideous crime; all the shame she must have suffered. It helped explain her mood swings and her inclination to smear animal remains in an attempt to frighten her unsuspecting mentees and drive them closer for her comfort and support.

She spoke to Vivian regularly, shared her plans and goals with her, and pledged to carry her carefree spirit in her heart. Her new purple suede handbag with its soft, swinging fringe hung on her shoulder; a small homage to her mentor.

'You sure you've got everything?' James was hovering, holding back the urge to check her boarding card. Again. They'd already run through his cockpit checklist on the way to the airport, and after a final reassuring hug, it was time for her to leave.

'Text me as soon as you get there.' He'd been so supportive, helping her plan this journey. The first of many, she hoped, and maybe soon she'd agree to them going somewhere together, but not yet. This was her time, and she knew exactly how she wanted to celebrate Billy's big birthday.

She'd read about Banksy's Bethlehem Hotel on her flight back from Spain, after her failed attempt to find Fleur. Back when her life was collapsing around her, when Fleur was central to everything she did. But she was finally accepting that it was time to live her own life. It was time to let Fleur go, and although she still woke in the night worrying about her, it wasn't so often now. But other things still bothered her, such as the thought that Shayne McGreal was still alive. Did he remember her role in the house fire? Would she ever be free from him?

On the plane, she finally relaxed, browsing through some details she'd printed off about The Walled Off Hotel in Bethlehem - '*Housing much of Banksy's latest art*'. The collaboration with other artists was designed to raise awareness of global political unrest. A perfect goodbye for Billy.

'You didn't fancy partying in Ibiza then?' James joked, reminding her she still didn't know where Ibiza was. But she would.

She dozed off to Billy's words: 'We're all a product of our environment, Anne,' and now she knew he was right. But she needed to expand that environment, to embellish it with colour and texture. Shafts of filtered lemon light streaked her skin, set off a glimmer of rich gems strewn through her hair. She felt perfectly content, and although travelling alone, she would be greeted by the work of her old friend. Banksy. Her true mentor, who would always be there for her, wherever she was in the world.

Epilogue

1981

Cerys' eyes, wild as a startled horse, are starting to make her friend anxious. It is a strange day, the normal flow of things disturbed by the frenzy that precedes a royal wedding. In this restless void, Cerys, giddy on cider stolen from the crates stacked ready for the street party, needs something to happen. Their eyes settle on a ribboned girl happily swinging on the proud old oak tree, where it is rumoured pit ponies were once tethered, and a coal miner had also swung after the pits closed.

It is eerily quiet for a Wednesday, with everyone packed into pubs in the pulsating build-up to the wedding, when a thud draws their attention. The girl has fallen from her swing, banging her head. Red, white, and blue ribbons are now staining pink, and Cerys is standing over the body. Her breathing is uneven. There is a bubble of spit at the corner of her mouth.

'Let's finish her off.'

'But she's hurt herself. Looks like she's cut her head or something ...'

'Makes it easy then.'

In the peace of the late July morning, it only takes one sweep, but the metal bar bounces back, making them both gasp, then watch in disgust as the limp body judders. The second girl watches trancelike as Cerys removes the girl's ribbons and trainers. With excitement sparking through their veins, they run under trembling bunting, past laden trestle tables, stopping only to gasp at the tiered cake topped with tiny figures of Prince Charles and Lady Di. And trays of wobbling red jelly and frothy spray cream. A fitting street party for a royal wedding.

Printed in Dunstable, United Kingdom

73127460R00228